A REFUGE OF CONVENIENCE

WIND RIVER CHRONICLES, BOOK 3

KATHY GEARY ANDERSON

PURPLE AUTUMN PRESS

Edited by Kristin Avila and Marjorie Vawter

Cover by Carpe Librum Book Design

This is a work of fiction. Where real people, events, establishments, organizations, or locales appear, they are used fictitiously. All other elements of the novel are drawn from the author's imagination.

Scripture quotations are from the King James Version of the Bible.

ISBN 978-1-7369207-4-9 (paperback)

ISBN 978-1-7369207-5-6 (ebook)

www.kathygearyanderson.com

To Jared and Megan, my two greatest gifts. I am beyond blessed to be called your mom.

CHAPTER 1

enver, Colorado, March 1902

D   Jonas was dead. There could be no doubt. No one took blows to the head like that and lived to tell about it. He certainly lay still enough.

Claire forced herself to move. Kneeling, she placed two fingers alongside his windpipe. No pulse, as she expected.

Except . . . maybe . . .

No. Nothing.

She'd never expected to see her husband again, not after two years of him not finding them. His appearance in her kitchen this morning had been a shock. More than a shock. Sheer terror. And now he was dead.

Blood pooled around his head. She hadn't anticipated all the blood. She should have. Head wounds were notorious. She pushed to her feet, wincing at the dark red stain now marring the front of her crisp white pinafore. Nurse Usher, her supervising nurse at St. Luke's, would not approve.

She glanced down at the rest of her nurse's uniform. Her bodice hung loose, torn from its high collar to her navel, exposing her chemise and corset. By evening she'd be sporting a black eye. No. Nurse Usher definitely would not approve. She bit back the laughter that threatened to escape. She couldn't afford hysterics. Not now.

A cry from Ella in the next room brought her back to the present. She couldn't let her daughter see this. Even though they'd run from Jonas long before Ella ever knew him, no child should see a scene like this. No child should see her *father* like this. She needed to focus. Plan.

"Sadie, we have to go."

She stepped over Jonas's body to where her sister stood frozen, iron skillet still clutched in her right hand. Prying it loose, Claire set it on the table, then thought better of it. They should take it with them. It was the murder weapon, after all.

No, not murder.

Self-defense.

But would the police see it that way? She wasn't about to take any chances. Grabbing a dish towel, she wrapped the skillet in it, then herded her sister toward the door.

"We need to pack. We need to leave. Now."

Sadie shot a glance back over her shoulder. "Is he . . . ?"

"Yes. And we have to get out of here as quickly as possible."

THIRTY MINUTES LATER, CLAIRE HOPPED OFF THE TROLLEY AT THE foot of Seventeenth Street and jogged toward the entrance of Union Station, Sadie at her heels. She ignored the stitch in her side and the weight of Ella held tight on her hip. They'd made it this far. Now to find a train. Any train. The first one leaving would be best.

Ella wriggled in her arms. Claire let her slide to the ground, holding fast to her hand as they slipped beneath the bell tower that marked the station's entrance. With any luck, they'd blend into the crowd, their anonymity guaranteed by the sheer number of travelers who came and went through this station every day. She hadn't time to plan a more elaborate escape, not like the first time. No disguises. No subterfuge. Hopefully, once they were out of Denver, she'd be able to formulate a better plan. For now, they just needed to leave.

"Do you have any idea where we're going?" Sadie switched her valise to her other hand and heaved the strap of her satchel back onto her shoulder.

"Not really. I'll decide when I get to the ticket counter. Maybe you and Ella should stay here while I get the tickets. The fewer people who see us together, the better."

Nodding, Sadie sank onto a nearby bench and pulled Ella onto her lap, letting her bags slip to the ground beside her.

Claire added her own heavy valise to the pile, then turned toward the nearest ticket counter. "I'll be right back."

Halfway across the great hall, she skidded to a halt. That man. The tall one on crutches leaving the counter. Wasn't that? No, it couldn't be. He wasn't to be released for another three weeks.

Claire studied the man's profile—wavy dark hair, straight nose, strong chin. As if sensing her stare, he turned his head and looked straight at her.

Drat. It *was* him!

Wyoming.

Ducking her head, she searched for a place to hide, but the wide-open expanse of the big hall gave her few options. She whirled around, panic seizing her breath. Had he recognized her? Wait. She swallowed a laugh. What was she doing? She was wearing the mourning hat from her Mrs. Dempsey disguise, complete with a heavy black weeping veil. Even if he had seen her from this distance, he would never recognize her as Nurse Monroe. People saw what they expected to see. Turning again, slowly this time, she saw she was right. He was already hobbling away.

What he was doing here was beyond her. He shouldn't even be on his feet yet, let alone trying to walk with crutches. She watched his precarious progress for a minute, then shook her head. He was no longer her concern. She joined the line at the ticket counter, craning her neck to see the train schedule.

"Look out!"

The shout drew Claire's attention back to the great hall. A man pushing a cart piled high with trunks and bags of all sizes careened toward Wyoming. Time slowed as the cart barreled forward. Wyoming lurched sideways but not fast enough. The cart clipped his bad leg, throwing him off balance. Crutches tangling, he twisted and fell. Claire cringed as his head hit the marble floor with a thud.

Not stopping to think, she jogged toward him and, for the second time in three hours, knelt beside a man's inert body. All those weeks in traction and now this. Gently lifting his head, she probed the back of his scalp. No blood, but a nasty bump was already forming. She applied pressure to the area, checking for any response. Nothing. He was out cold.

"Ya know this man?" The man behind the luggage cart peered down at her.

"Yes. He's my p—." A flash of red in her periphery alerted her to Ella pushing her way through the growing crowd, Sadie in tow. Sadie shot her an apologetic look as Ella tore out of her grasp and launched herself into Claire's arms.

"Mama. Mama," she cried, burying her head in Claire's shoulder.

"Hush, baby. It's okay." She stroked Ella's hair and gave Sadie a slight nod. They were just in time, really. She'd almost confessed this man was her patient, ruining any chance of anonymity. In fact, throwing herself in the middle of this drama had been a huge mistake. She looked down at Wyoming. He still hadn't moved, and she knew she couldn't leave him this way. But maybe she could use this to their advantage. Hadn't Mama always said the best place to hide something was in plain sight? If the police were to follow them, they would be looking for two women and a child, not a family of four, no matter how conspicuous they might be.

"He's my husband," she finished, praying Wyoming wouldn't gain consciousness any time soon. She pulled out her handkerchief and dabbed at her eyes beneath her veil. "His leg was just beginning to heal, and now this. We need to get home for Father's funeral. We must! Oh, oh, what will we do?"

As if on cue, Ella threw herself onto the floor and began to wail. Dropping to her knees beside them, Sadie pulled Ella into her arms and began to rock back and forth while the crowd around them grew even larger.

Luggage Cart Man pulled out his own red flannel handkerchief and wiped his brow. "I'm sorry, ma'am. Truly, I am." He shifted from one foot to the other. "I tried to avoid him, but the cart was just too heavy to stop. Don't ya cry, now. I'll get ya on your train if I have to carry your man on myself. When does it leave?"

Ignoring his question, Claire loosened Wyoming's collar and began to pat his cheeks. "Darling, please wake up. Please. I need you." If she was going to play the helpless wife, she might as well be convincing. Though what she would say to him when he did regain consciousness, she didn't know.

The crowd around her shifted as an elderly gentleman carrying a black doctor's bag pushed his way through.

"May I be of assistance?"

"Oh, yes. Please. He's hit his head, and if he doesn't wake up soon . . . well, we can't miss our train. We just can't!"

"Hmmph. Your husband has larger concerns right now than making a train." The doctor checked Wyoming's pulse, then pulled back his eyelids, moving his head from side to side. He lifted Wyoming's head, probing for the injury as she had done earlier. This time, Wyoming moaned the moment the doctor found it.

"Sir. Sir. Can you hear me?" The doctor turned to Claire. "Try calling your husband by name. Maybe he'll respond to your voice."

By name? She'd only ever called him Mr. Garrity. To his face, that is. Behind his back, he'd been Wyoming. Cora gave him that moniker the first day he arrived—a larger-than-life cowboy, as rough and wild as the Wyoming plains from where he hailed. He'd been so tall, they'd struggled to find a hospital bed to fit him. Of course, he had a first name. It was written at the top of his chart, but for the life of her, she couldn't remember it.

"Ma'am?"

She closed her eyes, willing her mind to see his chart the way she could often see a page of text when trying to remember an answer to a test question.

Dear Lord, if you ever truly hear my prayers, hear me now. What is his name?

Jackson! Jackson Garrity.

"Jackson, honey." She leaned forward again. "Jack. Wake up. Come on, now, sweetie. If you don't wake up, the doctor will send you back to the hospital."

That did it. His eyelids flew open, and she found herself gazing into those midnight blue eyes framed with dark, sooty lashes—eyes no nurse at St. Luke's was completely immune to, including herself. Confusion clouded his vision. If she didn't act fast, the game would be up. She pushed back her heavy black veil allowing him to see her face. Recognition chased the confusion but didn't completely dispel it.

"Jackson, the doctor needs to know you're all right so we can get you on the train." She held his gaze, willing him to understand her hidden message. *Don't give me away, Jack. Don't mess this up.* He'd always been a man of few words. The strong, silent type, as Cora liked to say. She hoped this blow to the head hadn't changed that.

"What your wife says isn't entirely true, sir."

Jackson turned his head to study the doctor, a frown creasing his forehead.

"I don't recommend you get on a train at all today. With your leg injury and now this blow to the head, what you need is bed rest and constant evaluation. Your travel will have to wait for another day."

"No." Jackson's voice may have been weak, but there was nothing weak about the look he gave the doctor. "I'm going home."

He rolled to one side, struggling to lift himself up. Claire took hold of his arm, signaling Sadie to take the other, and between the two of them, they managed to sit him up.

"We'll be fine now, doctor. Thank you."

"Ma'am, I beg you to listen to reason. Your husband has no business traveling. You need to see that he has suitable medical supervision, or I cannot guarantee there won't be dire consequences."

"I'm sorry, sir, but we must travel today. My father's funeral is tomorrow. I'll see that he rests on the train, I promise."

The doctor shook his head, pulled out his pocket watch, and flipped its lid. "If that's the case, then I wish you luck." His tone implied he didn't think that likely. "I have a train of my own to catch." With that, he pushed to his feet and took off down the great hall toward the departure gates, taking most of the gawking onlookers with him.

Luggage Cart Guy lingered still, though he looked about ready to bolt. Not if she could help it. Him they needed.

"Sir." She waved her hand at him to get his attention. "You promised to help us. Does that promise stand?"

"Yes. Yes, of course, ma'am, but . . ." He looked off down the hall. "I need to deliver this luggage first. When does your train leave?"

That bothersome question again. She didn't even know what train they were taking.

"10:40."

Oh. She'd quite forgotten Jackson was conscious now and could answer for himself.

"Very good, sir. That gives us a little less than an hour. Do you know your departure gate?"

"Gate four. To Rawlins."

"Right. Let me help you to that bench over yonder. Then I'll deliver this load and return with a conveyance that will get you to your departure gate in plenty of time. I promise."

Putting words to action, the man squatted down beside Jackson and threw one of his arms across his shoulders, beckoning Claire to do the same. Together, with Sadie pushing from behind, they were able to lift Jackson to his feet and maneuver him to the nearby bench. Then Luggage Cart Guy was off with a final promise to return soon. Claire hoped he was as good as his word. She also hoped she could convince the silent man next to her to allow them to join him on his journey.

At the moment, he didn't seem to notice her presence, just sat with his head cradled in his hands as if it was all he could do to stay upright. Given that blow to his head, it probably was. All the more reason for him to need her.

"Mama." Ella climbed into her lap and patted her cheek to gain her attention. "Why was that big man sleeping on the floor?"

"He wasn't sleeping, sweetie. He was hurt. And Mommy is going to try to help him feel better. But right now, I have an important job for you to do. Can you go with Aunt Sadie and help her buy our train tickets?" She pulled her wallet from the pocket of her skirt and handed it to Sadie. "I need to talk with Mr. Garrity for a minute."

"The 10:40 to Rawlins?" Sadie asked with a quirk of her eyebrow.

Claire nodded, and the two headed off toward the ticket counter.

"Mr. Garrity?" The man beside her did not move. "Mr. Garrity? Sir? May I speak with you for a moment?"

He turned his head marginally, peering up at her from between his fingers as he continued to cradle his head. His obvious pain gave her the courage to push forward.

"I'm sure you are wondering how I came to be here. I happen to believe it's more than coincidence. More like Providence, if you believe in such a thing, which usually I don't, but given the circumstances, I can't help but think . . ." She was babbling. She always did when she was nervous, but if she kept this up, she would lose him. She heaved a breath. "What I'm trying to say is, you need me. What the doctor said earlier is true. You have no business traveling in your condition. A concussion is not something you should ignore. You need someone who knows what signs to look for, who can watch over you in case you should lose consciousness again. I have medicine with me that could ease your pain. In short, Mr. Garrity, you need a nurse, and I, as it happens, need a job."

"No."

No? She hadn't even asked him yet. Not directly, anyway.

"Please? Just listen for a minute. For reasons I can't explain right now, I need to leave Denver. Today. The safety of my sister and daughter depends on it. I had hoped to find a nursing position before I left, but that's not possible now. That's why I believe my running into you was meant to be. You have to know you left the hospital far sooner than you were supposed to. In fact, I'm surprised they even released you."

"I released myself."

"Which is my point exactly. Your leg is barely out of traction. You still need weeks of supervised recovery and therapy if you ever hope to walk normally on that leg again. I know the exercises you will need. I know what procedures you would have undergone in the hospital. I can help."

He shook his head, wincing.

"Did I mention I have medicine that would help your pain? I wouldn't even need pay. Just room and board for my family and me. Please, Mr. Garrity. I wouldn't ask if I weren't desperate."

He heaved a great sigh. "I can't. I live with my father, and you wouldn't be welcome for reasons *I* can't explain right now."

Claire could tell by the set of his jaw he wasn't going to budge on this one.

"Very well. A compromise, then. Allow us to travel with you as far as Rawlins. I'll see you get the care you need on the journey in exchange for your protection."

"Protection?" He laced the word in sarcasm.

"Believe me, sir. Traveling in the company of a male, no matter how incapacitated, is far safer than the three of us traveling alone. Do we have a deal?"

"Suit yourself." He dropped his head back into the cradle of his hands. "And I'll take whatever it is you have for the pain."

CHAPTER 2

Jackson's head pounded in rhythm with the clanking of the train's wheels. The pain in his leg he'd long since learned to ignore. But this pain was relentless.

He leaned his head back against the seat, closed his eyes, and drew in long, slow breaths. The pain had abated to a manageable level with the powders Nurse Monroe had given him earlier, but those had long since worn off. He cracked his eyes to look at his traveling companions in the seat opposite—all asleep. Nurse Monroe's head rested on her sister's shoulder, who in turn rested her head against the window. The child slept in her mother's lap, sucking her thumb.

A pretty picture. One he might enjoy if it weren't for his throbbing head. He could wake the nurse, ask for more medication, but he didn't want to disturb her. She'd more than held up her end of their bargain, getting him transported to their gate and onto the train, settling him in his seat with pillows and blankets, propping the foot of his bad leg onto the seat beside her, providing a cold compress for his head. He'd been comfortable enough to sleep for a few hours until the pain returned in spades.

It would be so easy to wake her and beg for more medicine. His foot rested mere inches from her elbow. A simple tap with his casted foot, and he'd escape the pain again. But he wouldn't place himself any further in her debt. Because he wouldn't . . . *couldn't* . . . give her what she asked for—a job, protection, a home for herself and her family. He simply had nothing to give.

It hadn't always been this way. Before the accident, he'd had self-sufficiency, dreams, ambitions. A couple of kicks from a frightened horse, and now he was reliant on Pa for everything. And Pa . . . .

No.

Bringing the three of them home to Pa was beyond question.

Even if he could, he didn't know he *would* help this one. Nurse Monroe was a woman of secrets—dark ones that lingered in the recesses of those stormy gray eyes of hers. He'd known that from the first time he laid eyes on her back at St. Luke's. It wasn't that he didn't like her. He liked her fine . . . more than the other nurses who all tended to talk a body to death. Nurse Monroe was calm and competent. Her gentle touch had an uncanny ability to soothe. But she had secrets. Ones that apparently had erupted into trouble. There was no doubt she was deep in trouble now, from the soles of those sensible black half-boots to the tip of her ridiculous hat. And Jackson had about all the trouble he could manage in his life right now.

No. He wouldn't be helping Nurse Monroe, and because of that, he wouldn't be taking any more help from her. He'd just have to handle the pain without her.

The brakes squealed and hissed as the train slowed for the next station. Jackson covered his ears and closed his eyes against the sound. Breathing deeply again, he battled to regulate the pain that ricocheted inside his skull. *Please, God, make it stop.*

A tiny hand, soft as a bird's wing, tapped against his cheek. Turning his head, he looked into the eyes of the little one, now standing on the seat next to him. She was a beauty, with a halo of dark curls and gray eyes like her Mama.

"Mister, does your head hurt?"

He nodded and the pain ratcheted even with that slight movement.

"Ella help."

She reached her cool, tiny fingers up to his brow and began to massage it. Her touch was far too gentle to do much good, yet he found he didn't want her to stop. Something about the gesture brought a lump to his throat, making it difficult to swallow or talk.

Finally, after a minute or two, he reached up and took her hand. "Thank you, Ella. That's good." He hoped his gravelly voice didn't scare her.

"Better?"

"Yes."

She studied him a minute, then, apparently satisfied with what she saw, she climbed into his lap and sat down. Not easily scared, this one. He was far more comfortable with lambs and colts than baby humans, and ones of the female variety left him completely at a loss. Sure, he'd practically raised Gabe and Petie, but it'd been years since they'd been this young, and from what he could remember, they'd been entirely different creatures than this gentle little girl-child. They'd always been more interested in running, climbing, and generally getting into all sorts of mischief than sitting on anyone's lap.

"I sing for you?"

He glanced over at the two sleeping women across from them and put a finger to his lips. "Quietly. Don't wake the others."

She studied him with those smoky eyes, then began to croon in a voice barely above a whisper.

"Hushabye, don't you cwy.
Go to sleepy liddle baby.

When you wake, you shall have
All the purdy liddle horsies.
Dappas and gways
Blacks and bays
All the purdy liddle horsies."

She was singing him a lullaby. He couldn't remember the last time he'd heard a lullaby. Not since Ma, and that was years ago. The lump in his throat came back. His injuries must be making him soft.

Ella brought her song to an end, then stuck a finger in her mouth and looked at him. He should say something. But he never knew what to say to girls, no matter how small. Instead, he leaned his head back and closed his eyes.

"Do you like sleeping on the floor?"

What in tarnation?

"I'd rather sleep in a bed."

"But before. You were sleeping on the floor, and all those people were around you. Mama had to wake you."

Oh.

"I wasn't sleeping. I hit my head."

"Like the bad man?"

"What bad man?"

"The one at our house. He was sleeping on the floor too. And there was red paint all around him."

"Ella!" A shocked whisper cut into their conversation. "Mr. Garrity is not feeling well. He doesn't need you telling him one of your stories."

He opened his eyes just a sliver. Nurse Monroe was watching him, eyes wide and worried. Stories? Not likely. Secrets more like. Dark ones, as he'd suspected. If he weren't in so much pain, he might even care.

"Your head is hurting again, isn't it?"

And his leg and everything else. Now she was by his side, cool hand on his forehead. A stronger hand than her daughter's but no less gentle. She turned his head toward her and peered intently at his eyes.

"I'll give you something for your pain. It should help you sleep too."

He should fight it. He wanted to, but he didn't have it in him anymore. When she placed the glass at his lips, he swallowed, though he knew just by the smell that it wasn't headache powders like before. Laudanum. This round went to its sickly, sweet promise of oblivion. He'd fight another time. Just not today.

A SLAMMING DOOR AND DISTANT VOICES PIERCED THROUGH Jackson's drug-fogged brain. He opened his eyes to sunlight streaming through lacy white curtains. Where was he? St. Luke's? No. No beds besides his own filled this room. Stark white walls were replaced by dark, mahogany panels. Sensing someone with him, he turned his head. Nurse Monroe dozed in an upright chair next to his bed.

Memory returned in wisps. The accident in the train station, the pain-filled journey, laudanum, and blessed sleep. But somewhere within that sleep arose fuzzy memories of a laborious walk from the station in the dark of night and the final relief of a hotel bed. The Brunswick. He was staying at The Brunswick, waiting for Louis to come pick him up. But why was Nurse Monroe still here? Hadn't they agreed to part company once they arrived in Rawlins?

More memories surfaced, of bedpans and nausea, a steady arm bracing him, a cool hand at his forehead. And laudanum. Craving, even begging, for its sweet release. Embarrassment washed over him. It wasn't as if any of this was new to him. A man didn't spend six weeks in traction and not get immune to strangers caring for all his most basic needs. This was different somehow. Seeing Nurse Monroe outside the hospital setting and meeting her daughter and sister made it all more personal. She wasn't simply a nurse anymore. She was a woman, and a pretty one at that.

She needed to leave.

He'd be fine without her. Louis would be here soon. Or should be anyway, within a day or two. He'd sent the telegram as soon as he'd left St. Luke's. Yesterday, maybe? With any luck, Louis should arrive by Friday at the latest. Surely, he could manage on his own until then. He took quick inventory of his body. Head, no pain, thank God. Other than the grogginess left-over from the laudanum, everything felt completely normal in that area. Leg? The dull ache he'd learned to ignore remained, but not the wracking pain he'd felt after hobbling the block from the train station to the hotel. He should be fine once he got used to his crutches and gained a little strength.

Strength. That was his weak spot. The day Dr. Ferguson finally let him out of traction and the nurses helped him sit up, he'd been amazed at how little strength he had. He'd been as weak and wobbly as a newborn lamb. And today, after that harrowing train ride, his whole body felt heavy. Too heavy. He barely had the strength to lift a finger.

But he would manage. He had to, and once Louis got here, he'd have all the help he'd need. It was time for Nurse Monroe to go.

Placing his hands on either side of his hips, he struggled to sit up. Nurse Monroe jerked upright.

"You're awake," she said.

He would have laughed at the irony of that statement if she hadn't turned and faced him fully. Good God. A bruise shaded the circumference of her left eye and spilled down her cheek in varying shades of purple, blue, and yellow. She must have noticed him staring because she lifted a hand to shield her face, darting a quick glance toward the bureau atop which rested her large black hat. That explained the ridiculous veil.

"What happened?" His voice sounded angrier than he intended, but he couldn't help remembering Ella's "bad man." The little one hadn't been telling stories, no matter what her mother said.

Nurse Monroe stood and began to arrange the pillows behind him, allowing him to sit more comfortably. "Oh. I'm clumsy, is all. Hit a door jamb in the dark the other night when I was getting Ella a drink of water."

Either she or the door jamb had to be moving mighty fast to leave that sort of damage. If she'd added a galloping horse to the equation, he might have believed her. Might. As it was, he struggled with the slow burn that raged within him at the thought of a man—any man—leaving that kind of mark on her.

Oh, her secrets were deep, all right.

And she needed to go. The last thing he needed was a woman who couldn't be trusted in his life. And a woman with dark secrets was not someone he was likely to trust.

She turned to the small bedside table, poured some water from the pitcher, and handed him the glass. "You must be thirsty after all that laudanum."

He took the glass, letting the cold liquid soothe his parched throat. "Thank you."

"You look better today. Is your headache finally gone? You were out for so long. I was beginning to fear that blow to your head was worse than expected. You were pretty sick the first night we got here. Do you remember any of that?"

"Some. How long have we been here?"

"Three and a half days. You've been awake a few times here and there, but this is the first time you haven't asked for more pain medicine, so that must mean you're feeling better."

Three and a half days! Louis would be here sooner than he'd

thought. All the more reason to send Nurse Monroe and her family on their way.

He rubbed a hand across his face. Where to begin?

"You and your sister must be anxious to leave."

She shrugged. "We have nowhere to go."

"I told you in Denver, I can't hire a nurse."

She turned away, setting his glass on the bedside table. "Pity. You need one."

"I'll be fine once my brother gets here."

"Oh? And when will that be?"

"Soon. So, you need to think about moving on." That sounded rude even to his ears, but it needed to be said.

"I'm considering my options, Mr. Garrity. I will at least wait until your brother gets here."

"No need."

"No need?" She looked at him fully now, amused exasperation in her eyes. "Very well, then. I'll leave you to dress yourself and find your own lunch. Unless, of course, you aren't hungry. You did swallow a few sips of soup yesterday before you fell asleep again. I might warn you, though, the wait staff is very short-handed. In fact, the hotel's proprietress informed me this morning that if I expected to eat my meals in my room again today, I would need to fetch them myself. I wish you luck negotiating those stairs on your crutches while balancing a food tray. I know *I* could not manage it."

He must sound like an ungrateful jerk.

"Look. It's not like I don't appreciate all you've done for me. You've been great. But I can't hire you, and . . . and because of that, I can't let you help me anymore.

Her expression softened, compassion turning her eyes a soft gray. "I know it's hard for a strong man like yourself to accept help, especially from someone you barely know, but fate has put us together for whatever reason. Let me at least help out until your brother arrives."

18

"No." He had to prove to her he could manage by himself. Pushing himself off the pillows, he swung his legs over the side of the bed. He'd get up on his own. Then she'd see.

But he'd either not accounted for the weight of his splinted leg or the dizziness that hit him like a wave because instead of standing as he'd planned, he pitched forward into her arms. He thought for a moment they were both going over when his initial impact sent her back a few steps, but she managed to keep her balance and finally steadied them both. She was stronger than she looked.

He held onto her, struggling to retain his balance, and was suddenly aware of every curve, every soft valley of her body pressed against his. Didn't help that he was bare-chested. Or that her hair smelled as fresh as the spring winds off the Wind River mountains.

"Well, I'll be hog-tied."

His head jerked around at the sound of the familiar voice. He hadn't heard the door open, but there stood Louis in the doorway, looking like a spooked owl, eyes and mouth forming three perfect "O's." His brothers always did have lousy timing.

"Sorry. I . . . I didn't mean to interrupt . . . I . . . I'll come back."

As Louis turned away, Jackson pushed out of Nurse Monroe's arms and fell back onto the bed, his cast almost hitting her as he went down. Blasted leg. Why couldn't it cooperate?

"Get in here, Lou," he called to Louis's retreating back. "I need you."

Louis turned, his grin wide and mocking. "Doesn't look to me like you do."

"It's not what you think. Nurse Monroe was just helping me stand up."

"*Nurse* Monroe? That's not the story I heard."

"What do you mean?"

"Ran into Mrs. Peabody at the stage station in Rongis on my

way here. She's been in Denver visiting her daughter. Said she came in on the same train as you and that you'd taken a wife."

"What?" Jackson closed his eyes. Talk about lousy timing. Mrs. Peabody of all people. "Who else did she tell?"

"Who do you think? There's nothing that lady likes better than a juicy bit of gossip. And there's nothing she'd consider juicier than one of the Garrity boys taking a wife. 'Course *I* didn't believe it. Until I checked for you at the front desk, and they told me Mr. and *Mrs.* Garrity could be found in room 304."

Jackson groaned and fell back against his pillows. What a mess. The news would be spread from here to Lander by the time he got there. Pa would be . . . Blast! Pa.

"I'm afraid this is my fault." Nurse Monroe stepped from the corner where she'd retreated when Louis entered the room. Her hands trembled a bit as she clasped them in front of her. "You were so ill when we got here, and given the circumstances, I put both our rooms under your name. I didn't stop to consider the consequences."

She kept her eyes trained on the floor as she spoke. This was the first time he'd ever seen her react with anything other than poise and confidence. If he didn't know better, he'd think she was afraid of Louis.

He blew out a sigh. "Never mind. It's not the first time our family has been fodder for gossip. I'll set things straight when I get home."

Louis cocked an eyebrow at him. "So, you two aren't married?"

"No. I told you. She's my nurse. Or was my nurse. She was one of the nurses at St. Luke's. We happened to run into each other at the train depot in Denver. I was in pretty lousy shape, so she agreed to help me as far as Rawlins. That's all."

Louis crossed his arms, skepticism written all over his face. "Very considerate of you to take time from your journey to take care of my brother for so many days, Nurse Monroe. Where is it you are headed?"

"Wherever I can get a job."

"Let me get this straight. You left a job in Denver and were willing to travel to the middle of nowhere Wyoming with my brother but don't even have a job waiting for you?"

Jackson noticed Nurse Monroe kept the left side of her face angled away from Louis. He doubted his brother had noticed the bruising around her eye. If he had, he might not have been so inquisitive.

"Look, her reasons for leaving Denver are none of our business. Fact is, you're here now, and I no longer need her help." He turned back to Nurse Monroe. "As I was saying before Louis arrived, you are free to go any time."

She held his gaze for a moment, then nodded. "I wish you well then. Would you like me to leave the bottle of laudanum for you? I'm assuming you still have a bit of travel ahead of you before you get home. You'll need it before you get there."

"No. I'll be fine."

She returned to the bedside table, swept the items on it into her bag, then started toward the door.

"Wait." Louis stepped in front of her, freezing when the impact of her black eye hit him for the first time. He paused for just a heartbeat, then continued. "You should come with us. You said yourself you don't have a job, and I don't know of anyone in the area who needs nursing care as much as my brother does."

Jackson couldn't believe what he was hearing. "Are you daft? Pa would never stand for it, and you know it."

"He *might*. We'd never know unless we try."

"*I* know. And so do you. It's not going to work."

"Hear me out. I hate to say it, Jack, but that hospital didn't do you any favors. You look worse today than you did when I put you on the train six weeks ago."

"They saved my leg."

"Maybe, but you're nowhere near getting any use out of it. The way I see it, you're going to need a lot more care than Pa, the boys, and I can give you. You have a nurse right here who needs a job and knows more about the kind of care you need than anyone."

"Which is precisely what I've been telling your brother all along." Nurse Monroe's voice regained all its lost confidence.

"So, it's settled then? You'll join us?"

"No." Jackson hadn't meant to shout, but Louis must have taken that blow to the head instead of him. He could think of no other reason he'd suggest something so crazy. "Nurse Monroe also has a *daughter* and a *sister* in her care." He enunciated the words slowly to let them sink in. "I'm not taking all three of them two hundred miles from the nearest railroad on what we both know is a fool's errand. Much as you might not like it, Lou, your nursing duties start now. Nurse Monroe, you are free to go."

Glancing between them, she gave a quick nod, then slipped through the door that conjoined their two rooms.

CHAPTER 3

Claire leaned her head against the door to Jackson's room and let out a shaky breath. She'd been *so* close to getting that job, but maybe it was for the best. Were all the men in Wyoming as big as the Garrity brothers? She'd gotten used to Jackson's size, mainly because he'd been totally incapacitated for the majority of the time she'd known him. One didn't fear a crippled man . . . much. But when his brother arrived, and she saw what Jackson probably looked like before the accident— taller by four inches than any average man, powerful, and muscular, and . . . and downright big. The damage a man like that could do with just a flick of his wrist made her want to cast up her breakfast.

She walked over to the armchair and sank into its soft cush- ions. Thank goodness he hadn't been able to hire her. Really. Oh, he seemed harmless enough now, but Jonas had once seemed just as harmless. What did she actually know about him? No. This was best. He simply wasn't worth the risk.

The nurse in her hated leaving him with his health so fragile, though. From the sounds of it, he had many days of travel ahead of him. Hard travel. Not like riding a train, and he'd barely survived that. But their parting ways was for the best. The west-bound train left at ten o'clock tonight, and she and Ella and Sadie would be on it. They'd go as far as Ogden, maybe even Reno, and then she'd look for a job caring for some helpless old lady or spinster invalid—but *no men*. She'd find a job that would allow them all to live together for once.

Right.

And the moon really was made of green cheese.

She pushed herself out of the armchair and took down her valise. She might as well pack. They hadn't brought much in their haste to leave Denver. Still, any action was better than sitting and stewing about their situation.

She finished adding Ella's tiny dresses and underthings to the bag, then turned her attention to her gray traveling suit. Shaking out the skirt, she surveyed it for stains and wrinkles. Could be fresher, but it would have to do. She picked up the jacket but dropped it back onto the bed when the door to their room collided open with a bang.

Sadie stood in the doorway holding Ella on her hip, red-faced and panting as if she'd been running rather than taking the leisurely walk she'd intended.

"What in the world . . . ?"

Sadie let Ella slide to the floor, then quickly shut the door behind them.

"Go play with your babies for a minute, sweetie, while I talk to Mommy."

Ella trotted over to the corner where they had set up a make-shift nursery for her dolls. Sadie took Claire by the arm and pulled her to the other side of the bed.

"You're on a wanted poster," she hissed.

Ice coursed through Claire's veins tingling to her hands and feet. She sank onto the bed behind her.

"Me? Are you sure? Where?"

"At the depot. And it wasn't you, precisely. It was Mrs. Dempsey."

Claire let out a deep breath. It could be worse.

"How did it describe her?"

Sadie pulled a crumpled paper from her pocket and handed it to her.

"Sarah Rose Montgomery! You took it?"

"Shhh." She tipped her head in Ella's direction by way of warning. "No one saw me. The telegrapher had his back to me, and the waiting room was empty. You were right, by the way. Only two trains a day, and the westbound doesn't leave until ten."

Claire smoothed out the handbill.

Her eyes were drawn to the Pinkerton logo at the top of the page, followed by the words: *WANTED. $1000 REWARD. Seeking information into the whereabouts of a Mrs. Wilhelmina Dempsey of Denver, Colorado.*

One-thousand dollars! Someone was willing to pay a generous sum to find them. But then, a man was dead. Murder wasn't something the law took lightly. She drew in another deep breath and slowly let it out. Murder. Would she ever become accustomed to that word?

She scanned down to the description: Age forty to forty-two years, height five foot seven inches, weight around 160 pounds, red hair, gray eyes, light complexion, well-proportioned, attractive woman. Often wears a black bonnet and mourning veil. Could be traveling with two daughters, ages seventeen and three.

Mr. Hennessy must have provided the description. And found the body. Which is what they'd anticipated when they sent him that anonymous message before leaving Denver. Much as she would have liked the extra time to get far away before anyone started looking for them, she couldn't stomach the thought of Jonas lying undiscovered until Mr. Hennessy paid his monthly visit for the rent.

Thank goodness she'd decided to leave Mrs. Dempsey behind in Denver. All her dresses still hung in the wardrobe of the cottage they'd rented. Apart from the red wig which lay buried at the bottom of her valise and the widow's bonnet which was . . . drat, still on the bureau in Jackson's room. She'd need to retrieve that before they left and dispose of it somehow. She wanted nothing left to connect her to the woman on this handbill.

"So, what are we going to do?"

Claire looked up from the handbill into Sadie's worried eyes. "The first thing *you* are going to do is get out your paints and help me cover this bruise on my eye. If I'm not going to wear the widow's veil, I'll need something to hide it."

Sadie took hold of her chin and turned her face toward the light. "I'll be able to mask some of it, but we should alter your gray felt. It has a wide enough brim, and if I use some of the veil from your black, we can shade that side of your face so no one will notice."

Sadie was a master with shadows and veils. Mrs. Dempsey had been her brainchild two years ago when they'd fled St. Louis. Her expertise in turning her then twenty-two-year-old sister into a middle-aged widow could be attested by the fact that description appeared on the wanted poster. For two years, their landlord had never suspected the woman from whom he collected rent each month was anything other than she appeared. The fact no one in the Pearl Street neighborhood knew of Nurse Monroe and no one at St. Luke's knew of Mrs. Dempsey was the only thing working in their favor right now.

"We need to work out a new disguise. The husband-and-wife ruse has worked pretty well. Do you think you could make me up to look like a man?"

Sadie, who was now sorting through her paints and

powders, snorted. "I may be good, but I'm not that good. You're far too pretty to pass as a man, and I'm far too short. My vote is that you keep the disguise you're using right now."

"Nurse Monroe?" Claire shook her head. "Too easy to trace back to Denver. Much as I like the name, I'll probably have to let that one go." Monroe had been her mother's maiden name, which Jonas had not known. Paired with her middle name, Claire, it had kept her linked to her past and her real self. But now, like her earlier disguises, the name had served its course.

Sadie motioned her into the chair by the bureau and began applying cold cream to her cheek and eye. The cool lotion felt good against her skin. "I meant you should keep on being Mrs. Garrity. You said yourself the husband-and-wife role worked. Are you sure Mr. Garrity won't take us with him? He needs a nurse."

"But he doesn't want one. Besides, his brother came while you were out. As far as he's concerned, I am no longer needed. And it's just as well, really. We can't keep up the fake couple ruse. Not in his hometown."

"Maybe. But seeing that handbill has me spooked. I'd rather be heading to some remote ranch than continuing along the rail route. You know that handbill will be in every station."

"There's no way anyone will connect the description of Mrs. Dempsey with either of us."

"But the fact they already have a wanted poster out means someone is on the case. The handbill mentioned a Pinkerton detective. What if someone makes the connection between Mrs. Dempsey and Nurse Monroe back in Denver? You know they'll follow the rail route first. And this is a small enough town that if you come into town claiming to be Mrs. Garrity and leave four days later as someone else. Well, that's bound to stir up questions."

She made a good argument, but there was little they could do about it. "We'll just have to be discreet when we leave for the train station. It's late enough at night that maybe no one will really notice, and if Jackson leaves in the morning, hopefully, everyone will assume we went with him."

"If he leaves in the daylight, someone is bound to see him and notice we're not with him. I don't like it. Can't you ask him again if he will take us with him?"

"No, but I will ask him to leave before daybreak. It's the best I can do. When we get to Ogden, we'll find a way to disappear. Surely, we'll be able to think of another disguise by then."

Sadie applied a final layer of powder, then stepped back to survey her handiwork. "I think that will do. Especially if we place the hat and veil just right. I had to cover that bruise on your chin as well. He really did a number on you this time. I don't think I've ever seen it this bad."

"It's been two years. You've probably forgotten."

Sadie snorted. "Keep telling yourself that if you want, but I know what I saw when I walked into that kitchen. If I hadn't been there, you'd be dead right now." Her voice broke a little on those last words. She firmed her lips, blinked fiercely, then shook her head as if to shake off the thought. "Anyway, be sure to wear your high-collared shirtwaists, or we'll need to cover those bruises around your throat as well."

Claire reached out and pulled Sadie into a hug. "I haven't had a chance to tell you this yet, but thank you. I don't take what you did lightly. Believe me."

"What? Murdering your husband? Why, I'd do that for you anytime. Don't think of it."

"Not murder." Sadie might sound flippant, but Claire knew the word bothered her just as much as it did her. "Self-defense. There's no crime in killing if it's done to protect the ones you love."

"Which is precisely why we're running, right?"

"We're running because Jonas was a man, and we live in a

man's world. In God's eyes, you aren't guilty. Trust me in this, Sadie."

Sadie shrugged and pulled out of Claire's embrace. "It doesn't matter. I'm fine. No need to worry about me. Let's get packed."

~

A RAPPING AT THE DOOR WOKE JACKSON THIS TIME. APPARENTLY, hotels weren't the best places for daytime sleep. Not that he wanted to make a habit of sleeping the day away, but sleep was about all he seemed able to do these days.

"Come in." Even his voice sounded weak.

Louis had gone to see about supplies for their trip home. He supposed this might be Nurse Monroe and the girls, coming to say their final goodbyes. He hated that he found that thought depressing. They were no longer his concern.

But the weathered face that poked itself around the door was a far cry from Nurse Monroe's.

"Mr. Baldwin!"

"And the Missus." The man chuckled as he pulled his plump, pretty wife into the room after him.

Jackson struggled to sit up, glad he'd made Louis help him dress before he left. Mrs. Baldwin was as close as he had to a mother, but he still didn't want to greet her in his union suit.

"Oh, Jackson," she exclaimed as she swayed into the room. "What did they do to you at that hospital? Why, you're as thin as a rail." She placed her hand against his cheek and shook her head. "We'll have to see what we can do to get you fattened up again."

Mr. Baldwin came and stood at the end of his bed. "You are a bit more peaked than I was expecting. Are you sure they didn't dismiss you too early?"

"I dismissed myself."

"Ah. That explains it. You always were a stubborn one, but I have to tell you, son. This is one time you maybe should have listened to the doctor."

"I'll be fine now I'm shed of that place."

Frown lines formed between the man's dark brows as he surveyed Jackson's leg. "Still in a cast, then? I thought you might be out of that by now."

"No, sir. Just out of traction."

"You'll walk on it again, though, right?"

Jackson shrugged. "Doc said I would. No guarantees I won't always have a limp, though."

"Well, at least you still have the leg. When I first saw it after the accident, I wouldn't have bet you'd be able to keep it. I'm glad we sent you to Denver."

"Yes, sir. Thank you for that. But what are you doing in Rawlins? I didn't expect to see the two of you until I got home."

"We've been to Laramie for the annual sheep ranchers' convention. Got in this morning and decided to rest up before we took the stage home. Ran into Louis in the lobby. Could have bowled me over with a feather when he told us you were here. Figured you'd be in the hospital at least another month."

"Couldn't stomach it anymore. Besides, spring's coming."

Baldwin turned to his wife. "Didn't I tell you, Beatrice? Trying to keep Jackson in a hospital would be like trying to cage a mountain lion. The boy just isn't cut out for enclosed spaces." He turned back to Jackson. "I guess I should be surprised you lasted as long as you did. I can't say I'm sorry you'll be home in time for shearing and lambing, though. I could use your help."

"Don't know that I'll be much help this year." How he hated admitting that.

"Now, I wasn't expecting your help out on the range. Louis, and Gabe, and the other herders can help there. I'm talking about help with the record-keeping and numbers. It'll be good experience for when you run your own ranch someday. But as I said when you left for Denver. Your first job is to get well. Gain your strength back. You'll get the same pay, like I promised."

"I appreciate that, sir, but I don't feel right taking pay for doing nothing. You've already covered the hospital expenses. Why don't we wait until I'm back at work to talk pay again?"

"Office work isn't exactly doing nothing, son. Besides, you were hurt by one of my horses. And, from what I've been told, you may have saved Charlie's life. You'll take your pay just like before. No arguing."

No use trying, anyway. Mr. Baldwin was about the best boss a man could ask for. He'd taken him on when Jackson was just a scrawny kid and taught him everything he knew about the sheep business. Not only did his mentor know about his dream to someday run his own sheep ranch, but he also encouraged it. Jackson had hoped to be able to buy his first flock this fall, but when he broke his leg, he figured that dream was long gone. Now he wasn't so sure, especially if Baldwin continued to pay him. It would take a lot of work to get his leg back to where it once had been, but he'd do it gladly if it meant he could still start a ranch of his own in the fall.

A tap sounded on the door adjoining his room to Nurse Monroe's. Not waiting for his answer, she stepped into the room, stopping short when she saw the Baldwins.

"I'm sorry. I didn't know you had company. I left my hat here earlier. I'll just grab it and get out of your way."

"Why, Jackson Garrity." Mrs. Baldwin was suddenly all smiles. "Then the rumors I've heard are true. I never would have believed it if I hadn't seen it with my own eyes. You have a wife. Come here, dear, and let me look at you. My, but you're a lovely thing." She pulled the startled nurse into a warm and lengthy embrace. "You have no idea how happy I am that Jackson has finally married."

Nurse Monroe looked at him over the top of Mrs. Baldwin's shoulder, eyes wide and pleading.

He cleared his throat. "Um. No. There's been a mistake. We're not married."

Mr. Baldwin's gaze lingered on the door adjoining their two rooms. "What do you mean, not married?" His voice vibrated disapproval.

"She's my nurse. *Was* my nurse, back at St. Luke's. Then, I had another accident at the train station the day I left. Got run into by a man pushing a luggage cart and couldn't catch myself because of my leg. Knocked me cold. She happened to be there, traveling with her family, saw the accident, and came to help. Because I was in such bad shape, she agreed to stay and help me until Louis got here."

Mrs. Baldwin released Nurse Monroe and turned toward him, all her smiles long gone. "Jackson Alexander Garrity. What have you done? Staying four days in adjoining hotel rooms with a woman who is not your wife?"

"It's not like that. I wasn't even conscious most of the time, and Louis can vouch for the fact that I can't get out of bed without help."

"Whether it's like that or not, it's what people will think. Why, even we heard the rumors about the newlyweds on the third floor who hadn't left their rooms for four days. At the time, we had no idea it was you, but if you were to leave here and both go your separate ways, believe me, the rumors will fly. And they won't be pretty. We won't be party to this type of scandal, not after what those men did to our Mary. You *know* we won't. We can't." She turned to her husband, tears in her eyes. "Joseph, fix this." Then with a swish of her skirts, she left the room.

A knot formed in the pit of Jackson's stomach. She was right. Though his actions were nothing like the men who had ruined their daughter, the Baldwin's could never continue to hire a man known for having illicit relations with a woman, no matter how false those claims may be. His dreams of owning a ranch of his own faded to dust.

"I'm sorry, sir. I didn't think . . . I never meant . . ."

Mr. Baldwin held up a hand to stop him. "Doesn't matter. The deed is done. No matter how innocent you may be, people are going to believe the worst. There's an easy enough fix, though. We'll get you hitched tonight."

Nurse Monroe gasped. "Oh, no, sir. There's no need for that. I'm not here alone. My sister is with me. And my daughter."

"Ah. You're a married woman. Why didn't you say so?"

"No. I'm not married. I mean, not now anyway. I'm . . .," she cleared her throat. "I'm widowed."

"But you and Jackson haven't spent any part of the past four days alone together?"

"Not exactly. Sadie has taken Ella for walks on occasion. My daughter is only three and doesn't do well cooped up in a small room. And Jackson needed someone to care for him at night. He truly has not been well."

Mr. Baldwin shook his head. "Then I'm afraid marriage is your only choice." He pulled out his pocket watch and checked the time. "Since you're incapacitated, Jackson, I'll make the arrangements. Expect us back here by seven."

After he left, Nurse Monroe sank into the chair beside the bed and covered her face with her hands. "I'm so sorry, Mr. Garrity. I never thought I would cost you your job. I never even thought about how this would affect you. You were so sick that night. All I wanted was to get you settled in a bed as quickly as possible. I never supposed registering us all under your name would jeopardize *your* reputation."

She raised her head to look at him. A tear coursed down her left cheek, creating a dark channel in the white of her face. Was that paint? Of course, it was. He saw now that her bruise was covered. Great. A painted lady with a dark past that made what he was about to say sound crazy, but he wasn't ready to bury his ranching dreams just yet.

"Maybe we should do it."

"Do what? *Marry?*"

He held up a hand to stop the protest he saw coming. "Let me explain. I don't know what you're running from. Or who. I don't want to know. But I do know the three of you need a place to go. You've told me that often enough, and while my circumstances won't allow me to provide a *job* for you, maybe I could provide for you if we were married. Are you truly free to marry?"

For a minute, he didn't think she was going to answer, but then came a nod so slight it was barely perceptible. "But I don't *want* a husband, Mr. Garrity."

"And I don't *want* a wife. We wouldn't be the first couple in history to marry for convenience. We'd make it a marriage on paper, not in fact. The Baldwins will be happy, I'll keep my job, and you'll have a home for your daughter and sister. Problems solved."

"You can't possibly want to be tied to a fake marriage."

"I didn't say fake. The marriage itself will be legal. Like I said, we won't be the first couple to marry for reasons other than love."

Her face paled. "I won't be a wife to you in . . . in . . . the real way. Ever. I *can't.*"

Her revulsion ran deep. He had to believe it had everything to do with her past and nothing to do with him.

"Fine. You won't have to. I never planned on getting married anyway. So, I won't be giving up any dreams by marrying you."

"Children?"

"I'll have Ella."

"Most men would want a son to carry on their name."

"I have three brothers. I think the Garrity line is safe."

She stood and began pacing the room. Up and back. Up and back. Finally, she stopped at the foot of his bed.

"I can't. I'm sorry. I won't be trapped in another marriage."

Trapped. Right. Her secrets. He let out a sigh. It had been worth a try. Blast. He was so close. Five months, maybe six, and he'd have the money he needed to buy 2000 head of sheep. It wasn't much, but it was a start. But if Baldwin let him go now . . . with both his health and reputation in shambles . . . everything he'd saved so far would go to merely staying alive. Ten years of working and planning and saving. All for nothing.

"Six months." He hated that he sounded desperate. "Give me six months. By then, I'll have enough to buy my own outfit, and you'll be free to go. We'll get an annulment. Whatever. I give you my word."

"Your word." She stared at him as if she were trying to read his soul. Maybe she was. After what seemed an eternity, she closed her eyes and drew a deep breath. "Very well, Mr. Garrity. I'll take you at your word. I'll marry you for a safe place for my family as long as we both understand that after six months, I'm free to go."

"Deal." He held out his hand, and she placed her small one in his for the handshake. His ranching dreams were safe. Hopefully, they hadn't come at a cost greater than either of them was willing to pay.

CHAPTER 4

Widowed on Monday, married on Friday . . . only a fool would do that. But then, she'd been a fool before. Jonas was proof of that.

The wagon lurched and bucked. Claire tightened her hold on the man lying beside her to keep him from rolling.

Her husband.

Speaking of fools. The stubborn idiot. What had possessed him to dismiss himself from the hospital four weeks early, knowing full well *this* journey lay ahead of him? No amount of padding and blankets could make the ride comfortable, no matter how much she tried. Her own backside was bruised and aching, and she was able-bodied. She could only imagine the pain he was in.

Not that he complained.

But the pallor of his face and his clenched jaw told her all she needed to know. Still, he refused the medicine that could render him oblivious to it all. Of course, he did. Heaven forbid he should be so weak. Oh, he'd allowed the morphine the first two days, but since yesterday, he'd refused all medicine, preferring to lay there in stoic silence when she knew very well the continuous rocking and pitching of the wagon was wreaking havoc with his leg. But if he could be stubborn, so could she. Instead of relieving the monotony by walking alongside the wagon, as Ella and Sadie were doing, she remained by his side, trying her best to keep him from knocking around and praying this excruciating trip would be done soon.

The wagon crested another rise, the scene ahead suddenly different from what had gone before. So far, they'd seen miles upon miles of tan and brown grasses dotted with silvery green clumps of sagebrush and patches of white where the spring snows had yet to melt. And rocks. Plenty of rocks. Trees were practically non-existent unless a house or creek was nearby, and those were few and far between.

But ahead of her lay new terrain. Here, the road wound down into a gentle valley of yet more grass and sage but was bordered on the east by a line of scarlet cliffs, brilliant against the dull colors that had dominated the scenery thus far.

She turned to Jackson. "What's that called up ahead? That canyon there."

He opened his eyes, scanned the view, then closed them again with a sigh. "That's called home."

She could almost hear the relief in that sigh.

Home.

There was a beauty to it amidst the wild, untamed vastness. But home? Not for her. Not yet anyway. Yet somewhere in that wide valley was a place her husband called home. A place he was willing to endure great pain to return to. A place that, even in the middle of his terrible pain, put the slightest of smiles on his face. Would it be the same for her? Could it? Only time would tell. One thing was for sure. A person could lose herself in this immense wilderness. Which was exactly what she hoped to do.

She would never have agreed to this farce of a marriage, no matter how temporary, if it hadn't guaranteed an escape from civilization. And wanted posters. And Pinkerton detectives. But after three days of traveling through the most desolate country she'd ever seen, she was beginning to relax. Surely, no detective, no matter how good, would connect the current Mrs. Garrity of middle-of-nowhere Wyoming with the Mrs. Dempsey on that wanted poster.

She braced her legs against the side of the wagon as it lurched over yet another rock and began its slow descent into the valley ahead. Louis had said they'd be at the ranch by night-fall. One more day of this constant rocking and pitching, and they'd be done with it. She couldn't wait. Jackson moaned as the wagon gave another strong jolt.

"Are you sure you don't want some laudanum? It would ease the pain and make the day seem shorter."

He shook his head, eyes still closed. "Better not. You meet Pa today."

You meet Pa today. What did he mean by that? How could his taking laudanum in any way affect her meeting his father? She considered asking him but decided not to waste her breath. He had deflected every one of her questions about the ranch and his family so far. Given the pain he was battling today, she doubted he'd be any more obliging. The man was tight-lipped in the best of circumstances. She'd just have to wait until they got there to have her curiosity satisfied.

The wagon slowed and pulled to a halt beside Sadie and Ella, who had walked on ahead. They now sat on a boulder on the side of the road.

"Legs get tired?" Louis asked.

"Ella's did." Sadie handed Ella to her over the side of the wagon, then climbed up on the seat beside Louis. Sadie was far more at ease with both of the Garrity brothers than Claire was, but then, she wasn't married to one of them. Nor had she the history with Jonas that Claire did. She'd been just as trusting of men as Sadie was when she was her age. Sometimes she missed her own innocence.

Ella's sharp elbow poked Claire in the side as she settled in beside her.

"Why is the diwt wed, Mama? And those walls?"

"Those are cliffs, sweetie, not walls. And I guess they are red because God made them that way. Just like he made the sky blue and the grass green."

"But it wasn't wed before. It was bwown."

"Yes. He's painted it prettier here. He does that sometimes."

"Why?"

Ah. This game again. Ella was queen of the whys these days.

"I don't know, honey. He just did. Now, why don't you crawl under this blanket so you'll be nice and warm? It's time you took a nap."

"I'm not sleepy. Tell me a story, Mama."

"What story would you like?" As if she didn't already know. There was only one that Ella requested these days. She'd told it about ten times since their journey began. Luckily Claire knew it by heart and had no need to dig out the storybook buried somewhere in her valise.

"Wose Wed."

"All right. But you must close your eyes while I tell it."

Ella curled in close, resting her head on Claire's lap and closing her eyes.

"Once upon a time, there was a poor widow who lived in a little cottage with a garden in front of it. In the garden were two rose bushes, one red and the other white. She also had two daughters who were exactly like those rose bushes—one was called Snow White and the other Rose Red."

By the time she reached the part where the dwarf was caught in the tree, Ella was asleep. Claire pulled the blanket close around her and dropped a kiss onto her dark curls. Not all that happened with Jonas was bad. This little one was her life, and without Jonas, that life never would have been. Maybe now that

Jonas was dead, she could finally put the dark times behind her and focus only on the good.

As long as this new marriage didn't somehow turn bad, as well. *Trust me*, he'd said. But what if she had no trust left to give?

Jackson clenched his jaw to keep another moan from escaping. When had he become such a lightweight? Pain pulsed through his leg and up to his back with every heartbeat, intensifying each time the wagon rocked and bounced over rocks in the road. Just four more miles to the ranch. Surely, he could survive four miles. Maybe once he got home, he'd allow himself the relief of laudanum. Maybe. But not until Pa met the girls. He couldn't afford to have his brain addled for that. No telling how Pa was going to take his having a wife.

Wife.

The word still felt strange, especially since the ceremony itself seemed more of a dream than reality, mixed now with all the drug-induced images that had filled the days in between. He vaguely recalled insisting on standing with the aid of his crutches rather than lying like an invalid in bed, then feeling relieved that the minister kept the ceremony blessedly short so he didn't have the embarrassment of falling at the feet of his new bride. No man wanted to start a marriage that way, even if the marriage was just a farce. The rest was a blur, but it must have happened given the fact Nurse Monroe now sat in the wagon bed beside him, a simple gold band encircling her left ring finger. Where that came from, he had no idea. Mr. Baldwin must have arranged for it.

Jackson had told Claire the truth when he'd said he'd never planned to get married. The way he saw it, women were more trouble than they were worth. Oh sure, he knew of men who were happily married. Mr. Baldwin. His friend, Rob Skivington.

But Jackson had never been comfortable around women. He never knew what to say to them. And they never knew what to make of him either. As far as he was concerned, life was simpler without them.

But now, not only did he have a wife, he was also responsible for a daughter and sister-in-law. The magnitude of what he'd agreed to yesterday was beginning to set in.

He glanced back at Ella and Sadie following along behind the wagon again. Sadie held Ella's hand as she jumped from rock to rock. The little one had far too much energy to stay cooped up in the wagon for long. Guess the fact they were traveling at a snail's pace counted for something.

The wagon lurched over yet another boulder. He stifled a groan, bracing his good leg against the other side of the wagon as it turned to negotiate a steep patch in the road. A crack, loud as a shotgun blast, ripped through the air. The wagon careened sideways. They were going over!

He pulled Nurse Monroe into his arms and curled around her, hoping to shield her from the worst of the impact. His shoulder hit the ground with a thud, and then they were rolling. His casted leg slammed against a boulder sending a jolt of pain through his body so fierce he must have blacked out. The next thing he knew, he was looking into Nurse Monroe's startled eyes as she struggled to get up. He still had her clutched against his chest but, thankfully, hadn't landed on top of her. He loosened his hold, and she rolled off him.

"Mr. Garrity. Jackson." Her face hovered over his, one cheek scratched and bleeding. "Are you hurt?"

He took a quick inventory of his body. "I don't think so. Just . . . my leg . . ."

"Your bad one?"

He nodded.

"You probably jarred it in the fall. The cast should have kept it from doing too much damage."

"Claire!" Sadie came scrambling over the rocks toward them, white-faced and breathless, carrying Ella on her hip. "We saw the wagon tip and start rolling. Are you all right?"

"We're fine. Just a little banged up is all. Where's Louis?"

Sadie looked down the hill and screamed. "Oh, my stars!" She dropped Ella into Claire's lap and took off at a run.

Turning in the direction Sadie was running, Claire gasped and struggled to her feet. "Honey, stay here with Mr. . . . with Jackson. I need to go help Aunt Sadie."

Ella clung fast to her mother's skirts. "Mama. You're bweeding."

"I'm all right, sweetie. It's just a scratch. Stay here a minute."

Ella dropped onto the rock beside him, an obvious frown on her face. Jackson craned his neck, trying to see where the girls had gone, but he couldn't see over the rise ahead of him. Blast! Of all the times to be weaker than a mewling kitten. He couldn't even sit up by himself, let alone help Louis. He rolled onto his stomach, ignoring the shooting pain the movement initiated in his leg. Pushing up on his elbows, he belly-crawled until he could see down the hill in front of him. Debris lay scattered in all directions—blankets, luggage, boards—and there, about thirty yards ahead, lay the wagon, bottom side up, missing one wheel. The girls crouched beside something on its far side. Louis? He couldn't tell. He forced himself to roll two rotations to his left and tried again.

Yes. There. Louis. He lay face down and totally still. Dear God. No.

Wait. He moved. Just now. His head turned as Sadie rested a hand on his back. Jackson let out a pent-up breath. *Thank you, Lord.* But he needed to get down there.

"Whatcha doing, Mr. Jackson?" Ella plopped down on her belly beside him, her little face inches from his.

"Playing a game. Wanna help?"

Her dark eyes sparkled. "Wing awound the wosie?"

"No. This one's called Find Jackson's Crutches." He swept a hand toward all the debris spread before them. "Let's see which of us can be the first to spot them."

They lay side by side for a moment, scanning the scene.

"I see one!" Ella crowed.

"Where?"

She pointed across the scattered landscape to where the bottom part of a crutch peaked out from beneath a blue blanket.

"Good eye. And I see the other over there by your mother's carpetbag. Do you think you could get them for me?"

She was off before he finished his sentence, dragging one up the hill to him and running back down for the other. He rolled over onto his back and sat up. Bringing the crutches close, he used them to pull himself up, hand over hand, until he was standing, albeit clumsily. He hopped a bit on his good foot until he gained his balance and was able to wrestle the crutches into place. Then came the slow descent to the wagon.

By the time he reached his brother, he was sweating, and the girls had Louis sitting up.

"How're you doing?"

Louis gave a lop-sided smile. "Oh, peachy. Never felt better."

"He's dislocated his shoulder," Nurse Monroe said, "and probably broken a few ribs. If you help me, we can get his shoulder back in place. Sadie, give me your shawl." She wrapped it low around his waist and handed the ends to Jackson. "Here. Take these and just hold onto them a minute. Louis, I need you to lay down again and relax. I promise this will make it feel better. Now, Jackson, pull towards you with the shawl, and I'll just . . ." She slowly pulled Louis's arm at an angle toward her. "There. That's done it, I think. Did you hear the pop?"

Louis nodded.

"Try reaching over to touch your other shoulder. Yes, that's it. Back in place." She took the shawl from him and fashioned a sling. "You'll need to keep it immobile for a few days, but it'll probably be those ribs that give you the most trouble."

She sat on the ground beside Louis and looked around. He had a feeling it was the first thought she'd given to their situation since the accident happened. He followed her gaze as it took in the debris, scattered belongings, and broken wagon.

"Now what?" she said.

He wished he knew.

"Did Cain and Abel get loose?" Louis asked.

The mules. He hadn't even thought of them in all the excitement. They certainly weren't standing by the wagon, but if they'd gone down in the wreckage, the height of the wagon's edge would block them from their view. He took off as fast as he could hobble on his crutches, letting out a whistle in case they had gotten loose and were still nearby. An answering whinny came from the front of the wagon. As he drew closer, he saw one of the mules lying on his side, hopelessly entangled in the traces and reins.

"Hey, boy, hey," he levered himself down beside him, keeping his casted leg away from the mule's body. The mule turned his head, the star on his forehead identifying him as Abel. Jackson stroked his neck, crooning softly to steady him. A quick glance at his body and legs showed no visible injuries. "Easy there, buddy. We'll get you out of this."

Abel whinnied and kicked as Sadie and Nurse Monroe rounded the front of the wagon.

"Can we help?"

"Stay back a minute. He's pretty spooked."

"Where's the other one?"

"Not sure." He let out another whistle, hoping Cain was still within earshot. If not, he was probably halfway to the ranch already, provided he had his wits about him and wasn't injured. As he worked to untangle the reins from around Abel's legs, Nurse Monroe unlatched the traces from the wagon frame. A few minutes later, the mule was loose and scrambling to his feet. Jackson ducked and rolled to avoid getting trampled. Blasted leg was of no use around livestock.

Sadie helped him to his feet and gave him his crutches while Nurse Monroe stroked Abel's neck, her calming touch working the same magic on him as it did on her patients.

"Any damage?" Louis rounded the back of the wagon, holding Ella's hand and walking like an old man. The gray of his face testified to the pain he was in.

"He's probably in better shape than you are. Better sit down before you fall down, Lou."

"How far is the ranch from here?" Nurse Monroe asked.

"Four miles. Give or take."

"Then I'll take Abel and get some help."

"No." He and Louis answered her in unison.

A hint of a smile shadowed her lips. "Either of you have a better plan? Sadie's never ridden a horse. Jackson, you have a cast on your leg, in case you've forgotten, and Louis can barely walk. One second on this mule and those ribs will have you screaming in pain. By my estimation, we have about two more hours of daylight. Either you let me ride for help, or we're camping here tonight. I don't think any of us want that."

Jackson looked at Louie and caught the resignation in his eyes. She was right. They had no choice.

"All right, but listen. The ranch is about four miles up the road. You can't miss it. It'll be the first place you see, and there's a big 'G' hanging from the crossbar of the gate. Listen close, now. Don't go to the house. Stop at the barn only. Petie should be there this time of day. Tell him we need him to bring the buckboard, and then you come right back. No need to wait for him. He'll know what to do. You got that?"

She narrowed her eyes and looked as if she had a thousand questions. Luckily, she chose not to ask them. "Fine," she said. Taking Abel by the bridle, she led him to the side of the wagon, then climbed onto its upturned side and hoisted herself onto the mule's bareback, exposing a fair amount of shapely leg in the process. He wasn't prepared for the effect those legs had on him. He looked away, willing himself to think of something else. Anything else. This marriage of theirs had enough challenges without him thinking thoughts like those.

With a kick at Abel's flanks, she was off. Where she'd learned to ride bareback, he had no idea. She'd do nicely here in the west if she wanted to stay. But first, she needed to survive Pa.

CHAPTER 5

If the St. Louis society matrons could see her now, they'd have a heyday. Mrs. Jonas Fitzgerald. Riding a mule. Bareback and astride, no less. Mrs. Phineas McCallister would be especially pleased to see how far she'd fallen. She'd never forgiven Claire for marrying Jonas after she'd had him earmarked for her daughter Bethany. By the time Claire returned from her honeymoon, she'd have been more than happy to let Bethany have him. But by then, it was too late.

Little did those matrons know she'd far rather be Mrs. Jackson Garrity riding a mule bareback than the ever-so-proper, former Mrs. Fitzgerald. There was something so freeing about riding this way, far from the constraints and expectations Jonas had placed on her. Taking firm hold of Abel's spiky mane, she eased him into a trot and then a canter. Abel seemed just as happy to be free of constraints as she was. Either that, or he just wanted to get home.

They rounded a bend in the road. Up ahead, she could see a gate just as Jackson had described. Sure enough, as she drew closer, she could see an iron "G" swinging from the cross-post. As she slowed Abel to turn in at the gate, she noticed another sign nailed to the side post. The words "No Filese Ranch" were burned into the wood in uneven letters, almost as if a child had written them. Strange name for a ranch. She'd have to ask Jackson about it.

She could see the ranch house, long and low, nestled into the red cliffs behind it. A porch ran its entire length. Just off to her right stood an enormous barn. She headed the mule in its direction. She'd only gone a few paces when a boy emerged from its interior, leading a horse. He looked to be around fourteen or fifteen, tall and lanky, with arms and legs that went on for miles. Judging from his dark hair and height, he had to be a Garrity brother. Petie?

She called out the name, and he looked up and froze. She rode closer.

"Are you Petie?"

He nodded, casting a wary glance toward the house.

"I'm Claire." No need to mention her relation to his brother just yet. "Jackson and Louis sent me. There's been an accident with the wagon, and Louis is too hurt to ride. And with Jackson's leg." She shrugged. "They said you were to bring the buckboard to pick them up."

"I figured something was wrong when Cain came back all beat up and trailing his traces. I was just heading out to check." He sent another glance toward the house. "You'd best come on in the barn while I hitch up."

What was it about the house that had the Garrity boys so wary? She had half a mind to march on up to the door and find out, but her first priority was getting everyone back to the ranch before dark, especially Ella. Her curiosity would have to wait.

She slid off Abel and led him into the barn. Petie took his horse into a stall and came back for the mule.

"So, was Cain hurt?"

"A few scratches is all. Nothing serious."

As Petie put Abel into a stall next to his brother, the two mules greeted each other by touching muzzles. Guess they were happy to be together again.

"I'll take care of their cuts when we get back. Castor and Pollux will have to pull the buckboard," Petie said.

He disappeared into the dark recesses of the barn. Then he came back, leading two of the largest dapple-gray Percherons Claire had ever seen. While Petie worked, Claire took the opportunity to tour the barn. Judging by its size and the number of full stalls, the Garritys were not lacking in livestock. In addition to the mules and the Percherons, Claire counted five saddle horses of various colors and breeds. She stepped to the doorway of the barn and looked out. She didn't see a chicken house or any cows in the nearby pastures. Where did they get their milk and eggs?

Curious now, she stepped out of the barn and headed around to the other side. She found several corrals and a round pen, but no cows or goats penned in any pastures as far as she could see. Just a barn full of horses and farm equipment and a ranch house.

"I don't know who you are or what you're doing on my land, but you're not welcome here."

Claire whipped around at the sound of the harsh voice behind her. A bear of a man pointed the barrel of his shotgun straight at her heart. "I'll give you five minutes to hightail it out of here, or I'm going to shoot. Now git."

CHAPTER 6

C laire studied the man in front of her, trying to gauge the weight of his threat. It wasn't his size that bothered her, though he was massive. Nor was it his wild appearance. His unkempt gray and black hair hung in waves to his shoulders. A bushy gray beard hit him mid-chest and looked like it hadn't been trimmed in a decade. It wasn't even the shotgun, oddly enough. What bothered Claire was his eyes—stone-cold and full of hatred—and the very same midnight blue as Jackson's but oh so different.

She decided to fight his animosity with cheerfulness.

"Hi. I'm Claire." She held out her hand for him to shake. "You must be Jackson's father."

The gun didn't move a fraction. Instead, he growled, "I don't care who you are. The likes of you aren't welcome around here. Go on, now. Git."

The likes of her? What could he mean by that? She wasn't of a different race, which, sadly, she knew could set off some people. She might be a little travel-worn, but she was dressed as a lady, so surely, he didn't think she was *that* type of woman. Did he?

Truth dawned. This was why Jackson and Louis hadn't wanted her to come to the ranch alone. The man was crazy. And a crazy man with a gun was not to be taken lightly.

She drew in a shaky breath and released it. She'd dealt with crazy before. One or two had come under her care at St. Luke's before they'd been transferred to the asylum. She would simply humor him.

"You're right. I should leave." She sidled to the left, hoping he'd lower his shotgun. If she could just get around him and back to Petie, she could . . .

As if on cue, she heard the boy call her name. Then he came bounding around the corner, skidding to a halt when he saw his father.

"Pa! Stop. She's fine."

"She's not fine. She doesn't belong here."

"No, sir. I mean . . . yessir, I know, but she came to get help for Louis and Jackson. There's been an accident with the wagon, and they sent her for help."

"She's lying." The shotgun never wavered, nor did the man's steely gaze. "I don't know what your story is, lady, but we're not buying it here. There's no way either of my boys would have sent a woman to my ranch."

"They didn't want to. Truly. But they had no choice. Neither is able to ride a horse right now and the wagon's in shambles. I insisted they send me. There weren't any other options. Sir, if you care about your sons at all, you'll let Petie and me go help them."

"She's telling the truth, Pa. Cain came back to the ranch ten minutes ago, limping and dragging his traces. I'd just saddled Samson to go check on things when she rode in on Abel, who's also cut up. I have Castor and Pollux all hitched and ready to go. At least let me go see what happened. I'll take her with me and not bring her back. I promise."

Not bring her back? Well, that could be a problem. But she'd play along if it meant the man would lower that blasted shotgun.

He studied her again, eyes narrowed and wary, then waved her on with the tip of the gun. "Get along then. Go. But see that you don't come back. And, Petie, you be sure to tell your brothers that the rules are still in place."

Claire wasted no time scrambling onto the buckboard to take a seat next to Petie, who soon urged the Percherons into a trot. She didn't look back to see if the gun was still pointed her way, but she also didn't relax her shoulders. And she didn't breathe easy until they headed out the gate.

"What rules does he mean? The ones he said are still in place?"

"There's only one, really. Didn't you see it? There on the gate?"

"The name of the ranch?"

"Well, that. And what's written under it."

She looked back over her shoulder at the small sign, but if something was written on it, it was well hidden behind a clump of sagebrush.

"All I see is the name, No Filese. I've not heard that word before. What is a filese?"

"Fillies. Jackson wasn't too good at spelling when he wrote it. A filly is a female horse."

"Oh. I see. Because it was just you boys and your father?"

"And because of what's written underneath."

"And that is?"

"No girls allowed."

No girls allowed? Sounded like some schoolyard club, not a ranch of full-grown men.

"Is that a joke?"

"No, ma'am. Since Ma left, Pa hasn't allowed any females on the ranch. Even animals. We don't have cows, hens, mares, nanny goats, or ewes. No womenfolk allowed. At all."

She stared hard at the boy to determine if he was pulling her leg. If he was, he had an excellent poker face. And if he wasn't, well, that would certainly confirm her suspicion that the man was crazy. It explained some other things as well–like Jackson's reluctance to give her a job.

"I live with my father and brothers," he'd said. *"And for reasons I can't explain right now, you wouldn't be welcome."*

Reasons like his father was a nut case? She could understand the man being soured on women if his own marriage had ended poorly, but to ban *all* female creatures, even livestock? The man was batty. No buts about it. And if so, where did that put her and Sadie and Ella? There was no way she would subject her sister and daughter to another dangerous man. Not if she could help it. But if they couldn't stay at the ranch, where would they go?

She glanced to her left at the sun, hovering just above the horizon. Daylight was fading fast. Dear God, she didn't want to spend another night camped out under the stars, but the alternative wasn't looking very promising.

THE LAST STREAKS OF PINK AND ORANGE IN THE CLOUDS ATOP THE Winds were fading to gray when Jackson heard the creak of a wagon and the jangle of a harness. Finally.

Once Claire left, their group of four had broken into isolated segments. Sadie, wrapped tightly in a blanket, leaned her back against the broken wagon bed with Ella asleep on her lap. She'd spent the first half-hour gathering all their scattered belongings into a pile while he and Louis sat and nursed their wounds like a couple of wounded bears.

Louis lay on the ground not far from where Claire had mounted Abel. He hadn't shown any interest in moving since she'd left. Jackson didn't blame him a bit. He'd broken ribs before and knew the type of pain any movement could cause. Sadie had wrapped a blanket around him, and then they'd let him lie.

At first, Jackson had tried to help Sadie gather the belongings but soon found he and his crutches simply got in her way. So, he'd found this vantage spot on a rock where he could watch the road, and he'd waited. The ache in his leg was worse than it'd been before the accident, and he could barely stand it then. Now it was all he could do to think of anything but the pain. The sound of that wagon approaching was the sweetest sound he'd heard in a long while.

In the growing dusk, he could see them come around the bend, Petie driving Castor and Pollux, Claire on the seat beside him. Pa wasn't with them, thank God. With any luck, he still had no idea Claire existed.

Petie pulled the Percherons to a halt and jumped down.

"You all right?"

"Will be once you get us home."

"How'd it happen?"

"Axle broke when we were on that downhill stretch over yonder."

"Louis?" Petie tipped his chin toward where their brother lay. Louis had turned his head in their direction but otherwise made no effort to move.

"A few broken ribs. Dislocated shoulder, but he should be all right. Thanks for coming."

Petie nodded, then looked over at the girls. Claire had climbed down off the buckboard and was already laying her sleeping daughter onto one of its bench seats. Sadie had begun loading their luggage. They sure didn't waste time. They most likely wanted a real bed tonight as much as he did.

"Maybe you should go help the girls. The sooner we get loaded and on the road, the better. Daylight's purt near gone," he said.

"They coming with us?" He heard the doubt in Petie's voice.

"Didn't Claire tell you she's my wife?"

The shock on Petie's face answered that question.

"You're joshing me, right? What about Pa?"

Jackson shrugged and nodded toward the pile of luggage and supplies. "Let's get loaded up. I want to be home before it's full dark."

"Wait. Jack, you need to listen. Pa already saw Claire and came after her with his shotgun. He barely allowed me to come back with her. Said she was lying about you and Louis being hurt. When we left, he told her not to come back. Told me to tell you and Louis the rules are still in place."

"But he didn't know she was my wife."

"You think that'll matter?"

Probably not, but Jackson was too tired and in too much pain to argue.

"Just get the things loaded and help Louis and me into the buckboard. We'll worry about Pa once we get to the ranch.

But by the time they reached the ranch, he had only two things on his mind—a soft bed and laudanum. Each dip and sway of the wagon jolted pain through his leg so intense he was now fighting dizziness and nausea. On the wagon bench beside him, Louis alternated between groans and whimpers. At least he wasn't alone in his misery.

When Petie turned the horses toward the gate, Pa stepped out of the shadows, shotgun at the ready.

"Whoa. Hold those horses right there, Petie. You'll be wanting to let these ladies out before you take your brothers on up to the house."

"No." Was that guttural groan the best he could do? He drew a deep breath. "Stay in the wagon. Please," he said through clenched teeth. That last word was barely more than a whimper, but it drew the girls' attention, and neither of them moved.

"Claire's a nurse, Pa," he forced his voice to carry more strength. "Both Louis and I are going to need her help."

"I don't care if she's the Queen of England. She's not coming onto my ranch. Now you women get on down off that wagon."

Pa lifted his shotgun and pointed it straight at Claire, who held out a hand to ward him off. Slowly she started to rise.

Jackson lurched forward to try to stop her. A shard of pain bolted through his leg and up into his back, knocking him sideways. A wave of heat swept through him as his stomach roiled. There was no stopping it this time. He barely had time to lean over the side of the wagon before emptying the contents of his stomach onto the ground.

He felt her next to him, supporting him with an arm across his shoulders, as he heaved over the edge of the wagon. He was swimming in pain with her his only lifeline. Finally, the nausea subsided. He fell back onto the seat. Claire wiped his face and mouth with her handkerchief and lay a cool hand across his brow. He clung to her other hand, ashamed of his weakness but unwilling to let her go.

As if from a distance, he heard a gruff voice.

"Don't be such a crazy old coot, Henry. Can't you see your boys are suffering? Let that nurse get them settled, and then we'll decide what to do with the women. Here. Give me that shotgun. Petie, drive your brothers up to the house."

Sikes.

Thank God. No one but Sikes could get Pa to listen to reason. He breathed a prayer of thanks as the wagon started forward. His sole focus now was his bed and the hope that soon he'd have relief from the pain.

CHAPTER 7

The interior of the ranch house was a lot neater than Claire had anticipated, with its being a bachelor residence. This main room, anyway, where she and Ella and Sadie had been ushered, was almost spartan in its lack of furnishings. A large stone fireplace with a cheery fire was the most welcoming part of the room. The three of them gathered around it, letting its warmth dispel the chill of the early April night.

The short, thin, bald man who'd saved them from Jackson's father had told them to sit tight while he got the boys settled. Then he and Petie had helped "the boys" into the house, and they'd all disappeared down a long hallway in the opposite direction. She assumed getting them settled meant changing them out of their clothes and putting them to bed. She could have helped with that, but the little man waved her back when she started to follow. She'd stayed behind, not wanting to push her luck in this already tenuous situation. Hopefully, they'd call her soon. Both men needed relief from their pain, but Jackson was in a very bad state.

Her hands now warm, she opened her nurse's bag and located the laudanum. Might as well be ready.

"Mama. I'm hungwy."

"I know, honey. We all are. We'll get some supper soon."

Hopefully.

The reception they'd received so far left her doubting they'd ever be settled for the night.

"But I want to eat now." Ella threw herself against Claire's leg and started to bawl. She was beyond tired, as they all were, and a tired, hungry three-year-old was not to be comforted.

Claire picked her up and looked at Sadie over her shoulder. "Maybe we should try to find something in the kitchen."

"I'll find some supper for the tike if you'll take care of the boys." Their champion was back. He held out his arms to take Ella from her. Surprisingly, the child stopped crying and went quite willingly. Must have been the mention of supper because she usually was quite shy around strangers.

"I'm Sikes, by the way. Jedidiah Sikes." Holding Ella in one arm, he gave Claire a firm handshake. "Been Henry's business partner for years and his friend long before that."

Though much the same age as Jackson's father, this man was his friend's opposite in every way. Short where his friend was tall, bald instead of bushy, and generous with his smiles. Kindness shone in his pale blue eyes. The tension in Claire's shoulders relaxed a little.

"I appreciate that, Sikes. We haven't had anything to eat since noon, and I'm afraid she's pretty hungry. Could you get a little something for Jackson and Louis, as well? Cold meats would be fine, though if you had some broth, it would be better, and some milk for each of them so I can give them their medicine."

"I'll see what I can find. Maybe your friend here would like to help me?" He sent a questioning glance toward Sadie.

"Oh. I'm sorry. We never introduced ourselves. This is my sister Sadie. I'm Claire, and this is my daughter Ella. I was Jackson's nurse at the hospital." Best leave the explanations at that. No need to muddy the waters right now with the marriage news.

"Well, if you can help those two, I'd be much obliged."

"I'll do my best."

She found Jackson and Louis in the first bedroom on the right down the long hallway. Two oversized beds filled the area leaving room for little else other than a small table in between the two beds. Pegs on the wall held the men's pants and shirts.

Jackson lay in one of the beds, eyes already closed. His face was pale, but he seemed to be breathing easier. Louis sat gingerly on the side of the other bed.

"It hurts to lay down," he said, giving her a lop-sided smile.

"I'm sure it does. Let's see what we can do to relieve the pain."

She unbuttoned his nightshirt and slipped it off his shoulders. He winced as she pulled the sleeve off his left arm. A large bruise spread across his left torso. He flinched as she ran her fingers across it, probing as gently as possible for any sign of dislocated bone.

"Sorry. I know it hurts, but if the bones are out of place, they could puncture a lung." Luckily, there were no signs of any protrusions or indentions. "Looks like they're just cracked. I'll bind them up, and hopefully, you'll be able to sleep."

She took a roll of sticking plaster from her bag and tore off five long strips.

"Now, lift your left arm above your head. Take a deep breath then let it all out as far as you possibly can. There." She wrapped one strip of plaster from back to front in the direction of his ribs. "Don't breath now." Quickly she strapped the rest of his left side, then used a soft wool bandage to wrap his entire chest and cover the strapping.

Sikes appeared in the doorway just as she was finishing up, a tray with two bowls and two glasses of milk in his hand. A savory, meaty aroma wafted by as he set the tray on the bed table. Her mouth watered at the smell, but any thought of eating would have to wait.

"You're in luck," Sikes said. "Henry had a pot of venison stew on the stove. I siphoned off a bowl of broth for each of the boys."

"Oh, that will work wonderfully. Do you happen to have any extra pillows? Louis will probably rest better if we can prop him up, plus they will both need to sit up to eat."

Sikes nodded and left the room. A few minutes later, he returned bearing two more pillows. While he set to work getting Louis settled and then helping Jackson sit up, Claire measured a dose of laudanum into each of the glasses of milk.

"Drink these first," she said. "Then we'll see about getting some broth down the two of you before you both fall asleep."

She didn't have to tell Jackson twice. He took the cup from her hand and downed it like Jonas used to throw back a shot of whiskey. For a man who usually fought the laudanum, he certainly was happy to have it now. Pain would do that to a person.

"Here. Try a few bites of this." She blew on a spoonful of the broth and held it to his lips. "The laudanum will sit better if your stomach isn't completely empty."

But after only a few bites, he pushed her hand away.

"Are you feeling sick again?"

He shook his head. "Just want to sleep."

She didn't blame him. The last three days had been grueling for her, and she wasn't dealing with intense pain. She could only imagine the fatigue he must be feeling. Taking one of the pillows from behind his head, she propped up his casted leg with it.

"Rest now," she said. Brushing a stray lock of hair back from his eyes, she trailed her fingers across his face, lingering a bit on the raspy whiskers along his jaw. He hadn't shaved since their wedding. Their wedding. Was that even real? She still had a hard time remembering this man was her husband.

"Thank you." His voice was thread-thin. Hopefully, the laudanum would soon give him a few hours of respite from the pain.

With Jackson settled, she turned her attention to Louis. He was doing a much better job with his supper.

"Couldn't you have put at least a few chunks of meat in this bowl, Sikes?"

Clearly, the binding around his ribs was helping abate his pain. He almost sounded himself again.

"Tomorrow." She took the empty bowl from him. "Get a good night's rest, and we'll talk about solid food tomorrow."

She helped him settle back against his pillows. "Does this work, or do you want to try another position?"

"No. This is good." He grabbed her hand as she turned away. "Thanks, Claire. You're a brick. We're lucky Jackson made you family."

She shot a glance at Sikes to see his reaction to Louis's words, but he was busy stacking the bowls and glasses on the tray. "Just rest now. We'll talk more tomorrow."

She packed up her nurse's bag, turned down the wick on the lamp, and followed Sikes out of the room.

He led the way to the kitchen, where Sadie, Petie, and Ella were finishing up their supper. Henry was nowhere to be seen. Somehow that fact only made Claire tenser. Was he waiting outside for another chance to pounce on them, gun waving?

Sikes handed her a bowl of venison stew. "Best eat up. Henry's not going to stomach you girls hanging around all night."

Just as she thought. He was waiting . . . somewhere. If she hadn't been so hungry, the thought would have been enough to steal her appetite. As it was, she burnt her tongue in her hurry to comply with Sikes's warning.

"What's to be done with the three of you beats me." Sikes leaned a shoulder against the door jamb and crossed his arms, studying them as if they were specimens under a microscope. "I'm guessing from what Louis said back there, you weren't planning to go anywhere other than here."

Claire shook her head but continued to eat. She probably looked like a savage the way she was tearing into this stew, but it had been a very long day, and lunch had been little more than cheese and stale bread.

"Well, I told Henry this day would come. Can't raise four strapping boys without one of them wanting to bring home a wife someday. Just didn't figure Jackson to be the first to try it. Henry's not going to like it, not one bit, but I'll let Jackson be the one to tell him." He walked over to the table and began gathering the dirty dishes.

"I can take care of those," Sadie said, starting to rise.

"Now, you just stay put. Ain't the first time I've washed a few dishes." He took the bowls over to the sink and began to clean them.

Claire scraped the last spoonful of stew into her mouth and then brought her own empty bowl over to join the others. "Are you sure you don't want us to help?"

"Naw. You might want to gather up your bags, though. I'm thinking it might be best to have you girls stay out at my place tonight. I'll bunk with Petie. He's got an empty bed in his room what with Gabe being out at sheep camp for a few weeks. The morning's soon enough to get this all sorted. Petie, grab us a couple of lanterns, will ya?"

Ten minutes later, Claire picked her way across the darkened yard, trying to follow the path marked by the faint glow of lantern light. Each shadow felt ominous, as if Jackson's father was hiding, simply waiting for them to draw near before jumping out, shotgun aimed. Petie led the way carrying one of the lanterns. Sadie followed close behind, carrying a satchel and valise. Beside Claire, Sikes carried the other valise in his free hand, shining his own lantern on the path ahead of her. She carried Ella on her hip, the girl heavy in her arms. The little one had finally succumbed to sleep, and Claire could feel her soft breath against her neck as her head lolled against her shoulder.

Petie led them to the far side of the barn, the side she hadn't investigated earlier that day. She could just make out the dark shape of a small cabin tucked against the walls of the cliffs, its windows shedding a welcoming glow. At last. Like Ella, now they'd been fed, she wanted little more than to sleep and leave this grueling day behind.

She climbed the steps onto a small porch and followed Sadie into the tiny cabin. Like the main ranch house, the interior was clean but sparse. It consisted of one room with a cookstove, sink, and cabinet in one corner, a large bed and a table in the other. Not much, but better than sleeping on the ground as they had the two nights previous. She'd have slept in the barn tonight if needed. Yes, this would do.

Sikes set her valise on the table. "I know it's not much. Bachelor diggings and all. I promise we'll find a better solution in the morning. Outhouse is down the path to the left. The pump on the sink will bring you water."

"Thank you. I appreciate you letting us stay here."

The older man shrugged. "Sounds like Henry could use my help at the house anyway with both those boys laid up."

She'd left him her vial of laudanum with instructions on how to administer the correct doses. There was no telling if or when she'd be allowed back to give the boys any nursing. There was no sense in either of them suffering because of their father's insanity if it could be helped.

She watched as Petie and Sikes headed back down the trail toward the ranch house, then shut the door and dropped the bar in the latch. Somehow, knowing that crazy man was out there somewhere with his shotgun made her wary. She laid Ella on the bed, then sank into a rocker placed conveniently by its side. Sadie sat at the table, head resting on her hands.

She looked up and caught Claire's eye.

"So," Claire said. "Still think this hasty marriage was a good idea?"

Sadie shrugged. "I can't imagine any bounty hunter or detective finding us out here. I don't even know where we are. We're safe for now, and that's something."

Safe. Sure. Unless her new father-in-law decided to shoot them. With him lurking somewhere in the shadows, she felt anything but safe. But they had a roof over them and a bed that looked big enough for the three of them. For now, it was enough.

CHAPTER 8

J ackson woke to find Pa sitting in a rocker at the end of his bed, *Plutarch's Lives* in his hand. At his stirring, Pa put his book down and came to stand beside him, peering down at him through his bushy gray eyebrows.

"'Bout time you woke up, son. I was beginning to think that nurse of yours put something fishy in your medicine."

He turned to see Louis's bed empty. "How long have I been out?"

"Going on a day and a half now."

That long? He remembered very little about the night they got here other than the relief of finally sinking into his bed and letting the laudanum do its magic.

"Claire?"

Pa's expression darkened. "If you're asking about those womenfolk you brought home with you, Sikes has them boarding over at Granny Bascom's. Now that you're awake, I believe it's high time you sent them on their way. I don't know what you were thinking bringing that nurse with you, but let me make things clear. The rules haven't changed. No women on my ranch. Not now. Not ever. Sikes and I will tend to any nursing you need."

Jackson struggled to sit up. Clearly, neither Louis nor Pete had wanted to tell Pa that Claire was more than just a nurse to him. He would have to do it, but it wasn't a conversation he wanted to have lying flat on his back.

Pa helped him sit, then positioned some pillows behind his back. "See? I can play the nursemaid as well as any female. Now that you're awake, I'm guessing you'll be wanting some food. From the looks of you, that hospital must have been skimpy with its meals. I knew Baldwin was making a mistake, sending you all the way to Denver. Far as I can see, you'd have been a lot better off here at home."

"They saved my leg."

Pa's harrumph made it clear what he thought about that.

"You walking on it any?"

Jackson shook his head. "Just got out of traction the day before I left. The doctor said the cast should stay on another week yet, and that I shouldn't put any weight on the leg until the cast comes off. After that, there'll be exercises I'll need to do, but I should be back to full strength by the end of the summer, provided I'm willing to work at it."

"I reckon there won't be any question about that. If I were a betting man, I'd put my money on your being back on Boaz within a month."

The mention of his favorite horse had Jackson longing to head out to the barn right now. If only he didn't feel as weak as a nearly drowned pup.

"I hope you're right. How is he? Did he get fat and lazy with me gone so long?"

"Your brothers took turns riding him to keep him exercised, but he'll be mighty glad to see you. He's been moping around like a jilted spinster since you left. But enough jawing. I'll go get your lunch. And while I'm gone, I'll find you a pen and paper.

The sooner you tell that nurse and her kin to be on their way, the better."

Jackson sat a little straighter in the bed. It was now or never. "Pa. Before you go, there's something you should know."

Pa paused in the doorway and looked back.

"Claire isn't just my nurse. She's my wife."

Pa looked like Jackson had just punched him in the gut. "Your *wife?*" He spoke the word like a curse word.

"Yes, sir."

The color drained from Pa's face, leaving him older somehow. And gray. He studied Jackson for a few minutes as if willing him to say he was just fooling, then slowly shook his head.

"I might expect such foolishness from your brothers, boy. But you? I thought you were smarter than that." Turning, he made his way out the door and down the hall.

FIVE MINUTES LATER, LOUIS POKED HIS HEAD AROUND THE corner of the doorway. A look of relief flooded his face.

"You're awake."

"Where've you been?"

"Decided to try a walk to the outhouse. Getting mighty tired of the chamber pot."

Jackson knew the feeling, but it'd be several more weeks before he had that luxury. His brother lowered himself slowly onto his bed, holding his side and grimacing as he settled in and positioned himself on his pillows.

"You doing all right?"

"Tolerable. If I don't move."

"Just don't laugh or cough or breathe, and you'll be fine."

Louis shot him a glare. "So, what's with Pa?"

"What do you mean?"

"He's sitting in the kitchen with his head buried in his hands. For a minute there, I thought you might have kicked the bucket."

"He probably wishes I had. I told him about Claire."

Louis's eyes widened. "About the wedding?"

Jackson nodded.

"What did he say?"

"Not much."

"No yelling?"

"Not yet."

Louis leaned back against his pillows and closed his eyes. "Who knows. Maybe he'll come around."

"Yeah, and maybe the sun will start rising in the west too."

CHAPTER 9

"Now, take two of these spoons full of baking powder and add enough milk to make the mixture soft." Granny Bascom handed the pitcher to Sadie.

"How much is that?" Sadie hesitated before pouring.

"Just enough to make the dough soft."

"But how do you know how much that will be?"

Claire hid a smile. Sadie hated not being exact. And Granny Bascom had been full of "a pinch of this," "a dab of that," and several "just enoughs" since they started this impromptu cooking lesson.

Claire didn't mind. Cooking was Sadie's department. Had been since they set up housekeeping in Denver—two spoiled rich girls without so much as an inkling of how to boil water. Claire's job was managing the finances and figuring out a plan to bring money in for the future, while Sadie learned how to keep a home. As far as Claire could tell, her sister had learned just fine. Neither Sadie nor Ella had missed any meals, and the few meals she'd shared with them on Sundays were sufficient, if plain. If memory served her right, those first meals were very simple—a few slices of cheese on toast or a boiled egg or two, but once Sadie discovered a few cookbooks in the Denver Public Library, they'd gradually become more substantial.

Since then, Sadie was always looking for opportunities to improve her skills, so when Granny Bascom had told them today was her baking day, Sadie had jumped at the chance to help. Claire was content to let them work while she kept Ella occupied, rolling out animal figures from a mixture of flour, salt, and water.

"Look, Mama. A kitty cat." Ella held up a lumpy mass of grayish dough. Claire wasn't quite sure if the spiky points were ears or teeth.

"Very nice, honey. Can you make a bunny too?"

All in all, her inconvenient marriage of convenience was working out well. She never saw her husband, and for the first time in almost two years, she was able to spend time with her daughter, not just a few quick hours on a Sunday before she had to return to her work at St. Luke's. Her biggest regret these past two years was the hours of mothering she'd lost while trying to gain her nurse's license. But St. Luke's made no exceptions. All students must live and work at the hospital six days a week. Women with families were encouraged to stay home. As far as the staff at St. Luke's was concerned, Nurse Monroe was a single woman with no hindrances except for a sickly mother whom she was allowed to visit once a week.

She'd told herself the sacrifice was necessary in order for her to have a way to support the three of them once the money she took when she left Jonas ran out. Each week, though, it became harder and harder for her to go back, knowing how much Ella would change in a week, knowing all the milestones she was missing, knowing Sadie was more of a mom in Ella's eyes than she was.

But that was behind them now, thanks to Jackson and his woman-hating father. Really, the situation couldn't have worked out better if she'd planned it. She had the security of marriage with the freedom of single living. And there was no way some Pinkerton detective would track Mrs. Dempsey to this tiny cabin in the wilds of Wyoming. Mrs. Dempsey no longer existed.

"Would you like to try a batch, dear?"

Claire glanced up to see Granny Bascom looking at her. They'd only lived here a week, and already she was beginning to love this spritely little woman. She reminded her a lot of her own Grandma Monroe.

"Me? Oh. No. I'm not much of a cook."

Cooking hadn't been part of the nursing curriculum at St. Luke's because, according to Nurse Usher, if a family was financially able to hire a private nurse, they'd also have the wherewithal to hire a cook. None of the nursing students planned to remain at the hospital once they graduated unless they stayed to teach. The only money to be made was in private nursing. Student nurses staffed the hospital, and they weren't paid.

"All the more reason to learn. Someday soon, that husband of yours will be on his feet again and able to provide you with a home. You'll be needing to feed him and your little one."

Good Lord. She hoped not. Of course, she wasn't averse to Jackson getting well. But living as husband and wife, just the two of them and Ella? No. Hopefully, that would be many months down the road. Many, many months. Six months would be ideal. By then, this farce of a marriage would be over.

"Maybe I'll just watch you and Sadie this time. I'm sure to make a mess of things if I try."

"Nonsense. I'll tell you what. We'll finish this batch of biscuits, and then you and I will put together a simple white cake. Every wife needs to know how to bake a cake for her husband."

"You're making a cake too?" Claire looked at the six loaves of bread rising, the large batch of gingerbread, and the trays of more than six dozen biscuits. "How in the world do you expect us to eat all this?"

"Oh, we won't be eating it all, dearie. Most of what's here will go to the Garrity's."

"You do their baking too?" The mystery of how the Garrity men obtained their milk and eggs on a farm void of cows and hens became clear soon after they moved in with the older lady. Petie showed up the next morning with two empty pails and a basket. Granny Bascom took them and his quarter and scurried into her back room, returning a few minutes later with two full pails of milk and a basket of eggs. Two days later, Petie was back, and the process repeated itself. Apparently, Claire wasn't the only one profiting from Henry Garrity's hatred of women.

"How long have you known the Garritys?"

"Oh, ever since they settled in the area. Must be going on twenty-five years now."

"So, you knew Jackson's mother?"

"Isabel? Yes. As well as anyone could know her, I guess. She wasn't an easy woman to know."

"Jackson said she left the family. Do you know why?"

"He didn't tell you?"

Sadie snorted. "He didn't even tell her women weren't welcome on his father's ranch."

Not in so many words anyway. Jackson wasn't much of a talker, and they'd spent very little time together, especially since their hasty wedding. Those long days in the wagon didn't count. Jackson had hardly been coherent, using any energy he did have to cope with his pain.

"Well, seeings how you're family now, I suppose it wouldn't hurt to tell you a little of the family history. No one knows much, mind, but I probably know as much as anybody. Back in '77, the government opened up the land around here for settling through the Desert Land Act. A person could get up to 640 acres at twenty-five cents an acre if he promised to irrigate the land within three years. My husband and I took advantage of the opportunity, as did Henry Garrity and Jedidiah Sikes. Our plan was to build apple orchards. Garrity and Sikes had a bigger operation in mind. They wanted to grow enough produce to supply the miners in South Pass and the soldiers in Fort Washakie.

"Isabel and Henry hadn't been married long when they arrived in the area. Garrity and Sikes were old friends from during the war. The way Sikes tells it, he was on his way West to try his hand at farming when he stopped to see his friend who was living in Chicago at the time. Henry worked as a clerk for an insurance company and hated his job, so it didn't take much for Sikes to convince him to come West." Granny used her circular cutter to deftly cut a tray of biscuits. After placing the tray in the oven, she brushed the flour off her hands.

"Isabel, now, was another story. She was a city girl and never did take well to the farm life. I always got the feeling, talking to her, that being a farm wife was a huge step down for her. She didn't know the first thing about running a household on her own, and once the boys started coming along, she was even more overwhelmed. I did my best to help her out, send her some of my extra preserves at the end of a season, and give her cooking tips, but she'd have none of it.

"Since my Hiram and I never could have children of our own, I'd take to having the older boys over some days to give her time to rest, especially during her pregnancies. None of it helped. She just grew more and more discontent. Then one day, one of those traveling medicine men came to town. Oh, he was a looker all right and could talk real smooth. When he left town, Isabel disappeared."

"You think she left with him?"

"We didn't at first. She'd left Henry a note saying she was going back home, but when he telegraphed her parents, they didn't know anything about it. Then my Hiram was in

Cheyenne a few months later and saw a handbill of that same traveling medicine man. Seems he'd added a new talent to his show. A Madame Tralinda. Said she was a singer with the talent of Jinny Lind. Hiram told me the picture on the handbill was a dead ringer for Isabel. She always did have a right, pretty singing voice. In fact, Henry went so far as to order a piano delivered on one of those wagon freight trains one Christmas. Must'a paid an arm and a leg for it for all the good it did him.

"It kept her happy for a while, I guess. You could always hear her playing and singing any time you visited the ranch. But in the end . . . well, I guess there's no keeping someone where they don't want to be."

"And she never came back? Even to see her boys?" Sadie asked.

Claire looked over at Ella, her dark curls bent over her latest dough animal. There were reasons a wife would leave a husband. She knew that well enough. But to leave her children behind? She couldn't fathom the desperation that would make that possible.

"How long ago did this happen?"

"Let's see now. Petie was just learning to walk around that time, so I'd say it's been about thirteen years."

So, Petie would have been the same age Ella had been when she left Jonas. No. That part of Isabel's story Claire couldn't relate to. Besides, Henry wasn't a Jonas. Or was he? Like Granny said, no one knew the whole story, except maybe Henry and Isabel themselves. But she had to believe Isabel would never have left her boys behind if she hadn't known they'd be safe. She should probably give her new father-in-law the benefit of the doubt.

"And now, dearie. Let's get to work on that cake." Granny Bascom handed her a large mixing bowl.

She glanced over into Sadie's laughing eyes and shrugged.

How bad could this be? If it made their sweet little benefactress happy, it would be worth the effort.

~

THIS CAKE WASN'T HALF BAD, IF SHE DID SAY SO HERSELF. OF course, if she were to try to make it again without Granny by her side directing each step and regulating the heat of the oven, the results weren't likely to be anywhere near as good.

After a long day of baking and a simple supper, she and Sadie sat at the kitchen table, enjoying the fruit of their labors. They'd put Ella to bed an hour ago. Granny sat in a rocker beside the wood stove, knitting a pair of socks.

Claire took another bite of cake, savoring its soft sweetness. This life was sweet. Safe. Quiet. If she wasn't careful, she could get used to it. Begin to think of it as normal. That wouldn't do. Not for long, anyway. She was willing to give Jackson his six months, especially if she could spend them here in this haven of peace, but the truth was, they didn't belong here. They couldn't continue living a lie indefinitely.

She watched their hostess, rocking and knitting. So calm. So content. The tiny lady was a marvel. She looked to be in her eighties and was no bigger than a ten-year-old girl, yet the woman was still busy after a long day of work in the kitchen. Who knew who the socks were for. Probably one of the Garritys. Though no relation to the family of men who were her neighbors, Granny sure poured her life into their well-being. They were lucky to have her.

She and Sadie and Ella were lucky as well.

A pounding on the door shattered the peace of the evening. She saw Sadie tense and felt her own body readying to flee. Would they ever get past this feeling of being hunted? The door flew open, and Petie stood in the doorway, panting, wild-eyed. His gaze caught hers.

"You need to come quick. Louis is real sick. Pa went to get the doctor, but Sikes says to get you first, or it might be too late."

Claire jumped to her feet. "What happened?"

"He's got the fever and chills and can hardly breathe at all. Sikes thinks it might be pneumonia."

She took the steps to the loft two at a time to gather her nurse's bag and a coat. As she headed out the door, Granny handed her a loaded pillowcase.

"I put some flannel and cheesecloth in there and a few onions. Should get you started on a poultice if you need it. No telling what those men will have on hand."

"Thank you." She followed Petie out into the night.

Two horses were tied to the cabin's porch.

"I brought Malachi for you to ride. He's pretty gentle. And I found Ma's old side-saddle. Will you be all right riding, or do you want to ride behind me?"

"Malachi will be fine." A huge improvement over riding bareback on a mule. Petie helped her mount, then swung up into his own saddle and took off into a canter. Claire followed suit, keeping an eye on the lantern in Petie's hand and praying Louis wasn't as bad off as it sounded.

They made the two-mile trek to the Garrity ranch in good time, and soon Claire was following Sikes down the hallway again to the room where she'd last left the brothers. Was it only a week ago?

What she found when she stepped inside the room was a total reverse from how she left it. This time Louis lay prostrate, pale and barely conscious, while Jackson sat in a chair next to him, his casted leg propped on a stool. He turned his head as they came into the room, desperation fading to relief when he caught sight of her.

"You came."

"Of course." She walked to the other side of the bed and

placed her palm on Louis's head. Hot. "How long has he been this sick?"

"He's had a cough for several days. Just kept getting worse. Then yesterday, he started with the fever and chills. We thought he was some better today until a few hours ago. The fever came back, and he started talking wild. That's when Pa decided to go for Doc Stevens, and Sikes sent Petie to get you. Do you think it's pneumonia?"

"Could be." She took his pulse. Rapid. And his respirations were at thirty-five. She took her thermometer from her bag and shook it.

"Louis. I need to take your temperature. Can you hold this under your tongue?"

Louis whipped his head from side to side. "Blasted sheep. More trouble than you're worth. Get on with ya."

On second thought, she might have more luck getting a reading from his armpit. She pulled down the sheet, glad to see he was bare-chested other than the wrap she'd placed there last week. A small poultice had been applied to his left side, still warm to the touch. Both would need to come off, but she'd get the temperature first. She settled the thermometer in place on the arm closest to Jackson. "Watch that for me," she told him. "See that he doesn't knock it loose. There's no doubt he's running a fever, but I'd like to get an accurate reading if I can."

Probably was pneumonia, but she knew better than to diagnose an illness before a doctor had his say. The signs were all there, though. Cough. Rapid pulse and breathing. Flushed, dry, hot skin. Mild delirium. She'd treat it as though it was until the doctor told her otherwise.

She turned to Sikes, who hovered just at the end of the bed. "Could you get me a basin of tepid water? We need to get his fever down, if we can, to alleviate the delirium and allow him to rest. Also, if you could start some water boiling for a steam tent, that would be helpful. Oh, and Petie? Could you get that window open? We need as much fresh air in here as possible."

She set to work removing the straps around his chest.

"Why are you taking those off?" Jackson's voice was curious, not accusing.

"It'll help him breathe. He'll probably hurt, what with the broken ribs and all, but he needs to be able to take deeper breaths. What's in the poultice?"

"Flaxseed. Sikes makes it up. Uses it on the horses."

Claire couldn't help but smile. Granny had underestimated the resources of this bachelor household. She might have known they would know a few remedies to doctor their livestock.

"Should we not have used it?" Jackson sounded concerned.

"Oh no. It's exactly what he needs. I'll reapply one in a bit, but I want to get his fever under control first."

She took out the thermometer and glanced at the reading. 104. Worse than she'd suspected.

Right on cue, Sikes returned with the water she requested. "Thank you. Would it also be possible to get an ice bag for his head?"

The older man nodded and left again.

Claire brought the basin to the bedside and dipped a cloth into the water. Perfect. Not warm, but not cold either. Wringing out her cloth, she began bathing Louis around the face and neck. At first touch, Louis thrashed his head from side to side but soon gentled.

"Cool. Feels cool," he said.

"Yes. It will help your fever."

"Head . . . aches." He struggled to get the words out.

"I know. We're getting you something to help it feel better. Just rest now. You'll feel more comfortable soon."

Sikes returned with the ice bag as she was drying Louis's neck and shoulders.

She took it from him and placed it across Louis's forehead. "Here you go. This will help soothe your headache. Just lie still now, and we'll get you bathed."

But when she moved the sheet to start on his right arm, Sikes took the cloth from her.

"Jackson and I will handle the bathing. You said something about wanting to get a steam tent ready?"

She looked into the man's pale blue eyes, reading what he wasn't saying. She wanted to tell him that after two years of hospital nursing, there was nothing under that sheet she hadn't seen a thousand times but she held her tongue. His offer could very well be as much to save Louis from embarrassment as her. And it didn't hurt to share the work.

"I did. And I need to fashion a jacket poultice so we can cover more of his chest. The ice pack and sponge bath should help reduce his fever, but you might also try getting him to drink some cold water while I'm gone. I'll be back as soon as I can."

She took the bag Granny had sent with her and slipped out to the kitchen. A kettle of water was beginning to steam on the stove. Finding a knife, she chopped a quarter of one of the onions Granny had sent. Then she poured some hot water into a small pan, added a cup of flaxseed and the onion, and let them boil. Taking the flannel, she fashioned a double jacket open on the sides to allow the poultice in between and fastened it at the top and bottom with safety pins.

She worked quickly. The sooner they got his fever under control and his congestion alleviated, the better she'd feel. She hadn't expected to find him in such bad shape. Only a week ago, he was the strongest, most vital young man she'd ever met. If they'd told her Jackson was in bad shape, given what he'd gone through in the past six weeks, she wouldn't have been at all surprised. But Louis?

Once the poultice thickened, she strained off all the water

and spread the paste on two lengths of cheesecloth, covering them on both sides with a rubber sheet. She placed one in each side of the jacket, rolled it to keep the heat in, and placed it in a shallow washbasin. Gathering the basin, a towel, and the steaming kettle, she hurried back down the hall.

Some doctors today advocated using cold packs rather than hot poultices, but Papa had always favored heat for pneumonia. If it was good enough for him, it was good enough for her, at least until the Garrity's doctor told her otherwise. Even at St. Luke's the majority of the doctors on staff advocated for heat, so she couldn't go too far wrong.

She entered the room just as the men were finishing with Louis's bath. The sponge bath and ice pack were doing the trick. Louis was already resting more quietly.

She came to his side and placed a hand against his cheek. Yes. A bit cooler already.

"Help me lift him," she said to Sikes, "so I can put this poultice on him. Also, while he's sitting up, I'd like to try him in the steam tent for a few minutes. The more we can do to loosen the congestion in his lungs, the better."

She carefully settled the poultice jacket across Louis's shoulders, checking the temperature against the back of her arm before pressing it against his chest and back. Jackson piled a few pillows behind Louis's back to keep him sitting up while Sikes brought a lap desk to set across his legs.

Pouring the steaming water into the shallow basin, she set it on the desk, leaned Louis forward until his face was in the steam, then draped a towel over his head and shoulders. "I need you to breathe deeply now.

"Hurts."

"Yes. I know, especially with those broken ribs, but you have to do your best." She placed a hand against his left rib cage to give him a little extra support. "Come on now, Louis. You can do it. Breathe as deeply as you can."

After a few minutes, he began to cough up phlegm, groaning against the pain.

"You're doing great, Louis. See if you can cough a bit of that into this cup, and then you can lay back and rest a bit. There you go. You're doing famously."

As she expected, the sputum was a rusty brown. She set it aside to show the doctor.

"Let's lay him back now. Not all the way. Keep him elevated so he can breathe easier. That's it. Now, Louis, I'm going to give you a couple of drops of medicine for the pain, and I want you to try to sleep. There you go. And a sip of water. And another. Good. Rest now."

She settled the ice bag back across his forehead and placed her palm against his cheek again. The fever wasn't gone, but it certainly had abated. A quick check of his pulse showed his heart rate and respiration had slowed as well.

She sat down in the chair Sikes had brought her. She'd done all she could for now. Time would tell if it was enough. Glancing up, she caught Jackson's gaze on her.

"Thank you," he said.

"He's not out of the woods yet."

"Maybe not, but he's a lot better than he was. You're very good."

She shrugged. "I'm just doing my job."

He shook his head. "It's more than that. You have a gift. I noticed it back at St. Luke's. More than with the other nurses. Your touch brings peace. Healing." He looked down at his brother. "Look at him. Sleeping like a baby now. Sikes and I couldn't get him to rest before you came."

Claire felt her cheeks warm at his words. Who would have thought Jackson, the man of so few words, would say something that touched her so deeply? People had said things like that about her father. He had the healing touch. Could it be true? Did she have it too?

She pushed to her feet, breaking from Jackson's hypnotic gaze. If she didn't watch herself, the man would draw her in. She'd let a man's charming words fool her once before. Never again.

She began organizing her bag, cleaning and returning the thermometer to its proper place, sorting through her medicines, anything to make her look busy and keep Jackson from saying any more. Luckily for her, Jackson was never one to push conversation. When she finally allowed herself to glance back at him, she saw he'd taken up a book. Good.

Louis was still sleeping peacefully when Henry Garrity came back with the doctor. Maybe because of that, he didn't make too much of a fuss about seeing her there. She heard a gruff "what's she doing here" directed at Sikes, who was standing in the doorway, and Sikes's quiet rejoinder of "saving your son's life," but didn't pay either of them much heed.

The doctor was a pleasant, middle-aged man who asked for her observations after taking Louis's vitals. She told him how she had found Louis when she arrived, showed him her records of his temperature and pulse readings and the sputum specimen she'd procured. He nodded.

"You've applied a poultice."

"Yes. An hour ago. Flaxseed, with a little onion to help the congestion. And we had him under a steam tent for about ten minutes."

"Medicine?"

"A few drops of morphine for the pain."

He nodded and turned back to Henry and Sikes in the doorway.

"You were right, Henry. He does have pneumonia, but with careful nursing, which I see he is already getting, and the fact he's young and healthy, I see no reason to be alarmed. Of course, we'll know a lot more in a couple of days when he reaches crisis."

He looked at Claire. "You are a trained nurse, are you not?"

"Yes. I've had two years training at St. Luke's in Denver."

"Any private practice?"

"No, sir, but my father and my grandfather were both doctors, so I feel as if I've been around medicine all my life. My father would often take me on visits with him when I was young." No need to tell him the last ten years of her father's life, he'd been a surgeon in St. Louis. She'd had little to no exposure to that part of his medical life.

"The Garritys are fortunate to have you. You probably know the care guide as well as I do, but here's what I'd like to see. Poultices every four hours, temperature checked every four hours, keep the steam tent going. Stimulating liquids as often as possible. You know what to do if the temperature spikes. I'll leave this citrate of iron and quinine to be given as needed. Morphine for pain, especially in light of his broken ribs. I'll stop back in a couple of days to monitor his progress. From what you've told me, I'm guessing we can expect crisis by the end of this week. Then, if all goes well, another couple of weeks of bed rest, and he should be good as new."

He turned to Jackson, who had returned to his own bed when the doctor came in.

"And you, son? How is the leg?"

"Mending."

"When did they put the cast on?"

"Ten days ago, maybe?"

"Two weeks ago Thursday, as soon he came out of traction," Claire answered for him.

"Then it's time to take it off. I'll bring my tools when I come back, and we'll get you out of it. The sooner you start using that leg without the cast, the better. Your wife will be able to help with that, as well."

So, he did know her connection with the family. Not having lived in a small community before, Claire had been skeptical about Mr. Baldwin's and Louis's insistence that everyone would know about her and Jackson before they even got home, especially since the ranch was so isolated. She didn't think Mr. Garrity would have talked about her to the doctor. Given the option, he'd just as soon she would cease to exist. But if this doctor, whom she'd never met, knew Jackson had a wife, then the rest of the Lander area must know as well, just as Mr. Baldwin had predicted.

"His wife ain't staying. In fact, you may as well pack up your things." Henry looked directly at her for the first time since entering the room. "Doc can drop you off at Granny's when he leaves."

"I always knew you were stubborn, Henry," the doctor said. "But I didn't take you for a fool. Pneumonia's no walk in the park. You've got the gift of a trained nurse right here in your own home. If you let your pride stand in your way, you might end up with one son dead and the other crippled. I'll be back on Thursday, and I pray to God, I find this woman here when I come." With that, he brushed past Henry and Sikes and made his way out the front door.

She could tell by the set of Henry's jaw he didn't like the doctor's words any too well.

Sikes laid a hand on his arm. "Doc has a point, Henry."

Henry growled. "This is my house and my family, and no doctor's going to tell me how to run things. Petie, get the horses and take Claire home. She can come do her nursing during the day while Sikes and I are in the fields, but I'll be durned if I'm gonna allow a female to stay under my roof overnight." He stalked out of the room. A few seconds later, she heard a door slam down the hall.

Petie slipped from the room, and Claire turned to pack up her things. Sikes came up beside her. "Tell me what to watch for while you're gone."

"His temperature, mostly. If it spikes again, try another

sponge bath with lukewarm water. His poultice will need to be changed in about three hours and every four hours after that. Try to keep him quiet and resting as much as possible. I'll be back first thing in the morning, but if he suddenly gets a lot worse, promise you'll come get me?"

"We will. And Doc's right. We are lucky to have you. Thanks for what you did tonight. I'll talk to Henry. He's not a bad one. It's just . . . well, it's complicated, but I know he appreciates what you've done for his boys."

Claire wasn't as sure about that, but she wasn't going to argue. Compromise. She hated to leave a patient in Louis's state, knowing how fever often seemed to spike at night, but at least she could be here during the day. And if she was here when he reached crisis, all the Henrys in the world wouldn't be able to make her leave.

For now, Louis was resting quietly. It wouldn't hurt to get some rest herself.

CHAPTER 10

J ackson rubbed absently at his bad leg, which was propped on a chair in front of him. The numbers didn't add up. No matter how many times he tried, something just wasn't right. Gabe had dropped off Baldwin's books last week when he stopped by to pick up a fresh horse and some clean clothes. With both Jackson and Louis out of commission and lambing season starting up, Baldwin's son-in-law Preston, who usually handled the bookwork, had been pressed into lambing duty. As a result, Baldwin made good on his promise to keep Jackson busy and sent the books over.

At first, Jackson had welcomed the excuse to escape the sick room and put his mind to work, but after two hours of going over the numbers, he still wasn't anywhere near to making sense of it all. It wasn't the mathematics. It was the details.

He knew for a fact wethers sold at three and three-quarters last fall, yet here it was in black and white as three and a half. Why would Baldwin sell at a loss when he didn't have to? And some of the expenses didn't add up either. Surely, Baldwin hadn't paid almost twice as much for feed than the going rate last year.

His boss had always been sharp as a tack in his verbal negotiations, so why didn't that same savvy show up on paper? Throwing his pencil down, Jackson leaned back with a sigh and closed his eyes.

Blasted broken leg. This wasn't what he wanted to be doing today or any day. Numbers always had come easy for him but sitting inside did not. If he had his druthers, he'd be out with Gabe and the others helping with lambing. He wouldn't even complain about the lousy weather that always accompanied this time of year. Heck, he'd be willing to help Pa and Sikes with the planting if it meant getting out of the confines of this house.

When he left the hospital in Denver, he'd thought life would return to normal. Boy, had he been wrong. The truth finally hit home when Doc cut off his cast last week. One look at the shriveled, puny mess of a leg, and he knew getting back to his old life would be a long time coming.

They may as well have taken his leg as much use as it was to him. He could barely lift it in his own power, and Doc said he couldn't put any weight on it for another month. He'd go stark-raving crazy before then.

"Taking a break?" Claire's voice cut into his thoughts.

He opened his eyes to see her smiling at him from the doorway. Her smile had become the highlight of his days.

"Louis is sleeping," she said. "I thought I'd grab some tea. Did you want some?"

"Any coffee left?"

She walked over to the stove and tested the coffee pot. "A little. Shall I pour you a cup?"

"Please."

"Sugar? Milk?"

"Black's fine."

She brought him a mug, brushing his hand as she set it on the table beside him. Even that slight touch tingled. She smelled of fresh linen and something flowery.

The more she was around, the more time he spent watching her and thinking thoughts a man hadn't ought to think. Too much time on his hands was his problem. His mind knew their marriage was temporary. He *wanted* it to be temporary. A wife had never played into his dreams of the future. Pa had seen to that. But for some reason, ever since he'd said the words "I do," he couldn't help thinking of her as his wife and wanting to do all the things a man did with a wife. That kind of wanting was a very dangerous place to be.

She fiddled at the stove for a while and then came back, cup of tea in hand, to sit across from him at the table.

"How's the leg today?"

"Same."

"Now Louis is on the mend, we could start your rehabilitation. We'll set up a schedule at least twice a day, though three times would be best. Start with deep massage and stretching and, when you can handle it, work up to exercises that will bring back strength to that leg. Does that sound good to you?"

He nodded. Given his current frame of mind, the thought of her hands on his leg, two, maybe three times a day, sounded like the sweetest type of torture imaginable, but if that's what it took to get his leg back, he'd do it. Anything to get him out of this house and back on his horse.

"When would you like to start?"

"Today?"

"Today will work if you think you're up to it. We might be able to get two sessions in before I leave tonight. One for sure." She stood, teacup in hand, and made her way to the door. "Let me know when you are done with your work here, and I'll get things ready."

He cleared his throat. "Maybe after lunch."

"Perfect."

He watched her walk away, the sway in her hips mesmerizing. Fool. She wasn't planning to stay. He knew firsthand not to give his heart to a woman bent on leaving. Besides, the last thing he needed was the complication of a real wife and family. Which meant he needed to get this leg healed. Once he and Louis were mended, she could go back to living at Granny's, and he could get on with his life.

∾

"Tell me when it hurts." Claire lifted his leg and began to bend his knee upward.

"Hurts." The word came out like a whimper, and she'd barely moved his leg an inch. But after fifteen minutes of pure torture where she'd kneaded his thigh muscle into a screaming mass of pain, he was done being stoical. After her first touch on his leg, there'd been nothing the slightest bit sweet about this session. On the plus side, any amorous thoughts he'd had earlier had long since fled.

She gently laid his leg back down on the bed. "All right, then. Let's try this. See how far you can lift your foot off the mattress."

He tightened his muscle and bit down on his lip, but he couldn't quite bite back the moan that escaped as pain shot down his leg. As far as he could tell, his foot didn't move at all.

"Good. Now try making small circles with your foot. Any movement you can do will help strengthen your leg muscles. These are exercises you can do even when I'm not around. The more you do them, the more you'll eventually be able to do without my help." His face must have reflected his disbelief because she gave his toe a gentle tap and came up to stand by his side, gazing down on him with that look of sweet compassion. "I know it doesn't seem like you can do much at all, but this is the worst it will be. I promise it will get better each time. You'll see. We're done for today, though."

"Well, that's a relief," Louis grumbled from the next bed. "Hard to get any sleep around here with all that belly-aching."

"Belly-aching? Why he's hardly made a sound. I'd like to see you be as brave when I ask you to do your breathing exercises."

"I have broken ribs. How can you expect me to breathe that deep with broken ribs?"

"Well, Jackson has a broken leg. You should be sympathizing with him, not picking on him."

He had to admit. It felt good to have Claire taking his side, but he hated being so weak a woman had to fight his battles. He felt all of eight years old with Ma coming between him and Louis.

Claire pulled the covers over his leg, then tucked them in around his chin, making him feel even more like a child. He scowled. The last thing he needed was a mother.

"Now. I've worked you pretty hard today, so I'm going to give you a bigger dose of pain medicine before I go." Claire said. "Try to rest the leg but remember what I said. The more you do on your own, tightening and releasing your leg muscles, the sooner you'll be able to be up and around. I know it seems hard now, but it will come." She gave his hand a squeeze before turning to the table to measure out his medicine.

After today's session, he wasn't sure he was up to any more exercises. Hadn't she said they'd do them three times a day? He wanted to groan just thinking about it.

The front door slammed, and Claire jumped, spilling some of his medicine on the side table. He noticed her hand shake a little as she mopped it up. Though usually calm and confident in the sickroom, she was still as skittish as a spooked mare when she thought Pa was around. He wished he could somehow reassure her that Pa's bark was much louder than his bite.

Voices sounded in the hallway, and a few minutes later, Sikes poked his head in the doorway, bringing Mr. Baldwin along behind him.

"Look who I found wandering around in the yard like a lost

hen. Says he's here on business if you can believe that. Told him we didn't have no sheep around here."

Mr. Baldwin laughed. "Just two of my best sheepmen. Had to come check up on them to make sure they are on the mend. Can't afford to be without either of them for too long."

Jackson pushed himself up in bed, not wanting his boss to see him flat on his back. He might feel like a wrung-out rag after that session Claire put him through, but he didn't want to show it.

"So, how are your patients today, Nurse Garrity?"

"Both a bit grumpy to be honest, which, in my professional opinion, is usually a sign they're on the mend. If I were to predict, I'd say that in a couple of weeks, Louis will be back to his normal health, and Jackson will be putting weight on that leg of his."

"A couple of weeks? Well, that is good news. We'll be deep into lambing by then, and I could use Louis's help with the drop herds. Do you think he'll be up to it?"

"I don't see why not, as long as he takes it slow and wears his flannels. His ribs should be better by then also, but we don't want to risk a relapse, so maybe not too much too soon. We'll know more in a few weeks'time."

"And Jackson? Think you'll be able to help with shearing? Not the physical work, of course, but I could use you for the counting and recording. Oh, and I brought by those numbers you wanted from last year's shearing and the loose estimates the herders gave me on winter kill. Were you able to look over those books I sent you yet? Any questions?"

Plenty of questions, but none he could air in front of the others in the room. "Yes, sir. I did get a start on them. Maybe once I've had some time to look over what you've brought me today and finish with the rest, we could sit and talk."

"Of course, of course. No rush. I'll have the herders keep

their usual tallies during lambing, but we'll get our most accu-rate counts at shearing. Think you'll be up and around by then?"

Six weeks? He'd better be, or he'd be cutting this infernal leg off himself.

"I'll be there." His voice held confidence he no longer felt, not after today's less-than-promising start. But he had six weeks. Surely in six weeks, he'd see improvement.

CHAPTER 11

"Pa says you're not to come anymore." Petie stood in the doorway of Granny Bascom's, milk pails in hand. A glance over his shoulder told Claire he hadn't brought Malachi with him this morning.

She wasn't surprised. She knew this day was coming sooner or later, especially since Louis was back out with the sheep. Jackson's leg was getting stronger every day. In fact, Dr. Stevens had told him he could start putting weight on it as early as next week. Knowing Jackson, he'd be off his crutches in no time. She should be happy her services were no longer needed.

Except . . . she wasn't.

"How is Jackson?"

"He says to tell you he'll be fine."

Of course. And he would be. She'd only been visiting him a few hours a day anyway since Louis had left the sickroom, just enough time to massage his leg and help him with his exercises. He could do most of the exercises on his own now, and those he couldn't, well, Sikes or Petie knew what to do.

"I'll get the milk for you then, and you can be on your way." She exchanged the empty pails for the full ones Granny had left at the back door, then watched as Petie rode away. The day stretched empty before her.

She should join Granny, Sadie, and Ella out back. Ella liked to help Granny gather eggs, and Sadie was prepping the garden for planting. She'd been planning to help her with that this afternoon anyway. Now they could get an early start.

Instead, she poured herself a cup of tea and sat at the table. Why was she so sad about this? She was a nurse. She was used to watching her patients leave the hospital. But this was different. This time she had no other patients waiting in the wings. No other duties calling her. And to be totally honest, she'd been enjoying the hours spent with Jackson, especially once Louis had left, and it was just the two of them.

There was a comfort between them she hadn't expected, a sense of camaraderie as they focused on getting strength back in his leg. They were a team, working toward a common goal. She was going to miss that. But this was for the best. Really, it was. This place, these people, was a temporary stop on her journey. She'd promised Jackson six months. But six months was all she was willing to give. Come autumn, she, Sadie, and Ella were moving on.

She couldn't afford to get attached. The last thing she needed was to fall under the spell of another man. That road led only to disappointment and pain. Yes, Henry Garrity was right to call an end to the nursing. In fact, she should be thankful he hated women so much. This way, she and Jackson could get back to living their separate lives, and in six months, she'd be on her way. No one would blame her for leaving under these conditions. Jackson would keep his job. She and Sadie and Ella would get their six months of hiding where no lawman would think to look, and nobody would get hurt.

She pushed to her feet. No more moping. It was time to get on with life here at Granny's. She set her teacup by the sink and headed for the door.

~

"You stick the pea seed in the ground like so, then cover it over with the dirt. Like a blanket. You do it now." Claire watched Ella's chubby little fingers sprinkle dirt over the next seed and pat it down. "Good. Help me finish off this row, and then we'll give all the seeds a drink and let them rest. When we come back and check on them next week, maybe we'll see little pea plants starting to grow."

"Are they thirsty, Mommy?"

"I guess you could say that. Water and sunlight make them grow, like when you eat your dinner and drink your milk. That helps you grow."

She rocked back on her heels, happy to watch her daughter work. Ella carefully set each pea seed on the line they'd drawn in the dirt and poked it down. Then a sprinkle of more dirt and a pat. Planting with a three-year-old wasn't a quick process, but Claire wouldn't change it for the world. This was what she'd needed. Quality time with Ella, watching her learn and grow.

While she waited for Ella to finish the row, Claire took a moment to breathe in the beauty of the day. She'd always loved springtime. Everything so new and fresh. New birth, renewal, was something her soul longed for long before Jonas. Each year, as the world came back new and alive after a long season of winter, she heard the whisper of promise. Could her life do the same now that Jonas was gone? Be renewed?

She let her eyes scan her surroundings, the red cliffs bright against the blue in the sky, the fresh green of the grass, the smell of newly turned earth, and . . . Jackson? Her heart quick-stepped at the sight of him standing a mere ten feet away. He leaned on his crutches, a tentative smile on his lips as her gaze caught his.

"How did you get here?"

"Petie brought me in the wagon. I need your help."

She pushed to her feet, wiping the dirt from her hands onto

her already soiled apron. If only she'd put on something other than this old house dress this morning. Or at least spent more time on her hair. But really, what did it matter how she looked? What was good enough for Granny and Sadie should be good enough for Jackson.

He looked good. Dressed casually as well, in brown canvas pants, a chambray shirt, and a wide-brimmed hat, he looked stronger somehow and handsome. Not at all like the invalid she'd left a week ago. But as she drew near, she noticed pain etched across his face, lingering in those midnight-blue eyes of his.

"How's your leg?"

A corner of his mouth lifted in a half-smile. "Not so great."

"What's happened? Have you injured it again?"

"It's my knee. I'm having trouble bending it."

"Come inside, and I'll take a look." She turned back to Ella, who stood beside their row of peas, hands planted on her hips, watching them. "Sweetie, let's take a quick break while I help Mr. Garrity. Come along now. Maybe Granny will have a slice of gingerbread and some milk for you."

As she suspected, the word "gingerbread" had its effect. Ella barreled past them and up the steps into the cabin. Claire followed, allowing Jackson to navigate the three steps on his own time, knowing from experience he wouldn't appreciate her hovering over him.

"Hold on now," she said to Ella, who was already clambering onto the bench by the table. "We need to wash the garden dirt off our hands before we eat anything."

She looked over at Granny, who was helping Sadie roll and cut out biscuits. Sadie raised an eyebrow at her when Jackson hobbled into the room behind her.

"I promised Ella some gingerbread while I examine Jackson's leg. I hope that won't be a problem."

"No problem at all." Granny scuttled around the table. "Petie said he'd dropped you off. He's gone to gather the eggs. Can I get you anything?"

"No, ma'am. I'm fine."

Granny's cabin suddenly felt minuscule with the four of them plus Jackson all in one room. Claire hadn't thought about the lack of privacy when she'd asked him inside. The cabin's main floor was all one room with Granny's bed partitioned off in the corner with a curtain. She'd have to look at his leg there. He wouldn't be able to manage the steps to the loft, and asking him to drop his pants in front of Granny and Sadie was out of the question.

"Granny, would you mind if we used your bed for the examination?" She turned to Jackson. "You're going to need to take off your pants so I can see your leg." Her face warmed as she spoke the words.

Good grief. She was acting like a fourteen-year-old schoolgirl, not a seasoned professional. A *widowed* seasoned professional. She wasn't some innocent virgin who'd never seen a man's bare leg before. She'd seen Jackson's leg hundreds of times, but something about this cabin, with Granny and Sadie looking on, made it all feel more personal. More intimate.

"Why don't the three of us take a gingerbread break?" Granny looked toward Sadie and Ella. "You'd like some too, wouldn't you, Sadie? I know I do. And since it's such a nice day, we can eat out on the porch. We'll ask Petie to join us when he's done with the eggs."

Minutes later, Claire and Jackson stood in the kitchen alone.

"Guess we know how to clear a room," Jackson said. "Tell everyone I'm about to drop my pants."

Claire laughed, letting go of most of the awkwardness. "Get on with you then. You can change behind Granny's curtain and wrap one of her quilts around you if you like. You'll be able to manage?"

"Mostly. I may need some help with my boots."

She ended up helping with both the boots and the pants, but all awkwardness fled when she saw his knee, red, hot, and swollen three times its normal size. No wonder he couldn't bend it.

"Have you been resting your leg like I told you after each exercise session?"

"Some."

"Some? How often do you do the exercises?"

"Mornings mostly. Sometimes at night."

"And you're resting it in between?"

"Well, no. Not resting exactly."

"What have you been doing, then?"

"Helping out around the farm. In the barn, mostly. I've been working the horses."

"You're riding? How?"

"Not riding. Can't bend the leg far enough."

So, he'd tried.

"Just exercising them is all. On a lead rein. My horse, Boaz, and a few others that aren't being used to plow."

"How many hours would you say you're on your feet each day?"

"Seven, eight hours, maybe?"

"Jackson Garrity. No wonder your leg is swollen as big as a post beam. You've been doing too much. You should be resting with your leg up at least as often as you exercise. Have you been getting your massages?"

"Petie and Sikes tried a couple of times, but they're both so ham-fisted I made them stop. Besides, it's spring planting. No one has time to be giving massages."

"Your father should have thought of that before he told me not to come back anymore. Never mind. Lay back." She lifted Jackson's leg and began kneading the calf area, starting at the ankle and working her way up. Jackson moaned. "If this is too much for you, tell me, and I'll stop."

"No. Don't stop."

She continued to work on the calf muscle. "The massages aren't critical, though they would help keep the swelling down. What's most important is that you don't overdo it. I want you to promise me. For every two hours of standing or exercise, you spend one hour on your back with your leg elevated like I taught you.

"Your leg will heal, but it will heal a lot slower if you push too hard. I know you're anxious to be up and about and doing all your regular activities, but a break like this takes time. You already set your healing back by leaving the hospital too soon. Now you have a choice. Listen to your body and take it slow or go too fast and make the healing process even slower."

She skirted his swollen knee and worked his upper thigh, rubbing against the grain of the muscle where the break had occurred. Jackson sucked in his breath.

"Too much?"

"No. Hurts good."

She nodded. She knew what he meant. Like worrying a sore tooth, sometimes it just felt good to push against the pain. Nevertheless, she would send him home with some pain medicine. As long as it had been since his last massage, he would need it. Because of that, she made quick work.

"There. That should help for now. Let's get you dressed before the others come back in." She turned to reach for his pants, but he caught her hand.

"I promise to rest the leg and take it slow if you'll promise me two massages a week until shearing time."

"How? Your father won't let me on the ranch. And here . . ." She gestured to their tiny quarters. "It's too cramped. You'll have no privacy. Besides, we can't expect the others to leave the cabin every time you come."

"There's an empty potting shed on the edge of Granny's

property right where her land joins ours. You ride by it any time you come to the ranch."

"The little gray shack?"

"That's it. Meet me there on Tuesday around ten. Please?"

His thumb traced a slow pattern on her wrist, hiking her pulse. Mercy. He was nearly irresistible with that look in his eyes. Why did this feel like an invitation to a secret lover's tryst?

She glanced at his swollen leg and back into those hypnotic eyes. "All right. Twice a week until shearing time. If you promise no more eight-hour days on your legs. At least until you get your strength back."

"Promise."

Voices at the door told her their time was up. "Let's get you back into these pants and boots. With any luck, they've saved some gingerbread for us."

CHAPTER 12

He was late. Not that she minded, but in the three weeks they'd been meeting in this tiny shed, he'd always arrived before her. Funny how the shed seemed larger today without him in it.

There wasn't much to it, really. An eight-foot by ten-foot rectangle of weathered gray wood, the shed housed buckets and rakes, and shovels. A table that had once been used as a potting bench took up most of the space. Of sturdy construction, it was the ideal height for a massage table. Up until today, Jackson had always been sitting on it when she arrived.

Where was he?

She walked to the door again, looking out across the grassland that marked the beginning of the Garrity ranch. The shed was tucked at the edge of Granny Bascom's property in amongst a grove of apple trees. The Windsors and the Wealthies Granny called them. Though Granny no longer actively worked her orchards anymore, with Petie's help with pruning and the community's help at harvest, she managed to have a respectable crop each year. Enough, she'd told them, to make and sell her famous apple cider at the fair, but nothing like the operation Ed Young had going. Apparently, he was the apple orchard king of the Lander area, and Granny was willing to let him have that title.

Claire leaned against the door jamb and drew in a deep breath of the sweet-scented air. Truly, this spot Jackson had chosen could not be more beautiful. The walk to and from Granny's cabin through pink and white, blossom-laden trees had been a welcome treat, almost worth the mixed feelings she'd had about spending time alone with her so-called husband. Not that Jackson had ever been anything but a gentleman, but he *was* a man.

A big man.

A man who grew stronger and more able-bodied each week. Therein lay the problem.

A helpless, broken Jackson was one thing. This new stronger version of her handsome patient was a complication she'd rather not deal with.

A cloud of dust on the horizon materialized into a horse and rider. Claire ducked back into the shadows of the cabin's interior until she realized the horseman was Jackson. He rode with the ease of someone born to the saddle, he and the horse moving as one. They were a pleasure to watch. The horse was a sleek buckskin with dark legs, mane, and tail, as powerful and handsome as his rider.

Jackson cantered right up to the doorway of the shed and pulled to a stop, grinning down at her like an excited schoolboy.

"You're riding!"

"Yep."

"For how long?"

"Today's the first try. Had to adjust the stirrups some, but it seems to be working."

"Any pain?"

"A little getting on." He rose in the saddle and clenched his jaw as he swung his bad leg across the horse's back and stepped down.

"And off."

"Nothing I can't handle."

Of course not. The man was determined to be back tending the sheepherders by the end of shearing time, and though he still walked with a slight limp, she didn't doubt his ability to accomplish that goal. He was relentless in pushing himself with his exercises no matter how much they hurt. And he'd refused to take any more laudanum after that first massage three weeks ago. Probably for the best. She'd seen far too many become addicted.

"Well, come on in. We'll work out the kinks. If riding isn't too painful for you, it'll probably do your leg good. Could be another way to help build back your muscle."

"Let me get Boaz settled, and I'll be right in."

Boaz. Another gelding. And another Biblical name. She reached up and stroked Boaz's neck before Jackson could lead him away.

"He's beautiful."

"Don't be letting that get to your head and all, now, Boaz. 'Pretty is as pretty does,' they say, and you and I both know how ornery you can be."

"He's not the one who hurt you, is he?" She'd forgotten Jackson's injury had been caused by a horse. Her admiration of Jackson's ability to ride this morning ratcheted up a notch.

"Naw, that was one of Baldwin's. I'm not saying Boaz couldn't have done the same in his youth, but he wasn't the culprit."

Jackson led his horse to the nearest apple tree and tied him to a low-hanging branch. Limping a little, he walked into the shed and hoisted himself onto the table. Since the day she examined his leg in Granny's cabin, Claire hadn't asked to see Jackson's bare leg again. Somehow, in this isolated setting, she felt safer with him fully clothed.

"How's the knee? Have you had much swelling lately?"

"Some, if I work it too hard. But nothing like it was."

"Good. You may notice some tonight after riding for the first time, but if you keep the leg elevated and rest it like I've taught you, it shouldn't be a problem." She bent his leg, watching his face for evidence of pain. He'd never been good at voicing his discomfort, so she'd learned to read his face. She looked for a tightening in the jaw, any sign of a wince, no matter how slight. "Your range of motion has certainly improved. You're almost at a full ninety-degree angle." She didn't have to ask if he'd been doing his daily exercises. The improvement in his leg was proof of that. "Keep this up, and you won't be needing these massages much longer."

"Might be for the best. Don't know when we'd fit them in with shearing starting next week."

She squelched a pang of disappointment. Foolish girl. Ending these massages was a good thing. Not because she hated this time they had together, but because she was enjoying it far too much. Enjoying the feel of his muscled leg beneath her hands. Relishing the smell of him, all earth and grass and fresh spring air. Something about him drew her like a moth to a flame, and she refused to be a moth. Never again.

"Jackson?"

Claire jumped at the sound of a voice in the doorway. Mr. Baldwin stood there, eyes wide, jaw slack.

"What are you two doing way out here?"

The better question would be, what was *he* doing here? The man had a knack for turning up just at the wrong time. She glanced out the small window beside the door and saw a black horse tied beside Boaz. She hadn't even heard him ride up.

Jackson pushed himself to a sitting position on the table, a deep flush staining his cheeks. Claire felt warmth flush her own. How awkward this was.

"Claire's been treating my leg, helping me with my exercises."

"Exercises, huh? Is that what we're calling it these days?" He chuckled. "Never mind. I remember what it was like to be a newlywed, but you shouldn't tie your horse in view of the road if you want privacy. I saw Boaz tethered over here and thought someone had stolen him. Does this mean you're riding again?"

"As of today."

"Excellent. I was just headed to your Pa's to see how you were progressing. I can count on you for shearing then?"

"I'll be there."

"Good. Louis sent word that the last of the ewes should deliver within the next few days, so we'll plan to start on Monday. You can bring those ledgers with you, and we'll go over them in the evenings."

"Yes, sir."

"I'll leave you to your 'exercises' then." With another chuckle, he walked to his horse, mounted up, and rode off.

An awkward silence followed his departure. Claire resumed her manipulation of Jackson's leg, then began to massage his thigh, but in the aftermath of Mr. Butler's innuendos, she struggled to regain the impersonal nature of each touch. Mr. Baldwin's teasing reminded her this man was her husband. He had every right to demand certain privileges.

Had he changed his mind at all since their marriage? He'd been sick and weak back then, but Jonas had taught her it took very little—a random word, a touch, a look—to spark a desire for such privileges in an able-bodied man. What did she know of Jackson, really? He seemed a good man. But so had Jonas at one time.

She glanced at him, lying rock still and silent, one arm bent and covering his eyes. For all she knew, he could be sleeping. Somehow, she doubted it. The air around them fairly shimmered with heat. The walls of the tiny shed closed in, stealing her breath. Claire gave Jackson's thigh one last rub and stepped back.

"There. That should do it for today." She forced lightness into her voice.

Jackson lowered his arm and looked over at her, his eyes so dark they almost looked black. Those eyes. Their draw was almost irresistible. Almost.

She quickly turned away and began packing her bag.

"I didn't hurt you too much, did I? I can send some aspirin with you if you'd like."

"No. I'm fine."

He sat up, wincing a little as he swung his bad leg around, and stood. She always forgot how tall he was until he stood. Tall and strong and standing between her and the door. She had to get out of here. Now.

"So. I better get back. I'm guessing from what Mr. Baldwin said, this will be our last session?" She sidled around him as she talked, trying her best not to brush up against him, a surprising feat given the shed's tight quarters.

"I reckon."

"I'll be off then. Good luck with the shearing and . . . after. I'm sure we won't see much of you, you'll be so busy. If you need anything for the leg, let me know. Otherwise . . . well, I'm sure we'll see you around. Sometime."

She practically sprinted out the door and started up the path.
"Claire."

She turned to see him standing in the doorway, a slightly bemused expression on his face. Well, of course, he was confused. She was acting like a regular birdbrain.

"Thank you," he called.

Thank you? When had Jonas ever thanked her for anything?

"Of course. Take care, Jackson."

She forced herself to walk away slowly this time, but for the longest time, she could feel his gaze at her back. Thank goodness this session was their last. Today's awkwardness was a great reminder that the best way for them to survive this six-month marriage was separate.

CHAPTER 13

I t was good to be back. Sure, the sheds reeked of that familiar stench of shearing time—wool grease, dirt, and sweat. Had anyone told him a year ago he'd welcome that smell, let alone find joy in it, he'd have laughed in his face. Yet, after months of lying on his back, wondering if he'd ever walk again, the smell was pure delight.

Well, maybe not delight. But he was back. And not on crutches either.

His knee would give him heck tonight after all the standing and walking he'd been doing, but pain had been a daily reality for so long that it hardly mattered. He'd deal with it. Claire wouldn't be happy, but then, Claire wasn't here, was she? Now their therapy sessions had ended, she could no longer scold him for overdoing things. The thought didn't bring the satisfaction it should have, but he refused to dwell on the reason.

The less time he spent thinking about his pretend wife, the better. His marriage was doomed before he said, "I do." Like Father, like son, people would think, except unlike Pa, he knew to guard his heart. He was no fool, though folks around here might think him one when she left. He'd have his own flock by then. He was willing to pay the price of a little public humiliation to be an independent sheep owner.

"Sheep out!"

A call from the shed alerted him to let another fifty sheep into the holding pen. Fifty sheep in, fifty sheep out the other side in intervals of approximately thirty minutes. The shearing crew Baldwin hired was small, with only eight men shearing, but they were experienced. At this pace, they should easily have all the ewes shorn and back on the range by early June. He let the final ewe through and shut the gate.

Summer range was his favorite part of sheep herding—away from the heat, away from the dirt, just cool mountain air, and lush green meadows. Now that he could ride again, surely Baldwin would put him back on his camp tending duties. He really hoped so. If he had to spend the entire summer indoors looking over ledgers, he'd go crazy for sure.

So far, the rough tallies the herders had given him from the lambing looked promising. Baldwin had sent Louis and Tavis out to the grazing pens to get a more accurate count this morning. It helped to have all the sheep gathered in one area. Counting sheep in pens was hard enough. Keeping an accurate count on the open range, especially with the bands dividing and changing every day during lambing, was almost impossible. But if the preliminary numbers held, they'd come through lambing with only a six percent loss of both lambs and ewes. Not bad, given the dangers of open-range birthing.

If his leg could take all the walking, he'd have been at the pens with Louis looking over the new lambs. In January, before the accident, Baldwin had promised to sell him 2500 ewe lambs at the end of the summer season. He was itching to see the new crop. Maybe during lunch, he'd ride Boaz out that way. For now, he was content just to be back in the action, even if the only action he saw was opening and shutting a gate.

"Sheep out!"

~

"I GOT THOSE NUMBERS FOR YOU." LOUIS HANDED JACKSON A tally sheet.

"How'd that go for you?"

Louis shot him a dark look. "About like always when you try to count a flock of three-week-old lambs who can't find their mothers."

"But you managed."

"We managed."

"Just be glad you don't have to count their mamas too." Each ewe was counted as it was sheared, possibly the only accurate count a sheepman like Baldwin, who owned over 10,000 sheep, got in a year's time.

Jackson couldn't hear Louis's reply. Behind them, the bleating of the penned sheep rose to a cacophony as Tavis and Gabe released three hundred lambs into the pen for their lunchtime feeding. Jackson turned to watch. The reunion between the lambs and their mamas this initial time after they'd been sheared was always a spectacle. Jackson chuckled as lamb after lamb ran toward its mother's voice and skidded right past her, not recognizing her with her new hairdo. There was nothing cuter than a three-week-old lamb and nothing uglier than a newly-shorn sheep.

Shaking his head, Louis turned and headed toward the mess tent. Jackson caught up to him. He'd forgo riding out to see the other lambs for now. His leg needed a rest, or he wouldn't make it through the afternoon.

After downing a plate of lamb stew, he pulled out the tally sheet Louis had given him and scanned the numbers. Wait. This couldn't be right. He'd have to check when he got back to his bunk, but his memory for numbers rarely failed him. If these were accurate, their lambing loss percentage had more than doubled from the initial numbers the herders had given him.

"Did any of the herders mention more than normal predator activity?"

"Not that I know of. Why?"

"The numbers are off."

Louis shrugged. "Aren't they always? You know how hard it is to get a true count out there."

"Yeah. But we're talking differences of around 50. Maybe a hundred. This is three times that."

"You sure?"

"I'd bet my day's pay on it."

"Well, lambing was a mess this year with the two of us gone. When I finally got out there, Preston was trying to do your job, and we both know how worthless he is around sheep. I'm surprised they gave us any numbers at all."

Louis was right. Baldwin's oldest daughter, Jane, had met Preston Winthrop III when she'd gone back east last summer to visit relatives. Jackson had the feeling a tenderfoot easterner wasn't exactly Baldwin's first choice as a son-in-law, but being the only man in a house full of women, Baldwin pretty much gave his girls anything they wanted. Still. Putting the greenhorn in charge of even a few of the drop herds? It's a wonder the losses weren't even higher.

"That's probably it. Baldwin's not going to be happy to hear his losses are double what we thought they were, though. I don't know if he's ever had a twelve percent loss before."

"I've heard of winter kill as high as thirty percent this year up near Lost Cabin. At least we didn't get the snowfall they did. Might want to bring that up if he throws much of a fit."

CHAPTER 14

Jackson shoveled another bite of ham roast and potatoes into his mouth, savoring the flavor. The cornbread and beans Cookie served in the mess tent weren't nearly this good, but dinner with the Baldwins wasn't without its pitfalls. He kept his eyes trained on his plate, forcing himself to chew as slowly as possible to avoid being drawn into the conversation. It would never do to make eye contact or finish early. He'd learned that lesson long ago.

Shopping . . . Stacia Allen's . . . shirtwaist in blue or red . . . Lander on the Fourth . . . picnic . . . dance . . . . He let the words flow around him.

He'd been all of fifteen when he first discovered people actually *talked* to each other at the dinner table. When you competed for grub with three brothers and maybe as many farmhands, you didn't take much time to stop and jaw awhile. A fellow could stay pretty hungry employing that method.

Baldwin was a great guy, and he didn't have a problem with Beatrice most days, but the daughters were another story altogether. Four of them. Always talking. Always giggling. Always watching him with those cow eyes of theirs.

They were all just kids when he started working here. The older two, Jane and Mary, couldn't have been more than twelve and ten. But even then, he hadn't known what to make of them. They followed him everywhere those early years, asking all sorts of questions and whispering and giggling to each other behind their hands as he worked.

He reached for his glass of water and caught Mary's eyes on him from across the table. Her gaze skittered away the minute he noticed her. She hadn't always been so shy. Before that ugly business with those outlaws last year, she'd been as gabby as all the others. A kick at his ankle drew his attention to the girl beside him. Charlie held a cloth-covered basket out to him.

"Biscuit?"

Beatrice Baldwin made the flakiest biscuits this side of the Winds. He deposited three on his plate before passing the basket along to Preston.

Now, Charlie, he liked. No flouncy dresses and ribbons for that one. She wore britches more often than not and didn't talk about fripperies the infernal day long like the others. Most days, he'd find her in the barn with the animals, and their mutual love for all the critters had formed a bond between them. Too bad her sisters weren't more like her.

"... Jackson ..."

His attention caught at the sound of his name. He fought the urge to look up.

" ... is able to ride again, so will you please keep Preston off the range?" Jane sounded peeved. As if any of them really wanted Preston out with the sheep.

"The boys and I will discuss that later, Jane. You know I don't talk business at the table."

"But I need Preston home with me, Papa." Her voice took on a petulant whine. "After all, he'll soon be a father. He needs to be with his family."

Baldwin grunted. "Family? What family? Your baby won't be

here until December. It won't hurt for Preston to spend a few weeks this summer out at the camps if I need him."

"And don't forget Jackson's also a family man," Beatrice said. "His wife and daughter probably want him around too."

"I don't see why. They don't even live with him."

"What?"

Blast. This was just the type of talk he'd hoped to avoid. He could feel Beatrice's gaze on him.

"Jackson, is that true?"

Why it should matter to Beatrice was beyond him.

"*Is* it?"

He sighed. There was no avoiding Beatrice once she got a bee stuck in her bonnet.

"Yes'm."

"But where are they living?"

"Granny's."

"Why in the—? Oh, never mind. I know why. It's that stubborn father of yours, isn't it? Joseph, this is just not right. A man and wife should live together. What type of marriage can they have if they don't even live in the same house?"

"I suspect they manage." The smile in Baldwin's voice suggested he was thinking of that day at the potting shed.

"Which is exactly my point, Mother." Jane jumped back into the breach. "Preston should be working here at the ranch. Like he did before. Jackson will be fine."

Jackson actually agreed with Jane, which was a first. Unluckily for them both, her father was not one to let his wife and daughters manage his ranch. Other things, yes. But not the ranch. He hoped Jane's butting into the matter wouldn't jinx things for him.

"Like I said before. The boys and I will discuss work assignments later. No more ranch talk. I want to enjoy your mother's apple pie, and I'm sure the boys do too."

Jackson was happy to let the subject drop. He was mighty

partial to Beatrice's pie. The speculative gleam in her eyes as she studied him was worrisome, but not so much that he'd let it spoil his dessert.

～

JACKSON STARED AT THE NUMBERS BALDWIN HANDED HIM. TWO hundred and forty-eight ewes missing from the beginning of lambing to shearing time. Even without him and Louis on lamb duty, that number seemed high.

"How confident are you in the winter tallies? Could there have been a bigger loss to predators and weather this winter than the herders reported?"

Baldwin shrugged. "You know how hard it is to count out on the range. I've never seen the numbers off this far, though. One to two percent margin, maybe. This is a lot higher than that."

Adding in the lamb losses, which were almost as high as the ewe loss, Baldwin's overall loss came to well over eleven percent. Six percent more than any of the last three years.

"Was the lambing this year really that ugly?"

"I wasn't out there every day. The times I was, it didn't seem much different than usual."

"What do Tavis and Laraby say about it?" He figured Baldwin's two most experienced sheepmen would have mentioned something if the birth fatalities were higher than usual.

"Seems as if the heaviest losses were in Preston's bands. Both Tavis and Laraby reported the usual amount. There's always the breach births, the older ewes that don't make it, predator loss. But neither reported anything out of the ordinary."

"Chalk it up to inexperience then?"

"I guess we'll have to. Tarnation!" Baldwin threw his ledger onto his desk and began to pace. "Had I known how much that boy would cost me, I'd have hired someone from town with a little experience and kept Preston here at the ranch. I certainly didn't anticipate this many losses. It couldn't have been much worse if they'd had no supervision at all."

"He was in charge of the drop bands, then?"

"According to Gabe, he insisted on it. By the time Louis got out there to take over, the damage had already been done."

The thought of all those animals dying unnecessarily gnawed Jackson's gut. Seemed to him that even Preston should have known losing four to five sheep or more a night wasn't normal, and the daily losses had to have been that high to account for these numbers. What a waste.

"Well, it's all water under the bridge now. We'll hope for minimal losses this summer to make up for it. With you and Louis both back on the job, that shouldn't be a problem. Now, you said you had some questions about those books I gave you? Find a few mathematical errors, did you?"

Nothing that simple. And he hated bringing it up right on the heels of Preston's bungling the lambing so badly.

"It's not the math so much as—"

"Starting without me?" Preston sauntered into the room and threw himself into one of Baldwin's overstuffed leather chairs.

Great.

"About time you joined us." Baldwin's tone was decidedly frosty. "Jackson and I were just discussing the heavy losses we sustained during lambing. You wouldn't know anything about that, would you?"

"What is Jackson implying?"

"He didn't imply anything. The numbers speak for themselves. We had twice as many losses during lambing season than we've had in the past three years."

"You're not saying *I'm* to blame?"

"You tell me. How many ewes would you estimate you lost each day you were out there?"

"I don't remember. You have the tallies, don't you?"

"Yes. But if we go by your tallies and the tallies from Tavis and Laraby, there's about a hundred ewes unaccounted for. Care to explain that?"

"I wouldn't have any idea. There were so many count changes every day between groups breaking off to give birth and then being added back in. It's a wonder anyone kept an accurate tally."

"Apparently, no one did. So, either I lost a hundred head of sheep to poor birthing practices, or there's a band of sheep out there wandering around lost. Either way, I'm down eleven percent."

Preston shrugged. "I never said I knew anything about lambing or anything else to do with the herds. I told you then you'd be better off keeping me here at the ranch doing your books. It would have made your daughter happy too."

"Ah, yes. About those books. Jackson was just getting ready to tell me about some mistakes he found there."

"And you're taking his word for it? He has, what, an eighth-grade education? Need I remind you I graduated from Princeton?"

"No need. You've mentioned it often enough." Baldwin leaned back in his chair and huffed a sigh. "All right, Mr. Princeton grad. Let's put you to the test. I'll give you both three numbers to add. Whoever has the answer first is the one I trust when it comes to my books. Ready?"

"Hold on." Preston strolled over to Baldwin's desk and picked up a pad of paper and a pencil. "All right. Shoot."

"Three thousand twenty-one. Eighty-five hundred and sixteen. Fifty-two thousand two hundred and fifty-five." He paused as Preston wrote down the numbers, then turned his way. "Jackson, care to give us your answer?"

"Sixty-three thousand, seven hundred and ninety-two." Baldwin had been parading him out like a trained pig ever since the day he realized he had a head for numbers, but tonight he didn't mind so much. Preston and his eastern education deserved to be taken down a notch.

"Oh, come on. You expect me to believe he came up with that off the top of his head? Is this some sort of parlor game the two of you play?"

"You try. Give him any two random numbers and ask him to multiply them. Then work the problem yourself and see if he's right."

"Fine. One thousand eighty-five times four hundred and twenty-two."

"Four hundred fifty-seven thousand, eight hundred and seventy."

Preston began to work the problem. A few minutes later, he threw down the pencil. "Fine. Your camp tender's a math savant. So, what terrible errors did I make in the books? Did I forget to carry a three? Mistake a two for a five?"

"Naw, it's not the math so much. It's the details." He turned to Baldwin. "What price did you get for your wethers last fall?"

"We waited until the price hit $3.75, didn't we?"

"I thought so."

"I'm sure of it. Bunce sold at $3.50 and was kicking himself when we compared prices."

Jackson opened the ledger to last season's sales and showed him the number in the price column.

"Three dollars and twenty-five cents? That's not right. Preston?"

"Don't look at me. I just copied down the numbers from the receipts you gave me. A two and a seven can look a lot alike."

"Do we have the receipts?"

Jackson shook his head. "They weren't with the records you gave me."

"I'm sure they're filed with the bank statements," Preston said.

"Well, we can look those over later. Anything else?"

"Just some discrepancies between what you should have paid for feed and what you actually paid. About a four to five-cent difference per pound."

"Not in my favor, I suppose?"

He shook his head again.

"How do you know?" Preston was practically yelling now. "Do you have all of last year's prices memorized?"

Jackson couldn't blame the man for sounding defensive. Most likely, the errors were honest mistakes, as Preston said. A seven that looked like a two. Two numbers transposed. Not ever having worked with sheep before, he wouldn't notice the difference.

"Jackson has already demonstrated he has a head for numbers, and he's been in this business almost ten years," Baldwin said. "If he says the prices are off, you can believe they are." He slammed the ledger shut and shook his head. "Honestly, Preston, I'm not sure what to do with you. Mistakes like this will keep happening unless you know the business better, but it's obvious I can't just throw you out with a band of sheep on your own and expect things to go well. Maybe my best bet is to put you with Tavis or Gabe this summer and let you learn from the ground up like Jackson did."

"What? Me herd sheep? You've got to be kidding me."

"You told me you wanted to learn the business. Here's your chance to learn from some of the best herders in the county. If you'd rather not, then feel free to find a job in town, but I can't have you in charge of my books until you can recognize the going price for mutton and a fair price on a bale of hay."

"Fine." Preston spat the word across the desk and pushed to his feet. "But I'll leave it to you to explain to your daughter why her husband won't be home all summer." He shot a glare Jackson's way as he made his way out of the room. "Hope you're happy, Number's Boy."

Of course, he wasn't happy. Preston being out of the office meant he'd have to be in it. He felt the walls closing in already.

"Sorry about that," Baldwin said. "I'd like to help the boy get a start in this business, but frankly, I'm not sure he's cut out for it. We'll know more by the end of the summer, I guess. Now, about you. I'm sure you've already figured I'm going to need your help getting these books back in order. I don't know how much we'll need to refigure, but I do know you're the best man for the job." He held up a hand. "I know. You're raring to get back to camp tending. How about we compromise? I let you tend two of the herders, give Louis the other four, and in between trips to the camps, you help me get these books in shape. What do you say? Sound fair?"

Jackson leaned his elbows on his knees, rolling the brim of his hat through his fingers. It wasn't what he wanted, but the man had paid all his medical bills and kept him on the payroll for months when all he could do was lie flat on his back. He could afford to spend a few days a week in the office.

"Yes, sir. More than fair. Thank you."

"Good." Baldwin stood up and held out his hand. Jackson took it in a firm shake. "I'll see you back here bright and early Monday morning then."

CHAPTER 15

Jackson's leg throbbed, but he didn't care. He'd spent a week on horseback, moving sheep camps from one mountain spot to another. If Claire were here, she'd scold him. Tell him to rest his leg for at least a day, maybe more, before getting back on a horse. But Claire wasn't here, and this was his first day free in over a month. He was going to make it out to his land even if it meant he'd pay for it with a sleepless night of pain.

He hadn't been there since February, shortly after he filed a claim on it and right before his accident. One hundred and sixty acres of the nicest land on Cherry Creek. The original homesteader, a German fellow named Schmidt, had abandoned it before he'd proved the land. He'd left very little to show for his three years' labor other than a windbreak of cottonwoods and cedar and a tiny dugout with a dilapidated roof.

Jackson had planned to restore the roof last winter and live in the dugout until he could haul enough timber from the Winds to build himself a cabin. This infernal leg injury had postponed all his plans, but he wasn't giving up. Not by a long shot. He wouldn't have much time this summer, what with working Baldwin's books and moving two sheepmen around but come fall, he hoped to buy that band of ewes from Baldwin and winter them at his own place. It shouldn't take too much to whip the dugout into shape, even if he had to wait until fall to do the work.

Today he'd get a better idea of what needed to be done. The last time he'd visited the property, snow had filled a good part of the dugout, so he couldn't get a fair assessment of the work it needed. He hoped it was merely a matter of replacing the poles in the roof and adding a top layer of dirt.

He cantered by the Skivington cabin with a wave to little Hazel Long sitting in the doorway. He should stop and say "howdy," but Rob was probably out with the sheep, and he never knew what to say to the womenfolk. The Skivingtons were good people, though. Another reason this plot of land had appealed to him. A man couldn't go wrong with neighbors like Rob and Maddie.

Giving Boaz free rein, he urged him to a full gallop. He couldn't get to his place fast enough. Finally owning a ranch of his own was what he'd clung to all those long days in traction.

He pulled Boaz to a stop as he crested the next rise. His land spread before him just as he remembered it. Grass and sage flowed in waves through the valley, flanked on the east by the crimson cliffs and the blue peaks of the Winds on the west. Cherry Creek wound its way through the middle of it, like a silver ribbon snaking toward the south. Everything was exactly as he pictured it those long, trying days in the hospital, except for . . . a cabin?

He blinked. There ahead, right where he planned to build a cabin someday, just south of the windbreak Schmidt had planted, sat the beginnings of a cabin. Men swarmed all over it, placing logs, and pounding nails. Two were working a double saw.

Squatters? If so, there was a whole army of them. He spurred

Boaz into a gallop again, rapidly closing the distance between himself and the men. As he drew close, he recognized Louis's curly, black head of hair, and the boy working the other side of the saw looked suspiciously like Gabe. What the devil was going on?

He cantered into the yard, spraying dirt and pebbles on both brothers as he reined to a halt. Louis grinned and yelled over at the men on the cabin walls, "Pay up, boys. He's here."

Baldwin popped his head over the top of the highest log. "Today? I thought for sure, he'd use his first day off to go see his bride."

A grizzled head poked around the doorway. Pa? And Sikes was coming around the building. And there was Petie with Rob Skivington, and Smiley and Bob, two of Baldwin's ranch hands.

"You kidding me?" Louis crowed. "Jackson? His land comes before any woman. You all owe me fifty cents."

"What's going on?" He didn't care if he was shouting. This was his land, and he'd be hogtied if he'd sit here and let everyone continue talking about him as if he wasn't there.

"You'd think it'd be obvious, Jack. We're building you a cabin. It was supposed to be a surprise for you and Claire, but I knew you'd show up long before we finished. We had a pool going on what day each of us expected you, and I won. Thank you for being so predictable."

"When? How? Why?" He sounded as flabbergasted as he felt. "How long have you been at this?"

"Since the day after shearing ended. There were a few who foolishly bet you'd swing by here on your way out to tend to Laraby and Tavis, but I figured you'd at least wait until your day off."

He ignored Louis's boasting to look at the work in front of him. They'd done all this in a little over a week? It would have taken him months to accomplish this much on his own. He couldn't believe what he was seeing—a half-completed, two-story log cabin. Here. On his land. Another day's work and they'd be adding the roof.

"But . . . *why?*"

"You can thank Baldwin for this one, son. He's the one who rounded us all up to come help build it," Pa said.

"Now, no need to thank me. We all know this particular project was the brainchild of my wife. The minute she learned you weren't living with your new bride, she began picking at me to do something about it. It was either come out here and build this thing or find a new home for myself."

That explained Baldwin's involvement, but Pa? He would never have expected Pa to have any part of this. He turned toward him, not even sure how to ask.

Pa must have read the question on his face because he shrugged. "I think you're all kinds of a fool for taking a wife, but now the deed's done, I don't have a problem with you living with her. I just don't want her living with me. Now, enough jawing. If we're going to get this place built by the end of this week, we'd better get back to work."

Louis poked at him with one end of his two-handled saw. "Since you're here, you may as well make yourself useful. Gabe, you and Petie bring us another log. Jackson and I will show you how it's done."

GRANNY SAID DAYS LIKE TODAY ALMOST MADE UP FOR THE Wyoming winters. Almost. Since Claire didn't plan to experience a Wyoming winter, she didn't care how bad they got. She was fully content to enjoy this day to its fullest, including the sunshine that warmed her skin and the gentle breeze that kept the heat from becoming too intense. She bounced and swayed on the hard seat as the wagon careened over rocks in the now-familiar red dirt road that cut through the valley connecting the scattered ranches along the Red Canyon.

Petie was driving them to a neighbor's housewarming—their first social outing since arriving in this far-flung community. Other than the Garrity household, Claire had met very few of the neighbors. Mrs. Baldwin and two of her daughters had dropped by early on. And she'd met one of the Baldwin's ranch hands. Smiley, Granny, called him. He'd stopped in out of the blue one day asking to see the nurse. He hadn't said much, just held out a mangled hand, angry and red with infection. Said he'd caught it in a coon trap a week back. She'd cleaned it with alcohol and wrapped it with gauze soaked in carbolic acid, and he'd smiled through the entire process. The land out here sure raised them tough.

Other than that, her days had fallen into a quiet routine. Work in the garden with Sadie. Daily walks on the prairie with Ella. With three grown women in such a small cabin, housework was a breeze. Even wash day lacked its usual dreariness with both Sadie and Granny to help. For the first time in two years, she had time to herself to read, sew a few dresses for Ella, or crochet.

Best of all was the time spent with Ella. Not a snatched hour or two a week like in Denver, but full days and weeks watching her daughter learn and grow. She knew these halcyon days could never last. At some point, they would move on, and her nursing duties would resume. But right now, on this glorious summer day, she wanted to do nothing but enjoy.

"How many neighbors will we meet today?" Sadie quizzed Granny, who sat on the front bench beside Petie.

"I'm not right sure. The Baldwins will all be there. The Skivingtons too. Possibly the Cullens. Mostly folks along Cherry Creek. Oh, and the Garritys, of course."

Claire hadn't seen Jackson in almost a month, not since that awkward day at the potting shed where she'd all but run away from him. She didn't mind his absence. In fact, she'd come to count on it. So far, their marriage of convenience offered everything he'd promised her—no expectations, plus a safe place to hide while the ugliness back in Denver blew over. Most days, she didn't consider herself married at all.

That being said, was it wrong to be glad she'd allowed Sadie to trick out her simple straw boater with new ribbons and that she was wearing her blue and white striped shirtwaist with extra lace on the collar instead of her everyday white? That the thought of seeing Jackson again made her think about her appearance should be concerning, but she refused to dwell on it. Every woman wanted to look her best, especially when meeting new people. The fact that Jackson would be there had little to nothing to do with it.

She could tell herself that anyway.

Ella wriggled on the bench next to her, a basket of Granny's famous dried apple pies at her feet.

"Are we there yet, Mama?"

"Soon, baby girl."

"When is soon, Mama? Now?"

She pulled a piece of string from her pocket. "Long enough to play a game of cat's cradle. Shall we?"

After five minutes of cat's cradle, a couple of stories, and a game of "I Spy," Petie finally turned off the road toward a brand new, two-story log cabin protected along the north by a stand of cottonwoods and cedar. A group of women gathered around a long table. Dresses and white tablecloths fluttered in the breeze. The men stood closer to the cabin, most looking it over, though a few seemed to still be working on its construction. Claire spotted Jackson straddling the roof's ridge pole. Louis squatted at his side, both dark heads bent over a stove pipe.

Crazy man! On a roof with that leg? She shook her head and forced her eyes away. Even from this distance, he looked good—

tanned, healthy, strong. He'd come a long way in the past month.

As she and Sadie scrambled from the wagon, Mrs. Baldwin bustled over to them, arms outstretched and a smile as wide as her round face.

"Here you are at last. You look lovely, dears. And sweet little Ella. Such a doll. Come. You must meet the other women. They're dying to get acquainted with our newest neighbors."

Claire glanced at Granny, who Petie was helping out of the wagon.

"You run on along, girls. I'll be right over as soon as Petie gets my pies. No need to wait on my slow bones."

"We don't mind," Sadie said.

"No. Now shoo. I'll be right along."

Mrs. Baldwin linked an arm through hers, letting Sadie and Ella fall in behind.

"Here she is, ladies. Isn't she just as pretty as I said? And Doc Stevens sings her praises as a nurse. Our Jackson has found himself quite the catch." Claire felt her cheeks warm at Mrs. Baldwin's praise. She hadn't expected this kind of reception. But of course, the neighbors would be curious about Jackson's new wife.

This wide-spread Wyoming community might be a far cry from the close-knit St. Louis social scene, but she knew as well as anyone the gossip and speculation a new arrival stirred within any community. She attempted her friendliest smile and tried to focus on each new name and face as Mrs. Baldwin introduced her.

She'd already met the oldest Baldwin girls, Jane and Mary. Now she met the younger two, Emily, who looked to be about fourteen, and the littlest, Charlotte, who might be ten or eleven. Next was Mrs. Skivington, tiny, pretty, gracious, and very pregnant. Claire guessed her to be early in her third trimester. Her little sister, Hazel, who lived with them, was about Charlotte's age, but the two girls could not look more different. Hazel's tidy brown braids hung to the middle of her back, tied together with a jaunty red ribbon. A crisp white pinafore covered her pretty red print dress. Charlotte's untidy braids looked as if they hadn't been combed in days. Judging from the girl's boyish attire —overalls over a cotton shirt—ribbons did not spend much time in her hair or on her mind. A smudge of dirt graced the end of her pert little nose. Both girls, however, seemed fascinated with Ella.

"Can we take Ella to see the chickens, Mrs. Garrity?" they asked in unison.

"Please, call me Claire." She barely remembered she *was* Mrs. Garrity. Chances of her answering to the name were slim. "And, of course, you can take her. Just be sure to watch her around the horses."

The three girls skipped off, each of the older ones holding one of Ella's chubby little hands. Claire smiled. Today would be a rare treat for Ella as well. She couldn't remember when her daughter had played with anyone other than herself and Sadie. Well, and Petie, of course. She'd taken to following him around like a lost puppy on the mornings he stopped by Granny's. Petie was always a good sport, but seeing Ella with other girls made Claire's heart sing even if they weren't her age.

Another wagon pulled into the yard, and a large family piled out.

"Ah. The Cullens did make it," Granny said. "I wondered if they might."

"Have you ever known Daniel Cullen to pass up free food?"

"Now, Jane."

"You've said as much yourself, Mother. Can't get him to show up for the work, but mention a party, and he'll be there."

"Rob said he was quite helpful when it came time to put the roof on last week." Mrs. Skivington struck Claire as a woman who tried to have a kind word for everybody.

Jane sniffed. "Just my point. One day's work out of twelve, and yet he shows up for the party."

"I'm afraid Sadie and I have done even less work than that, but here we are."

"That's different. You're the–."

Mrs. Baldwin cut her daughter off with a sharp look. What was that about? Claire's speculation was cut short as the Cullens bustled up.

Mr. Cullen greeted Mrs. Baldwin, then headed off toward the men over by the cabin. Almost as tall as the Garrity men, he had a far beefier build. Jane's comment about him not missing food might have some merit. In contrast, Mrs. Cullen was rail thin and harried. Large strands of dark blond hair had escaped her pompadour, leaving her looking like she'd been in a windstorm. She carried a baby on her hip. Another boy, about a year younger than Ella, clung to her leg. Three other boys trailed after their father–all tow-headed and freckled. If you were to line them up, they'd look like stair-step copies of each other. Five boys under the age of seven. No wonder the poor woman looked harried. She must be exhausted.

"I meant to bring my sourdough biscuits, but Billy here," she placed a hand on the head of the toddler clinging to her leg, "got into the flour. Had it spread across the whole kitchen when I'd only turned for one minute to make sure Baby didn't crawl too close to the stove." Mrs. Cullens shifted her baby to her other hip. "I'd no sooner got that cleaned up when Tommy runs in from the barn, crying and bleeding. The goat had kicked him. Mercy, the way he was caterwauling, you'd think he'd been shot. By that time, Daniel was in wanting his breakfast, and I had to round up the other boys from the back pasture. I finally told Daniel we were either coming empty-handed, or we weren't coming at all."

"Oh, I'm so glad you decided to come after all," Mrs. Skivington said. "We have plenty of food for everyone."

"Corinne," Mrs. Baldwin cut in. "I haven't introduced you to Jackson's new bride. This is Claire and her sister Sadie."

Mrs. Cullen held out a limp hand for her to shake. "To be honest, I thought Daniel was pulling my leg when he told me Jackson had married. I didn't know Jackson could even talk to a woman, let alone marry one." She laughed. "I know I've never heard him say more than two words in succession. How you can stand all that silence, I'm sure I don't know. Now, my Daniel. He's a man who can talk. A real conversationalist. It's one of the first things I liked about him. Why, just the other day . . ."

If that were true, it's a wonder either of them heard a word the other one said. Surely, one would have to talk over Corinne Cullen just to get a word in edgewise. Claire tuned her out and let her eyes wander over the crowd. A thought niggled. Who was this new cabin for?

Granny had told them Mr. Baldwin was building it as a surprise for a young couple, yet everyone here already had their own homes. Except. Oh, of course! Who else would Mr. Baldwin want to surprise other than one of his own daughters? Jane was newly married and expecting her first child. Naturally, she'd want a home of her own.

A whoop from the roof drew everyone's attention. Louis pumped the air with his fist while Jackson grinned down at the men on the ground. Apparently, the stovepipe was finally set. Louis scampered down the ladder. Jackson followed at a slower pace, but not bad for a man whose leg was in traction a little over four months ago. Dr. Ferguson would either be proud of his recovery or appalled at his utter lack of caution. Maybe both.

Once Jackson reached the ground, Mrs. Baldwin called the men over to eat. Soon, everyone was milling around the table that practically groaned with food. Fried chicken, sandwiches of all varieties wrapped in wax paper, cold veal loaf, salads, stuffed eggs, buttered biscuits, stewed fruit, cake, and, of course,

Granny's dried apple pies. They'd also brought along several bottles of her famous apple cider. Mrs. Skivington had brought a cherry cordial, and there were several pots of coffee. No one would go hungry today.

A quick scan of the crowd located Ella, still tucked between Charlotte and Hazel. Her daughter basked in their attention.

"Looks like Charlie's found a few new friends."

Claire jumped at the deep voice in her ear. Jackson. He'd startled her, was all. No other reason for the thrill that raced down her spine.

"Charlie?"

"Baldwin's youngest."

"I thought he only had daughters."

"He does." He nodded toward Ella, Charlotte, and Hazel.

"You mean Charlotte?"

"She prefers Charlie."

Not surprising. The name suited her.

"So, you're climbing roofs now? Your leg must be doing really well, though I'm not sure Dr. Ferguson would approve."

"Don't see Dr. Ferguson anywhere around here, and Doc Stevens said I was fine to resume my regular activities."

"And by regular activities, he meant climbing ridge poles?"

His face reddened beneath his tan.

"I reckon he meant anything that needed to be done. Even climbing ridge poles."

She laid a hand on his arm. "I'm only teasing. Honestly, Jackson. I'm glad to see you getting around so well. You've made a remarkable recovery."

"Leg still hurts like h—, sorry, hurts *a lot* some days, but it's nothing I can't handle."

"Well, if you need a massage now and then, you know where to find me."

His gaze settled on her hand, still resting on his arm. The air heated around them. Her mind conjured up the feel of his leg muscles beneath her fingers the last time they met in the potting shed. He cleared his throat, and she jerked her hand away.

"Um, Claire," He took off his hat and ran his fingers through his hair. He chewed on his lower lip a second, then took a deep breath. "There's something you should know—"

"Jackson," Mr. Baldwin called across the crowd. "You two get over here and get some grub. There'll be time enough to make sheep's eyes at each other later."

Louis, who was standing nearby, came and locked arms with both of them and sashayed them over to the table, bowing to Mr. Baldwin as he delivered them to the food line. "One set of newlyweds, signed, sealed, and delivered."

Claire wished she didn't blush so easily. But then, what did it hurt to let these people believe they were a young couple in love? They were Jackson's neighbors and friends. She owed him at least the image of a happy marriage, for now, anyway. Time enough for the truth to come out later.

A few hours later, full of chicken and apple pie, Claire and Sadie followed the others as Mr. Baldwin led them on a tour of the new cabin. Larger than Granny's, the interior boasted a kitchen and sitting area plus a small bedroom on the first level. The second floor housed a large open area big enough for several beds. Apparently, Mr. Baldwin had his eye on future grandbabies.

A modest barn and a chicken coop completed the exterior buildings. Everything was simple. A bed, a few rough furnishings, and a new cooking stove were the only things inside for now, but what was here would allow the young couple a wonderful start on making a home of their own. The cabin could be lovely with a few curtains at the windows and some colorful throw rugs on the floor. She almost envied Jane the privilege of making this rough homestead into a home.

She turned to the girl, who stood just to the right of Sadie.

"It's lovely. The men have done a wonderful job."

"I suppose. It's a little primitive for my taste, but Father will be glad to know you like it."

Why in the world should her opinion matter? Hopefully, Jane would be able to muster up more enthusiasm when her father revealed his surprise. Surely, she understood all the work that had been done on her behalf.

Claire glanced around, still unable to locate which man among the group was likely Jane's husband.

"Is your husband here today? I'd love to meet him."

Jane scowled. "Father sent Preston out to the sheep camp with Tavis for the summer so Jackson could be close to you and your daughter. I'm surprised he didn't mention it."

That made no sense. Mr. Baldwin knew she and Jackson weren't living together. What difference would his absence make to her? Jane must have misunderstood. But if Jane's husband was truly with the sheep for the summer, why all this work to build them a cabin? Jane would be better off staying on her parent's ranch so she could have help when the baby came.

Doubt prodded at Claire's complacency. What if she'd been wrong and the cabin wasn't for Jane and Preston? What if?

No.

Surely, they hadn't. They wouldn't. But her gut told her they had.

The cabin walls closed in, making it impossible to breathe. She needed air. She headed for the doorway, only to be caught on the threshold by Mr. Baldwin.

"Now, don't you be leaving just yet, Miz Garrity." He tucked her hand into his arm and turned her back into the room. "I have a surprise for everyone and would like for you to stand beside me when I reveal it."

His words confirmed her suspicions. Dear Lord, no. Please, no. Everything had been going so well. Her silent prayer must have fallen on deaf ears because as they made their way through the crowd, Mr. Baldwin snagged Jackson with his other hand and drew them both to the center of the room.

"Listen up, folks. There's something I'd like to say." He shouted over the voices in the room.

Claire's cheeks heated as everyone's gaze turned her way. A quick glance out of the corner of her eye at Jackson told her he was as uncomfortable being the center of attention as she was. He kept his eyes glued to the floor and his Western hat clenched tightly in his fists as Mr. Baldwin continued.

"I'm guessing everyone knows why we're here, except for this pretty little lady here. My original plan was to make this a surprise for both her and Jackson, but I might have known I couldn't keep the man off his own property long enough to pull it off. No matter. His help came in handy when we got to the roof."

A few chuckles followed that comment.

"Claire, I'm sure you've guessed my surprise by now. These neighbors and I wanted to do something for both you and Jackson. A wedding gift of sorts. This here cabin is for you. The land is Jackson's, but until a few weeks ago, all it had on it was a dugout with a broken roof. Not a fit place for a wife and family, as he may have told you. When we heard there wasn't room for all of you at the Garrity ranch . . ."

No room? Well, that was one way to put it.

"We decided to do something about it. Jackson's had a run of bad luck this year, but the way I see it, that luck changed when he met you. Now, raise a glass with me, everyone. To the new Mr. and Mrs. Jackson Garrity. May their life on this ranch be long and prosperous."

"Here, Here." Cheers and applause broke out all around the room. Granny grinned at her from her spot near the door, and for the first time since she'd met him, Henry Garrity wasn't glowering at her. There might even be the slightest hint of a smile underneath all that hair in his beard. Until today most of the people in this room were strangers, yet they'd built an entire cabin for her. Well, not really for her. For Jackson. She wished they hadn't, but she wasn't blind to the magnitude of the gift. What must it be like to truly belong to a community such as this?

"Thank you." Jackson's voice was tight with emotion. "I . . ." He cleared his throat. "I . . ."

Louis walked over and draped an arm across his brother's shoulders. "What my big brother is trying to say is, if any of you need anything ever, the Garrity boys will be there to return the favor."

Jackson nodded emphatically and reached out to shake Mr. Baldwin's hand. Then, he made the rounds of the room, thanking each of the men individually. For his sake, she was glad. He deserved a place of his own. She caught Sadie's gaze on her from across the room, one eyebrow raised in question, and shrugged. The situation was far from ideal, but at least she still had Sadie and Ella to serve as buffers. It wasn't like she would be living with Jackson all alone. She could handle even this . . . for a few months, at least.

CHAPTER 16

"What do you mean you won't be staying?"
"Granny said we should leave the two of you to
yourselves for a few days. We never packed a bag for Ella and
me. Just you. Granny said you and Jackson deserved a
honeymoon."

If she didn't know better, she'd say Sadie's voice held a hint
of a smile when she said the word honeymoon. But Sadie would
never betray her that way.

"But *you* know better. Help me think of something . . . some
reason why you and Ella need to stay tonight. How about this?
We tell her I can't possibly be away from Ella, that I never have
since she was born."

"Except she knows that's not true. We told her all about
those nights I took care of Ella when you were in nursing
school. Remember?"

"Well, we have to think of something. You can't leave me
here alone."

"Jackson's not Jonas, Claire."

"We don't know that. Not for sure."

"Have you seen him around animals?"

"What do animals have to do with anything?"

"Animals can sense things. If a man can hurt an animal, he can easily hurt a human being as well. Remember Winston?"

Father's beloved basset hound. Sadie insisted she'd seen Jonas kick him the first time he visited the house, but Claire hadn't believed her. She hadn't listened to anyone who said anything against Jonas in those days. She'd been so infatuated, so bewitched by the idea that a man like him would choose her. But Winston had hated Jonas, and the feeling was mutual as far as Jonas was concerned. She hadn't thought anything of it at the time. Not everyone liked dogs. But when Winston turned up dead, poisoned, within a week after they returned from their honeymoon, she'd wondered.

"Look. It's just for a few nights." Sadie took Claire's arm and turned her from the crowd. "If we make a fuss, people are going to get suspicious. That's the last thing we need. Right now, everyone thinks Jackson went to Denver, fell in love with his nurse, and brought her back. Fun story, but nothing out of the ordinary. If you start acting like you don't want to be alone with him, people will wonder. And when people wonder, they talk. What if that detective tracks us to this area? That kind of talk could get us noticed. Is that what you want?"

"Of course not." But the chances of a detective finding them out here in the middle of nowhere, especially when he thought he was chasing a forty-year-old woman and her daughters, were next to nothing. The threat of having to stay in a small cabin alone with a man she hardly knew—a big, strong one—was far more real to Claire right now.

"Here you are, dearies." Granny bustled up, Petie and Ella in tow. "Best get our good-byes in now and be on our way if we want to get home before dark. Did you give your sister her bag?"

"Yes. She's all set."

"But there's no need to take Ella with you. She can stay with me." She had to make one last attempt. Although she was only three, her daughter made a very effective buffer.

"Now, don't you worry about Ella. She'll be fine. Honeymoons are no place for children, which is why they usually don't come until after." Granny laughed at her own joke. "We'll have her back to you at the end of the week when Jackson heads out to the sheep camps. In the meantime, you enjoy that new cabin of yours and your man."

Claire's cheeks heated at Granny's not-so-subtle innuendos.

The little lady pulled her into a hug, then allowed Petie to help her into the wagon. Sadie held Ella out for a hug and kiss, then hoisted her up and climbed in beside her. They were abandoning her, all of them, without even a care. Claire hadn't felt this alone since her wedding night with Jonas.

Oh, dear Lord, please don't let tonight be a repeat of that.

She swiped away the tear that *would* fall even though the occupants of Granny's wagon had only turned to wave at her once—once!—before heading on their way. Unfeeling was what they were. She sensed someone beside her and turned to find Maddie Skivington, empathy shining in her golden-brown gaze.

"It's hard to watch our loved ones leave, even if it's for a short time. I remember the day we left New Jersey. Why, I must have cried the entire morning, maybe the whole day. And I tried so hard not to. I wanted to be brave for Rob, but I failed miserably." She reached out and touched Claire's arm. "It'll get better. I promise. This place . . ." She made a sweeping gesture with her hand. "So large and empty. Takes a bit of getting used to if you've been raised in the city like we were. But give it time. Soon it will feel like home. And if you need anything . . . a cup of sugar, a bit of flour, or just someone to talk to . . . we aren't that far away. Feel free to drop by any time. That's what neighbors are for."

"Thank you." Claire pasted on the smile she'd used all afternoon. Hopefully, this sweet lady didn't recognize how false it was. "I'll be sure to take you up on that. I'm glad you will be my closest neighbor." That much was true. Had the Cullens or even the Baldwins lived closer, she wasn't sure how neighborly she would want to be, but this woman, with her empathetic eyes and gentle nature, might someday be a friend. And Lord knows, she might need all the friends she could get trapped out here alone with a man she barely knew.

"I'm glad too. Since Hazel and the boys joined us, it hasn't been nearly as lonely, but I'm looking forward to having another woman close by. It'll be a treat. Now, Rob and I will be heading out as well. I wanted to tell you goodbye and let you know we left most of the leftover food for you and Jackson, so you won't need to worry about cooking right away. Also, Mrs. Baldwin made sure you were stocked with all the basics, but if you need anything, be sure to let me know. Once Jackson leaves again for the sheep camps, I'll check back to make sure you're doing all right."

Seems like everyone thought she and Jackson needed to be entirely alone this week. Everyone but her.

"You're too kind."

"Not at all. We have a long way to go to repay Jackson for all he did for us when we first arrived. We were two greenhorns from Newark foolish enough to buy ourselves a herd of sheep the first month we were out here. If it hadn't been for Jackson, we never would have survived that first year. He brought us our supplies, our letters from home, newspapers, and magazines, but most of all, he taught us how to herd sheep and survive in the Wyoming wilderness. I'm just glad we can do something, even if it's just a little, to help him in return. So, anything you need, anything at all, you hear?"

What would this kind lady say if Claire asked her for a place to sleep other than this brand-new cabin everyone had worked so hard to build? But she wouldn't do that to Jackson, who'd done nothing to warrant her fears. As Sadie said, Jackson wasn't

Jonas. She had to believe that. And, somehow, she had to make it through the next few days. Then Ella and Sadie would return, and things would seem more normal.

～

SOMETHING WAS BURNING. JACKSON COULD SMELL IT FROM THE yard as he washed up at the pump before heading in for breakfast. Smoke billowed from the kitchen window. Still dripping, he broke into a run.

Had they not set the stovepipe properly? Had Claire accidentally knocked over a lantern? He burst into the cabin to see her bent over the oven, gray clouds of smoke rolling around her. He pushed her aside, grabbed a nearby towel, and pulled out a skillet filled with a blackened, burning mass. Two long strides took him back outside, where he dumped the contents of the pan onto the dirt, stomping out any remaining embers. What in the world was it? Biscuits? Whatever they were must have been burning for some time. He left the pan and the mess on the ground and headed back inside, leaving the door open and raising the back windows to let the room air out.

"What happened? Did you forget they were in there?"

Claire stood by the stove, wide-eyed and pale. A tear trickled down one cheek.

"What's the matter? Are you hurt? Did you burn yourself?" He started toward her. She backed away, trembling from head to foot. If possible, she turned a shade paler.

"I'm sorry." Her voice was high-pitched. Child-like. "I d-didn't mean to. Honest. I know it was stupid. I'll do better next time. I promise. P-please, please don't hit me."

Her words stopped him in his tracks. Hit her? What kind of monster did she think he was? Oh. A memory of her bruised and beaten face surfaced. Somehow over the past six weeks, he'd forgotten about her secrets—the dark ones that sent her running from Denver, the ones that made her desperate enough to agree to a marriage like theirs. He'd grown accustomed to her confidence and quiet strength as a nurse . . . as a mother. He'd ignored those fleeting glimpses she sometimes gave of a terrified woman.

No glimpses today. The terror flowed off her in waves. He held his hands out, open at his waist, and slowly inched back, just as he would in the face of a wild horse.

"Hey, now." He kept his voice low and calm. "No one's going to hit anyone here. It was a mistake. No harm done. You aren't the first to burn something in the kitchen, and you won't be the last. It's just a pan of biscuits. Nothing to cry over. I promise."

She watched him like a rabbit would a hawk. He took another slow step backward. "Why don't I make breakfast this morning? You can watch. We'll keep it simple. Bacon and eggs. Nothing fancy." Eggs. What had he done with the eggs? Oh, right. He'd left them by the pump when he'd stopped to freshen up. "I'll just go get the basket of eggs I left outside."

He backed slowly out of the cabin, then loped toward the pump.

Lord, how can I help her? They should have sat down and talked last night after everyone left. Women liked that. The talking. Ma had said it to Pa often enough. "You never talk to me, Henry. How am I supposed to know what you're thinking?"

He'd seen how jittery Claire was, blindsided by the surprise of the cabin, but he hadn't known where to start. He never knew how to talk to women. He was like Pa in that way. But she hadn't made it easy either—pleading a headache, then disappearing into the bedroom and shutting the door. He'd planned to try again at breakfast. But now this.

"So, Lord. What do I do?"

Treat her like Duchess.

Duchess? Where had that thought come from? God wanted him to treat Claire like a horse? Jackson hadn't thought about that mare in weeks. He was still new to this praying business. Maybe he'd misunderstood. He'd only begun these conversations a little over a year ago when Rob Skivington had explained to him how God actually *wanted* to talk . . . *wanted* a relationship with him. Thankfully, these newfound conversations had gotten him through the grueling months of traction, the trip home, the rehabilitation. However, there were still times he wasn't sure if that quiet prompting he felt were his own thoughts or truly the voice of God. But surely, he never would have thought to equate Claire to Duchess on his own, would he?

Mainly because he didn't want it to be true. Duchess was damaged. Probably beyond repair. Was that true of Claire too? He hoped not, but what did he really know about this woman who was his wife? How easily he'd forgotten that black eye she'd been sporting the day they left Denver. Who had beaten her? Her father? Her husband?

No, not a husband. She'd told him she was free to marry, and he didn't think she'd lie about something as big as that. Whoever it was, he had an overwhelming urge to hunt him down and make him pay for whatever he'd done to turn the beautiful, confident Claire into that terrified little girl he'd seen in the kitchen.

He picked up the basket of eggs and slowly made his way to the cabin. He still had no idea what to say to her. How to begin. *Treat her like Duchess.* A lot of help that was. The last time he'd tried to help Duchess, he'd ended up in traction. Why did he have this gut feeling that if he tried to help Claire, he'd be the one getting hurt?

CHAPTER 17

Claire heard him come in but didn't raise her head from where she had it buried in her arms on the table. She couldn't face him. Not yet. Maybe if she didn't look at him, he'd turn around and go away. What a fool she'd made of herself. Crying. Begging him not to beat her. What must he think?

In her head, she knew normal men did not beat their wives for burning biscuits. Of course, she did. But when he'd rushed toward her, so big, so loud, she hadn't been thinking, just reacting. She saw Jonas, not Jackson. Jonas. Bent on teaching her a lesson. For smiling too long at the waiter. For not smiling enough at him. For wearing her hair too tight, too loose, too curly, too straight. She never knew what would provoke a lesson. She just knew when he turned to her and came at her like that, it was coming. Jackson must have thought she'd lost her mind.

She heard him humming something soft and low. He had a nice voice. She could tell he was fiddling with something on the stove by the rattle of the cast iron. Was he really going to cook breakfast?

She had to sneak a peek. Sure enough, he stood at the stove, his back toward her, towel tied around his waist like an apron, shirt sleeves rolled up, baring his strong forearms. He looked completely at home.

He dropped a pat of butter into the skillet, then turned and caught her looking at him. She was tempted to duck her head back into her arms but hated to seem so cowardly, so instead, she sat up straight.

"Ca—can I do anything to help?" If he could pretend all was normal, then so could she.

"If you could find me a bowl and a fork and a little bit of cream, I'll get these eggs whipped up. And maybe some ham or a slab of bacon?"

She walked to the cupboard for the bowl and fork, then located the other items in the icebox. Mrs. Baldwin had been more than thorough when she'd stocked the kitchen. If only Claire had been equally as thorough when it came to paying heed to Granny's instructions in the kitchen these last few weeks. Instead, she'd all too often left the cooking to Granny and Sadie to spend her time in the garden or playing with Ella.

"I'm sorry about the biscuits." Might as well address the elephant in the room. "I'm afraid I haven't spent a lot of time in the kitchen."

"Like I said before, you're not the first to burn a pan of biscuits. When Ma left, Pa made our female cook leave as well. None of us knew Jack squat about how to cook a meal. Those first few weeks weren't pretty, but we got the hang of it over time. If you'd like, I could teach you what I know. It's nothing fancy. Just basics. But me and my brothers haven't starved yet."

His smile invited one of her own.

"Thank you. I probably should have paid more attention to how Granny did it. I remembered her recipe for the biscuits. They just cooked a lot faster than I expected."

"Now, see, that's on account of the stove. Learning a new stove is always tricky. Seems like they never put the levers in the same places. You had the drafts opened up all the way. See, over here on this side? Made the fire burn too hot. Close them about halfway next time, and you won't have a problem."

The drafts. Of course. She'd forgotten all about them. Had she made such a foolish mistake around Jonas, she would have had to pay for it for months. But Jackson just shrugged it off. Sadie was right. Jackson wasn't Jonas. She had to quit equating the two, or the next few months would be a nightmare.

"If you'd like, you can warm up those ham slices in that pan over there while I cook these eggs. The stove's cooler on that side since it's so far from the firebox. Shouldn't need to worry about them burning, especially with us right here watching."

And now he was teasing her, much like Papa used to tease her when she was a child. If she didn't watch out, she was going to find herself liking this man. And that would never do. Time to remind him, and herself, of the ground rules.

"I don't plan to stay, you know."

Nothing like just blurting it out. She hadn't meant it to sound quite so harsh, but it was the truth. Might as well make sure he knew her intentions hadn't changed. Silent seconds ticked by with no response.

"After the six months, I mean."

"I know what you meant." His words were quiet, measured. He pulled the pan of scrambled eggs off the cooktop and deposited them into a large serving bowl. "Why don't you bring the plates and ham to the table. We can talk while we eat."

Why? Had he changed his mind? He couldn't hold her here, could he? Not unless she agreed. She followed him to the table. The aroma of eggs and ham that had smelled so good just minutes before suddenly turned her stomach. Oh, why had she said anything at all? She should have let it go, waited it out, then, after the allotted six months, just up and left one day. He would have known why. Why even bring it up?

She jumped when his fingers brushed against hers on the table. He pulled his hand back.

"Sorry. I thought we'd say Grace before we ate. You don't have to hold my hand."

Grace. Of course. Granny always held their hands when she said the blessing. Must be a practice around here. Claire didn't mind holding Granny's and Sadie's hands, but she drew the line with Jackson. She clasped her hands tightly in her lap and bowed her head. She figured he'd get the message. Apparently, he did because he began to pray after a slight pause.

"Lord, thank you for the food you provided this morning. Thank you for this new cabin and the kindness and generosity our neighbors showed in building it for us. I know for sure I don't deserve these blessings, but I'm sure glad you gave them to me anyway. Amen."

The prayer suited him. Honest and simple with no flourishes or facades. And, certainly, no more words than necessary. For someone who said they would talk over breakfast, he was doing a good job of eating without talking. Normally, she didn't mind his silence, but there were times like right now when she wished she could hear what was going on in that head of his.

"You said we would talk?"

He swallowed his bite of eggs, took a sip of milk, and nodded.

"Should have talked it out last night, I guess. I know this cabin was a surprise. Surprised me too. Sure makes a marriage like ours a whole lot easier if you don't have to live in the same house, but I meant what I said in Rawlins. I won't hold you to any more than six months. Well, three months now. I'll have the money for my own herd by fall, and if you want to leave, you can. But I won't kick you out either. You can stay in this cabin as long as you need."

"Oh, I won't—"

He held up a hand to stop her. "Let me finish. I know you're not real comfortable around me, but I promise it'll get better. Baldwin insisted I take this week off, but I'll hardly be around after that. I spend most days at Baldwin's if I'm not out at the sheep camps. You, Ella, and Sadie will have full run of the cabin, and I promise not to bother you. I'll sleep upstairs. I'll stay out of your way. As far as I'm concerned, this cabin is yours."

"Oh, you don't—"

Again, his hand came up. "If you don't hear anything else I'm saying, hear this. I will never hurt you. I will never touch you in any harmful way, and I will never do anything to cause you pain. You are safe here. And if there's ever a time you feel unsafe, tell me, and *I'll* leave."

His gaze held hers, honest and pure. Sadie was right. He wasn't Jonas, but that didn't mean she could stay. In fact, more than ever, it meant she must go. He deserved a real marriage with a wife who would love him the way he deserved to be loved. She couldn't be that wife any more than she could promise not to cause him pain. She was a fugitive, an accomplice to a murder, and because of that, come September, she would leave.

THE NEXT DAY SMILEY SHOWED UP WITH DUCHESS. GOD WAS LIKE that sometimes, using multiple methods to get Jackson's attention. Probably because he knew Jackson was too thick-headed to get it the first time.

"Boss says he don't want her around the ranch no more," Smiley said. "Since you didn't want her put down, he said to tell you she's yours."

Suddenly, Baldwin's insistence that they build a corral last week made more sense. He'd told his boss he wasn't planning to bring in a string of horses until the fall, but the man had persisted.

"Never know when you'll need to train a horse," he'd said.

Right. Looks like he had a horse to train.

But first, he'd need to build a gate.

"I'd best get her to the barn, then."

As he took the lead rope from Smiley, Duchess reared back, kicking out with both front legs. He stepped to her left shoulder and let her have some rope. Thankfully, he hadn't been near enough to get kicked, but the action sure hiked his adrenaline. He needed to stay calm, though, or he'd never be able to help her.

"Don't envy you working with that one," Smiley said. "Should'a just let Baldwin shoot her after she almost killed you."

"She didn't almost kill me."

"Well, she certainly didn't do you any favors. And you know as well as I do, she'd 'a killed Charlie if you hadn't stepped between them."

He shrugged. The truth was, it wasn't the horse's fault, and he'd be hogtied if he'd let them kill a horse for something it couldn't control. Even if he couldn't rebuild her trust, he wasn't going to stand by and see her put down.

After Smiley rode out, Jackson led Duchess to the barn and stabled her beside Boaz. Two horses, six chickens, a rooster, and a new house. Two months ago, he didn't even know if he'd ever walk again. God had been good. Very good. But now it was time he got to work.

CHAPTER 18

"I've brought you some lunch if you'd like it."

Claire.

He'd forgotten all about her.

And the time.

Jackson glanced at the sun's position. Well past noon. He hadn't even noticed he was hungry until now. He'd been too caught up in Duchess. She was coming along, though, not shying from his touch when he stroked her legs and belly like she had before.

And, as he walked toward Claire, he could feel Duchess at his back. Following. A good sign.

"Who's this?"

"Duchess. Baldwin sent her over for me to work with."

"She's beautiful. Why does she need work?"

"It's a long story. You said something about lunch?" He was suddenly ravenous and far more interested in finding out what was in that lunch bucket than discussing Duchess.

"Yes, of course. I brought you some food, in case . . . in case you wanted to eat out here instead of inside. You never came in, so . . ."

"Sorry. I lost track of time." Something was off. Something in the way she was looking at him, or, in fact, not looking. Her face was flushed, and her focus was somewhere off his left shoulder. He glanced behind him and then down. Oh. His shirt. He'd stripped to his undershirt in the heat of the day, forgetting he wasn't alone. She must think him uncouth standing here half-dressed.

He grabbed his shirt off the fence post and held it in front of him. "I'll . . . I'll just wash up. Get presentable."

"Th—that's fine. No hurry." But she still would not look at him, and her cheeks glowed crimson.

He dunked his head under the cold water from the pump, letting the morning's sweat and grime slough off him. Skittish was what she was. He knew skittish. Hadn't he been dealing with it in Duchess all morning? But why? This new side of her perplexed him. The Nurse Claire he knew was confident. Calm. In charge. She'd never blushed once, no matter how many times she'd bathed his battered leg and sick body. He shook the water from his hair and rubbed it dry with the towel he kept nearby.

Something was spooking her. Maybe the circumstances—their being all alone here, so far from the others, but he thought he'd made it clear last night she had nothing to fear. Guess, like Duchess, it would take time to gain her trust. He slicked back his hair, then pulled on his shirt, buttoning it all the way up before heading back to where he'd left her.

"A—are you all right with eating out here? You were so busy, I thought y—you might like it rather than coming inside. But if you . . . if we . . . you can eat inside if you'd like."

There it was again. The uncertainty, the hesitation. He liked the confident Claire so much better.

"This is fine. We can sit in the shade by the barn if you don't mind sitting on the ground. I eat outside most days when I'm at the sheep camps."

He led her to the shady side of the barn and took a seat in

the grass, leaning his back against the barn wall. She spread a cloth on the ground and began to empty the pail she'd brought.

"It isn't anything fancy. Just some chicken from the party, a boiled egg, and a slice of Granny's pie. But I did try another batch of biscuits." She pulled out a couple of golden biscuits and added them to his plate.

"Looks great." He looked at the single plate. "Didn't you bring anything for yourself?"

She ducked her head. "I—I already ate. I h—hope you don't mind. I wasn't sure . . . when you didn't come in . . ."

He held up a hand to stop her. "It's fine. You shouldn't have to wait for me to eat. Next time I don't come in for a meal, just holler out the door that it's ready or let me go hungry. Truth is, I'm not used to having someone around to take care of me. Not that I'm complaining. Thank you."

He dove into the food, glad she'd brought two large pieces of the chicken. Mrs. Baldwin was a master when it came to fried chicken. And Granny's apple pies were the best in the county. Soon, they would need to cook something for themselves, besides biscuits and eggs. For now, he was grateful for the generosity of their neighbors. Claire's biscuits weren't half bad either. A little crunchy, but after yesterday's ashes, these were a huge improvement.

He popped the last bite into his mouth and leaned back against the log wall, satisfied. He loved summer afternoons like this. It was a bit warm in the sun, maybe, but it was perfect here in the shade. When he was a kid, he'd spent afternoons like this stretched out in the shade, looking for cloud pictures and dreaming of the day he'd have a ranch of his own. Those dreams rarely included a wife and family. Not after Ma left. Certainly not after the Lillie May debacle back in school. But here he was, a married man, sitting in the shade of his own barn. All he lacked was a herd of sheep.

"So, tell me the story."

Her voice startled him. Once again, he'd almost forgotten about Claire. "What story?"

"About the horse. Duchess, is it? Why do you need to work with her? Is she one of those wild horses Granny says live in the mountains around here?"

"No. She's a thoroughbred. Baldwin bought her back east and shipped her here as a present for Beatrice. I remember when he first brought her to the ranch. The prettiest little filly I ever did see. So sweet and gentle. The girls loved her."

"But she's not now?"

Jackson sighed. The story was an ugly one. One he'd rather not tell, but Claire was bound to hear it one way or another. It wasn't likely she'd give up her questioning if he ignored her.

"Last year, things got pretty ugly around here between the sheep ranchers and a few of the cattle ranchers. One rancher, in particular, had a passel of lowlifes as ranch hands. They didn't take well to sheepmen using the range, even though the public lands are open to everyone. So, they started pestering some of the herders."

He rubbed his bad leg, kneading against the ache as he talked.

"Rob Skivington was one of the ones they harassed. Maybe because he was new to the area. Anyway, they shot up a bunch of his sheep and threatened his life. They also stole the payroll from a rancher named Bunce and set fire to a load of wool headed to market. But the worst was what they did to Baldwin. His middle daughter, anyway."

"Mary or Emily?"

"Mary. She was out riding Duchess one day, like all the girls did from time to time, but she didn't come home. So we organized a search party and scoured the area but couldn't find her until the next day. She was tied up in an old miner's shack, bruised, beaten, and in a terrible state. Turns out she'd run into a group of those scoundrels. They used her like no woman ought ever be used, especially one so young and innocent. I've never seen Baldwin so cut up."

Claire paled and bit her lower lip so hard he was afraid she might draw blood. He shouldn't be telling her this story but didn't know how to tell Duchess's story without telling Mary's too.

"Did they find the men? Get justice?" Claire's voice was low, hard.

"Not right away. See, at the time, we had no idea who was behind it all. The men wore masks and rode horses no one recognized. Rob guessed the identity of one of the men who attacked him, but he had no proof and no way of knowing he was part of all the other stuff. That didn't come out until months later when they tried to pull off a train robbery. The ones who weren't killed in the shootout following the holdup were finally caught and are now serving time at the State Pen, though you can be sure Baldwin would rather have strung them up himself if he could. We all would."

She nodded and turned away, blinking back a sheen of tears. "And Duchess?"

"She disappeared the same day Mary did. We didn't find her for months. Then early this year, I was riding fence on Baldwin's property and came across a horse caught in some barbed wire, half-starved and scarred all over. I almost didn't recognize her until I saw the blaze on her nose. Her scars were old, like someone had whipped her something fierce. But who had her and how long she'd been wandering, trying to find her way home, is anyone's guess. I brought her back to the ranch and doctored her up. Pretty soon, she was back to her old weight and health, but her inner scars were harder to heal, I guess.

"We didn't realize how bad those were until Charlie came to the corral one day wanting to ride her. I was leading her out of the gate so she could be saddled when she just erupted. Charlie had raised a hand to pet her, but she had a riding crop in her hand. Spooked Duchess something fierce. I barely had time to get between her and Charlie. Probably would have been fine if a wagon hadn't been parked right by the fence. She caught me up against it and leveled several kicks at my leg before anyone could pull her off me."

Claire gasped. "She's the horse? The one who broke your leg?"

"Yep."

"My God. And Mr. Baldwin is making you work with her? That doesn't seem fair."

"He's not making me. I didn't want her put down, which was what he wanted to do with her, so he gave her to me."

"He gave her to you." Claire closed her eyes and shook her head. "And you took her?"

"She's not a monster, Claire. Damaged, maybe, but that's not her fault. She's a victim, just like Mary. Neither one deserves to be thrown aside as if they no longer have a purpose."

"Is that what people say about Mary?"

"Some."

She shook her head again. "It's a crazy world."

"Yes."

She laid a hand on top of his. "I'm glad you want to help her. I hope you can."

Slowly, he turned his hand over until he held hers, a little surprised she didn't flinch or draw away. Her hand felt good in his, soft and cool.

"I hope so, too," he said.

CHAPTER 19

The next few days passed much like the first. Claire found a cookbook on a shelf in the kitchen and spent her mornings reading through it. With its help, she managed to prepare a few simple meals of eggs or canned meats and vegetables. She was not anywhere near Granny's or even Sadie's level in the kitchen, but she hadn't repeated the biscuit debacle. And Jackson never complained. Runny eggs, slightly singed toast . . . he accepted each meal with a thank you and not one word of criticism. Claire didn't know what to make of it. Was he that easily pleased or just extra cautious after her breakdown over the biscuits? Whatever the case, Claire would be glad when Sadie returned. They both could use a good meal or two.

Jackson spent most of his daylight hours outside, taking care of the few livestock they had—a cow, chickens, horses. He'd bring in fresh milk and eggs before breakfast each morning. He'd also started fencing in a pasture area in addition to the small round corral where he worked Duchess, so both the horses and their cow would have room to graze. Afternoons, he trained Duchess.

As soon as she finished washing these dishes from lunch, she would join him. Somehow the relationship between Jackson and that horse fascinated her. Had a horse injured her the way that one had hurt Jackson, she wouldn't have gone within ten feet of it. But day after day, Jackson continued to work Duchess with patience and gentleness. Already she was responding.

Claire laid the last bowl in the drying rack and dried her hands on her apron before hanging it across the back of a chair. Today was another beautiful, sunny day. She couldn't wait to get out and enjoy it. Surprising how quickly she'd adjusted to this wide, open country after living her whole life in the city.

As she hurried up the path to the corral, she saw Jackson exit the barn, a whip in his hand. Wait. A whip? After all Duchess had endured and what he'd told her about the cause of his accident, why was he approaching that horse with a whip? She quickened her steps, intercepting him just as he reached the gate to the corral.

"What are you doing?"

Maybe she'd said that a little too forcefully because Jackson took a step or two back, eying her much as he did Duchess each time she reared to attack.

"I was fixin' to work Duchess for a while."

"No. I mean the whip. Why would you take that near her, knowing how much she hates it?"

Understanding dawned in his eyes. "I'm not going to use it on her. I'd never whip a horse."

"Then why take one near her at all?"

"Because she's a horse, and she lives in a world of whips. If she continues to fear the whip, she'll never be of any use. What if I was riding her in Lander or Dallas and came up next to a freighter using a bullwhip or a stage driver or coachman urging his horses into a trot? If I can't reverse her fear of a whip, then she'll be stuck on this ranch the rest of her days. She'll be held captive to fear. That's no life for a horse. That's no life for anyone."

"How do you know she won't attack you again?"

"I'm figuring she'll put up a fight at first. But as long as I know it's coming, I can protect myself. And hopefully, by the time we're done today, she'll know she can trust me not to hurt her."

Claire wished she shared his confidence. She took a seat on the hay bale Jackson had set outside the fence for her, prepared to watch and help if needed. Though, what she'd be able to do if the horse got out of control was beyond her. Hopefully, Jackson had an escape plan.

As he had the past two days, he started by making Duchess run the perimeter of the corral, first in one direction, then the other. He guided her with a flick of his wrist and a click of his tongue. He'd told Claire that this was his way of reminding Duchess he was the one in charge. If he could control her movements, he was the leader. After a few minutes of running her, he stopped and called Duchess to him. She stood without a flinch as he attached the lead rope to her neck and followed him as he walked toward the gate where he'd left the whip. He sent her backward until there was about six feet between them, then bent and picked it up.

Duchess watched, curious but not panicked until Jackson flicked the end of the whip into the dirt about two feet from her legs. She reared and bolted. Jackson planted his legs and kept a firm grip on her rope, allowing her to circle him, all the while keeping a steady whack of the whip in the dirt by her side. After a few seconds, she stopped, legs twitching, eying him cautiously. As she gentled, Jackson stopped whacking. Seconds later, he started in again. This time, Duchess's reaction was less intense. She circled Jackson only a few times before stopping, eyes still wary but not as panicked. Again, Jackson stopped flicking the whip.

They continued this process over and over until Jackson could flick the whip louder and closer to Duchess, and she would not flinch. By the end of thirty minutes, Duchess was even allowing Jackson to stroke her neck, legs, and belly with the whip. Watching the two of them, Claire could hardly believe this was the horse that still caused Jackson to walk with a limp. All those months in traction, all that terrible pain, and yet he handled her with calm confidence. And she responded, eyes always trained on him, waiting for his direction. Why, to look at the two of them now, you'd think they shared a bond and a history as long and deep as the one between him and Boaz.

They stood now, side by side. As Jackson stroked the white blaze on Duchess's nose, she lowered her head and leaned into his hand. Tears pricked the backs of Claire's eyelids as she watched them. Jackson's gentle touch, the horse's tentative trust, so freely given. She swallowed and looked away. She felt the pull. There was something very attractive about strength tempered by gentleness. But she'd felt the pull of attraction before and been burned. She wasn't about to let her guard down now to a man she barely knew, no matter how different from Jonas he seemed.

"Mama!"

Her head jerked toward the house. She'd been so engrossed in Jackson and Duchess she hadn't noticed a wagon approaching. Ella stood on the seat between Sadie and Petie. She squirmed in Sadie's arms, waving and calling to her.

They were here. Finally! As Petie drew the wagon to a stop, Claire ran toward them, catching Ella in her arms as she leaped from Sadie's hold.

"Mama. Mama. I missed you."

"Oh, baby. I missed you too."

She inhaled Ella's little girl scent, a mixture of gingerbread and sunshine, and kissed her soft curls. Oh, how she'd missed her.

"Mama. You're squishing me."

"I'm sorry, baby. I'm just so glad you're here.

Ella's little hand patted her cheek. "Don't cwy, Mama. I won't leave you ever again. I pwomise."

"Promise?"

"Yes."

"Good."

"Did you miss me too?" Sadie had climbed down from the wagon and pulled her into a side hug.

"You know I did. We haven't had a decent meal since you left."

"So, I'm simply a cook to you?"

"You're so much more than that, and you know it."

Sadie held her gaze, eyes searching.

"The week went well?"

"Everything's fine. But I'm glad you're here."

Which was only the truth. Not because she needed protection from Jackson. She needed protection from herself. A man that handsome who also seemed good and honorable was a very dangerous thing. Sadie and Ella were just the buffers she needed to keep her from making another mistake.

CHAPTER 20

Something was off. Jackson sensed it the moment he rode into Tavis's sheep camp. Tin cans and bottles littered the ground around a stone-cold fire pit. In all the years he'd known him, Tavis had never left as much as a cup out of place in his wagon.

Whoever made breakfast this morning had left a mess. Bacon grease congealed in one skillet. Another bore the remains of some blackened scrambled eggs. Only a fool would leave food at an untended campfire. And Tavis was no fool. Something was definitely wrong.

"Halloo." He bellowed the greeting. Though the camp seemed deserted, someone might be within hearing distance.

"In here."

He almost missed the thready reply coming from the wagon itself. He pulled open the door, eyes adjusting to the wagon's dim interior.

"Tavis?"

The sheepherder lay flat on the bunk, older and paler than he'd ever seen him. Jackson walked in and took a seat on the bench beside the bed.

"Are you sick?"

"Nae. Fell and wrenched me back. Four days ago. Havena' been able ta move since."

"Is Preston with the sheep?"

"Aye. If there be any sheep left."

"Why? What's happened?"

"What hasna' happened? Och, mon. The lad's an *eejit*. First, it was the Death Camas. The lee side o' the first hill was covered with it when we arrived. I'd pointed it out to him that first day. Said, whatever you do, don' let sheep be grazing in that area. The next day, I stayed behind to clean up after breakfast. Sent him and the dogs on ahead. Sure, eno'. I come around the bend no' an hour later, and what do I see? Thirty head or more wandering free on the lee side o' the hill. I chased 'em out of there, but too late for at least half. Took the sickness that night and died."

Tavis shook his head and closed his eyes as if, even now, the thought was too much for him to handle.

"Then there was the band he let run up and over a cliff. Twenty gone that day." His voice quivered. "Couldna' chase them because his knee hurt, he says. And he canna' get the dogs to do what he tells them. Mostly because he can't remember what to tell them. Three commands is all he needs, but can he remember a one? Nae."

Jackson had never heard Tavis talk this much or this fast. The Scot's accent was so thick, he could barely follow.

"Then earlier this week, a band o' coyotes came snooping aroun' after dark. Instead o' coming to get me, he fires the rifle hisself. Killed off three sheep, but no' a single coyote. So, the next night, I hear the dogs a'barking and hurry out so he don' try shooting on his own again, but he'd left a pile o' firewood right at the bottom o' the wagon stairs. Knocked me legs out from under me and put me flat on my back. Haven't been able to walk aboot since."

Tavis clutched onto Jackson's hand. The strength he'd always known in the man was still evident.

"Ye've got to save me lambs, laddie." His voice wavered again. A sheen glistened on his ice-blue eyes. "It's been four days. No telling the mess he's got 'em into."

"I'll tend to them in a bit. First, let me help you." He went to the cupboard over the stove, sorting through the contents for medical supplies. "Do you have anything in here for pain?" How he wished Claire was with him. She would know what to do.

"Don't mind me, mon. I've gone this long. I can hang on a bit longer. I need ye to save me sheep."

"He can't have killed them all. He's been bringing them in at night, hasn't he?"

"Aye, but no telling how many or what shape they be in. I tell ye, I haven't moved from this bed in four days. He killed off fifteen o' them the first half hour I left him unattended. Please, Jackson. Go find me sheep."

Jackson heaved a sigh. Tavis loved his sheep like children. Unlike many who herded sheep just to have a job, he was a good shepherd. The best Jackson had ever worked with. No way the man was going to rest easy until Jackson came back with word on his sheep.

"Hang tight, then. I'll go round them up."

HE FOUND THE SHEEP, OR A SMALL BAND OF THEM ANYWAY, before he found Preston. He heard bleating and the tinkle of the sheep bells first, then turned a corner to find them trapped on a steep incline between a rushing stream and Laddie, Tavis's black and white collie, who patrolled the ridge top. Hopefully, this was a small, runaway band and not a remnant of the larger herd that might have crested that ridge before Laddie could stop them. Jackson hopped across the larger boulders in the stream and wended his way through the writhing, noisy mass until he reached Laddie. Peaking over the boulders at the top of the ridge, he released his pent-up breath. No white bodies lay dashed on the rocks below.

"Good job, Laddie." He gave the dog a well-deserved head rub. "That's a good boy. Now let's get these scallawags out of here."

He signaled Laddie in one direction while he took the other, pushing the band down the embankment and up against the stream. Like the dumb sheep they were, none of them wanted to be the first into the water. He grabbed the lead ewe by her collar and dragged her in. A slap to her backside sent her rushing to the other side, the rest following. Laddie rounded up stragglers, nipping at their heels and barking. Soon they had the band on clear, flat ground and heading toward pasture.

Half a mile later, they found Preston stretched out in the middle of a large, empty pasture. He sat with his back against a boulder, hat down over his face, fast asleep. Other than the small band Jackson had rescued, there wasn't a sheep in sight. Not surprising. By the looks of it, this field had been grazed out days ago.

Jackson kicked the bottom of Preston's boot.

"Preston. Wake up. Preston!" He kicked again, harder.

The man lifted his hat and looked up, bleary-eyed. "Huh?"

"Where are your sheep?"

Preston sat up and took off his hat. After a slow look around the pasture, he scratched his head and then pushed to his feet. "When did you get here?"

"Couple hours ago. Found this band down the road a ways. How long you been asleep?"

Preston shrugged.

"So, where's the rest of them? You do have more than just that band, don't you?"

Preston scowled. "Of course, I do. Blasted critters. They never stay put."

"Yeah. They'll do that when the feed's lousy. Can't you see the ground's played out? They won't stick around if there's nothing to eat. Come on. We better go find them if we're going to get them rounded up by nightfall."

"Dang sheep. All I do is chase 'em. My knee gave out on me after the first week, I've been walking so much. And the dogs are useless. Now with Tavis complaining about his back, I've been trying to keep this whole operation together by myself. It's impossible, I tell you."

Jackson bit back the words he wanted to say. All the yelling in the world wasn't going to change the fact they had about two thousand head of sheep to find and only a few hours of daylight left to do it.

"Where's Roy?"

Preston looked around the pasture. "He's gone too? I told you those dogs are worthless."

"He's likely keeping the rest of the herd alive like Laddie was doing when I found his group. Come on. We're wasting daylight."

They finally found the rest of the sheep stretched out in a verdant valley about two miles up the trail. As he expected, Roy stood guard. He exchanged barks with Laddie, who ran to join him. Jackson did a quick count of the marker sheep. About 300 head were still missing.

A glance at the waning sunlight told him there'd be no time to find them today. If he was lucky, he'd have time to get back to Tavis and move the entire camp here before full darkness set in.

"You think you can keep the sheep here while I go get Tavis?"

"You're bringing him here?"

"Might as well. I was planning to move the sheep this direction tomorrow anyway. Easier to move the camp this way than then move the sheep back and forth. There's plenty of food for them, so they shouldn't wander off. Just stay alert to predators and let the dogs do their work."

"How long's it gonna take you? I'm half-starved."

"Hour and a half. Maybe two."

"Two hours? I have to wait two hours to eat? Are you kidding me?"

Jackson pulled a piece of jerked beef from his shirt pocket and handed it to Preston. "Now stay put and keep those sheep here."

Turning, he half jogged back down the trail ignoring the tightness in his bad leg. He'd been on his feet too long already today, which meant his knee was beginning to swell. Tonight would be a long one, in more ways than one.

JACKSON HEADED OUT OF BALDWIN'S RANCH HOUSE, AN ANGRY Preston on his heels.

"I don't care what you say. I'm not responsible for all those sheep dying."

Except he was. Almost two hundred head of sheep. Gone. In the space of two weeks. Jackson had never seen such incompetency. Or heard so much belly-aching. The man hadn't let up once in the past four days, grueling days spent hunting down lost bands and moving two camps. They'd found one band of sixty sheep littered on the rocks beneath a hundred-foot drop. Another ninety or more were still unaccounted for. Once he'd rounded up Tavis's remaining herd, joined them with Juan and Gabe's so Tavis could have some help, and set out to look for them, they were long gone.

The best he could do was leave the remaining 3500 sheep with the three seasoned sheepherders and bring Preston back to the ranch. Though Tavis could barely hobble, he refused to leave his sheep, and none of the men wanted Preston to stay. It was either bring him back home to Baldwin or lose Baldwin's three best herders.

Baldwin hadn't been any too happy to see him, but that wasn't Jackson's concern. He didn't blame Tavis for not wanting him to stay at sheep camp and couldn't fault Baldwin for not wanting him back at the ranch. All he knew was his time babysitting the man was over. All he wanted was to go home and forget the week's disasters.

"Don't walk away from me when I'm talking to you." Preston grabbed Jackson by his upper arm and swung him around. "I'm telling you, I'm not taking the blame for this."

"Then who should we blame, Preston? The sheep? Everyone knows sheep are the dumbest critters alive. That's why they have herders. So, if they eat poison weed, jump off cliffs, or are decimated by predators, the person in charge of them isn't doing his job."

"Blame Tavis, then. I wasn't alone out there."

"You want me to blame our best sheepherder? A man who has never lost more than fifteen head of sheep in the ten years I've known him? Are you serious? He can barely walk because of you! Face it, Preston. It's all your fault."

"Why, you—" Preston swung a fist, but Jackson caught it mid-punch.

Instead of backing down, Preston swiped at him with the other fist. The blow glanced off Jackson's ear as he ducked.

Enough was enough. The ache in his bad leg was bone-deep after days of traipsing through the mountains in search of lost sheep. He was tired, dirty, hungry, and he wanted to go home.

He grabbed Preston by the shirt, lifted him off his feet, and threw him in the nearby horse tank. A shriek from the porch and a chorus of guffaws from over near the barn told him they had an audience.

Jane tore across the yard toward him, fire in her eyes.

"Jackson Garrity. You will not treat my husband that way."

Ignoring her, he whistled for Boaz and climbed into his saddle. Jane snatched at Boaz's bridle and stepped in front of him.

"Where do you think you're going? Get off this horse and apologize to my husband."

Apologize? Ha. When hell freezes over. Every time he looked at Preston, all he saw was the lifeless bodies of all those sheep at the bottom of the cliff. Tavis had cried when he told him how many they'd lost. Cried! Preston was lucky to have only suffered a dunking.

Sidestepping Boaz around Jane, Jackson urged him into a trot and headed for the gate, paying no mind to Jane's cries of outrage. Preston was Baldwin's problem now. He had two days off, and by God, he planned to enjoy them.

The sun was low over the Winds but still far from setting as he headed up the red canyon road toward his cabin. The cliffs on his left glowed a deep scarlet in the waning light. Summer days were long, and this one had seemed like an eternity, but finally, he was on his way home.

Home.

That word evoked equal amounts of anticipation and dread. For the first time in his life, he had a cabin of his own. And a family, of sorts, waiting on his return. He'd always imagined himself a solitary man. Had never expected to need or even want a family of his own. Now, he found himself looking forward to seeing them. All of them. But he'd been gone for more than a week. Would he even be welcome?

Claire invaded his thoughts as she had so many times over the past days. Those beautiful gray eyes, her smile, that way she had of tipping her head when she studied a problem, her gentle touch on his leg. He'd craved one of her massages for days as he'd struggled to sleep at night due to the ache in his leg.

Had she thought of him too?

Not likely. And he needed to stop thinking about her. Her

stay was temporary. Getting attached was a fool thing to do. Except his heart didn't seem to care. In fact, his heart was beating altogether too fast at the thought of seeing her again. He needed to rein himself in. More than likely, she wouldn't even smile to see him.

Finally, his cabin came into view. Smoke curled from its chimney. Soft light glowed from the windows. He spurred Boaz into a gallop, but when he reached the yard, he didn't call out or make himself known. He headed to the barn first. As long as it was still daylight, he'd take care of Boaz and clean up a bit before seeing the ladies.

Half an hour later, he stood on the front step, hand on the door handle, reluctant to turn it and go in. What if they didn't want him here? What if he didn't know what to say to them? Would it just be one long night of awkward silence?

Taking a deep breath, he pushed open the door and called out, "Hello?"

A heady aroma of roast beef greeted him as he walked in. His stomach growled at the thought of a meal ready and waiting for him.

"Jackson!" A curly-headed bundle of energy attacked and wrapped herself around his knees.

He swung Ella up and pulled her into a hug. Her little arms caught him in a chokehold. Her silky curls brushed his chin.

"You're scratchy!"

"Sorry. I haven't had a chance to shave." At least his head and upper body were clean, thanks to a dunk under the pump out back of the barn.

"It's okay," she said, patting his cheek. "It tickles."

He let out a little growl and rubbed his cheek against her neck just to hear her squeal. Cautiously, he let his eyes drift behind Ella to where Sadie and Claire stood in the kitchen. Whatever their initial reaction might have been, they both appeared pleased to see him now. Nothing like the enthusiastic welcome Ella had given, but he'd take it.

"We thought you might be back today," Claire said. "Good thing you are, since we cooked up a feast. Are you hungry?"

"Starved."

"It'll be ready in a few minutes if you want to take your bag upstairs first."

He let Ella down then limped toward the steps. Darn. The way his leg was feeling, those steps were going to be a challenge.

"I think I'll wait and take it later. I'd like to sit for a minute, if that's all right?"

He turned to see Claire studying him, head tipped to the side just as he remembered.

"Ella, why don't you take Jackson's bag up to his room for him. Can you do that?"

"Uh-huh." The little girl pulled the saddlebag into her arms and scampered up the steps before he could tell her to stay.

"I could have done that."

"I know. But she loves to help. Now come sit down before you fall down. We'll get some supper in you, and then we'll see about that leg."

He might have known she hadn't missed his limping. He tried, without much success, to walk with a normal gait over to the kitchen table. Claire pulled out a chair for him and all but pushed him into it, then turned another toward him and helped prop his leg on it. She ran her fingers over his thigh and knee, leaving a trail of fire.

"Feels a little swollen. Did you have to walk much?"

"Too much. Had to track down about a third of Tavis's sheep."

"Goodness. What happened?"

"Preston."

"Jane's husband? Is he not good with sheep?"

As far as Jackson knew, he wasn't good with anything. "You

could say that."

"Did you find them?" Sadie asked from over by the stove.

"Some." No need to mention he hadn't found them all alive. Ella had come back and climbed into his lap. No need for her to hear the gruesome details. She reached up with her tiny hands and patted his cheeks again, seemingly fascinated with his whiskers.

Sadie placed roast beef and a large bowl of potatoes on the table. Claire followed behind her with a bowl of green beans and a plate of golden-brown biscuits. No burned ones tonight.

"Ella," she said. "Climb down now and wash up. It's time to eat."

As soon as the girls were all seated, he prayed a quick blessing over the food and dug in. A meal like this could keep a man happy any day of the week, but after a week of camp food, it was absolute paradise. He was content to let the girls chatter while he ate and ate and ate.

Between the three of them, they filled him in on what had happened since he left. Claire had finished planting her garden. The cow got out one day and ended up all the way over at the Skivington's before they found her. Ella gathered eggs every day and wasn't a bit afraid of the rooster anymore. And Hazel had given Ella the cutest little orange kitten that now lived in the barn and went by the name of Mr. Cuddles. Somehow their talking didn't bother him like the Baldwin girls' chatter did. In fact, he kind of liked it.

He'd reached the end of his second helping and was contemplating the wisdom of licking his plate. Had he been alone, he would have. The gravy was that good.

"I hope you saved room for dessert." Sadie took his empty plate and replaced it with a bowl of apple Brown Betty.

So, no licking the plate, but this would do. Yes. It would do quite nicely. He let the cinnamon richness settle on his tongue a brief second before swallowing.

"This is great, Sadie. All of it. Thanks." He smiled at her before shoveling in another bite.

"Oh, I didn't make it. Tonight's meal was Claire's doing."

He glanced at Claire seated beside him, the pink in her cheeks telling him Sadie wasn't kidding.

"Sadie's been teaching me to cook. It's easier than I thought it would be once you get a handle on how hot to heat the stove."

"Sadie must be one heck of a teacher. These biscuits couldn't possibly be something you made." He caught her eye and winked, loving how her eyes flashed at him.

"Hey, now."

He grinned at her. "I'm kidding. The whole meal was great. Thank you."

As he stood to carry his plate to the sink, he caught Sadie eying him like he was a cipher she couldn't figure out. What was that about?

Later, after Claire had kneaded the knots from his leg and left him to the soothing warmth of a hot water bottle while she put Ella to bed, Sadie pulled up a chair beside him.

"You better not hurt her." Her voice was low, fervent. "She's had enough of that."

He didn't ask what she meant. He'd known from the beginning—the bruises, the secrets, Ella mentioning a bad man in the kitchen. Someone had done a number on her. He turned and held Sadie's gaze.

"You're safe here, Sadie. All of you."

She gave a wry smile and shrugged. "Is anyone ever truly safe? But I believe you'd like to keep us safe. I guess that's enough for now."

Such cynicism in one so young, but her words reminded him not to get too content with the way things were. This home, this make-shift family, was temporary. If he'd learned nothing else from Ma, it was that. Good things didn't last forever. Not for him, anyway.

CHAPTER 21

"Another slice of gingerbread?" Claire held the platter out to Jane and Mary Baldwin. They'd ridden over, along with Charlotte, for a visit. On the way, they'd stopped by the Skivingtons and asked Maddie and Hazel to join them. The two younger girls had immediately taken Ella out to the barn to play with Mr. Cuddles while the rest of them sat around the kitchen table, drinking tea and talking.

She'd come to enjoy the casual nature of these impromptu neighborhood gatherings. One never knew which day they might occur. Thankfully, Sadie had made fresh gingerbread this morning, so they had something to serve.

"None for me, thank you." Jane laid a hand on her stomach. "This little one is still making it hard for me to keep anything down." She turned to Maddie, who had just taken her third slice. "How long did it take for you to get over your morning sickness?"

"Somewhere in the fourth month, maybe? It took me quite a while to realize I was in the family way, so those early months are a little fuzzy in my memory. Lord knows I haven't had any trouble eating lately. Seems like it's all I want to do." She laughed. "I'm blaming you today, Sadie. This gingerbread is delicious."

"I must confess," Jane said. "I wasn't entirely sure of our welcome here today."

"You are always welcome. Why would you think otherwise?"

"Well, after that ugly business between Jackson and my Preston, I wasn't sure how you would respond."

"I'm afraid I don't follow. What ugly business?"

"Jackson didn't tell you?" Jane firmed her lips. "No. I suppose not. He wouldn't want to put himself in a bad light. He attacked Preston. Right in our front yard."

"Attacked?" Suddenly that last bite of gingerbread didn't sit so well for her either. Attack was such a violent word. Would the Jackson she thought she knew truly *attack* anyone?

"Jackson? I don't believe it." Maddie set down her teacup with a sharp click.

Somehow, the fact that Maddie, who had known Jackson for over a year, had her doubts made her breathe a bit easier.

"I'm telling you, he manhandled my poor Preston. Just picked him up and threw him. I was terrified. And he refuses to apologize."

"What did Preston do?" Sadie also sounded skeptical, bless her.

"After Jackson threw him?"

"No, before. He must have done something to make Jackson mad."

Jane raised her chin. "Nothing that merited what Jackson did to him, I assure you."

Mary let out a faint snort.

"What was that for?" Jane gave her sister a glare.

Mary glanced at her sister, then down at the tea in her cup.

"If you have something to say, Mary, say it."

Mary kept her eyes trained down. "You know what Preston did. We were both on the porch that day and saw what happened. He threw a punch at Jackson. Twice."

"Only because Jackson said such vile things about him to Father. A man has a right to defend his own name. Oh, I wouldn't expect you to understand. You always were sweet on Jackson. In your eyes, he can do no wrong."

Mary shot a horrified look at Claire and flushed a bright, fiery red. Trust Jane to make things awkward. Claire tried to smile at the girl, but she'd already looked away.

Claire looked back at Jane. "I suspect frayed emotions were driving both our husbands. Was this after Jackson's last supply trip a few weeks ago? He did mention having had a rough time of it that week." Though he'd never given any specifics, surely nothing about a fight. "Something about some lost sheep?"

"And that's just it. He shouldn't put all the blame on Preston for those losses. Tavis was the experienced sheepherder. Preston was supposed to be learning from him. Besides, all herders suffer losses throughout the summer. It's part of ranching."

"No one has lost a couple hundred head before. Not in two weeks." Mary's comment was spoken under her breath, as much to the floor as to anyone in the room, but they all heard it.

"A couple hundred? How in the world?" Maddie turned to Jane, eyes wide.

Maddie was a herder's wife and had lived in a sheep camp for over a year. If she was shocked at that amount of loss, no wonder Jackson lost his temper. From the little Jackson said to her that night, she knew he lay the full blame on Preston. He must have had a reason.

Jane tossed her head. "I'm sure I don't know the particulars. What I'm saying is Jackson had no right to treat my husband that way, but I certainly don't hold that against you and Sadie. I hope we can still be friends, though I won't be coming to visit as often now that we're leaving the ranch."

"You're leaving?"

"Yes. Preston and I will be moving to Lander to take care of some of Father's town interests. Preston's far better suited for that line of work than ranching anyway. He's a Princeton graduate, you know. His skills are wasted in a job any foreigner or common laborer could do. He needs to be challenged."

Obviously, sheep ranching required more skill than Jane let on if her Princeton-grad husband could fail so miserably in his first try at the profession. She opened her mouth to defend Jackson, then closed it when Charlie, Hazel, and Ella burst into the room.

"Ella wanted some gingerbread, so we came back. I hope that's all right," Charlie said.

"Of course. Why don't you three wash up and come join us?"

While the girls took Ella to wash at the pump in the kitchen, Claire cut three more slices of gingerbread. Still a little damp, Ella scrambled onto Claire's lap and took hold of her thick slice.

"Did Jane tell you Jackson threw Preston into a horse trough?" Charlie said around her bite of shortbread.

"What's a horse trough?" Ella chirped.

"Charlotte." Jane sounded anything but pleased. "Don't talk with your mouth full of food. And there's no need to bring up that topic again. We've already discussed it."

Only she'd neglected to tell them about the horse trough. Claire choked back a laugh. Throwing someone in a horse trough didn't sound nearly as violent as attacking them. Especially if the other man threw the first punch. Any uneasiness she'd felt toward Jackson dissipated as her mind conjured up a wet and flustered Preston. She'd never met the man, but she'd heard enough about him to believe his pride had taken a pounding even if his body hadn't.

"What's a horse trough?" Ella wasn't one to give up easily.

"It's where the horses drink, baby. Boaz and Duchess have one out by the barn."

"Can Jackson throw me into it?"

"You wouldn't want him to. It would be wet and cold."

"Was Pweston wet and cold?"

Jane huffed. "See what you've started, Charlie? Someday you will learn to keep your mouth closed."

Charlie shrugged, not at all concerned by her sister's displeasure. "I thought they'd like to hear about it, is all. Did you tell them about Granny?"

"What about Granny?" Sadie asked.

"Well, no, I hadn't gotten to that yet. Turns out Granny slipped off a ladder trying to trim one of her apple trees last Monday and broke her wrist. Doc Stevens came out and set it for her, but she won't be able to use it for several weeks."

Sadie gasped. "Which arm?"

"Her right one, unfortunately."

"Oh, no. How is she managing?" Maddie asked.

"Ma was over there yesterday," Jane assured them. "And, of course, Petie's been helping out with her chickens and cow. I suspect the neighbors will each take a turn."

Sadie turned to Claire, pleading in her eyes. "I should go back and stay with her, Claire. As soon as Jackson gets back from his supply trip. Do you think he would take me? I could cook for her, help her clean, just like before."

Jane beamed at Sadie. "Now, I'm surprised Ma and I didn't think of that. It would be the perfect solution. *I* wanted to help, of course, but with our upcoming move to Lander and my delicate condition . . . well, Ma didn't think it would be wise. And, of course, Mary will never leave home. But you've lived with her before. You'd be the perfect choice."

"What do you think, Claire?"

Lose Sadie again? No. Please, no.

"I think we should both go see her, but we have no way of getting there until Jackson gets back."

"Now, I wish we'd brought the wagon today instead of riding over. We could have taken Sadie with us on our way home." Jane said.

"Sadie could ride back behind me," Charlie volunteered.

"That wouldn't be very comfortable for her. Besides, she'll need to pack a bag if she's planning to stay for a few weeks. No. We'll send Petie to get her tomorrow. No need for all three of you to go, though, at least before Jackson returns. I'm sure your husband wouldn't thank us if he came home to an empty house."

Would these Baldwins ever stop arranging her life as if she were some pawn in their chess game? But she was being uncharitable. Granny had done so much for them. And Sadie would be a great help for her. But she wanted Sadie here, as a buffer when Jackson was home, as a companion when he wasn't. She stifled a sigh.

"Thank you, Jane," she said, hoping she sounded more gracious than she felt. "We'll look for Petie tomorrow then."

After their company left, Sadie put her arm around Claire's waist as they walked back into the cabin.

"You don't mind my going to Granny's, do you? I wouldn't go if I didn't think you'd be fine without me."

"Of course not. I'll be fine." She had to be. "I'll miss you, though."

"I know it gets pretty quiet around here when Jackson's gone, but it's only a short walk to Maddie's if you get to feeling lonely. And I'll be back in a couple of weeks. I promise. I just can't let Granny fend for herself right now. Not after all she's done for us."

"I agree. And once Jackson gets back, I'll have him bring me to Granny's for a visit. I'd like to see how she's getting along for myself. In the meantime, I'll put together a bag with some pills and herbal teas you can give her to help with her pain."

If Sadie wasn't worried about Jackson's potential violent

streak, she wouldn't be either. After all, Sadie had been a much better judge of Jonas's character early on than she was. Much as she hated it, she'd have to trust Sadie's instincts over her own this time. Lord knows, her own had failed her before.

CHAPTER 22

Claire woke with a start. Heart racing, she struggled to catch her breath. The nightmare was back. Not that it had truly ever left, but without Sadie to talk her down from its aftermath, Claire was sure she wouldn't be getting more sleep tonight.

She pulled a sleeping Ella close, finding calm in the warmth of her little body. Thank goodness she hadn't cried out and frightened Ella with her sobs and thrashing. That had happened before, though, between the two of them, she and Sadie could usually pass it off as something silly Mommy sometimes did at night. But there was nothing silly about that dream.

Claire shuddered. It always started the same way. A knock at the door, Jonas on the other side, blood dripping down his face. He'd smile that mocking smile of his. The one that froze her blood.

"Didn't think I'd find you, did you? Slut! Did you really think you could kill me? Marry someone else? I'll teach you. You won't get away with that kind of behavior."

And then his hands would be around her neck—squeezing, choking, cutting off her ability to breathe—exactly like that last morning in Denver. Claire touched the skin around her neck, almost expecting to feel the bruising. It was a dream. Just a dream. Then, why did it feel so real? Would she never be free of Jonas and the terror he caused her?

A thump, seeming to come from the direction of the kitchen, put all Claire's senses on alert. Had she really heard something, or was it her imagination? With both Jackson and Sadie gone, every creak and pop the cabin made at night seemed magnified. Especially on the heels of that dream. Claire listened, but no sound followed. Easing Ella out of her arms, Claire got up and tiptoed to the door. But once there, she couldn't bring herself to open it. What if there was someone on the other side?

She and Ella were utterly and completely alone here. If someone were to come across this cabin in the night and decide to enter, who would stop them? And she had nothing to use for protection. Oh, why hadn't she asked Jackson to leave them a gun? Something. Anything. She was completely defenseless.

She listened intently for a minute or two. Nothing. It was probably just the cabin settling. A pop from the rafters. She was being a ninny. But ninny or not, there was no way she was opening that door.

Just to be safe, she dragged the heavy ladder-backed chair from the corner and wedged it under the doorknob. Then, climbing back into bed, she pulled the covers tight around her and Ella. That chair wouldn't keep anyone out long term, but at least she'd be warned. And it wasn't likely, between her dream and the noises, she'd be sleeping anymore tonight anyway.

COFFEE. THAT'S WHAT SHE NEEDED. NORMALLY, SHE AVOIDED IT, not particularly fond of its bitter flavor, but she needed something hot and bracing this morning. Something stronger than the tea she usually drank. Claire placed the tin coffee pot under the sink pump and began to fill it.

In the clear light of morning, last night's terror seemed ridiculous. Toward morning, she'd managed a few hours of sleep. When she woke and saw the chair still propped against her bedroom door, she couldn't help feeling silly. As if that would have kept anyone out. As if there was anyone to keep out. Jonas was dead. And nothing and nobody came to this God-forsaken bit of country. Very few people even knew their cabin existed. The noises she heard weren't real. Just her fear-laden brain playing tricks on her.

A bootstep sounded in the doorway behind her. She shrieked and whirled around, sloshing all the water from the coffee pot down her front. The cold water and her fright stole her breath before realization set in. Jackson.

"I didn't mean to scare you."

"No. It's . . . I'm . . . I didn't know you were back."

"Got in late last night. Thought you might have heard me."

Yes. Well. So, she had. Suddenly last night's fear seemed even more ridiculous.

"Maybe I . . . um . . . I should come back later." Jackson's voice sounded somewhat strangled. His eyes were glued to her front.

She glanced down. Oh, good grief. She stood as exposed as Bathsheba on the rooftop, the wet front of her cotton night-gown clinging like a second skin. Gasping, she whirled around and grabbed the hand towel. What must he think of her? Bare feet. Hair down. She could almost hear Jonas's voice in her ear, "Brazen hussy!"

She dabbed at her wet nightgown. "Sorry. I'm not usually so . . . I just had no idea . . ." She risked a glance at him over her shoulder. Thankfully, Jackson looked almost as mortified as she felt, easing her own embarrassment a bit.

"I . . . I'll just . . . " He inched his way backward.

She fought back a laugh. Could the two of them be any less coherent?

Jackson backed the rest of the way toward the door and bolted, slamming it behind him in his haste. She sank into a chair, covering her face with the wet hand towel. Lord. This inconvenient marriage has just reached a new level of awkwardness. Why, oh why, had she ever let Sadie leave?

###Wow. He had no idea. Shoot. He'd had *some* idea, but his imagination had never done reality justice. He hadn't been prepared for the sight of her standing there, sable hair cascading down her back in shining waves, her curves silhouetted beneath the sheer cotton of her nightgown. And then when she'd turned, the wet fabric plastered to her—well. He shouldn't have seen that, but now that he had, he couldn't not see it. The memory turned his mouth dry.

He'd been a fool to think he could make this fake marriage work. Sure, it was easy to promise a celibate marriage when you weren't actually living together, but to be in such intimate contact with someone as beautiful as Claire day after day? Not possible. What had possessed him to even try? The entire male population would be laughing at his folly if they only knew.

He dropped onto a nearby bale of straw and pushed the heels of his hands into his eye sockets as if he could somehow erase what he'd seen. What had Jesus said? If your eye offend you, pluck it out? He didn't think plucking out his eyes would do one iota of good. Her image was seared on his brain. Was it a sin to lust after your wife? Maybe. Maybe not.

No, in this case it definitely was. Because she'd never agreed to *be* his wife. Not in that way. Besides, she was leaving. He needed to remember that and not let her get under his skin.

He gave a snort. Too late for that. How was he ever going to face her again after acting like some awestruck schoolboy?

He'd keep his distance. That's it. Lord knows, Claire wouldn't mind. He'd seen how skittish she was around him. Staying away from her shouldn't be that hard. He was gone half the time anyway. The rest of the time, he'd keep busy. Get up early, come in late. The less time he spent with her, the easier it would be.

That's the ticket. Stay busy. He'd start with the morning chores. Gather the eggs. Milk the cow. From the looks of it, the woodpile needed some serious tending. He could use up half the morning just doing chores. And then there was the general ranch work he could do—train Duchess, finish building a larger corral. Yep. That's what he'd do. Keep his distance.

He'd split about half the logs in the woodpile when Ella showed up. Unlike the last few times he'd come home, she didn't scream out his name and throw herself at him. She simply stood by the corner of the corral, finger in her mouth, staring at him with those large dark eyes of hers. He wouldn't have known she was there if he hadn't spotted her white pinafore when he'd turned to heft another log for splitting.

He sent her a nod. "Morning, Ella Bella."

She didn't smile or respond.

He set down the ax and walked over to her, squatting to look in her eyes. "What's the matter? Cat got your tongue this morning?"

She shook her head.

"You sure? Maybe you should stick it out for me so I can see."

The pink tip of her tongue darted between her lips, then vanished.

"Ah. You're right. It is there. Playing the silent game then?"

She shook her head again.

"No? Could have fooled me."

"You didn't come in for bwekfast."

"Well, no." Like the coward he was, he'd left the eggs and milk on the back step and got right to work on the woodpile.

"I didn't know you were here."

"I got in late last night. When you were sleeping."

"You didn't want to see me?"

"No, Ella. Of course, not." He kneaded the muscles at the back of his neck and blew out a long breath. This was going to be more difficult than he'd thought. Truth was he'd wanted to see her and Claire. More than anything. Part of the reason he'd come home in the wee hours of the night was he hadn't wanted to wait until today to get here. He'd wanted to spend his full two days off with them. But that was the problem. He couldn't allow himself to become any more invested than he already was. Spending more time with the two of them was simply too dangerous.

But how was he going to explain that to Ella? He looked into her pretty gray eyes, so much like her mother's, and knew no matter what happened between now and then, watching her and Claire leave in the fall would be the hardest thing he'd ever had to do. Even worse than watching Ma leave. He was already too invested.

Unless . . . a thought that had been pricking at the back of his brain ever since he started chopping wood forced its way forward. What if they didn't leave? What if he could convince Claire to stay? What if he could convince her to make theirs a real marriage instead of a farce?

Just thinking about it made his stomach churn. How in the blazes would he accomplish that? He hadn't the foggiest idea how to woo a woman. But . . . he did have a home to offer her and security. She seemed happy enough here. Maybe . . . just maybe. He had to at least try.

"I'm sorry I didn't come into breakfast, Ella girl. It's just that I wanted to get all my chores done today, so we can spend tomorrow doing something special."

Ella's eyes widened. "Will we play hunt the penny?"

"No. Something better." He had no idea what it would be.

Something women liked. As if he had any idea what that was. He would come up with something. He had to. "So you need to let me finish splitting this wood and getting my other chores done. Then you, me, Sadie, and your mom can spend all day tomorrow together. Okay?"

"Aunt Sadie isn't here."

"She's not?"

"No. She's at Gwanny's."

This was a new development, a puzzling one, but not necessarily a bad one. Not having Sadie's critical eyes on him while he tried to woo Claire might be a godsend. He'd sort out the whys of her absence later. For now, he had wood to split and a hundred other tasks to finish in order to free up tomorrow. And he had to think of something a woman and her little girl might like.

He could do this. He had to. The alternative–watching Claire and Ella walk out of his life—didn't bear thinking.

CHAPTER 23

This was the stupidest idea he'd ever had. He must have been out of his ever-loving mind to think he could court a woman, especially one as beautiful and independent as Claire. When he'd suggested a horseback ride and picnic yesterday, Claire had been visibly reluctant. If it hadn't been for Ella squealing in excitement and begging to go, he doubted they would be here. Might have been best if they weren't. Neither he nor Claire had exchanged a single word for a full twenty minutes.

She didn't seem unhappy, though. After their initial debate about whether it would be safer for Ella to ride with him on Duchess or with her on Boaz, she'd mounted up and followed him out of the barnyard at a canter. He liked that she was comfortable on horseback. If she truly were to stay and become a rancher's wife, she'd need to be. *If she were to stay.* Who was he fooling? Did he really think he could convince her to make their marriage a real one? He couldn't even talk to her.

He thought he'd learned his lesson about trying to woo a girl years ago. Lillie May Stevens. Doc Stevens's oldest girl. She was the prettiest girl in Cherry Creek school. Her blond curls and big blue eyes had drawn him in. Made him think having a girl of his own wasn't such a bad idea after all.

He was all of fourteen, but still thought himself man enough to try courting. He'd be finishing school that year. Getting a real job. He'd left flowers on her desk, and a piece of taffy from a batch Granny had made them. One day he mustered up the courage to walk her home from school. She was all smiles and coy glances. He hadn't been brave enough to tell her how he felt, but he could tell she knew and felt the same. At least, he thought he could.

How wrong he'd been. The next day, as he was coming around the corner of the schoolhouse, he'd heard her and her friends talking on the front porch. He'd stopped to listen when he heard her say his name.

"Court Jackson Garrity? I'd never!" Her scornful laugh cut him to the core. "He might be handsome enough, but the boy can't string more than two words together at a time. He's like a big, lumbering ox. Why, I'd put a crick in my neck just trying to kiss him."

He didn't stick around to hear any more of the girls' laughter. He'd heard enough to know Ma was right. He was just like his Pa, and women didn't stay married to men like Pa.

He snuck a look at Claire. Maybe she hadn't noticed his silence. It wasn't like she'd been trying to talk to him. Thank goodness Ella was along. She'd done enough talking for the three of them.

He tightened an arm around the little girl as she twisted her body nearly sideways to follow the path of a rabbit they'd scared out of the long grasses.

"Did you see that, Jackson? A wabbit. Will there be wabbits at our picnic? I hope so. I want to catch a wabbit. Do you think I can? If I catch a wabbit, I'm going to name it Willie. I'll bring it home and make it a nice soft bed. I'll let him live in my room, and I'll love him always. Do you think Willie and Mr.

Cuddles will get along? I think they will be great friends." She reached forward and patted the side of Duchess's neck for the twentieth time. "Duchess can be their friend too. You're a nice horsie, Duchess. Isn't she a nice horsie?" She picked up a tuft of her mane. "Mama, who has the pwettiest hair? Duchess or Boaz?"

"Coat, sweetheart. A horse's hair is called its coat."

"Which coat is pwettiest, Mama?"

"Which do *you* like best?"

"Duchess's. I like her white nose. Which one do you like, Jackson?" She twisted around again to look up at his face.

"I've always been partial to sable." He glanced over and caught Claire's eye. The memory of dark curls against white cotton strong on his mind. He banished it to a deep corner.

"Stable?" Ella broke into giggles. "Not their house. Which horsie coat?"

"Sable, not stable, sweetie. Sable *is* the color of Duchess's coat. Jackson is telling you he agrees with you."

Ella tilted her head to stare at Boaz. "What's Boaz's coat?"

"Buckskin."

"Sable. Buckskin. Sable. Buckskin. Dappas and gways." Her singsong chant slipped into a song. "Blacks and bays, All the purdy liddle horsies."

The same lullaby she'd sung to him on the train. Had that only been three months ago? He swallowed against the sudden tightness in his throat and pulled her a little closer. He couldn't bear the thought of losing this little one. Somehow in the span of three months, she and her mother had taken a piece of his heart. He had to find the words that would get them to stay.

He cleared his throat. "Sounds like Hippolyta's band."

"Hipporites band? What's that?"

"It's a band of wild horses way up there in those mountains. Maybe someday I'll take you and your mama to see them."

"Today?"

"No. Not today. It's too far, but we're almost to today's surprise. Should be just over this rise."

He'd seen the spot as he'd headed out to the sheep camps last week and thought it might have potential. Hopefully. As they topped the rise, he let out his pent-up breath. Yep. A carpet of yellow flowers with patches of purple lupine and blue sage filled the valley below. Girls liked flowers, right?

A soft gasp beside him was the response he'd hoped for. "Oh, Jackson. It's gorgeous."

Ella bounced up and down on the saddle in front of him. "Mama. Mama. It's a fairy field. Can I run in it? Please, Mama?"

"There's a stream at the bottom of the valley. I'll let you down when we get there. We'll have our picnic there, and you can run all you want."

As soon as he lifted her down from the saddle, Ella took off, flitting from flower to flower like some overgrown butterfly.

"Help me find the fairies, Mama," she called.

Claire laughed. "You won't find them that way, sweetie. You have to be very quiet. If they hear you coming, they will hide."

Ella ran back, grabbed her mother's hand, and pulled her along. "Help me, Mama."

With the ladies occupied with their fairy search, Jackson tied the horses in a stand of cedars next to the stream and began unpacking the picnic lunch. He spread the tablecloth Claire had brought and set out the ham sandwiches and boiled eggs. Three tin cups to hold cold water from the stream and donuts from breakfast rounded out the meal. Not a feast, but enough to satisfy their appetites.

Claire and Ella returned with their arms full of flowers.

"After we eat, I'll show you how to make a daisy chain," Claire said to Ella. "You can wear a crown of flowers in your hair like a fairy princess. Would you like that?"

"Yes. And one for you too, Mama."

"Shall we make one for Jackson?"

"Yes, for his hat. And one for Duchess and Boaz."

Claire held out one of the small yellow flowers to him. "These look like tiny yellow daisies. What are they called?"

Jackson shrugged. "Folks around here call them golden weed or yellow sunshine."

"Yellow sunshine. I like that. It's like the whole field is glowing. This is so beautiful, Jackson. Thank you for bringing us here."

He nodded, wishing he could think of something gallant to say. Compare her beauty to that of the flowers or something like that, but that would sound ridiculous coming from him.

"Ready to eat?" There's romance for you.

"Of course. Come, Ella. Let's rinse our hands in the stream, and then we'll have our picnic."

He gave them each a tin cup to fill and followed them down to the water. Maybe all he'd need was the flowers and the setting to woo her. If he said too much, he was liable to scare her away. But if he didn't tell her he wanted her to stay, how would she know? Maybe after they ate, he would think of a way to let her know.

"Now we push the last stem through this slit like so," Claire guided Ella's little fingers with hers, "and voilà, we have a crown."

She placed the crown on Ella's soft curls. "What do you think. Do you like it?"

"Oh, yes, Mama. Now one for you."

"Of course. Shall I show you how to braid them this time?" She picked three flowers from the pile and began to braid their stems. "Now hand me another, and we'll add it to the chain, like so. See, this stem goes this way, and that stem goes that way. Now another flower."

Ella handed her a flower then leaned against her side. "Tell me a story, Mama."

"What sort of story?"

"A fairy princess story. About flowers."

"Hmmm. Let's see." Ella was always wanting stories. Any story would usually do, but she loved made up ones the best. Claire looked out over the field of flowers, seeking inspiration. "Once upon a time, in a field much like this one, there lived a village of flower fairies. Every time a flower grew, a baby fairy grew with it. Whenever a baby fairy was two weeks old, it would grow a pair of wings and leave its flower bed, but it would never leave the field. All of the flower fairies learned very early how to hide way down among the leaves of the flowers whenever any human came near, so hardly anyone could ever see the fairies, but they were there."

Ella picked up one of the flowers they'd picked and looked deep into its leaves. "I don't see any."

"No, you hardly ever do. They are very good hiders. Now, the prettiest of all the flower fairies was a princess fairy named Blossom. She wore a dress made of sunbeams and the tiniest flower crown just like this," Claire tapped Ella's flower crown, "only teeny tiny."

"Did her Mama have a cwown too?" Ella took the crown Claire had just finished and held it up. "Put it on, Mama."

Claire placed it on her head. "Of course, the Queen Fairy, Floriana, also had a flower crown and a dress made of purest gold. She was in charge of all the other fairies and made sure the flower field was a place of beauty and peace. But one day, a large woolly beast wandered into the field and began to eat the flowers."

Ella's eyes grew round. "Did it eat all of them?"

"Not quite, but he might have if the fairies hadn't fought back. Each of them had a silver sword about the size of a sewing needle. Queen Floriana organized the fairies into bands of warriors. Hour after hour, they would attack the woolly beast with their swords, pricking at its ears and nose, and feet. The beast would toss his head and stamp his feet, but he never left off eating the flowers. Pretty soon, another woolly beast and then another found the flower field until the fairies quite despaired of saving their home."

"Did all the flowers get chewed up, Mama?"

"No, because Blossom knew of a secret weapon. She had a special friend, a little black and white collie named Rosie."

"Like Mr. Skivington's Rosie?"

"Exactly like that Rosie. So Blossom flew and flew until she reached a meadow of grass where Rosie was guarding a flock of sheep. She whispered in Rosie's ear. 'Your sheep are in the flowers, and they need to come home.' Well, Rosie jumped up, just as fast as fast can be, and ran behind Blossom as she flew back to the flowers. When they got to the flower field, Rosie barked and ran and nipped at the heels of the woolly beasts until they all turned and ran back home. And the flower field was saved."

Ella clapped her hands. "I like that story, Mama. Tell another?"

"Maybe later. Right now, let's make a couple of necklaces for Duchess and Boaz to wear. Do you think they'd like that?"

Ella nodded.

"You'd better gather some more flowers, then. And while you do, see if you can find some fairies. Remember, you have to be very quiet, or they'll hide from you."

Ella was off with a bound, looking under each clump of flowers before she picked them, humming as she went.

"She sure likes to sing. Does she get that from you?"

Claire startled. She'd almost forgotten Jackson was with them. He lay stretched on the ground beside her, head resting on a rock, hat down over his eyes. She'd assumed he was napping.

"Definitely not me, but you're right. Ella has always liked to sing. I can't remember a time when she wasn't humming or singing something, even when she was really little."

"My Ma was like that. Always singing."

He'd never talked about his mother before. She'd assumed the topic was off limits. Now that he'd brought it up, curiosity got the better of her.

"What was she like?"

"Beautiful." He sat up and placed his hat on the ground beside him. His gaze met hers, those deep blue eyes of his, once again, drawing her in. "I know most kids think their Ma is the purtiest thing around, but she really was the most beautiful woman in the county. She had this long black hair she wore wrapped around her head in a braid, kinda like a crown. Her eyes were about the color of those lupines over there. Amethyst, Pa called them. And when she sang, everyone stopped to take notice. When I was little, she and Pa used to have these parties, invite all the neighbors, and at some point during the night, she'd pull out the songbooks and urge everybody to sing. It wouldn't take long before everyone just wanted to hear her sing. She was that good."

Jackson leaned back, propping himself on his hands and staring off into the distance. This was the most she'd ever heard him say, especially about his childhood. She was reluctant to comment for fear he'd stop.

"After Gabe came along, they didn't have the parties so much anymore. She said us kids plumb wore her out." He gave a wry smile. "I suppose we did. Then, right before Petie was born, Pa bought her a piano. Every afternoon when we came in from school and chores, she'd be playing and singing. I used to make Louis and Gabe sit with me outside by the window so we could listen. Otherwise, if she knew we were there, she'd stop."

"How old were you when she left?"

"Ten."

Ten. Much too young to lose a mother. She shook her head. Four boys, ten and under? How could a mother leave them?

"I sometimes wonder if we had been different . . . if we hadn't been so loud, if we hadn't tracked dirt in the house, if I hadn't wrestled with Louis and Gabe so much, would she have stayed?"

Claire reached out and placed her hand over his. "Trust me when I say this. It wasn't you or your brothers who made your mother leave. A mother might leave for many reasons, but it wouldn't be for how her kids behaved. And, for what it's worth? She missed out on a lot. Any mother would be proud to call you and your brothers her sons."

He turned his hand under hers until their palms were touching. His hand felt strong, calloused, yet comfortable, somehow. His thumb caressed the skin between her own thumb and forefinger. A flurry of tremors flitted through her belly. She snatched her hand away, immediately regretting it when she saw the hurt in his eyes.

"I'm sorry," he said. "I shouldn't have . . ."

"No. You didn't . . . I mean, I didn't . . . it's just that . . ."

He reached out and caught a strand of her hair that had fallen from her pompadour. She was suddenly very aware of her ramshackle appearance—grass-stained skirt, flower crown, unkempt hair. He pulled the strand slowly through his fingers before tucking it behind her ear.

I've always been partial to sable. His earlier words and the look he'd given her when he said them sprang to mind.

She cleared her throat and looked away, breaking the tenuous bond between them.

"You and Ella are safe here, Claire. You know that, right?"

She looked off toward the Winds in the distance, unable to look him in the eye. "I know."

But she didn't. And he was wrong. *This* wasn't safe. Not safe at all. If she let this attraction or whatever this was between them grow, neither of them would be safe. Love was never safe. Love was pain. Hadn't he experienced that already? With his own mother, no less?

No. She was leaving. She had to. She couldn't afford to let herself fall in love. Nor could she let him fall in love with her.

She stood up, breaking the spell.

"I'd better go help Ella with her flowers."

As she walked away, she could feel his gaze following her. But she wouldn't turn around. She couldn't afford to.

CHAPTER 24

The summer sun warmed the back of Claire's neck as she worked her way down a row of strawberry plants in Granny's garden. Jackson had dropped her and Ella off for a visit on his way to Baldwin's ranch this morning. After making sure Granny was comfortably settled in her kitchen rocking chair, she and Sadie went out to harvest the strawberries that loaded Granny's extensive strawberry patch. The plan was to make a couple of strawberry pies and several jars of preserves before Claire left this evening. Ella had helped for a few moments, though, in reality, she'd probably eaten more berries than she kept. Now she was off chasing a butterfly that flitted through the hollyhocks.

"I've decided to stay at Granny's." Sadie's announcement broke the quiet peace of the morning. "At least for the summer."

"*All* summer? Why?"

"Because she needs me."

"*I* need you." Claire hadn't meant for that to sound so petulant, but the truth was, she did. She couldn't imagine facing an entire summer alone in Jackson's cabin with just Ella for company and on occasion, Jackson. She didn't know which she feared most—Jackson's presence or his absence. Both were fraught with perils of their own.

"You don't, though. Not really. Not as much as Granny needs me. Claire, she can't even use her right arm. You remember what that's like."

Unfortunately, she did. Just a few months after Ella was born, Jonas had thrown her against her wardrobe with such force, she'd broken her forearm. He'd told everyone she'd had a riding accident. A careless young mother, he'd called her. She'd spent two months in a sling. The worst was not being able to pick up Ella. She had to rely on others to place her baby in her arms, and Jonas discouraged even that.

"That's why we hired a nursemaid, my dear," he'd say. She'd always suspected it was his way of keeping her from bonding with Ella. Well, it hadn't worked. Thank God.

She sighed. "Of course, I remember. And I want you to help Granny. I do. But . . . it's the nights. When Jackson's gone. I can't —" She cut herself off. She'd told herself when she ran from Jonas the first time, she wasn't going to whimper and beg. Never again. Besides, Jonas was dead. She had to stop letting him control her life. "Never mind. I'll be fine."

Sadie rocked back on her heels to study her across her row of strawberry plants. "The nightmares again?"

Claire nodded.

"When?"

"Last night, two nights ago, twice last week."

"Same as always?"

She nodded again.

"Maybe when Jackson leaves for his next trip, you and Ella could come stay here with Granny and me. We made it work before."

"And how do you think all the neighbors are going to feel about that? They took considerable time and effort to make sure we had a place to stay so we wouldn't all be crammed in with Granny. I thought our goal was to stir up as little talk as possible. I can just hear the tongues wagging now if we decide, after one short month, to go back to the way things were."

"I think they'd understand if you told them you didn't like to stay at the cabin without your husband."

"Or the tongues will wag even more about what a little ninny Jackson married. Folks are tougher out here." She shook her head. "It's all right, Sadie. I'll get used to it. It's only for a few more months anyway."

"You're still thinking of leaving here in the fall?"

"Aren't you? You know the agreement. I promised Jackson six months to get his sheep ranch started, and he promised me my freedom. Nothing's changed."

"You sure about that?"

"Of course, I'm sure. Why?"

Sadie shrugged. "I guess because I've seen the way Jackson looks at you."

"What do you mean?"

"He gets this look. Oh, I don't know how to describe it, but he looks at you like he sure wouldn't mind if you stuck around. Like he wouldn't mind if the two of you made things permanent."

"You're crazy." Though there was whatever that was that passed between them the day of the picnic. The way he'd held her gaze as he touched her hair. The way his fingers had lingered. She hadn't imagined that, had she? "I don't want a husband, Sadie. You of all people should know that."

"And yet, you have one. And you know as well as I do, Jackson isn't anything like Jonas. If you ask me, this is the perfect situation—an obscure sheep ranch 130 miles from the nearest railroad. Who's going to find us here? It's not like you've been hunting for a nursing position lately. Do you even have a plan for where we'll go when we leave?"

"Actually, I have been looking, but it's complicated." Because all the ads she'd found for private nurses wanted single women or widows without encumbrances. Encumbrances. As if Ella and Sadie could ever be labeled encumbrances. But the truth was, finding a position where they could all live together was proving harder than she expected. She didn't want to go back to what they had in Denver, where she only saw Ella one day a week.

The perfect position would be one where she could live at home and help out an over-worked local doctor in some small town—someone like Doc Stevens. But she couldn't exactly approach him or ask for references without raising questions about her marriage. She'd promised Jackson six months. She'd give him that full six months without cause for gossip. But after that, they were leaving.

"Just don't get too attached to this place, Sadie. You might think we're safe, but that security won't last forever. Jonas found us in Denver in less than two years. Our best bet is to keep moving, to never stay in one place very long. Comfortable as this place is, we can't forget we're fugitives."

"What's a fujatif, Mama?"

Shoot. She hadn't realized Ella was so close. How much of their conversation had she overheard?

"It's someone who likes to travel and see new places." Sort of. And, hopefully, it was a word Ella would forget by the end of the day. "Look, sweetie, Aunt Sadie and I have picked two really big bowls of strawberries. Shall we go in and make strawberry pies?"

"Stwawbewwy pie! I love stwawbewwy pie! Can we make one for Petie? And Jackson?"

"I'm sure there will be enough pie for everyone, but you'll have to be a big helper so we can get it all done before Jackson comes back."

"I help, Mommy. I pwomise."

As she watched her daughter skip ahead of her into the

cabin, she couldn't help but wish they didn't have to leave. Sadie was right. They'd landed in an almost perfect situation. But there was no escaping the truth. They were fugitives, and fugitives didn't get the luxury of perfect situations. Not long term, anyway.

SHEER DESPERATION HAD DRIVEN HER TO TODAY'S VISIT. JACKSON had been gone a full week on another sheep camp run. With Sadie at Granny's, Claire didn't think she could take another day of three-year-old prattle without some adult conversation mixed in. So, after a quick lunch, she and Ella had made the half-mile hike to the Skivington's cabin, where Maddie and Hazel greeted them with open arms.

"I'm so glad you decided to drop in today. Rob's out at the sheep camp with the boys and isn't due back for several days. Hazel and I had talked about coming to see you, but I decided I couldn't waddle that far."

Guilt pricked. She should have stopped by sooner. She and Maddie were essentially in the same situation, with their husbands traveling every few weeks to supply herders. However, Rob's trips were shorter since he only visited one camp. Each time she visited Maddie, she liked her more and more. Had their situation been different, she would have been eager to cultivate a friendship. But deep friendships and secrets didn't mix . . . neither did leaving, so she'd fought to keep her distance. Today, loneliness had won over practicality, but she was glad that it did, for Maddie's sake anyway.

Maddie led them into her cozy, one-room cabin, her large belly leading the way.

"How are you feeling?" Claire asked.

"Tired. All the time. I can't seem to get comfortable enough to sleep for very long."

"Oh, yes. I remember." During those final months of pregnancy, she'd been so big and ungainly that Jonas had refused to visit her room at night. Said she was too ugly. Too clumsy. Those had been the best months of her married life. But she also remembered the discomfort. She'd been torn between wanting her baby to come and wishing she could stay pregnant forever.

"Also, we've been getting ready for Mother Skivington's visit, setting up a room for her." Maddie gestured toward a door newly cut in the back wall.

Claire had noticed on the walk over that the Skivingtons had added a large canvas tent to the back of the cabin. Now she understood its purpose.

"Is there something I can do to help? What were you planning to do with your afternoon before Ella and I dropped in?"

"We were just sitting down to do some sewing. Hazel is working on a sampler, and I have some diapers to hem. But don't worry about that. We certainly can take some time off for a visit."

"Or we can visit while we work, and the diapers will be done in half the time."

After a few feeble protests from Maddie, the four of them set to work—she and Maddie on the diapers, Hazel on her sampler, and Ella sorting through buttons in Maddie's collection.

"So, your mother-in-law is coming? Will your own mother also be making a visit?"

A shadow crossed Maddie's face. "Mother passed five years ago. Only a year before Rob and I married."

"I'm sorry."

"She never would have survived a trip out here anyway. She was of delicate health all the years I knew her, and after Hazel was born, she slowly declined. That's probably why I've always felt more like a mother to Hazel than a sister. That, and the fact I'm fifteen years older."

Claire nodded. "Sadie's always telling me I mother her far

too much. She was only seven when our mother died. At twelve, I took my mothering duties very seriously, I'm afraid."

"Twelve is a hard age to lose a mother. Oh, I suppose any age is hard, but at twelve, you're old enough to know what you've lost, yet too young to process it well. Was her death sudden?"

How do you tell a pregnant woman that your mother died in childbirth? Simple. You didn't. "Like your mother, she also was of delicate health." Four miscarriages in three years would do that to a woman, but Mother had been determined to give Father a son. "But her death was not expected, and I know my grandfather and father both felt it should have been prevented. They each blamed the other, though I suspect, essentially, they each blamed themselves."

"I don't understand. What could they have done?"

"Oh. I forgot you didn't know. Both my mother's father and my father were doctors. Grandpa was a general practitioner in a small town in eastern Missouri. My father trained to be a surgeon. When he married my mother, she convinced him to join my grandfather's practice rather than work in a big city hospital. I remember he and Grandpa disagreed on just about everything. Father thought Grandpa was old-fashioned and backwards. Grandpa thought Father was young and reckless. Naturally, they disagreed on how to treat mother. Her death was the final tear in an already rocky relationship."

Essentially, she'd lost her only living grandparents and both her parents the day Mother died. Mother was barely in the grave before Father packed them up and moved them to St. Louis. He took a job as a surgeon for City Hospital and left her and Sadie in a huge, empty house under the care of a house-keeper, a cook, and a maid. He'd see them a few nights a week at the evening meal, but the father they knew and loved was gone. And they never visited Grandma and Grandpa Monroe again.

Maddie nodded. "Death is hard. We all grieve in different ways, and sometimes those differences cause friction. My younger sister, Edie, passed away last fall from scarlet fever." Tears welled in Maddie's eyes.

"I'm so sorry."

Maddie used the diaper she was working on to wipe at her eyes. "Thank you. Obviously, I still have trouble believing she's gone. But what I was saying was, her passing caused a rift between our family and her husband simply because he didn't feel we were mourning her passing the same as him." She shook her head. "As if you can truly judge the depths of another person's grief. Anyway, I'm praying that rift can soon be healed. I'd hate the thought of never knowing my nephew, but living as far away from everyone like we do . . ." Her voice broke. "Well, it's hard."

"You've had a lot of loss in your family." Hearing her story made it seem even more unfair that Rob should have tuberculosis. As a nurse, she'd seen many succumb to the ravages of consumption, and from what she'd seen this summer, the Wyoming air was not providing the cure Rob was seeking.

"You've suffered great loss as well, though I imagine your latest loss was the hardest."

"Yes, Father's loss was hard, but it's been almost five years now. It's not as fresh. And being older, maybe I was able to handle it better than I did Mother's." Or maybe his loss had been compounded with all she lost by marrying Jonas. The two events happened so close together that it was hard to separate the pain.

"You've lost your father too? I'm so sorry. Actually, I was referring to the loss of your first husband." She glanced at Ella. "Surely, his death was more recent?"

"Oh. Yes, of course. Jonas's death was by far the hardest." Claire struggled to make the words sound sincere.

"Has he been gone long?"

"Two years." She and Sadie had decided it was best to mark Jonas's death as the day they had first run from him. If they were going to lie, their stories needed to agree. Also, the less their story linked them to that fateful day in Denver, the better.

"Illness?"

"An accident." If one could call being beaten over the head with an iron skillet an accident. She firmed her lips and blinked rapidly, hoping to appear overcome. "I'm sorry. It's not something I like to talk about."

"No. Don't be sorry. I'm not even sure how we got ourselves onto such gloomy topics. Let's talk about happier things. Did I tell you we're planning a small party once Mother Skivington arrives?"

"Is there anything I can do to help? That's a lot to take on so close to your time."

"Oh. It won't be that much trouble. Simply a small gathering of neighbors is all, so Mother can meet all the people we've talked about in our letters. I know for certain she'll want to meet Jackson. Do you know when he's due home again?"

"I'm expecting him by the end of the week." It usually took about ten days for him to get his supplies in Lander and then make the rounds of the two sheep camps. "After that, he'll be home for a couple of weeks before he heads out again. When does she arrive?"

"Early next week. I'll let you know the exact date of the party after she comes."

"So, how can I help? I could make some pies. Also, Granny sent me home with five jars of strawberry preserves. I can bring a few with a couple of loaves of bread."

The rest of their time was spent on safer topics, recipes and gardening, and preparation for the baby, but as she gathered her things to leave, Claire's eye caught on a framed sampler hanging above the door. Stitched within a border of dainty flowers and vining leaves were the words, *Earth hath no sorrow that Heaven cannot heal.*

"That's pretty."

A gentle smile lit Maddie's face. "It's from a hymn. Maybe you've heard it? We sang it at my sister's funeral. Since then, the second verse has become my lifeline. *'Joy of the desolate, light of the straying, Hope when all others die, fadeless and pure; Here speaks the Comforter, in God's name saying, Earth has no sorrow that Heaven cannot cure.'"* She sang the words quietly, in a soft soprano.

"It's lovely." And it was—both Maddie's singing and the sentiment.

"I don't know how I would cope with this world's sorrow," Maddie said, "if I didn't have the hope that this life isn't all there is. But *you* know. You've had much sorrow too."

Yes, but not the hope. Not since Jonas, anyway. There was a time—right after Father died and she'd felt so lost and alone—when she'd foolishly thought Jonas was an answer to her prayers. But the reality of their marriage changed everything. And if heaven truly was her only answer to this life's sorrow, then she was out of luck. She knew the words Jesus had spoken to his followers in his sermon on the Mount of Olives. *"If you do not forgive others their sins, your Father will not forgive your sins."*

She'd determined early on in her marriage that she could never forgive the things Jonas had done to her. Never. She couldn't. She wouldn't. Besides, could God forgive a murderer? She might not have wielded the skillet that killed Jonas, but she'd wanted him dead. And she'd never once been sorry that he died.

No, the hope Maddie clung to was not for the likes of her. Not anymore.

CHAPTER 25

"We've decided to leave Wyoming."

Rob's announcement stopped Jackson midstride. "What?"

He and Rob were heading toward Rob's sheep pens to check on a bummer lamb. The party for Rob's mother was taking place in the cabin behind them, but Rob had pulled him aside and asked for his help.

Rob kept walking, so Jackson caught up.

"I'm selling out," he said.

"You're headed back to Newark?"

"No. I haven't given up my quest for health just yet." Rob's tone was wry. "We're moving to Denver. Truth is, I don't think I can handle another Wyoming winter. Not if it means being out in it every day taking care of sheep. And it's not fair to make my brothers do all my work. They have their own lives to live. Denver has doctors—good ones that specialize in t.b. I'm still not willing to check into a sanatorium, but it wouldn't hurt to be closer to good health care."

Jackson looked closely at his friend. Always a thin man, Rob was looking even more peaked than usual. Why hadn't he seen it? He knew Rob had suffered another setback late last winter and that he'd chosen to stay at the cabin with Maddie this summer rather than follow the sheep up the mountain, but he hadn't realized it was this serious.

"When?"

"After the baby comes and is old enough to travel. I imagine it'll be sometime in early October. Time enough to cull the herd and send the wethers to market."

"The boys leaving too?" Rob's two brothers had come out about a year ago to help Rob with the sheep. The two had become proficient herders, enough so that Rob had left them in camp on their own this summer.

"George says he'd like to stay. Hire out to another rancher. Fred will go home when Ma does." They'd arrived at the pen where Rob had corralled fifteen or more three-month-old lambs. A lean-to shed provided shelter from the sun. Not many sheep ranchers would spend the time and effort for the runts and orphans, but with a small herd like Rob's, every birth counted. Rob pointed toward the far side of the pen. "There's the lamb I was talking about. Over there by the shed. I'd say it was something she ate, but she's had the same feed as the others, and none of them are showing any signs of trouble."

Jackson crossed the corral and knelt beside the lamb. "Now then, little missy. Let's see what ails you." He lifted her head and examined her mouth. Cool. A little drool. Her stomach was definitely distended. "She's been dumpy, you say?"

"Yes. Just in the last few days. Lays around. Doesn't run and play like the others."

He pushed on her distended belly. "Looks like she's blocked to me. An injection of soapy water should do the trick, but you could also mix castor oil with some oats and see that she eats it the next couple of days. If that doesn't do the trick, let me know."

Rob squatted next to him. "How much soap?"

"Put a bar in a basin of hot water until the water gets cloudy. Let it cool until it's just warm, then squirt it up her with a syringe. I'll do it for you if you'd like."

"Naw. I'll take care of it after everyone leaves. This is a party. You came to enjoy the food and fellowship, not give a lamb an enema."

Jackson gave a hard stare and inched his left eyebrow up a bit.

Rob laughed and pushed to his feet, holding out a hand to help Jackson up. "I know. You'd rather stay here with the sheep, but Maddie will miss us. And Claire won't thank me for keeping you from her side."

As if Claire had even noticed he was gone. Seems like the more he wanted her to notice him, the less she did. Jackson brushed the dust off his pants and followed Rob from the corral. He was going to miss this. Miss Rob. For the past two years, he'd been helping him learn to be a sheepherder while Rob, in turn, had been teaching him to be a man of faith. They might be an unlikely pair, but they were friends, and Jackson didn't have so many friends he was willing to lose one.

As they walked toward the gate, Rob stopped him with a hand on his arm. "Before we head back, there's something else I wanted to talk to you about. In fact, it's why I really pulled you away from the party. Baldwin mentioned you might be ready to start a herd of your own. Would you be interested in buying me out? After market, I figure I'll have around 2000 head. I'd be willing to sell them to you for an even $5000. You could give me half the money when you take them over and the other half after sheering in the spring."

Jackson couldn't believe what he was hearing. He'd all but given up hope of buying any of Baldwin's herd, given the losses the man had suffered this summer. He'd figured he'd have to pay full-market value in Lander and start building his herd slowly, but here was Rob offering him a full herd for under-market value. "That's mighty generous. You know you could easily get $5500-$6000 for them."

"Maybe. But there's no one I'd rather have them than you."

Jackson understood. A good sheepherder became pretty attached to his herd. Rob had always been a good sheepherder, even early on when he was as green as the spring grass.

"I'll take your offer if you let me pay $5300. I'll give you $3000 now and the rest in the spring."

Rob held out his hand. "Deal."

Jackson took the handshake, not even trying to hide his grin. He was a stock owner. He already had the $3000 saved. He could quit his job with Baldwin tomorrow if he wanted to. But he wouldn't. He would keep his commitment to his old boss through the summer, but knowing that he'd accomplished his dream, that a ranch of his own was a reality, was a heady feeling. He couldn't wait to tell Claire.

Claire. Wait. Should he tell her?

Now he'd reached his goal and no longer needed Baldwin's approval, would she stay, or would she see this as an opportunity to leave? She'd promised him six months, and technically, he wouldn't have the sheep until October. Could he still convince her to stay until then? Lord, he hoped so. He needed more time if he were to convince her to stay permanently. He knew his chance of that was a long shot, but why not? One of his dreams had come true today. Why not dream some more?

CHAPTER 26

Hooves clattered against rocks as Claire urged Boaz up the steep incline after Duchess and Jackson. She shouldn't be here, but what she *should* do and what she *did* do were becoming more and more at odds these days.

"Want to come with me to find some wild horses?" Jackson had asked two nights ago as they sat on the porch watching sunset and dusk settle over their valley.

"Yes." The response had slipped out before she had a chance to think. For a moment, she'd felt like herself again—the girl she was before Jonas—the adventure-seeking, confident one who never took no for an answer. She hadn't seen that girl in a long, long time. Part of her welcomed her return, but a larger part of her cautioned against it. She'd learned the hard way that grabbing what you wanted without counting the consequences came at a cost.

There were so many reasons not to take Jackson up on his offer—Ella, for one, as well as her duties at home. The biggest reason was her ever-growing need to distance herself from Jackson. Still, for some reason, his invitation, coupled with a hint of a challenge in his magnetic eyes, was impossible to resist.

So, they had solicited Granny and Sadie to take Ella for a few days and set off for the mountains on their own this morning. The hazy purple of the Wind River Mountain range had been beckoning her for months. They'd spent the morning climbing steadily through foothills and lower mountain meadows, but now she could finally say she was in the mountains. Even though she'd lived in Denver for the last two years, she'd never seen mountains this close. They were harsher than she'd expected, jagged and craggy. Traces of snow still hugged the ridges and divots of some of the higher peaks.

She followed Jackson over a ridge and down into a meadow dotted with wildflowers. Since lunch, they'd been tracking along a stream that Jackson said led to a small lake where he'd recently seen a band of horses. Now that their path had widened, she cantered Boaz so she could ride abreast with Jackson.

"Do you think the horses will still be there?"

"Hope so. It's Hippolyta's band. Some of the prettiest and healthiest mares I've seen."

"Hippolyta? Like Queen of the Amazons?"

A slight flush crept up Jackson's neck. "Yep. That's what Louis and I named her when we first ran across her six years ago. Seemed to fit. A band of beautiful mares. Strong. Independent. I told Louis that I was coming back to get them when I had my own ranch."

"Will you try to capture all of them?"

"Not this trip. There are around twenty horses in her band. I'd be happy to bring home one this time. Train that one first, and then maybe go back for more. We'll see. Hippolyta's been around these mountains for a long time. She's a crafty one and won't be easy to catch. I'm hoping some of the younger ones might be if she lets us get close enough."

"Have you captured wild horses before?"

"A few times. Ranchers around here tend to build their stock that way. Feral horses are free for the taking if you know how to capture and train them."

Their path narrowed as they followed the stream into a valley. She pulled Duchess back to walk single file behind Jackson again. Claire didn't mind the silence. She reveled in the beauty around her, the glimpses of mountain peaks through the trees, the rippling of the stream as it flowed over the rocks, the sharp scent of pine. Her soul drank in the calm.

A low rumbling in the distance drew her attention. Was that thunder? *Please, God, no. Not today.* But when they broke into the open again ten minutes later, she could see dark thunderheads building over the mountain range to the west.

"Is it going to storm?" She tried to mask the panic building inside.

"Looks that way. Don't worry. There's a spot up ahead where we can shelter. We should get there before the rain starts."

"What if we don't?"

Jackson glanced back at her, a slight grin on his face. "What's the matter? Afraid of getting wet?"

He had no idea what she was afraid of, but he might soon find out.

No. She could do this. She *could* keep it together. It was just rain. Nothing more.

A flash up ahead and another rumble sent all her assurances flying. Lightning. Still a way off, but . . . *lightning.* She urged Boaz forward, concentrating on taking slow, deep breaths. In. Out. In. Out. Her heart raced, disregarding any attempt on her part to control it.

"Can't you go any faster?"

Jackson glanced back again, his grin fading to perplexity. "Are you all right?"

No. And she would be even less than all right if they didn't make that shelter soon. "Just hurry. Please?"

He kicked Duchess into a trot, and she followed suit. Soon, Jackson pointed to a rocky ridge about a quarter-mile ahead.

"We'll need to climb a little in case the stream rises, but about halfway up that ridge is an outcropping we can use for shelter."

She didn't wait for whatever else he had to say. Lying low on Boaz's neck, she urged him into a gallop. Duchess ran right beside her, the staccato of both horses' hooves beating in time with her heart. Jackson shouted for her to slow down when she reached the rocky face of the ridge, but she ignored him. Instead, she pushed Boaz forward. He navigated the first boulder with ease, but seconds later, his foot slipped on some loose shale, bringing him to his knees. Claire pitched forward, somersaulting over his head and onto the rocks just as another clap of thunder reverberated through the canyon. Screaming, she curled into a fetal position and let the tremors take over her body.

"Claire! Are you hurt? Claire!" Jackson's voice sounded as if it were miles away. She didn't even try to answer. Squeezing her eyes shut, she gave in to the voices.

Blew his boots right off him.

What is she doing in here? This is no place for a child.

Afraid of thunder? Don't be such a baby. Fitzgeralds don't show fear. I should just leave you out here until you can stop this ridiculous shaking.

But she couldn't. Stop the shaking. It was as if her body had a mind of its own. She clenched her jaw and tightened her muscles, but the tremors continued. She felt strong arms wrap around her and pull her close.

"It's all right. I've got you." A low voice murmured in her ear.

Papa? No, of course not. Papa was gone. The arms tightened and cradled her as they lifted her up and carried her. A splash of cold water hit her cheek, then another. She turned her head into the broad chest smelling of sun-dried linen and leather. Jackson.

Somehow just knowing he held her brought her calm. Breathe in. Breathe out. She felt him stoop low, then set her down. She opened her eyes to see they were in a shallow alcove carved into the side of the ridge. An outcropping of rock above them sheltered them from the rain, which had advanced from mist to a gentle sprinkle. This must be the shelter he had mentioned.

Jackson squatted next to her. "Are you doing all right? Did you hurt yourself when you fell?"

She'd all but forgotten her tumble from her horse. She sat a little straighter. "No. I mean . . . nothing major. A bruise or two I might feel in the morning."

"Good. I should go back to get our packs and check on the horses before the rain comes down in earnest."

Suddenly, a lightning flash lit the sky followed almost directly by a boom so loud it echoed off the rocks around them. A scream tore from her throat. She clutched at Jackson's arm. "No. Don't leave me."

The tremors were back with a vengeance rippling through her body in waves. She couldn't breathe. Couldn't think. She was going to die. They were both going to die.

Jackson pulled her into his lap, cradling her body between his knees and chest.

"Hush now. Shhhh. It's all right. Everything's going to be all right. I've got you. We're safe." He rocked back and forth, gently stroking her hair, her back.

She curled into him, listening to the steady beat of his heart, letting that sound drown out everything else—the rain, coming down in torrents now, the occasional claps of thunder. She squeezed her eyes shut and focused on that one sound. The sound of life. Blub, blub. Blub, blub. Count the beats. Steady. Slow. Breathe in. Breathe out.

Words her mother used to whisper on stormy nights came back to her. *The Lord is my rock, my fortress, my deliverer. My God is my rock, in whom I take refuge . . .*

Breathe in. Breathe out. *Please, God, don't let me die.*

SHE WOKE TO THE SMELL OF WOOD FIRE AND THE CLATTER OF TIN. For a moment, she struggled to get her bearings. Rock surrounded her. Jackson stirred something in a pot over an open fire. Ah, yes. The mountains. The storm. The panic. How long had she been asleep? Rain pattered outside their little alcove, but the storm's intensity was gone.

As she struggled to sit up, Jackson turned to her. "Feeling better?"

She nodded. She could hardly feel any worse than before. What must he think? She pushed the hair out of her face, realizing her chignon was far more down than up. She pulled out the remaining hairpins and brushed through the tangles with her fingers. She must look as crazy as she'd acted.

"What time is it?"

"Around seven. May as well camp here tonight and get a fresh start in the morning. Hungry?"

"Starving. What are you making?"

"Depends on who you ask. Cookie, Baldwin's range cook, calls it Bouillabaisse. Like giving it some fancy French name makes it special, but most of us just call it fish stew. Ain't nothing fancy, just fresh fish and whatever we might have on hand in our tins. Tonight, it's tomatoes, corn, and onions."

"Smells good. But where'd you get fish?"

"Caught a couple of trout in the creek while you were sleeping."

Apparently, he'd been busy doing a lot of things while she slept. He'd brought their packs and saddles into the shelter, built a fire, and caught some fish. Knowing him, he'd cared for the horses as well.

"Boaz wasn't hurt from his fall, I hope?"

"A few scratches. Nothing serious."

"I'm so sorry. I shouldn't have pushed him so hard. It's just that I . . . well, I'm . . ."

". . . afraid of storms?" Jackson gave her a lopsided smile.

"If there's thunder and lightning, yes."

"Good to know." He filled two bowls with soup, handed one to her with a spoon, then sat down beside her with his back against the rock wall. "I probably should mention that thunderstorms are common in the mountains this time of year, especially in the afternoons. If we go all the way to where the horses run, there's a chance we could have another one, maybe two. Still want to go?"

She blew on her soup and tested its heat. *Did* she want to go on? The thought of living through another experience like today was terrifying, and yet . . . this. Soup made with freshly caught fish cooked over a campfire. The mountains. The adventure. And she wanted to see those wild horses. She wanted that so much. Somehow, giving up on that meant Jonas had won and still had control of her life. That, more than anything, shaped her response.

"Yes. I want to go. Today was bad because I wasn't expecting it. And we were out in the open with nowhere to hide. I'm not always this bad."

"There's an abandoned trapper's cabin I'd planned to use. Not too far from the lake. We can easily make it there before the storms roll in tomorrow. If we make that our home base, do you think it would help?"

"I think it might. I do want to go, Jackson, and I'll try my best not to be such a coward next time."

Jackson swallowed a spoonful of soup, then another. Finally, when she thought he wasn't going to respond at all, he said,

"Being afraid don't make you a coward. Just makes you human. It's what you do with your fear that matters." He turned to look her in the eyes, his gaze steady, serious. "For as long as I've known you, you haven't backed down from anything. But if the thought of another thunderstorm is more than you can handle, we'll go back. Simple as that."

Claire blinked and looked away. If only he wasn't so kind. Did he have any idea how attractive that made him? She swallowed hard. She wasn't going to cry. Not here. Not now.

"Thank you." Despite her efforts, the words came out wobbly. She took another bite of her soup, hoping he hadn't noticed. They finished their meal in silence, then worked together to wash up the dishes and prepare their bedrolls for the night. The rain had stopped, so Jackson went out to check on the horses one more time and returned with an armload of wood.

"Found a couple of branches down under some rocks. They're not perfect but should be dry enough to keep the fire going for the night."

Now that the sun was completely down, she could feel the chill in the air. The mountain air had to be at least ten degrees cooler than the temperature back at their cabin. Though she had a blanket and warm jacket, she'd be glad to have the fire's warmth as well.

They sat watching the flames flicker and pop for a while. The cocoon of the cave wrapped her in safety.

"The first time I saw a dead body, I was five years old," Claire spoke into the silence. She didn't know why, but something compelled her to share this part of her story with Jackson. Maybe talking about where the fear all started would help him understand, at least a little bit.

He turned his head to look at her, his eyes black in the fire's low glow.

"We had just come to live with my mother's parents. My

grandfather was a country doctor, and my father had just grad-uated from medical school. Most of the time, my father and grandfather did their doctoring away from home, traveling to the houses of those who were sick. In emergencies, though, the sick would come to them. Grandpa had a room at the back of the house with a separate door to the outside. The infirmary, he called it.

" I usually stayed in the front rooms, but I remember hearing voices and a lot of commotion coming from that area one evening and must have decided to investigate. A body lay on the examining table covered in a sheet. I knew it was a body because its feet were sticking out. Big, white feet. One of them had a large hole in it, black and charred like someone shot a bullet through it. On the floor beside the table, I saw a pair of worn leather work boots. As I walked closer, I saw one of them had these strange black marks on its inner sole.

"I don't know how long I stood there, staring at those shoes . . . those big, white feet. I couldn't figure out why the man wasn't moving or complaining about the hole in his foot. Finally, Great Aunt Margaret found me and shooed me out. 'No place for a child,' she said. I wondered why until I heard the rest of the grownups talking. Turns out the man on the table was Mr. Patterson, our neighbor, and he was dead."

Jackson leaned forward and threw another log on the fire. "How'd he die?"

"They said a lightning bolt hit him while he was plowing his back field and killed him dead. Struck his right shoulder and went clear through his body. Blew his boots right off him.

"Mr. Patterson was the biggest, strongest man I'd ever seen. I was at his house the week before playing with his daughter, Bessie. I remember Mrs. Patterson scolding him for bringing mud into the house on his boots. He winked at me as he walked back outside to take them off. All I remember thinking that day was how Mrs. Patterson wouldn't be scolding him about the mud on his boots anymore."

Even after all these years, the memory of those big, white feet haunted her. Before that day, she hadn't even known lightning *could* kill. Mr. Patterson was happy, healthy, large as life, and then he was dead. Just because of a bolt of lightning.

"I didn't like storms much after that. When I was little, and a storm would be brewing, I'd run to my room and put my head under my pillow until the storm had passed. I got better as I grew older, but even then, I never really wanted to be outside. If there was going to be a storm, I'd find an excuse to stay home. Stay inside. But that fear was manageable. Then, the summer I turned seventeen,we had a storm to beat all storms. Ever hear of the Great Cyclone of '96?"

"In St. Louis?"

She nodded.

"Read about it. You were there?"

She nodded again. "Father was working at City Hospital by then. I'll never forget the day the cyclone hit. It was so hot and muggy that day. My friend Katie Beth Bentley and I had gone downtown with her mother to shop for new spring hats."

She'd been so young and carefree that summer with little on her mind other than finally wearing her hair up and lengthening her skirts. She and Katie Beth were planning their come-out in December and could talk of little else those days other than parties and boys and dances. If only life had stayed that simple.

"When we came out of Barr's, I noticed the clouds right away. They were dark and heavy, and the sky had a greenish look to it. Mrs. Bentley bustled us into their carriage. We barely made it back to their house before the wind picked up. We all rushed into their basement just as the storm hit. I'll never forget how loud it was. How the walls shook. I thought for sure the whole house was going to come down on us and kill us, like

Samson in the Bible." She shuddered, the terror of that night coming back.

Jackson put his arm around her shoulders, pulling her close. She felt safe, protected. She sat in silence for a few minutes, wishing she could somehow draw the strength of his presence deep into her being.

"Did the house fall in?"

She shook her head. "Not in the basement anyway. When the wind let up, we ventured upstairs. The entire side wall of their kitchen was in shambles. Rain was blowing in torrents into their kitchen and dining room. Thunder and lightning rumbled and flashed. Our house was two blocks over from the Bentleys. I remember taking off at a run. Katie Beth's mom called for me to stop, but I didn't listen. I had to know if Sadie and the others were all right.

"Half of the houses between the Bentley's house and ours were just heaps of rubble, but thankfully our house, which was further south, was intact. The large oak in our front yard was uprooted and resting on our porch roof, and the stable in the back had been hit, but the house was fine other than a few windows that had blown out. Sadie and Mrs. Shaughnessy and Rosie, our housekeeper and maid, were all fine.

"We took in a lot of our neighbors that night, though there were a few who would rather camp outside in the rain than risk coming inside and having a roof fall in on them again. We heard that City Hospital had been hit and feared for Father until a messenger arrived to say he was all right. We didn't see him again for days, though. There were so many people injured. He worked at the hospital non-stop, eating and sleeping there as well. I'll never forget the terror of that night. Fires broke out all over the city from lightning strikes and downed wires. Bells tolled for days honoring the dead.

"Next day, the damage was unbelievable. Trees had snapped like match sticks. Telegraph poles and wires were strewn and twisted all over the roads. Roofs had blown completely off churches and houses. Entire walls, in some cases entire houses, were gone, leaving only heaps of rubble." She gave a short, dry laugh. "A grand piano ended up in the pond at Lafayette Park."

"No kidding? I've been in some bad storms, but nothing like that."

"It was crazy. But, even then, I could handle my fear. I did what I did before. Stayed home when the weather threatened to be bad. Stayed away from windows when there was thunder and lightning. But I never had a full-blown panic attack. Not like I did today. Not until Jonas."

"Jonas?"

"My . . . my first husband. I guess I've never told you about him. He was . . . he was . . ." A monster. But Jackson didn't need to hear that. "He didn't tolerate weakness of any kind. When he realized I was afraid of thunderstorms, he decided he was going to cure me. 'Fitzgeralds don't show fear,' he liked to say." He never had shown fear, anyway. Not around her. "One afternoon, he insisted I come for a drive with him. A storm was building in the west so, of course, I didn't want to go, but he wouldn't take 'no' for an answer. He drove us out past the edge of town to this large empty field. Then, he climbed down and told me to get out. 'Come walk with me,' he said. 'You need to learn to face your fears head on.'"

She could still picture the area. No trees, no buildings, nothing for cover as far as she could see, just dark, threatening clouds. The rain had already been hitting the curricle's top before they'd even stopped.

"I pleaded with him to take me home, but he wouldn't listen, kept insisting I get out. As soon as I stepped down out of the curricle, he hopped back in and slapped the horses into a run. It all happened so fast that I didn't have time to react. I tried running after him, but it was too late. All I could do was watch him disappear over the ridge."

"He left you there?" Jackson's question was more of a growl.

She nodded. "I didn't know what else to do, so I started walking, but the storm was gathering strength, and I hadn't gone very far before the thunder began. One crack sounded so close. I could swear it was right above me. The lightning flash followed almost immediately. I dropped to the ground, rolled up in a ball, and covered my head with my hands. I couldn't think. I couldn't breathe. I just knew I was going to die." She gave Jackson a wry smile. "I probably reacted a lot like I did today."

He reached his free hand over and took hold of hers, entwining his fingers with hers. She felt cocooned in his embrace.

"I can't believe anyone would do that to another person. Did he never come back?" His thumb gently stroked the top of her hand, making it hard for her to concentrate.

"Um, yes. Actually, he did. He probably wasn't gone more than fifteen minutes. It just seemed longer."

When he came back, she'd still been in a heap on the ground, soaked and shivering like a drowned rat. He'd called her a baby and threatened to leave her there all night if she didn't stop shaking, but Jackson didn't need to know that. He didn't need to know any more of the humiliation she'd endured with Jonas. That was over now. Dead, like the man himself.

A vision of Jonas lying in a pool of his own blood came to mind. She shuddered.

Jackson's arm tightened around her. "Five minutes would have been too long. No one should treat another human being like that, especially not his wife. I want you to know–" He was silent so long that she looked up at him. His eyes locked on hers, dark and fervent. "I . . . I can see why you said you didn't want to marry again, but I'd never do anything like that to you. Never. You're safe with me. Do you believe that?"

She fought the desire to reach out and touch his cheek, to

pull him down into a kiss. Turning away, she swallowed against the lump in her throat. A tear slipped out, then another. She pulled her hand from his and brushed them away. Why, oh why, couldn't she have met Jackson first? Dead or not, Jonas would forever come between them.

She leaned forward, pulling away from where his arm still rested across her shoulders. The loss of contact left her cold, numb. "Of course, I believe you." She forced a light tone into her voice. "Don't worry, though. I won't take advantage of your generosity forever. I'll be out of your hair by October. I promise."

"What if I want you to stay?" The words were so soft she almost wasn't sure he'd said them.

She glanced back. His eyes, dark and intense, held her gaze, and pulled her in. With great effort, she made herself answer.

"I . . . I can't, Jackson. I'm sorry." He deserved so much more than a wife who was on the run from the law. She broke the connection and turned away. "I think I'll try to get some sleep now."

She turned to her bedroll, not wanting to look at him again because if she saw any trace of hurt or disappointment on his face, she wouldn't be able to stay strong. And she needed to be strong—for both of them.

JACKSON ROLLED ONTO HIS SIDE AND STARED AT THE DYING embers of the fire. He couldn't sleep. All he could think of was Claire lying mere inches away. She'd felt good in his arms. Too good. He almost wished another storm would roll in so he'd have an excuse to hold her again.

No, that wasn't true. He hated seeing her like that. So panicked. So terrified. That first husband of hers, Jonas, was it? If the man weren't dead, Jackson would be tempted to hunt him down, and give him a taste of his own medicine. He suspected tonight's story was just the tip of the iceberg of all he'd done to Claire.

Treat her like Duchess. Those words were beginning to make a lot more sense. But what if he ran out of time? Just like with Duchess, gaining Claire's trust had been a slow process. What if fall came around and she was still too afraid to stay? Could he really let her go?

She'd opened up to him tonight. A little, anyway. And she hadn't pushed away when he'd held her. It wasn't much, but it was something. Enough to spark a flicker of hope.

He blew out a heavy sigh. He was probably the world's biggest fool for thinking so.

Rolling over onto his back, he stared at the rocky ledge above him. Claire's soft, even breathing taunted him. The fact that she could sleep when just the thought of her lying this close to him aroused a wanting so strong he ached wasn't a good sign.

He sighed again. Tonight was going to be a very long night.

CHAPTER 27

They reached the old trapper's cabin early the next afternoon. It wasn't much, a simple one-room structure, but the roof was sound and would offer protection should another thunderstorm roll in. Claire seemed pleased with it. She'd said very little on their morning ride. Claire wasn't the talker some women were, but today she was abnormally quiet. And that bothered Jackson. Enough, in fact, that he'd tried to find something to say to fill the silence. Tried and failed miserably. It was as if, after telling her he wanted her to stay, anything else he might say seemed irrelevant. Inadequate. So, he hadn't said much of anything at all. It had been a quiet ride.

He stood at the door of the cabin, watching as she set things to rights, swiping dust from the table and chairs and sweeping the floor. Though abandoned by the trappers years ago, the cabin was used as a hunting shelter by most of the local ranchers, so it was still in pretty good shape.

He cleared his throat. "I thought I'd hike over to the lake. See if I can spot any horse sign. Would you like to come?" He didn't expect she would, not after their quiet morning.

"I'd like that. Do you think we'll see any?"

"If not this afternoon, we'll probably see them this evening when they come down for water. We can search out sign, anyway."

She nodded and set aside the broom. "Do I need to bring anything?"

"Just a good pair of eyes. We'll have to walk. Our horses might spook the band, but it's not far."

She hesitated in the doorway, eyes to the sky. "Any chance it might storm?"

"Some. I'll keep a watch out. If I see something building, we'll head back. Like I said, the meadow's not far from here."

They struck out through the trees. Before long, he spotted horse droppings and, a few feet later, hoof prints in a muddy patch left from yesterday's storm. Horses had been through here within the last twenty-four hours. Hopefully, it was Hippolyta's band.

He held a finger to his lips to caution Claire to silence and pointed to the tracks. She nodded, eyes bright, and stepped quietly behind him. They hadn't gone more than a couple of yards when his eyes caught movement in the trees to their left. He held up a hand to stop Claire, then crept slowly in that direction, placing each step carefully so as not to make any noise. He glimpsed a grayish-white form through the branches ahead of them. A rock? No. It was moving.

Creeping forward, he inched back one of the larger branches and peered through. A horse lay on its side, legs waving, belly straining. A foaling mare. A bit late in the season, but not unheard of.

"What's wrong with it?" Claire breathed in his ear.

He pointed to the white birthing sac between the mare's legs and watched Claire's eyes go wide. She nodded her understanding. He turned back to the horse. Something wasn't right. At this point in the birthing, the sac should be moving forward, but much as the mare strained, the sac remained barely visible between her legs. He crept forward to get a better view.

Blast! Only one foreleg protruded beside the foal's head. He'd seen a birth like this only once. Old Hinricks, Baldwin's best horseman, had talked him through it that time, but he'd been Petie's size back then. There was little chance his hand and arm would fit up the birth canal as easily today.

He glanced at Claire. Her slim arm would fit, and as a nurse, she probably wouldn't balk at the thought like many women might. He motioned her back and followed her out onto the trail.

"That foal's coming out wrong. One of the forelegs is folded back inside," he said, keeping his voice low.

"What will happen? Will she still be able to deliver it?"

"She'll probably die first. Unless we intervene. I've seen a birth like this before, but I'll need your help."

She nodded. "Of course."

"It'll be messy, though. And risky. A horse's contractions are mighty strong."

She studied him a minute, one eyebrow lifting when realization set in. "You want me to go inside her?"

"My arm won't fit."

She gave a quick nod and turned back toward the cabin. "Give me a minute. I've got some things in my bag that will help."

Ah. Her nurse's bag. He'd teased her when she packed it into the saddlebags, but she'd been right. You never knew when you'd need first aid on the trail. He just never expected they'd be using her supplies on a horse.

She returned a few minutes later with a bottle of iodine and a jar of petroleum jelly. "Do you think she'll let us near her?"

"Only one way to find out. She looks pretty spent, so I'm hoping. I'll approach her first and let you know if I think it's safe for you to follow."

They retraced their steps. When they reached the clearing where the mare lay, Jackson motioned Claire to stay back. Skirting around, he stepped through the trees close to the mare's head, slowly putting one foot in front of the other. The mare threw her head back and eyed him, the whites of her eyes showing.

"Easy now. Steady. We're here to help." He stopped, waiting to see how she'd react. Another contraction hit, and she huffed a soft moan. He crept closer to her head. "Easy now. Easy." He crouched and gently stroked her neck. Her eye caught his, not as panicked, more pleading than anything as if to say, "make it stop."

He held her gaze. Nodded. Then waved Claire in. "Slowly," he cautioned. "And watch those back legs." He noticed Claire already had her sleeves rolled up and her arms and hands lubricated. She gave the legs a wide birth and squatted behind the mare's tail. The mare took no notice of her.

"First off, you'll need to push the foal's nose back up the birth canal. Go ahead and tear away the sac. It won't hurt the foal, and you'll need to be able to feel the head and leg."

Claire followed his instructions and soon had her arm up to her elbow in the horse's belly. The mare struggled as if to get up, but Jackson settled her by stroking her neck.

"Can you feel the other foreleg?"

"I . . . no . . . wait, yes! I found it."

"Good. Now grasp it just above the fetlock and push the joint up. Imagine a horse taking a step and try to mimic that motion. Then slide your hand down and cup the hoof. Flex the fetlock back. All right. Now slowly bring it forward until the leg is straight. Careful. Don't let the hoof scrape the birth canal."

Claire's face took on a look of intense concentration. She struggled for a second, then two, until finally, "Got it!"

"Good girl. Now pull both legs forward until they are out and rest a minute. We'll see if she can take it from here."

Claire sat cross-legged in the dirt, and they waited through two strong contractions. The nose appeared. Then more straining and the head was two-thirds through.

"She's weakening. Been at this too long, haven't you, girl?" He crooned. "Go ahead. Give her some help. Pull gently but steadily. That's the ticket."

Claire was back on her knees, pulling on both forelegs. The foal advanced, slow, steady. The mare must have felt the progress because she gave another mighty push and the shoulders were through. Within seconds the rest of the foal followed suit. Both horses lay on their sides, exhausted. Jackson inched to his feet and motioned for Claire to follow him back through the trees.

"Best leave them to themselves now," he said. "No telling how the mare will react once she recovers."

Claire nodded, wiping her hands and arms on a towel she'd left beside her supplies. One thing about nurses. They came prepared.

"You did great back there," Jackson said.

"I wouldn't have known what to do without your instructions. We make a good team." She glanced back at the mare. "Do you mind if we watch for a moment?"

He shook his head. "I was kinda hoping you'd say that."

Claire smiled.

Crouching down, they peered through the branches. Both horses still lay on their sides, but the foal's head was now bobbing side to side. A new birth never grew old, no matter how many times he was a part of it.

They sat in silence five or more minutes before the mare began to stir. She'd had a hard time of it, but she had warrior blood in her veins. A few times, she would pick up her head and look back at the foal as if to assure herself it was there. By now, the foal had both forelegs splayed in front of it and was already making feeble attempts to rise. Finally, the mare struggled to her feet, breaking her last connection to the foal. Turning, she began to lick her baby, working its head, then its body. The foal pushed up on spindly legs, an exact replica of its mother, silver-white with a black mane and tail.

Thunder rumbled in the distance, piercing Jackson's concentration. He glanced at Claire, still engrossed in the two horses. No panic evident, but maybe she hadn't heard it.

He gave her a gentle poke with his elbow. "We'd better head back," he said.

"What?"

He tipped his head skyward as another rumble sounded. "Storm's rolling in."

Claire's eyes widened. "Oh."

"Ready?"

She glanced back at the mother and baby. "They'll be all right?"

"Right as rain." Maybe not the best analogy. "They'll be fine. They're used to the elements. Don't worry. That mama horse will know what to do."

Claire pushed to her feet and gathered her supplies. Though the thunder was rumbling closer and sounding more consistent, she still showed no panic.

"You gonna be all right?"

She smiled up at him. "Yes. I think I am. After the thrill of that–l," she gestured toward the mare and its foal. "Nothing else seems to matter."

He knew the feeling. Was glad they shared it. But a raindrop hit his cheek, followed almost immediately by another. He took her free hand and led the way down the trail, the tree branches and undergrowth making it almost impossible to hurry. The rain was coming down harder now, though the trees blocked some of it. Still, he was getting plenty wet.

He glanced back at Claire. "We're almost to the clearing. You want to shelter here until the rain lets up or make a run for it?"

"May as well keep going. I don't think I could get much wetter."

She was wrong. The minute they stepped into the clearing, the heavens opened, and the rain came down in torrents. He broke into a sprint, but Claire tugged on his hand and then let go.

He turned, almost expecting to see her dropping into a fetal position as she had the day before. Instead, she stood with arms outstretched, face to the sky, laughing. Slowly, she began to twirl, faster and faster.

"Look at me, Jackson. I'm invincible."

She twirled into his arms and fell against him, clutching his shoulders to stay upright. She laughed up at him, the rain flowing down her face, glistening in droplets from her eyelashes, plastering wet strands of her hair to her cheeks. He'd never seen her so happy, so alive. So . . . beautiful.

He pulled her close. "Maybe you just needed to replace the bad memories with a good one."

She stilled, eyes widening. "Maybe I did." Determination settled in her eyes. "Maybe I do." Reaching up, she cupped his cheeks and brought his lips to hers.

Shock coursed through his body, then heat. Her kiss was everything he'd imagined. Soft. Sweet. Silky. Intoxicating. He breathed her in, pulling her rain-soaked body against his until there was no space between them. He was liquid and fire all at the same time.

The desperation in her kiss fed his own, making him believe she wanted him as badly as he wanted her, making him believe in forever.

Forever.

Using every ounce of willpower in his body, he pulled back breaking their connection a mere fraction of an inch.

"Claire," her name came out in a hoarse whisper. "What are we doing?"

He rested his forehead against hers, chest heaving.

"What do you mean?" Her voice sounded dazed, breathless. Part of him relished the fact he might be responsible for that.

He lifted his head to look fully into her eyes. "Don't get me wrong. I'm enjoying this. I am. Too much, maybe. Last night you said you couldn't stay. Has that changed?"

He saw the minute clarity set in and hated himself for it. She dropped her arms and stepped back.

"No." Her head drooped. "No. Nothing's changed. I . . . I'm . . . I should . . ." She glanced toward the cabin.

"Go on. I'll check on Boaz and Duchess."

"Jackson . . ."

He ignored the plea in her voice and took off toward the back of the cabin. He couldn't look back. He couldn't waver because, if he did, he'd pull her back into his arms and take whatever she was willing to offer, no matter the consequences. He couldn't afford to let that happen. If forever wasn't in the cards for them, then neither was this. It was that simple. And that hard.

WHAT A MESS SHE'D MADE OF THINGS.

Claire peeled off her sodden shirtwaist and stepped out of her heavy broadcloth skirt. Thank goodness she'd packed an extra shirtwaist and skirt, or she'd have been relegated to wearing her nightgown for the rest of the day. As if she hadn't made this situation awkward enough, parading around in front of Jackson in her nightgown would be the topping on the cake.

Why in the world had she kissed him? Obviously, she hadn't been thinking straight. She'd been feeling invincible. Bringing new life into the world . . . that sweet baby foal. The joy of that experience had spilled over, making her laugh at the storm, laugh at her past.

And kiss Jackson.

But what a glorious kiss it had been, as exciting and perfect as all her girlhood dreams, dreams that had died on her wedding night with Jonas.

Maybe you just needed to replace the bad memories with a good one. His words replayed in her mind. They'd made such sense in the moment, but at what cost? She groaned, remembering the hurt in Jackson's eyes when she'd told him nothing had changed. Because it hadn't. Much as she might want to, she couldn't erase the past. The fact was, she was a fugitive. If she decided to stay here with Jackson, make theirs a real marriage like he'd asked, she'd have to tell him the truth. She couldn't start a real marriage with a lie. And if she told him, one of two things would happen.

Being the honest man he was, he would probably insist on her coming clean and turning herself in to the authorities. If it had been just her, she'd have done it long ago. But she couldn't let Sadie's life be ruined. She couldn't allow her sister to pay for a crime that was essentially all her fault. And she *wouldn't* leave Ella without a mother. Not if she could help it.

The only other option would be if Jackson agreed to keep their secret. Not likely. And if he did, then Jackson would cease to be the man of integrity she'd come to love.

Love? Wait. No. She didn't *love* him. That was dangerous thinking. But she had come to care for him. Very much. And because she did, she couldn't ... *wouldn't* ... embroil him in her mess. No matter how much it might hurt him for her to leave, he was better off without her ... without all of them.

But, oh, it was going to be hard to say goodbye.

She pulled the pins from what was left of her bun and wrapped her long curls in her damp towel, squeezing out as much moisture as possible. It would be a mess to comb as tangled as it was, but she needed to hurry so Jackson could change out of his wet things. Earlier, Jackson had rigged a blanket on a wire to conceal the side of the cabin that held the one cot, giving her a level of privacy, but she knew he wouldn't venture in until he knew she was dressed. She tried to pull her comb through the rat's nest of curls, then gave up.

Rain still pattered against the metal roof of the cabin. Striding to the door, she pulled it open and called Jackson's name. There was no need for their both catching a chill and getting sick just because she'd created an awkward situation.

A minute later, he stood in the doorway. Lord. How could she have forgotten how his wet shirt clung to the muscles in his chest and shoulders, how his gorgeous blue eyes looked almost black when he looked at her, how his lips . . . his lips.

She turned and almost ran toward the stove. "You should change out of your wet things." Why did she sound so panicked? "I'll get a fire started."

"Claire."

She waved him toward the curtained alcove. "Change first. You don't want to catch a chill."

She heard him sigh, then cross the floor and pull back the curtain. Only then did she release the breath she'd been holding. This was impossible. How on earth was she to survive this night if just looking at Jackson made her want to throw herself into his arms and forget all about her past? With trembling fingers, she began tearing the sheets of the newspaper she found piled beside the kindling box and wadding them into balls.

Concentrate on the task at hand, not on the man behind the curtain. Taking a deep breath, she arranged the wads of paper along the bottom of the stove and placed kindling on top.

Stack the logs. Open the flu. Strike the match.

As the fire leaped to life, she closed the door to the firebox. She'd heat some water. Boil some tea. Yes, tea would be good. Warming and calming both. Lord knows, she could use some calm.

"Claire."

She jumped at the sound of her name by her right ear. "Jackson. I didn't hear you come up."

He gave a rueful grin and pointed to his feet. "Bare feet are quieter, I guess. Can't put my boots back on until they dry a bit."

Bare feet. Great. Did every part of this evening have to feel so intimate? But she understood his plight. Had she not packed a second pair of thick wool socks, she would be barefoot as well. Wouldn't that have been cozy? She turned away and began filling the teapot from the bucket of spring water he'd set on the counter earlier.

"I thought I'd make some tea. Do you want some?"

"Any coffee?"

"I'll check." She placed the kettle on the burner, then opened the small cupboard beside the stove. After rummaging for a few minutes, she pulled out a small sack of Arbuckle's Ariosa.

"Looks like you're in luck. Not sure how fresh it is."

"Doesn't matter. Long as it's hot."

She busied herself at the counter, measuring the coffee into a battered tin pot and arranging their two cups. Then rearranging them. Then digging in the cupboard for sugar. Anything to keep from looking at him.

"Can you come sit a minute? We should talk."

No. No, they shouldn't. No amount of talking was going to solve this. And the fact that Jackson, man of few words, thought they *should* talk made it all the more uncomfortable.

"Claire?"

He wasn't giving up. Fine. She pulled out a chair across the table from him and sat, forcing herself to meet his eyes.

"I don't know what got into me out there." Might as well broach the topic head on. "The rain . . . the adrenaline . . . I'm . . . I'm sorry."

"I'm not complaining." He gave a boyish smile. "Should I apologize for kissing you back?"

"No. I mean . . . No. I didn't . . . it was . . ." Her cheeks burned so hotly he could probably feel their heat across the table.

"Claire. You don't need to be afraid. I told you last night, I'll never do anything to hurt you, and I mean it." He reached out to cover her hand, which she hadn't realized until then she'd been tapping repeatedly against the table. His touch sent a jolt through her. She swallowed hard and looked away.

Afraid? She almost laughed. He thought she was afraid of him? Maybe she should be, given her past, but she'd never felt anything but safe with Jackson. No. The only person she was afraid of was herself. She couldn't allow this attraction she had for him to continue. It was fruitless, and it needed to stop.

She pulled her hand away and stood up. "I'm not afraid of you, Jackson. It's just . . ." She walked to the stove where the teapot was whistling and took it off the burner. She continued talking with her back to him. It was easier that way. "Although my first marriage is in the past, the consequences of that marriage are not. I can't explain it. Just try to understand. Those consequences will always stand between us. I can never have a real marriage with you. With anyone."

"He hurt you."

"Yes. Often." She risked a glance back at him. His face was ashen. His jaw clenched.

"If he weren't already dead, I think I could kill him for that." His voice came out low and raw.

"No, you wouldn't. You couldn't. You're not like him, Jackson. That's what I lo—like about you. That's also why I can't stay. You're too good of a man to get caught up with me. You deserve someone as good and pure as you are."

She heard the scrape of his chair, and then his hands were on her shoulders. Gently, he turned her. Using the tip of his knuckle to lift her chin, he forced her to look him in the eyes.

"Listen to me. Not a single one of us is good and pure without the grace of God and the sacrifice of our Savior. So, don't you let me hear you saying anything about who deserves what. You are a smart, beautiful, courageous, loyal, amazing woman, and any man would be lucky to call you his wife. I know I am. And that's why I'm asking you to give us a chance. I know you're not ready to promise anything permanent. I won't push you. I'll never demand anything from you that you aren't willing to give. I just want you to give us time. Don't leave this fall. Stay through the winter. If you still feel you can't leave your first marriage in the past by next spring, then I won't try to stop you. I promise. I'll let you go. Please, Claire? Can't you give us a little more time?"

Try as she might, she couldn't stop the tears from falling. If only. She swallowed against the thickness in her throat.

"I'll think about it, Jackson. I will. But I can't promise anything tonight."

Cupping her face with both hands, he wiped her tears with his thumbs. "I'm not asking you to promise. All I'm asking is for six more months. Just consider it."

When she nodded, he pressed a kiss to her forehead, then stepped back, dropping his hands to his sides.

"Time for coffee?"

She gave a watery laugh. "And tea."

She turned back to the stove.

Six months. The idea was tempting. Too tempting. To not have to worry about finding a job or a place for the three of them to live for another six months? But at what cost? She wasn't sure she was strong enough to leave Jackson today. How much more pain would an additional six months cost them? A million reasons told her she couldn't stay. But her heart didn't want to listen to any of them.

CHAPTER 28

C laire crept along behind Jackson in the semi-darkness of predawn. They were back on the trail of the wild horses heading toward the lake they didn't get to yesterday. The mare and her foal were a good indication there were horses in the area, so Jackson's plan today was to get to the lake before dawn, when the horses were most likely to come down for water.

After their talk yesterday, things had settled back into a more normal pattern between the two of them. Ever patient, Jackson hadn't brought up the topic of her staying again. They'd prepared and eaten supper in comfortable companionship, made their plans for today's excursion, and sought their beds early. Given the unsettled battle between her heart and mind, she'd thought she might have trouble sleeping, but the whirligig of emotions from the last two days must have worn her out. Seemed as if she'd barely hit her pillow before Jackson was shaking her awake and asking if she still wanted to join him on his hunt for the horses.

Of course, she had. She didn't know what it was about this band of wild horses, but ever since Jackson had told her of their existence, she had longed to see them. Maybe it was the thought of their freedom, or maybe it was their elusiveness. Whatever it was, she hoped Hippolyta's band was truly in the area, and they'd catch a glimpse of it today.

Pre-dawn was lighter than she'd anticipated. As long as she kept a close eye out for rocks in the path, she was able to follow Jackson through the forested area quite easily. Before long, they broke through the trees into an open meadow. In the distance, a heavy mist hung between them and a ridge of tall rocky cliffs.

Jackson pointed toward it and whispered. "That's the lake over there. The horses should come down out of those mountains as the sun rises. Once we get to the lake, we'll try to skirt around it until we find a place to hide in the trees on the other side. Wind's in our favor, so hopefully, they won't smell us when they come down to drink. Just follow me."

They set off across the meadow, picking their way between boulders that glowed white in the dim light. Soon they reached the band of trees that flanked the lake. Jackson struck off to the left. Claire could see the edge of the water now, though the mist still hung heavy on its dark surface. She picked her way over fallen logs and through heavy branches until Jackson motioned for her to hunker down beside him behind a large boulder at the water's edge.

Jackson leaned close and spoke softly in her ear, his warm breath sending a shiver through her. "There's a narrow passage between those two cliffs." He pointed to the rocky ridge in front of them. "The horses should come through any minute now. *If* they come. Don't make a sound."

She zeroed in on the dark area Jackson had pointed to and waited. Birds called to each other in the trees around them. Water lapped on the shore. And then, out of the mist, a shadow gradually took the shape of a horse. One first, then another, until a slow parade of shadow horses made their way down the mountain to the shoreline. Claire held her breath.

They were beautiful.

Otherworldly.

Like phantoms in the pale morning light.

Sunlight slowly filled the valley, burning off the mist and revealing a band of horses in a variety of colors. Blacks, bays, sorrels, and every shade in between. And there, just at the water's edge, a mare and her tiny colt, both silver with black manes and tails.

She nudged Jackson and pointed. He nodded, and they shared a grin. The colt teetered on spindly legs and gingerly dipped its nose in the water. It's first morning drink! She couldn't be prouder if it were her own child. They'd done this. She and Jackson. Took two creatures from the brink of death and gave them life in this magnificent valley.

"Hippolyta's band?" she murmured.

Jackson nodded and pointed to a magnificent sorrel mare with black mane and tail that stood a few feet from the others, surveying the herd like the queen she was. While the others frolicked in the water, drinking, splashing, and kicking at each other, she kept a lookout, her ears constantly moving forward and back. Did she sense they were there?

Claire could have watched the herd for hours, but after a few minutes Jackson breathed in her ear again. "I'm going to try to make it to that outcropping over there." He pointed to some rocks at the edge of the trail where the horses had entered the valley. "If I make it without them spooking, head back toward the break in the trees where we came in. Make whatever commotion you want to let them know you're there. They should head back the way they came. I'm going to try to rope one when they go by."

"Do you know which one you want?"

"Hippolyta's filly." He pointed to a pretty young sorrel standing a few feet from the mare.Her mane and tail flaxen, whereas her mother's were black.

Claire was a little disappointed he wasn't going to try for

Moonshadow and Lightning. Yes, she'd named them already. But she also understood why he'd chosen a healthy young filly over an older mare and her fragile foal.

"Good luck," she murmured as Jackson took off. He eased himself quietly into the trees and disappeared into the forest. She didn't know how he did it, but she couldn't even hear a footstep as he left. Not the crack of a branch or a slipping rock. Only bird song.

Minutes later, he appeared on the far shore, inching his way up the rocks toward the outcropping. None of the herd seemed to notice. Hippolyta was facing away from him. The others were busy pawing at the water, drinking, and eating from the vegetation along the shoreline. As Jackson stretched out along the top of the outcropping, Claire eased to her feet and started back the way they had come. She wasn't nearly as silent as Jackson, but when she came to the clearing in the trees, the herd was still as she'd left it.

She let out a high-pitched whoop and threw one of the largest rocks she could find into the water. The far shore erupted as Hippolyta reared, turned, and led the herd back toward the jagged cliffs. Claire held her breath as Jackson rose, swinging his rope above his head and aiming it into the multi-colored stream of writhing bodies. How could he even see the filly in all the chaos? Dust raised by dozens of pounding hooves obscured her view.

When it cleared, the shoreline was empty, and Jackson stood, gripping the end of his rope with all his might. At the other end, the sorrel filly pitched and bucked, but the line held tight. When she settled, Jackson wrapped his end of the rope around his waist and tied it. Claire guessed he was securing it to free his hands for his descent.

Just then, a flash of black raced along the opposite shoreline. The largest horse Claire had ever seen headed straight for the filly, snorting and nipping at the young horse's legs. The filly reared, knocking Jackson onto his back and dragging him across the ledge as she tried to run. He was going to be dragged off the outcropping. If the fall didn't kill him, the hooves of the two horses below surely would.

Claire screamed, a high-pitched, blood-curdling scream that bounced off the walls of the cliffs and echoed back across the lake. Both horses stilled, the black's ears flicking forward and back. She screamed again, and the black took off up the path and through the narrow opening between the cliffs where the others had disappeared. The filly tried to follow, but by this time, Jackson was able to sit up and grab onto the rope with both hands. His heels dug in and held. The filly gave a few more kicks, then stood still.

Claire hitched up her skirts and took off at a run back the way she'd come, hurdling rocks and logs. By the time she broke through the trees on the other side, Jackson had already climbed off his perch and was slowly bridging the distance between him and the sorrel. Claire stopped to catch her breath and watched him work. He kept the rope slack, allowing the filly to run circles around him as he slowly drew closer.

She'd seen him use the same technique while working Duchess in the round pen at home. Soon he was at the filly's head, stroking her neck and murmuring in her ear. A tremor stuttered along the young horse's body and flank, but she held still. Turning, Jackson started walking slowly toward Claire. The sorrel followed. When they reached her side, Claire wanted to let out a victory cheer. Instead, she kept her voice low.

"We got her."

Jackson grinned. "We got her."

Tentatively, Claire reached out and touched the filly's shoulder. "She's beautiful."

"Yes."

"That black horse. The one that charged you. Who was that?"

"Theseus. The stallion. It's his harem."

"I thought you said it was Hippolyta's band?"

"It is. The lead mare's always the one in charge. She keeps Theseus around for one thing and one thing only." A slight flush stained his cheeks. "Well, that's not entirely true." His smile turned sheepish. "He also provides protection."

"I'll say. He about knocked you off that rock."

"Yeah." He caught her gaze, the intensity in his eyes drawing her like a magnet. "Thanks for that scream, by the way. That was some quick thinking."

Was it wrong to want to kiss a man so badly it ached? When had Jonas ever thanked or praised her for anything? She forced herself to break free from his gaze, looking at the filly instead.

"What will you name her?"

"I don't know yet. I'm thinking something simple, like Belle."

"What?" She turned back to him in mock horror. "And break with your family's tradition of biblical and mythical names?"

"I've already broken tradition."

"How's that?"

"She's a girl."

Oh. Well, yes. There was that. But still.

"You can't name her Belle. Not when you've already named her parents Hippolyta and Theseus. She needs a name in keeping with her heritage."

"Like what?"

"Merope? Maia?"

He shook his head. "Maybe Blanche."

"Blanche! You should be ashamed putting a name like Blanche with this beauty. How about Callisto? I've always thought that was a beautiful name."

"Naw. Maybe Gertrude. We could call her Trudy."

"Now you're just being ornery. You know you're not going to name her Gertrude."

He laughed. "Come on. We better get back to the trapper's

cabin if we want to be out of the mountains before the daily showers hit."

She didn't want to leave. Even the threat of another storm wasn't great enough to make her want to go. If only they could live out here, wild and free, like Hippolyta and her band. Just her and Jackson. No barriers. No past. No lawmen. No guilt.

But that would mean abandoning Ella and Sadie. She could never do that. But maybe, just maybe, she *could* stay with Jackson through the winter. Six more months. Was that really too much to ask, God? What could it really hurt if they stayed six more months?

CHAPTER 29

Claire sank into her rocker on the front porch and fanned herself with her hand. What she wouldn't give for a breeze right now. Even a slight one. But the laundry was done for another week. And, despite the heat, she was glad to be back outside. She pushed the rocker languidly back and forth, content for the moment to just sit and watch Ella, who was busy with her own wash day activities.

Her daughter sat a few feet away, dark curls bent over a child-sized tub where she scrubbed at a pile of doll's clothes. She hummed while she worked, hanging each tiny garment on the makeshift line they'd strung across the end of the porch. Ella's dress was about as wet as the clothes she was washing, but it was a hot day. The dampness wouldn't hurt anything.

In fact, Claire was tempted to join her. Had the water been colder, she might have. Maybe later, they would both walk over to the pump by the barn and wash their hands and faces in the ice-cold water from the well. Yes. It was good to be free from their self-imposed confinement.

She was probably being a ninny, but what she'd seen, or thought she'd seen, from her kitchen window two mornings ago had spooked her. At first, she'd thought it was just a shadow moving amongst the chokecherries down by the stream. A man-shaped shadow, to be sure, but probably nothing more than a play of shadow and sunshine off the branches of the trees. She tended to be jumpier when Jackson was gone. Regardless, she'd kept Ella inside most of that day. Then, she'd discovered a man-sized footprint in the mud next to the stream later that evening, just a few feet from where she'd seen the shadowy form. She'd taken Ella to the house, locked the door, and hadn't ventured out again until this morning.

Thank goodness Jackson had installed a lock on the door on his last trip home. He'd told her he wanted her to feel safe while he was away. She hadn't mentioned anything about her fears. About how the cabin seemed so vulnerable and isolated when-ever he was away. About how the nights were endless and filled with strange noises. Somehow, he just knew. One more example of the man's observant nature and thoughtfulness. One more reason for her to be looking for a new place to go. She was becoming far too complacent. Too open to the idea of staying with him through the winter. The man by the stream was a good reminder of how she couldn't afford to let her guard down.

The creak and rumble of a wagon drew her attention to the canyon road that ran the length of the valley. She was about to call Ella to come inside when she recognized the horses. It was hard to mistake Castor and Pollux for any other team, but instead of Petie at the reins, Jackson's father turned the horses down their lane. No mistaking that beard for anyone else's.

Claire hadn't seen him since the housewarming. Based on their past interactions, she didn't figure he planned to visit. Maybe he didn't know Jackson was gone. The wagon was loaded with hay bales and grain sacks, so she supposed he was simply dropping off some feed for Jackson. She hoped he'd simply take the supplies to the barn and be on his way. Petie, who usually made the deliveries, would always stop to talk, but there was no need for him to do so.

She raised her hand in a brief wave as he drove by on his way to the barn. He gave no response. Good. He wasn't likely to stop for a chat, then. And she certainly wasn't going to seek him out. She'd waved. She'd done her part. He couldn't say she hadn't tried.

Fifteen minutes later, he drove his empty wagon back up the lane, pulling to a stop in front of them. Drat. He was getting down. What in the world was she going to say to him? He didn't strike her as a man who liked small talk.

As he dropped into the rocker Jackson usually occupied, Ella came over and stood at his knee.

"Are you Jackson's Daddy?"

"Yes."

"Jackson's away."

"Figured as much."

"Did you come to see him?"

"Nope. Came to talk to your mama."

Ella tilted her head to one side. "And me?"

"Mostly your mama."

"We've been doing wash." She pointed to her washbasin at the end of the porch.

He glanced at the tiny clothesline and its tiny occupants. "I can see that."

"Maybe you should finish your laundry, sweetie, while Mr. Garrity and I talk."

Ella pursed her lips and placed two chubby fists on her hips.

"Ella." Claire made her voice stern.

With an obvious pout, Ella made her way back to her wash, but she was humming again within seconds. Mr. Garrity rocked back and forth, watching Ella at the washbasin, expression inscrutable. Why didn't he say something? He said he was here to talk.

Finally, she could stand the silence no longer. "My, it's been hot lately, hasn't it?"

Mr. Garrity turned his gaze her way, eyes hard as agates, their midnight blue so like his son's but their expression so very different.

"Had a visitor the other day."

So, no small talk. "Oh?"

"Ever heard of a Mrs. Dempsey?"

Claire felt the blood drain from her face.

"Hmmm. Looks like you have. I don't know who this Mrs. Dempsey is. Don't want to know, in fact. But there's a Pinkerton detective in the area looking for her. Seems to think she might be traveling with two other ladies and a child. Said their names are Anna and Gabriella Fitzgerald and Sarah Rose Montgomery. His description for Mrs. Dempsey didn't ring a bell, but the picture he showed me of Anna and Sarah Rose did. Any reason that might be?"

Claire swallowed hard and forced a shrug.

His stare was relentless. "I sent him packing. Said no one by those names had been seen around here. With any luck, any other folks he may have talked to told him the same. People around here tend to take care of their own. Just to be safe, I had Petie follow him when he left our place. Said he got on the stage heading west yesterday without talking to anyone else. Maybe he'll be back. Maybe he won't. But here's what I came to say. I knew you were trouble from the day I met you. I don't give a rat's ass who Mrs. Dempsey is or how she's connected to you. What I do care about is how it affects my son. If there's trouble following you and it in any way can hurt him, then maybe it's time you moved along."

He was right. They had to leave. The man in the trees had to have been the same man who visited the Garrity ranch. She was glad now she hadn't ventured outdoors after seeing him down there, but what if he had seen her or Ella before she'd seen him?

But, if he had, why would he have left? The fact he had tracked them here, so many miles from any railroad, was unsettling. Could it be a coincidence, or were he and maybe others following all travel routes from Denver? No. That was ridiculous. Surely, they didn't have that many men or that amount of time to put toward this one case.

No. Somehow, he'd followed their trail. And somehow, he knew their real names. Mrs. Dempsey was still a red herring, but he knew they were connected to her. He'd be back. It was only a matter of time. He'd connected too many links. Eventually, someone was going to give them up.

They hadn't even lasted six months.

She glanced at the man beside her. Did the panic show on her face? Most likely. He watched her as if he could read her innermost thoughts.

She cleared her throat. Attempted a smile. "Thanks for letting me know. Did he . . . um . . . did he mention why he was looking for these women?"

"I'm figuring you would know more about that than I would. All I want to know is this. If he was to come back, would it mean trouble for my son?"

She held his gaze. "No. If he comes back, your son will not be in any danger at all."

She wished she could say the same for herself and Sadie. They'd have to leave. Part of her wanted to rush into the house right now, pack her and Ella's bags and run, but given it had only taken five months for someone to track them to this Godforsaken place, where would they go? One thing was certain. They had to have a better plan. And better disguises.

Mr. Garrity pushed to his feet. "I'll be on my way, then."

"Could I ask a favor of you?"

He turned and looked down at her, face like stone.

"Could you tell my sister I'd like her to come visit when she gets a chance?"

"I'll have Petie bring her tomorrow."

She felt her cheeks redden under his piercing stare. "Th . . . Thank you."

After he left, Ella climbed into her lap and took her face between her chubby little hands.

"Mama sad?"

"Yes, Ella. Mama's sad."

Because now that she no longer had a choice, she knew for certain what she wanted. She wanted to stay.

"So, you saw him? Down by those trees?" Sadie shaded her eyes and looked toward the line of chokecherries in the distance.

"I saw his boot print in the mud."

"How long ago?"

"Four, maybe five days. It was right after Jackson left for his supply run."

"And Mr. Garrity says he was a Pinkerton?"

"It had to be the same man. There's little chance two separate strangers would be snooping around this area all in the same week."

"But he didn't see you."

"I don't think so. I stayed inside. Purposely fed the horses and chickens before dawn and after dark so they wouldn't see me if someone was watching. Petie watched him leave on the stage two days ago. If he had seen me, don't you think he would have stayed? Approached me or something?"

"I don't know. Maybe he's reporting back to whoever hired him."

"But why leave? Wouldn't that be too risky? Why not just send a telegram? Besides, he was headed west. Wouldn't whoever hired him be in Denver or St. Louis?"

Sadie shrugged. "I suppose. So, what are you saying?"

"I think it's time to leave. Don't you?"

"I don't know." Sadie rested her arms on the upper pole of the corral fence, her eyes on the two grazing horses. Sounds of an ax hitting wood drifted from over by the barn where Petie was splitting wood while Ella sat nearby talking to him a mile a minute.

"You don't *know*? Sadie Rose, we can't stay here if a Pinkerton detective is nosing around."

"That's just it. He's not nosing around. Not anymore. He left. If he didn't find what he was looking for the first time, why would he come back?"

"But why did he come here in the first place? And how did he know our real names? Somehow, he's already connected Mrs. Dempsey with who we really are, not the names we used back in Denver. And something led him here." She paced back and forth. How could Sadie be so relaxed? "He knows too much. It's too risky. Our best bet is to disappear before he decides to come back and do some more investigating. Who's to say he didn't already talk to someone in the area who recognized our descriptions and wasn't as close-lipped as Mr. Garrity? Why else would he have been snooping around in our trees?"

Sadie sighed. "But where will we go?"

"I've been thinking about that. We need a better plan this time. I'm pretty sure that's why it only took five months for him to track us down. The first time we ran, we had disguises in place from the start. And we ran to a bigger city. The disadvantage of coming to a place like this, even if it is in the middle of nowhere, is that everybody notices newcomers. We can't simply blend in like we did in Denver."

"So, a city? Boise?"

"No. I think we should go east. Mr. Garrity said the man was headed west. Why follow? I thought we might head to Chicago. We could easily lose ourselves in a city that size, and it would be easier for me to find a job. Our biggest problem will be getting there without leaving an easy trail to follow. We may have to backtrack. Leave a false trail like we did the first time. Put on disguises. Maybe even split up." She stopped at the panic on Sadie's face. "Just for a day or two. Just so we can arrive in Chicago from different directions. We won't stay separate."

"How are we going to afford that? We used up all our money just getting here." Sadie dropped her forehead onto her forearms. "Maybe I should just turn myself in. All this running . . . hiding. It's no way to live a life. You and Ella shouldn't have to suffer for what I did."

Claire walked over and took her sister by the shoulders, turning her so she could look in her eyes. "Sadie, look at me. Don't even think that way, you hear? We're in this together. We always have been. After everything you've done for me, there's no way I'm going to let you take all the blame for this. Do you really think I can have a happy life knowing you were paying the consequences for my bad decision? I won't do it, so get that thought out of your mind right now."

Sadie nodded, tears gathering at the corners of her eyes. She swiped at them. "I'm not sorry I did it, you know. I'm not. I should be, but I'm not. I'd do it again in a heartbeat. If God somehow gave me a chance to go back anddo that day over, I wouldn't change a thing. If I hadn't . . . he . . . he would have kil . . ."

Sobs choked off the rest of her words. Claire pulled Sadie into her arms.

"Hush, now. I know. I know. We'll get through this. We will. We've done harder things than this before and survived. We're smart. We're going to figure it out."

She looked over Sadie's shoulder and froze. Petie stood a few yards away, watching them. How much had he heard?

"She going to be okay?" He asked.

"She's fine. We're fine. It's just . . . it's the anniversary of our father's death. We're feeling a little emotional."

"Aunt Sayie sad? Mama sad?" Ella ran over and hugged them both around the knees.

Sadie's sobs melded to laughter as she bent to hug Ella back.

"I'm fine, Ella girl. Thank you for your hugs, though."

"Aw better, Aunt Sayie?"

Sadie glanced up at Claire and gave a short nod. "All better."

CHAPTER 30

S omething wasn't right. Claire had barely spoken to him since he got home. It wasn't that she was cold towards him. Just distant. Preoccupied. And just now, when he came in, she'd thrown down the paper she'd been reading and jumped up, almost as if she were guilty of something. But if she wanted to read a newspaper in the middle of the day, who was he to tell her no? Why would she even think he'd want to?

Maybe her response had nothing to do with him. Maybe her reaction had something to do with that blackguard who was her first husband. Jackson's gut burned at the thought of the man. If only there were a way to wipe out his imprint on Claire once and for all. But he couldn't change the past. All he could do was convince her to let him be part of her future. Though, judging by how she was responding since he'd come home again, the chances of that happening looked slim.

"Are you hungry?" Her bright tone sounded forced. "I've made lunch if you'd like some."

He nodded. "Thanks."

She called to Ella, who came running from the bedroom,

calling out his name and wrapping her arms around his legs when she saw him. He swung her up into his arms.

"Can we go see the horsie now, Jackson?"

"Let's eat first, and then we'll go. I promise." He'd been putting up fencing on the far edge of his land this morning in preparation for the arrival of his sheep, but he'd promised Ella at breakfast that she could watch him work the new filly this afternoon. He was almost as anxious as Ella to get started but not anxious enough to miss a meal and another chance to coax Claire out of her shell.

"Mama says the horsie doesn't have a name."

He glanced at Claire, hoping to catch her eye, but she kept her gaze firmly on the plate she was fixing for Ella. They'd spent most of their trip home from the mountains teasing each other about the filly's name. Secretly, he agreed with Claire. That beautiful horse deserved a name equally as beautiful. Still, he'd enjoyed their back-and-forth banter too much to give in. Claire had listed names of all the muses, nymphs, and demigods she could remember. He'd countered with the names of girls he'd gone to school with. The plainer and more ordinary, the better.

He sat Ella in her chair and took his own seat. "Your mama's wrong, Ella. The filly does have a name."

That got Claire's attention. She looked up, one eyebrow raised.

"I've decided to name her Calliope." He hated to cut short the smile she gave him but couldn't resist. "We'll call her Callie, for short."

She shook her forefinger at him. "*You* can call her Callie. *I* will call her by her full and proper name and give her the respect she deserves."

Then she laughed, and he joined in. Relief coursed through him. She was back. He reached for the platter of chicken. Now, he could enjoy his meal.

His peace was soon cut short by a shout from outside,

followed by a pounding at the door. Claire jumped up, then stood frozen in place, face white as the tablecloth.

Odd.

"Sit tight," he said. "I'll see who it is."

He opened the door to find George Skivington, hand upraised for another knock.

"Good. You're here." He looked over Jackson's shoulder toward Claire. "Maddie says the baby's coming. I'm off to get the doctor, but she'd like for you to come right away. Says she'd like your help in case we don't get back in time."

"Of course. Let me get my bag." Claire slipped by him into her room and returned with her nurse's bag. "You go along now, George."

The boy didn't have to be told twice. He leaped onto the horse he'd left by the porch and was off down the road like a rattler was on his heels.

"Do you mind if I take Boaz? There's no need for you to come right away. You and Ella finish your meal and spend some time with Calliope like you planned. It'll probably be a while before the baby's here."

"I want to see the baby, Mama."

Claire bent down to give Ella a hug. "You will, sweetie. Let's give her time to get here. You and Jackson can come by later to meet her."

Jackson saddled Boaz, then sent Claire on her way. As he and Ella walked back into the cabin, he couldn't help but marvel at the mix of emotions Claire had shown him in the past half hour. From aloof preoccupation to friendly, open banter. From terror to calm competence. He shook his head. She was a mystery, no doubt about it. A mystery he was determined to solve.

∾

DUSK WAS QUICKLY FADING INTO NIGHT AS THEY MADE THEIR WAY home that evening.

Claire rode beside him on Boaz while Ella dozed in his arms. He couldn't remember a time he'd felt more content. He glanced over at Claire.

"You've delivered two babies this month, Nurse Monroe. How does that feel?"

She turned to him, her smile wide on her beautiful face. "Wonderful."

He was glad to see her smile. Glad the easy comfort between them was back.

"Isn't Stanley Robert just the sweetest? So tiny. I'd forgotten how tiny a newborn can be. But a handsome little one, don't you think?"

"Seemed awful red and wrinkly to me."

She shook her head. "You men always say that. He's beautiful."

He shrugged. "His parents seem to think so. I guess that's all that really matters."

"I suppose this means Rob and Maddie will be leaving us soon."

"Rob said in about six weeks. Gives the babe time to grow and Rob time to sort his wethers for market. I told him I'd buy his sheep wagon along with the remaining herd, so he doesn't need to worry about getting that sold."

"How does it feel to own your own herd?"

"Wonderful." He echoed her word back to her.

"I'm so happy for you, Jackson. You've worked hard. You didn't let your leg injury set you back. Dr. Ferguson would be amazed to see how much you've improved. I don't think he held out much hope of you ever walking without a serious limp. And now you own your own ranch and can ride and walk as well as ever. All your dreams are coming true."

Not all of them. Funny how his dreams had changed since

meeting Claire. The sheep, the ranch, the cabin—none of it meant anything if he couldn't share it with her. He was tempted to tell her that but held back. The distance she'd shown this morning was gone for now. No reason to risk bringing it back.

They rode the rest of the way in comfortable silence. One of the many things he loved about Claire, she wasn't one of those women who chattered away about nothing just to fill the silence.

When they reached the cabin, he waited until Claire dismounted, then handed the sleeping Ella into her arms. He was about to take the horses around to the barn when he noticed the stranger. The man rose from his seat on the porch just as Claire turned toward the door.

She froze as he stepped forward. Tall and slender, the man had city stamped on him from his bowler hat to his wingtips. He leaned against the porch post and looked down at Claire and Ella.

"Hello, Anna," he said. "Surprised to see me?"

Claire clutched Ella tight to her chest but didn't reply.

Anna? Why had he called her that?

Jackson leaped off Duchess and came to Claire's side, putting an arm around her waist. She leaned into him as if she were about to fall.

"Kinda late for visiting, don't you think? Maybe you should come back another time. My wife has had a hard day."

"Your *wife*, huh?"

Jackson didn't like the sneer in the man's voice.

"What do you say, Anna? Do I have to come back? I don't believe you'll want to wait to hear what I have to say."

Claire straightened and pulled away. "Of course not, Miles. We'll talk. Tonight. Jackson, maybe you should see to the horses."

She was dismissing *him*? Uh uh. Not so fast. He crossed his arms over his chest and stared down at her.

"Maybe you should tell me what's going on."

She shifted Ella in her arms. "I will, Jackson. I promise, but I need to lay Ella down. You take care of the horses and let Miles and I talk a bit. Then I'll explain. I promise."

He didn't want to leave her with this man, but the pleading in her eyes was impossible to resist. He sent the man—Miles—a hard glare.

"I'll be back," he promised, pouring every ounce of warning into his gaze. If Claire had shown any sign of fear, he wouldn't have given in. As it was, Duchess and Boaz would have to be satisfied with minimal care tonight. No way was he leaving her alone with this guy any longer than he had to. He knew just enough of Claire's past to know this man could only mean trouble. And, as long as he lived and breathed, he planned to keep Claire free from that kind of trouble ever again.

CHAPTER 31

M iles.
Here.
They should have run. The minute Mr. Garrity warned her of the Pinkerton detective, they should have run. But she'd wanted to have a perfect plan in place. Wanted to see Jackson one last time. Wanted to figure out a way to leave that wouldn't hurt him or anyone else. Now it was too late. Her past had caught up with her. There was no running now.

But Miles was the last person she'd expected to see. The last time she'd seen him was at her wedding five years ago. She hadn't expected then to ever see him again. Yet here he was, looking just enough like his uncle to send a chill down her spine. But this was Miles, not Jonas. She had to remember that. Jonas was gone. Whatever threat Miles presented, at least she had that.

"Have a seat," she told him as he followed her into the cabin. "I'll put Ella to bed and be with you in a minute."

She laid Ella on her bed and pulled off the girl's shoes. She'd let her sleep in her dress tonight. She'd worn herself out this afternoon playing with Hazel and barely stirred when Claire laid her down. Claire tucked a soft blanket around her and dropped a kiss on her forehead. If only she could climb into bed beside her. Ignore the man in the next room and everything he represented. If only this new life she'd carved out for the two of them could go on forever. With a deep sigh, she forced herself to her feet and out the bedroom door.

Miles sat in one of the rockers by the woodstove, taking in his surroundings.

"You've come down in the world, my dear."

"You think so? Actually, I feel just the opposite."

"Yes. I suppose that mastiff you're living with now is a far cry from my uncle. Seems quite loving and protective."

"Why are you here, Miles?"

"I thought that would be obvious."

She dropped into the empty rocker beside him. "Obvious? We're a thousand miles from St. Louis on a ranch in the middle of nowhere. I haven't seen you in five years. Why in the world would your being here be obvious? What could you possibly want from me?"

"Absolutely nothing. Fact is, I came to give you something I don't want."

"You're not making any sense."

"Then let me be clear. The reason I've spent a considerable amount of my time and money finding you and have traveled into this godforsaken wilderness to meet with you is because I want to give you back the thing I want least in this world . . . my uncle."

"Wha—? I don't . . . I don't understand." Surely, he hadn't brought her Jonas's dead body.

"Really? I'm surprised. You've always seemed quite clever. You know how I hate the man. Always have. As I told you, I'm more than certain he killed my mother, as well as his first wife. At the very least, he made both of their lives a living hell, so I simply refuse to be his caregiver. I'm only his nephew. You're his wife . . . and, quite conveniently, a nurse. Yes, I know all about Nurse Monroe. If anyone should be saddled with him, it should be you."

"But . . .he's . . . he's dead!"

"Oh. Is that what you thought? You thought you'd killed him? No. I hate to be the bearer of bad news, but the murder didn't take. You probably shouldn't have sent that note around to the landlord if you'd really wanted him dead. Should have let him wallow in his blood for a few days, maybe weeks. As it is, he was found too soon, so no. Not dead. Changed, yes. Irrevocably, changed. But not dead."

Claire dropped her head into her hands. This was her nightmare come to life.

Jonas. Wasn't. Dead.

Her stomach roiled. She battled to keep from vomiting. This could not be happening. It couldn't be. Part of her wanted to cry from relief. Sadie wasn't a murderer. They were no longer fugitives. The other part wanted to scream in agony. If Jonas wasn't dead, then she was still married.

To Jonas.

Not Jackson.

The bleakness of that truth was too awful to consider.

She drew in two long, slow breaths. Then she lifted her head and looked at Miles. He stared calmly back as if he hadn't just shattered her world.

"Changed how?" She had to ask it. Had to know.

"Let's just say he's incapable of hurting you or any other woman ever again. Of that, I'm certain. He'll require a good bit of care, but you won't need to worry about the beatings anymore."

"You knew."

"Of course, I knew. Or suspected, anyway. I knew how he treated my mother . . . his own sister . . . how he treated Aunt Margaret. I had no reason to believe he wouldn't treat you the same way. You can't say I didn't warn you. You simply didn't believe me."

No. She hadn't. She'd thought, at the time, he was exhibiting a classic case of sour grapes because she had chosen his uncle over him. What a conceited little fool she'd been.

She stood up and began pacing. "I won't do it. You can't make me. I don't care how incapacitated he is. I won't be the one to care for him. I'll divorce him first."

"On what grounds? The fact he wouldn't die when you tried to kill him? The only one in this marriage with grounds for divorce is him. Unlawful desertion and all that. Yet, oddly enough, he never divorced *you*. Just told everyone he'd been forced to send you to an asylum for your failing mental health. Oh yes, my dear, he played the part of a grieving husband quite well. You'll find very few who will sympathize with your case."

He pierced her with a dark stare so like his uncle's that Claire felt the bile rise in her throat again. "I'm sorry, Anna. I'm not giving in on this. Either you take him, or I'll turn your sister in for attempted murder."

Claire gasped. "Sadie has no part in this."

"Doesn't she? My Pinkerton fellow certainly seems to think otherwise. He could present a pretty convincing case if I were to allow it. He's very thorough. Besides, the Pinkerton agency has been working on your case for years. I imagine they could charge you and Sadie with all sorts of crimes, including theft, fraud, assault, and even bigamy, at this point. What would happen to poor Ella then? Her father incapacitated . . . her mother and aunt in jail." He shook his head in mock sorrow. "I'm sorry, my dear, but you have no choice."

Claire's hands tightened into fists. How she wished she could smack that smug expression off his face. But he held all the cards. He also knew her far too well. If taking care of Jonas meant keeping Ella and Sadie safe, of course she'd do it. As he said, she had no choice.

Miles stood and scooped his bowler off the table. Placing it on his head, he strode to the door. "I'll bring him to you tomorrow. And I'll tell the Pinkertons I won't be pressing charges."

"Jonas is *here*? In Wyoming?"

Miles turned, one hand on the doorknob. "Of course. Once my detective told me your whereabouts, I packed up and brought him with me. Believe me, I wasn't about to make that bone-crushing ride across this god-awful country twice. We're staying over at the stage station in Derby. Not the best accommodations by a far stretch, but they'll do short-term.

"What you do with Jonas now is up to you. I brought his lawyer with me. He'll fill you in on all Jonas's financial affairs when we come tomorrow."

He opened the door and stepped past Jackson, who stood sentinel on the porch, arms crossed, jaw tight. He tipped his hat to him before climbing on his horse.

"I'll let your *wife* fill you in on the news. See you tomorrow, Anna."

Jackson watched Miles ride off into the night, then turned. "What's going on, Claire? Why does he keep calling you 'Anna'?"

"Anna is my name. Anna Claire is my full name. Come. Sit down while I make us some coffee. It's going to take a while to explain."

He followed her into the room. "Tell me this, first. Is he a threat to you? He said he'd be back tomorrow. If you don't want that, I'll see that it doesn't happen."

If only it were that simple.

She shook her head. "No. He's not a threat. But he didn't bring good news either. I'll tell you everything in just a minute, but I really need a cup of coffee."

Jackson took a seat at the table, not saying anything more until she set his coffee in front of him and sat down herself. Then he reached across the table and took both her hands in his.

"Claire, whatever you have to tell me, it will not change how I feel about you. Whatever is in your past is the past. You and I. We're the future."

Tears stung the back of her eyelids. How she hated hurting him. She stared at the flame in the lamp on the table, willing its brightness to dry her tears. Then, she pulled her hands from his grip and cupped them around her coffee mug.

"No. I'm sorry, Jackson, but we have no future."

"You said that man wasn't a threat to you."

"He's not. But my past is still a very big part of my future. I can't just walk away from it. Oh, Jackson, I'm not even sure where to start with this." She drew in a shaky breath. "There's a lot you don't know about my past. A lot I wish you never had to know, but you deserve the truth. Before I begin, let me just say, these past five months have been some of the happiest months of my life. You've given Ella, Sadie, and me a safe refuge when we dearly needed it, and I'll be forever grateful." Her voice broke, and she struggled for composure. After a few minutes, she tried again. "You're a truly wonderful man, Jackson. In fact, you've restored my faith in the possibility of there being good men in this world. I pray that someday you find the happiness you deserve with someone truly worthy of you, but . . ."

"You're leaving me." His words came out tortured.

"I don't want to. Please believe me. I have no choice. But you'll see it's for the best. Really. You deserve someone whole and worthy. Someone so much better than me."

Jackson started to speak, but she held up a hand to stop him. "Hear me out first. Then if you still have something to say, I'll listen." She took a sip of coffee, letting its heat burn its way down her throat. If only she could burn away the past as easily. "I met Jonas when I was eighteen. I was home for the Christmas holidays after my first semester of college. I had big dreams back then. I planned to get my undergraduate degree in science and then apply to medical school. I wanted to follow in my father's and grandfather's footsteps and become a doctor. The first lady doctor in the family."

How naive she had been, so sure of her path and her future.

"My father was one of the leading surgical physicians at City Hospital in St. Louis. Jonas had recently been hired as the hospital's administrator. He wasn't as old as my father, but he was his colleague and, obviously, a lot older than me. He was handsome and sophisticated, but most of all, he showed an interest in me I couldn't explain. He seemed fascinated that I was pursuing a career in medicine. He praised my intellect and would seek me out at social functions to discuss my plans and dreams.

"You have to understand that my father rarely had time for Sadie and me after my mother died. Before that, Father and I had been very close. I used to accompany him on his doctor visits. I told him I wanted to be just like him when I grew up, but once we moved to St. Louis, it was as if I didn't exist to him anymore. Nobody did. When my mother died, the father I knew died with her."

She took another sip of her coffee.

"Having someone like Jonas pay attention to me was like a long drink of water after years of drought. When I went back to school, he encouraged me to write to him, which I did. He would write back—words of advice, words of encouragement, words of admiration. All that attention went to my head. I felt so grown up and important that a man like Jonas would value my ideas, my input.

"His attention was even more focused when I came home for the summer. We weren't officially courting. I don't think I even saw him in that light back then, but whenever I was with him, I felt valued. I felt seen. Then in the first semester of my sophomore year, my father died suddenly of heart failure. Sadie and I were devastated. Though he'd been distant, he'd still been our provider. Our rock. I was so lost. I had no idea how to deal with finances, manage servants, or even plan a funeral. Jonas stepped up, filling the void, and when he asked me to marry him a few months later, I said yes. I gave up college, my dreams, everything for him, but I was happy to do it. At the time, I felt like the luckiest girl in the world that a man like Jonas would want me to be his wife."

She closed her eyes. If only she didn't have to tell Jackson just how foolish she had been. But he deserved to know the truth. All of it.

"There were warning signs, but I ignored them. Sadie despised the man. I laughed it off as little sister spite. Miles, who you just met, warned me that Jonas was not to be trusted, even went so far as to tell me he suspected Jonas had killed his first wife. I found that laughable and attributed it to bitterness on Miles's part because he and Jonas were estranged. Then, the night of our engagement party, Jonas flew into a rage because I danced with so many of our guests. I'd never seen him like that before, but he convinced me it was only because he loved me so much and was insecure about our age difference. He apologized so sincerely and seemed so broken. I believed him and forgave him everything."

Claire stared into her now empty coffee cup.

"As soon as we were married, things changed. Even as early as our honeymoon, Jonas changed into someone I barely knew. He demanded I do things that hurt me. Things I found degrading, demeaning . . . painful. It was almost as if the more I hurt, the more pleasure he had. At first, I protested, but he laughed at me for being so young and naive. He said it was all a part of being married. That it was my duty as a wife. But I hadn't been entirely sheltered as a college student. I knew what was considered normal behavior between married couples." She couldn't look at Jackson. The shame from those moments was overwhelming. She didn't want him to see in her eyes how dirty and damaged she was. She cleared her throat. "What he asked of me was not normal."

"Claire, I—"

"No. Jackson. Let me finish, please. In addition to *that* part of our marriage, he became increasingly unreasonable. Before, he'd had nothing but admiration for me. After, he could find nothing but fault. I didn't know how to run a household. I spent too long on my toilette. I gave undue attention to other men. I couldn't even smile at another man without him calling me a wh —, a . . . a vile name. At first, his punishments were verbal, but soon they became physical. He'd hit me in a fit of rage, then apologize in the morning in a way that made me believe it had been my fault he'd lost control.

"Other than Sadie, I had no one to turn to. He gradually isolated me from all my former friends. Any colleagues of my father were also colleagues of his. I remember once trying to talk to my father's best friend, Dr. Renfro. He was a renowned psychologist. I thought he'd be able to help. Instead, he ended up prescribing me medicine to treat female hysteria. I was pregnant with Ella at the time, and he tried to tell me my hormones were causing me to imagine things that were untrue.

"I don't know how long I would have gone on, ignoring the bruises, trying to make him happy so he wouldn't have reason to hurt me if it hadn't been for Sadie and Ella. Shortly after Ella was born, when Jonas was raging at me for something I did or didn't do, he made a threat that scared me. He told me he would have me committed to the asylum if I didn't do what he asked. I knew it wasn't an empty threat. He was already telling our friends and acquaintances that my pregnancy had left me with a nervous condition. It was a convenient excuse for when I needed to stay home to hide the bruises that were becoming more and more frequent.

"I was terrified of what would happen to Ella and Sadie if he were to have me committed. That very day, Sadie and I began plotting our escape. I knew Papa had hidden some money in a safe behind a fake wall in his study. He had lost a good bit of his savings during the crash of '83 and never totally trusted the banks again. That money was his safety net, our security, he'd told me. Several years before he died, he'd shown me the safe and given me the key to unlock it.

"I never told Jonas about that money. All Papa owned passed to Jonas when we married. I had no access to funds of any kind unless Jonas gave them to me, and he was very careful with every dime. The money in the safe was our lifeline.

"When Jonas left for a week-long hospital convention in Kansas City, Sadie and I took the money, packed a few clothes, and boarded a train to Chicago under some pretty obvious aliases, making sure the porter noticed us as he punched our tickets. Then we left the train at the next stop and donned disguises in the ladies' retiring room. We gave ourselves new aliases, better ones, and bought tickets heading in the opposite direction.

"We stopped running when we got to Denver. I knew the money we took would eventually run out, so I enrolled in nursing school while Sadie stayed home with Ella. We figured if I could bring in a little money through nursing, we could make the money stretch much further. We also lived as frugally as possible."

The coffee was beginning to sour in her stomach, but she had to make it through this next part. She set down her empty cup and clasped her fingers in her lap.

"After two years, we'd become pretty comfortable in our new life. I thought for sure Jonas would never find us. That he'd given up. But then, one morning, I stepped into the kitchen to start breakfast, and there he was. I had never seen him so angry. He was like some insane beast." She shuddered, remembering the crazed look in his eyes as he attacked. The strength of his hands around her throat. "He started choking me, screaming at me to give him his money back, calling me all sorts of vile names. I couldn't breathe. I couldn't fight him. I truly thought I was going to die. I probably would have if Sadie hadn't heard the commotion. She ran in, picked the iron skillet off the stove, and slammed it into his head, over and over, until he loosened his grip and fell. He was dead. I swear he was. I felt his pulse, or tried to, but there was nothing. So, we ran." She stopped, not wanting to look at him, not wanting to see the horror and disappointment that most surely would fill his expression. "And that's when we found you."

After several silent minutes, she forced herself to look up. Jackson stared back at her, white-faced and grim, but instead of the horror she expected to see in his eyes, she saw compassion. She hadn't known she was crying until he reached across and wiped a tear from her cheek.

"I wish you had told me sooner."

"I wanted to. I did. But I couldn't stand for you to find out what I had done. What I am."

He pushed his chair back from the table and came to squat beside her.

"What you are? Claire. What you are is an incredibly brave and strong woman, and I'm proud to call you my wife."

"But that's just it. I'm not your wife." She burst into tears. He stood and pulled her up into his arms.

"Hush now. Of course, you are. Nothing you've told me is going to change that."

She sobbed harder, knowing she had to tell him but not being able to stop the flow of her tears. For a minute, she simply let herself be held. She sobbed until she was spent, then rested against his chest, listening to his heartbeat, relishing the safety of his strong arms, knowing it was the last time she'd be this close to him. Finally, she summoned every last bit of strength and pushed away. She forced herself to look him in the eyes again.

"What you don't understand is this. Jonas didn't die. That's why Miles is here. He's coming back tomorrow and bringing Jonas with him."

"Like hell he is. That man is never coming near you again. Not as long as I live and breathe."

"No. Jackson. It's not like that. He's alive, but he's not the same. Miles says the brain injury left him incapacitated. He is not a threat anymore. But he *is* my husband. So, you see, it's a good thing we never made our marriage real because it never really was."

Jackson pulled her against him again, stroking her hair. His breath shuddered in her ear. "But that's where you're wrong, Claire. It was real to me. It was very real to me."

It had been real to her too. It was a hundred times more real than her marriage to Jonas had ever been, but it was over now.

CHAPTER 32

C hanged. Irrevocably changed. That's what Miles had promised.

But what if he wasn't?

Claire stood on the cabin's porch, watching a closed black carriage bounce its way down the red canyon road. Red dust swirled around it, partially concealing it.

Jonas.

Alive.

She wanted to turn and run for the mountains.

Jackson came out of the barn and headed toward her, taking a position against the porch post below her, arms crossed, face solemn, as the carriage turned down their lane.

Neither of them had slept. Jackson had promised her at some point during the night he wasn't leaving her side until he knew for sure Jonas would not be a threat. Though a part of her knew she should tell him to go, knew it was unfair of her to prolong the inevitable, the part of her that was weak couldn't tell him no.

Jackson's presence was a comfort, but it didn't stop the tremors in her hands. She clutched them together, willing her body to still. If Jonas hadn't changed, the last thing she should do was show fear.

The horses drew to a halt, and Miles climbed out of the carriage, followed closely by a short, thin man she'd never met. The driver jumped down and went to the back of the carriage to untie a wheeled invalid chair strapped there. He brought it around, then climbed into the carriage to return a few minutes later with Jonas in his arms. He handed him down to Miles, who settled him into the chair. Soon he was wheeling him across the yard toward the porch, the short man following along behind.

Miles rolled Jonas to a halt in front of her.

Changed.

Yes, changed indeed if he couldn't even walk. He'd gained some weight, especially around the face. His jowls were heavy. His jaw somewhat slack. He held his right arm bent and curled, not unlike the claw of a giant bird. He lifted his head and looked at her, head slightly cocked. His eyes caught on hers and held. His eyes had not changed. Dark as the pits of hell, they sent a clammy chill through her.

She couldn't do this. She could not. How could Miles ask it of her? To live with this man again, take care of him, after all he'd done to her? She wouldn't do it. She opened her mouth to tell them to take him away but stopped as Ella came to the door of the cabin and peeked out at the men gathered by the porch.

Ella.

And Sadie.

For their sakes, she had to find a way.

Dear God, help.

As Miles stopped the chair just short of the steps leading up to the porch, Ella ran over and hid behind her skirts. She had told her earlier that a sick man was coming to stay with them. She hadn't told her the man was her father. Some day she would have to know, but not today.

"Jonas," Miles said. "I'd like you to meet Nurse Claire and her daughter Ella. Nurse Claire is going to be taking care of you."

"Ah-na. Gab-ree-ella."

Claire's shocked eyes met Miles's. Though garbled and labored, Jonas's words were clear enough. He knew who they were. What else did he remember?

"You said he wouldn't be a threat."

"Does he really look like he'd be a threat? He can't even move unless someone helps him." To prove his point, Miles lifted Jonas into his arms and carried him into the cabin.

Jackson came up beside her as she followed Miles.

"Don't worry," he murmured in her ear. "I'm not leaving you alone with him."

His words were small comfort because, at some point, he'd have to leave. The situation was untenable. Jackson had a ranch and sheep and a life to get back to. At some point, she would be alone with Jonas. The very thought chilled her to the core.

After settling Jonas in the rocking chair, Miles turned to her.

"Shall we get down to business?" He gestured to the gentleman beside him. "This is Mr. Thaddeus Tate of the law firm Beckham, Griswold, and Brown. He has graciously agreed to come and explain Jonas's financial situation to you."

Mr. Tate's salt and pepper mustache twitched as he greeted her in a high, reedy voice. His mannerisms reminded Claire of a rabbit.

"How do you do, Mr. Tate. I know Mr. Beckham well. Are you also a lawyer at his firm?" Mr. Wade Beckham had been Papa's lawyer and a close friend of his. He'd often dined at their house.

Mr. Tate cleared his throat. "I'm . . . I'm a junior associate there. I work for Mr. Beckham in clerical work mostly."

Which explained why she had never met him and why he, rather than his boss, was the one charged with the thankless job of traveling across the country to meet with her.

"I see. Well, shall we sit at the table then? Would either of you gentlemen like some coffee?"

As they settled into their seats around the kitchen table, Jackson brought over the coffee pot and four cups, then sat beside her, taking hold of her hand under the table. Out of the corner of her eye, she watched Ella pull up a small stool and sit down beside Jonas, prattling on to him with no regard to whether he was listening or not. Jonas stared off into space, slowly rocking back and forth.

"Shall we begin?" Miles asked. "Sorry to rush things, Anna, but Tate and I hope to catch the stage to Rawlins this afternoon."

Mr. Tate set down his coffee cup and pulled a stack of papers from his leather satchel. "Yes. Well," he said. His mustache twitched again. "The terms of your father's will are a little convoluted, but I will try to be brief."

Papa's will? What did Papa's will have to do with Jonas's assets?

"At the time of your father's death, his total assets, including the house in Compton Heights, came to $70,000. Twenty-five percent of that amount, along with the house, passed to you and subsequently to Jonas upon your marriage. The other twenty-five percent was held in trust for your sister to be used for her care and upkeep until she reached her majority. Jonas had access to those funds until your sister left his care shortly after you were . . ." Mr. Tate cleared his throat. "You were . . . uh, institutionalized. And may I say, Mrs. Fitzgerald, how happy I am to see your health restored."

"I was never institutionalized, Mr. Tate. Nor was I ill. If Jonas told you that, he was lying."

"I . . . uh . . . yes . . . uh . . . I see."

Did he? She doubted that he did. But she was hardly going to belabor it now.

"So, my sister's portion of the inheritance is still available to her?"

Mr. Tate gave a quick nod. "Yes. Once Mr. Fitzgerald could no longer prove Sarah Rose was physically living under his care, Mr. Beckham denied him further access to her account."

That would have made Jonas livid. No wonder he was so adamant about chasing them down.

"You may be wondering what happened to the other fifty percent of your father's estate." Another twitch of the mustache.

"I'm assuming he left that to charity?" Her father had always been a generous man, lending much support to the various hospitals and orphanages in St. Louis during his lifetime.

"Twenty percent, yes, along with gifts he left to the servants."

Yes, she remembered now. Mrs. Shaughnessy, Rosie, and Trenton had all mentioned her father's generosity to them shortly after his death. She'd been too consumed with her grief and her plans to marry Jonas to pay much attention at the time. Now, she was glad to know their faithfulness had been rewarded.

"The final thirty percent was held in trust. You and your sister were to each gain a half of that portion when you reached twenty-one. The stipulation on this trust was that it could not be accessed by a spouse. The funds were for you and your sister alone. If you and your sister were to both die before receiving those funds, the money in the trust would be held for the care and education of any future grandchildren or passed along to charity."

Why did she not remember any of this from the reading of Father's will? She remembered hearing Mr. Beckham read it but very little about the specifics. To be fair, those days following Father's death had been dark. She'd been in such shock over his sudden death, in such a fog of grief, she hadn't noticed much of anything. She'd been totally unprepared at the time to handle any of their finances which is why she'd turned to Jonas so quickly, allowing him to take on so many of the details surrounding Papa's death. He hadn't attended the reading of the will, though. He hadn't been family then.

Had he assumed that most, if not all of Father's estate would come to him in the marriage? Possibly. No wonder he'd been so angry those early days of their marriage.

"And Jonas's assets?"

Mr. Tate's mustache twitched so rapidly that she almost expected him to turn and hop away. "I'm afraid your husband has very little left other than the house itself, and its furnishings, of course. Most of his remaining money has been used to settle his hospital expenses."

"Even the share he received from Father's estate when we married?"

"All gone."

"How can that be?"

"Gambling would be my guess," Miles interjected, rocking back in his chair. "That's how he lost his first wife's fortune. I'm guessing that behavior didn't change upon marrying you. None of his other vices did."

Gambling.

If what Miles said was true, it would explain a lot. Jonas's frequent trips out of town. His foul moods or high spirits on his return from those trips. She'd never been able to enjoy the reprieve his travels provided for fear of what his mood would be on his return. How she'd prayed in those days that he never would return. Those prayers, like so many others, fell on deaf ears.

"My advice to you, Mrs. Fitzgerald, is to sell the house. A house in that area of St. Louis, plus all the furnishings, Jonas's carriages, and his roadster, will bring you a nice sum. If you were to buy a smaller home, live modestly, there's no reason the money you have left, including the portion put in trust for you and your sister by your father, would not serve you well for years to come."

She agreed. Three years ago, she would not have known the first thing about living modestly, but having made the $1,800 they took from Father's safe stretch almost three years, she knew the numbers Mr. Tate had quoted would be more than enough to keep her, Jonas, and Ella comfortable. Sadie would be free to do whatever she wanted with her life.

No more running.

No more hiding.

That part of this whole nightmare felt wonderful, knowing Sadie would have her life back. She was no longer trapped by Claire's impulsive choice of a husband.

"Would you like me to initiate the sale as soon as I return to St. Louis? Or maybe you would like to return first, pack up any personal items you might want to keep?"

She'd said her goodbyes to that house and everything in it when she left Jonas. Did she want to revisit all of that? She glanced over at Jonas, still rocking and staring into space. Traveling with him in his condition would not be easy. Leaving him here on his own was impossible.

"No. I won't be returning. Feel free to put it on the market. If there is anything Sadie or I want, we'll write to Mrs. Shaughnessy and let her know. She can see to shipping those things here to us."

"That's settled then." Miles pulled his watch from his pocket and glanced at it as he pushed to his feet. "Looks like we'll have time to make that stage, Thaddeus, if we leave right away."

Mr. Tate cleared his throat and twitched a small card out of his pocket. "Well, then, Mrs. Fitzgerald, I'll be in touch as to the specifics of the sale. If you have any questions, you can write to me or Mr. Beckham at this address. Please let me know when or if you have a change of address."

"Thank you, Mr. Tate. I will."

Within minutes the two men were out the door, and the carriage, once again, raised dust clouds on the red dirt road. Claire watched it from the doorway, sensing the presence of both Jonas and Jackson in the room behind her. If only they could all go back a day. Had it really been less than twenty-four hours since she and Jackson rode home from the Skivingtons? How peaceful life had seemed then. And how terribly dark it felt now.

CHAPTER 33

I f she let herself, she could easily imagine nothing had changed. Deep down, in a place she didn't let herself go these days, she knew the truth. She was in denial. Had been since Jonas arrived two weeks ago. Though she knew the facts, she refused to let herself believe them.

On the surface, nothing much had changed. Oh, sure. Sadie had moved back as soon as she heard the news. The three of them, she, Sadie, and Ella, now lived in Jackson's space upstairs while Jonas occupied the first-floor bedroom. Jackson had moved to the barn. But he still came in for meals. They still sat in the rockers on the porch after Jonas and Ella were in bed, reading, talking, and watching the sunset. He could still make her laugh.

At night, when she climbed into the bed he used to sleep in, she sometimes got a whiff of his lingering scent—clean linen, and leather. She'd breathe in deeply and imagine him beside her, arms pulling her close as he had that night of the storm in the rocky alcove.

In her mind, Jonas was merely her patient. A job, nothing more. If she allowed herself to think of him as her husband, to face the truth, there could be no future for her and Jackson. She would fall into a pit so dark there'd be no escaping it.

Yes.

Denial was necessary. Denial was safe.

So, yesterday, when Jackson asked if she wanted to accompany him into Lander this morning to restock their essentials, she'd jumped at the chance. Even Sadie had encouraged it.

"Go. Get some fresh air," she'd said. "A change of scenery will do you good. I can handle the invalid."

Before daybreak, she'd put on her prettiest skirt and shirtwaist, dug out her favorite hat, and climbed onto the wagon bench next to Jackson, determined not to think about Jonas the entire trip. She needed this. She deserved this. And she wasn't going to let reality ruin these precious moments alone with Jackson. Because deep down, she knew they couldn't last.

"Are you warm enough?"

"Yes, I'm fine." But she was glad she'd worn a coat. After weeks of blistering heat, a front had moved in two days ago, bringing storms and cold winds. The morning air had a definite chill to it, but the day promised to be glorious. The sunrise rivaled the color in the red cliffs to the east. Touches of yellow gilded the cottonwoods growing in clusters along Cherry Creek. Fall was on its way. Her absolute favorite season.

She drew a deep breath, letting the anticipation of this trip into town seep deep into her soul. When was the last time she'd been in a town? March? April? If Jonas's return had brought anything good, it had at least brought a release from the fear of being caught. No more hiding. She could shop, visit town, and be a part of society again.

"How long will it take to get to Lander?"

"Should be there by noon as long as the road is good. The mud could slow us down a bit."

They talked of everything and nothing as they drove along, with plenty of silence in between. She'd come to expect those quiet moments with Jackson. Somehow, the quiet with him was never awkward. Peaceful, companionable, like an evening on the porch, but never awkward.

They stopped along the banks of the Popo Agie at the eastern edge of Main Street to eat the lunch she'd packed. Lander's business district stretched in front of them toward the foothills of the Winds to the west, a miscellaneous collection of wooden false fronts and two-story brick structures that ran several blocks. Main Street was a wide, muddy mess after the rain, but boardwalks ran the length of the street on both sides. Electric light poles and wires proclaimed a town with modern amenities. The town bustled with buggies and wagons. Men and women strolled the boardwalk and hurried in and out of the stores. Claire couldn't wait to join them.

"Where would you like to go first?" Jackson asked.

"I need to replenish my medical supplies now that Jonas is here, so a pharmacy, for sure. Then, we'll need sugar, flour, yeast, sewing supplies, maybe some material for some winter dresses, and a coat for Ella."

"We'll start at Palace Pharmacy and go from there. I'll let you off on the boardwalk so you don't have to traipse through that mud, then I'll join you to carry your packages, as long as you let me treat you to a slice of peach pie later. The Lander Café makes the best in the county. Don't tell Granny I said that, though. I'll deny it to my dying day."

She laughed. "I won't breathe a word. I promise."

Several hours later, after they'd stopped at the café for that slice of pie, which was every bit as good as Jackson promised it would be, Jackson dropped her off at Bossert's to look for Ella's coat while he finished up some errands of his own.

As she sifted through the ready-made coats, torn between red or robin's egg blue, she couldn't help but overhear two women in the next aisle.

"Did you see her? Holding on to his arm and flirting like

that? And her a married woman. Why the brazen hussy!"

"Can you blame her, though? Daniel tells me her husband . . ." The woman's voice dropped to a low murmur.

"I don't care if he is addled. He's still her husband. Carrying on with another man like that just isn't seemly."

Why did that last voice sound so familiar? Curious, she peeked around the corner.

"Why, Jane! And Mrs. Cullen. What a happy coincidence. I hadn't expected to run into you here."

Jane reddened and looked away. Corinne Cullen let out a nervous giggle.

Jane darted a glance over Claire's shoulder. "Is Jackson with you?"

"No. He's at the livery getting some work done on a harness." But how did Jane know she'd come to town with Jackson? Suddenly, the conversation she'd overheard took on new meaning. Had they been talking about her? Was *she* the brazen hussy?

She forced herself not to show her mortification, dredging up from long experience the expression she used on amputees when they first woke from surgery. She'd used it also on families whose loved one had but hours to live, a mask of peace that said everything was all right when clearly it was not. She'd been pretending to herself all day. She might as well continue a few minutes longer.

"You're looking well, Jane," she said, forcing lightness into her voice. She refused to return their nastiness with some of her own. "Not too much longer now until your baby arrives, is it? How have you been feeling?"

Jane's shoulders relaxed slightly. "Like I've been carrying this child forever." Her voice took on its familiar whine. "The heat this summer was awful. Thank goodness cooler weather is back. And I'll be moving back to the ranch next week when Preston takes the sheep to market. It will be so much better having Mother around to help."

"Yes. Mothers are a godsend. And you, Caroline? How are your boys?"

"Oh, you know my boys. Not a one of them can stay out of trouble for a moment's time. We, um . . ." She exchanged a look with Jane. "We heard the news about your first husband. Does this mean you will be leaving us soon?" She gave a short laugh. "Well, of course, it does. What a silly thing to ask, right? You can't possibly continue to live with Jackson now your husband has returned."

Claire forced a smile. "No. Of course, not. Jackson has been generous enough to let us use his house as long as we need it, but we'll be leaving once Jonas is stronger. We won't force Jackson to live in his barn forever." Though, deep down, she'd known the truth of that statement since the day Jonas returned, she'd never voiced it until now. Somehow, saying it out loud made it real.

These women and their catty comments had been like a slap in the face, but it was the slap she needed. Her days of pretending were over.

"I HAVE A FAVOR TO ASK." ROB SKIVINGTON LEANED AGAINST THE outer wall of the stall where Jackson was rubbing down Calliope. He'd ridden over about half an hour before and had watched while Jackson worked the young filly in the round pen.

Jackson looked up. "What do you need?"

"I was hoping you'd take my sheep to market for me."

"You too?" He'd had the same request from Baldwin last week. He'd had the ability to refuse him since the man was no longer his boss. Rob would be harder.

"Baldwin?"

Jackson nodded. "I told him no."

"I know the timing's not the best, but listen. George has

never been to market. He has no idea how to work with the commissioners or even who to see. Besides, you know he can't handle all those wethers on his own. I need Fred here with the rest of the herd, and I can't go. I don't have the stamina to make that trip and then the move to Denver the next week." As if to prove his point, Rob broke off into a fit of coughing. "Besides," he continued once he got his breath back. "I don't want to leave Maddie with all the preparations for our move plus all the work a newborn takes. She needs me here."

"I could watch your herd. Free up Fred." It was only a matter of weeks until the herd was his anyway.

"I thought of that, but Fred and George on their own in South Omaha? The city would eat them alive."

"They're city boys. They'd be fine."

"It's not the size of the city that worries me. You know what South Omaha is like. Newark may be larger, but it's nothing like that. At least not the parts Fred and George knew."

Rob had a point. Other than the stockyards, South Omaha had little to offer. Or maybe too much to offer fresh-faced kids like George and Fred, especially Fred, who attracted trouble like a sheep's carcass attracted flies.

"I can't leave Claire. I promised her I'd stay close until things settle a bit."

"I know you want to help her. And I understand. I do. She told Maddie her whole story shortly after her first husband returned. But most folks don't know that part of the story. And they're beginning to talk. The idea that she's still living with both her old husband and her new one doesn't sit well with them."

"Most folks can go to perdition. I'm not going back on my word."

Rob sighed and pushed away from the stall's door. "Would you at least talk it over with Claire? You might not care what people say, but I'm pretty sure she does. Besides, hard as it is, you're going to have to make the break sometime. You have a ranch to run and a life to live that doesn't include Claire anymore. Maybe getting away for a couple of weeks will help you let go."

"And if I don't want to let go?" He rounded on Rob, words firing like bullets. "What then?"

Rob held up a hand as if to fend them off. "Look, I understand. I know exactly how hard it is to let go of dreams . . . of a future you had all mapped out." He coughed into his handkerchief again, his thin body wracked by the hacking. Slowly, he folded the handkerchief and returned it to his pocket before looking Jackson in the eyes. "Believe me when I tell you, the harder you try to hold on to something not in God's plan for you, the more it hurts when it's ripped from your hand. Sometimes you just have to surrender, even when you don't understand. You have to believe God knows best."

Jackson scraped his boot against the straw on the floor, feeling a little ashamed at his outburst. Yeah, the man probably did know a thing or two about broken dreams, but at least he still had Maddie. The thought of life without Claire was like a heavy blanket pressing into his chest. He couldn't fathom it. He didn't want to.

Rob walked over and clapped a hand on his shoulder. "Look. Just think about it, will you? Talk to Claire. We won't leave her vulnerable. I promise. Either Maddie or I will stop by to check on her every day. And remember, she has Sadie with her. Will you at least think about it?"

Jackson forced a nod. He'd think about it, but the answer was still no.

Rob squeezed his shoulder and let go. "I'll be praying for you. For both of you. This life . . . well, it's not easy. Probably wasn't meant to be, but I do know it's nearly impossible without God's help. Seek Him in all of this. It's the only way."

CHAPTER 34

T here was a time a trip to South Omaha was the highlight of Jackson's year—a welcome escape from the day-to-day routine of sheepherding. Not this trip. The past week and a half had been nothing but torture. First came the long drive to Casper, followed by the tedious wait for railcars to come available since every rancher in Wyoming must have decided to send their livestock to market on the same week. Next came the sorting and loading and the slow train ride to the stockyards. Every moment of every long, tedious day, his mind was on Claire.

He shouldn't be here . . . wouldn't be here if it weren't for Sadie. When he tried to ask Claire what she thought of his taking this trip, he hadn't received much response. Something had happened on their shopping trip to Lander, something she wasn't telling him. At first, that day had been wonderful, just like old times between them. But when he met up with her at Bossert's, she'd changed.

From that moment on, she'd retreated into a shell he couldn't penetrate no matter how he tried. She was present in the body, but Claire, the real Claire, was gone. An automated

Claire had taken her place, going through the motions of each day with little care or notice of anyone around her. The fact he didn't know how to get the real Claire back was killing him.

But it was Sadie's argument that had turned the tide. She'd also heard the gossip making its rounds through their small community.

"You should go," she'd said. "If you want us to have any chance of staying in this area, you need to leave the ranch."

The threat of Claire leaving Fremont County and riding out of his life for good was more than he could bear. He'd headed over to Rob's that very day and told him he would go to Omaha.

But now, ten days into this interminable trip, he was no longer sure he'd done the right thing. What if Claire left anyway, took off while he was gone, not even giving him the chance to say goodbye? If only there was a way to know what was happening back home. He should have left Rob or Sadie with instructions to telegraph him if anything changed.

Or what if Fitzgerald really was a threat and had taken vengeance on Claire and Sadie while he was away? The 'what ifs' were going to drive him crazy.

To add to his misery, the rain hadn't stopped since they stepped off the train last evening. As he slogged through the mud toward the sale pens, rain dripped off his Stetson and his boots caught and held into the five-inch-deep mud with each step. Thankfully, he'd remembered to pack a slicker and some rubber boots.

The air was ripe with the odor of livestock and wet wool. The smell of South Omaha on a good day was foul. Today it was almost unbearable.

"So, you'll be taking over Skivington's herd when he leaves?" Commissioner Reeves mucked along at his side, also decked out in a slicker and rubbers. "I'm happy for your good fortune, but I'm sorry to hear Rob's leaving. He's a good man. His health still failing, you say?"

Jackson nodded. "He's counting on this fall's sale to help pay for his family's transition to Denver. Did you hear he's had a son?" Reeves was a trustworthy sales agent and had become a good friend over the years. He knew the man would give them a fair price for the sheep but figured it didn't hurt to remind him of why this sale was so important.

"No. I hadn't heard. Good for him. Give him my congratulations when you see him." Reeves turned to Preston, who floundered along beside them, trying without success to avoid the worst of the mud. Unlike Jackson, Preston had not packed a pair of rubber boots, and the look on his face was everything you would expect from a man watching his favorite pair of boots ruined by the mire. "I hear you're about to become a family man, as well."

"What? Oh, yes. Should have a squalling brat in the house within the next month. Couldn't come any too soon for me, let me tell you. Jane's confinement period has been a beast. I'm hoping

I won't have to go through that again any time soon."

Reeves, an avid family man with six lively children and a wife he adored, gave Preston a perfunctory smile and turned back to Jackson. Why Baldwin chose to send Preston as his representative was beyond him. Sure, the man was his son-in-law and had handled the fall sale for the past two years, but after all the mistakes he'd made this summer and the money he'd cost the operation, Preston was the last person Jackson would have chosen for the job.

Of course, his old boss *had* asked him to take on the job first, and he had turned him down. There hadn't been time to inform him he'd be making the trip after all before they took off. By then, Preston had been given the responsibility, and it was probably for the best. Jackson didn't work for Baldwin anymore. The sooner he made the break, the better.

They finally reached the pens where the Skivington and

Baldwin sheep were held. After several minutes of haggling, Reeves settled on a price Jackson felt was fair to everyone. Not as good as last year's prices, but given the current market trend, they were near the top end of what they could expect. He was satisfied.

Reeves shook both their hands. "I have another man to meet a few rows over, so I won't walk you back. You can pick up your checks at my office later this afternoon. I'm assuming you want them divided the same way as the past two years, Preston? Seven percent for you?"

"Yes. I ought to add the price of a new pair of boots to my cut because that's what today's walk through this hellhole is going to cost me."

"You'll have to take that up with your father-in-law," the commissioner said.

"Don't think that I won't. Anyway. You two can stand here jawing in the rain all you like. I'm off for drier, warmer pastures."

He took off at as fast a clip as was possible, given the mud. Jackson wasn't surprised. Though they'd spent the past ten days together, Preston had ignored him whenever possible. He supposed that dunking in the water trough was still gnawing at him, but Jackson still couldn't bring himself to apologize.

"Seven percent cut?" Jackson let out a low whistle.

"Yes. I was surprised when Baldwin authorized it several years ago. Seems pretty high for the amount of work the man does, but sons-in-law, right? There are advantages to marrying the boss's daughter."

Except none of Baldwin's books mentioned any such cut. He should know. He'd spent weeks going through every one of them. Could that be where the discrepancy lay in the past two years' sales numbers? Seven percent would about cover it. He was surprised Baldwin hadn't thought of it. Seemed strange he wouldn't have included it in his sales numbers.

Unless . . .

What if Baldwin hadn't really authorized that cut? Jackson shook the thought from his mind. Preston wouldn't stoop so low as to steal from his own father-in-law, would he? Besides, Baldwin's books were none of his business anymore.

All he wanted now was to finish this job and head home to Claire. Giving Reeves a farewell nod, he headed toward his room in the Exchange Building hotel, more than ready to get out of the rain.

ONE THING WAS CERTAIN. THE PORTERHOUSE STEAK AND trimmings served in the Exchange Building's dining room were worth every bit of the forty-five cents he'd paid. Jackson savored the juicy flavor of his last bite, then pushed away his plate and leaned back in his chair. Despite the rain and gloom, today was turning out to be one of the best he'd had this week. Skivington's sheep had netted a good profit, his dinner had been top-notch, and tomorrow he'd be on his way home. Though the trip would take a good three days, at least he was on the downhill side. Soon he'd see Claire again. Soon he'd know if she was all right.

He wouldn't let his mind dwell on what would happen after that. Just to see her again was all he wanted for now. The morning train to Casper could not come soon enough.

Beside him, Tavis and George were still working on their steaks. Maybe he'd splurge and order a slice of apple pie and ice cream. He didn't get to the big city often, and the thought of ice cream sure was tempting.

"So, ye got a good price for the sheep today, did ye?" Tavis asked.

Jackson nodded. "Three seventy-five for the ewes and four for the wethers." Four was almost top price for wethers in this market. Rob should be pleased. His sheep had fattened nicely on the summer range and hadn't lost much weight on the drive to market.

Tavis frowned into his meat. "I'm surprised Preston couldn't do as well with our sheep. Seemed to me they were just as fat and healthy. And no scabies to be found in any of them. We dipped 'em twice, we did."

"But you did do as well. Reeves offered Preston the same prices he did me. He even paid four twenty-five for the choice wethers."

"That's no' what Preston said. Said he got three-fifty on the ewes. Three seventy-five on the wethers."

"You sure?"

"Sure as I'm a'sittin here."

That was strange. Why would Preston lie to Tavis? Unless. Jackson did the math in his head. Yes, the numbers matched. The numbers Preston had quoted were seven percent off the original prices. He'd taken his cut out of the equation when he gave Tavis the numbers. But why would he do that? All the herders were paid a set price of $1 per day. Tavis's cut didn't change no matter how much Baldwin gave his son-in-law.

Something didn't ring true. His suspicions from earlier that day nagged at him. Did Baldwin know about this cut, or was Preston dipping his hand in the pot? Had the skewed numbers the past two years been Preston fixing them to hide the seven percent he was taking?

Drat. He was going to have to get involved after all.

"Where is Preston, anyway? Either of you know what room he's staying in?"

He and Scully, who'd accompanied Tavis as the second stock handler on the trip, had been very scarce since they'd arrived. Not surprising, really. South Omaha had its fair share of entertainments for ranchers visiting the city, most of which a man would be wise to avoid. Neither Preston nor Scully had ever struck Jackson as wise.

"They're not staying at the exchange," George said around a big bite of biscuit.

"They're not?"

"Nuh-uh. Last night, Scully said they were headed to the Atlantic. Said the beds were better there. Told me I should come with them, but I knew you already had rooms for us here." George shrugged. "Beds seem comfortable enough to me."

Jackson exchanged a glance with Tavis. Rob was right. George and Fred would have been chewed up and eaten for lunch had they come on their own. The Atlantic was one of the many bawdy houses in the area. He wasn't surprised at Scully's interest. Most of the single sheepherders would spend a large portion of their yearly pay on women and booze once they hit the city, but Preston was a married man.

"Well, if either of you see him around here later, tell him I'd like a word with him."

As it turned out, he and George ran into him later that day. After they picked up Rob's check at the commissioner's office, they'd headed downtown. They'd treated themselves to haircuts and shaves at Goodwin's and browsed through Flynn's department store, where Jackson bought a doll for Ella and some trinkets for Sadie and Claire. Had he still been married to Claire, he'd have bought her the seed pearl brooch shaped like a bouquet of wildflowers he saw there. Instead, he limited his purchases to a few ribbons and some lacy handkerchiefs for both girls. George picked up a few items for Maddie and his new nephew.

As they headed back toward the stockyards, they saw Preston and a group of other stockmen standing on the porch of the Riley's Saloon.

"There he is, boys." Preston made a grand flourish in his direction. "That's the man I was telling you about." His words slurred as he spoke. "He's a new kind of Mormon. 'Stead of being the husband of several wives, his wife has two husbands. All living together as happy as can be."

Jackson lowered his head, determined to ignore the man as he stalked on by.

But Preston wasn't giving up. "If you're feeling kinda left out now that the first husband has returned, Jackson, let me know," he called out as they passed. "I'd be glad to introduce you to a lovely lady you could have all to yourself. You too, Georgie. You oughta have yourself a little fun now that you're in the big city."

"Naw. I'm good." George called back, but after they started across the tracks, he touched Jackson's sleeve. "Hey, didn't you say you wanted to talk to Preston?"

"Waste of time. I'll wait until he's sober. What do you say we check out those horse barns? I hear they do a good business here on western horses. Wouldn't mind bringing a few in myself, maybe later this fall."

He didn't get another chance to talk to Preston until the train ride home. They were about an hour out of Casper when the stockholder's car they'd been traveling in cleared of all other passengers except an older gentleman several rows up. Preston was seated on the bench across from Jackson, legs extended, hat over his eyes—most likely sleeping off the alcohol from the night before.

He gave Preston's leg a sharp kick with the toe of his boot.

"Hey," Preston lifted his hat just high enough to glare at him. "I'm trying to sleep over here."

"Don't care. We need to discuss a few things."

"Like what?"

"What prices are you going to tell Baldwin you got for his sheep?"

"Why are you asking that? You were there. You know we got the same prices Skivington did."

"But those weren't the prices you quoted Tavis."

Preston shrugged. "Tavis doesn't need to know."

"Why not? Is it because the price you quoted him was the price Baldwin makes after you skim off your seven percent? Are you trying to hide something?"

"I didn't skim anything. I made that deal with my father-in-law two years ago, and it's none of yours or anybody else's business."

"Then why doesn't it ever show up on the books? It's funny how you didn't remind your father-in-law of it last May when it could easily explain why his numbers were off. Makes me wonder if there ever really was a deal."

"You're a blasted busybody, you know that? You don't work for us anymore, Garrity. So I suggest you keep your nose out of our business."

"First off, I never did work for you, Preston. And secondly, Baldwin is my friend, so if you are skimming money from him, you better believe I'm going to make it my business. Tell you what, I'll give you one week from the time we get home to come clean. After that, I'm asking him about it. Got it?"

Preston sat forward, a sneer on his face. "No. I don't 'got it,' because if you so much as breathe a word to him, I'll be telling the county a few of your little secrets. I'll bet the neighbors would be mighty interested to know sweet little Sadie and your poor, dear Claire aren't anything close to innocent. Imagine their surprise when I tell them how Claire's brain-addled husband was somehow left for dead in a rented house in Denver just days before she and her sister showed up in Rawlins with you. Too bad for all of you that murder didn't take, right?"

Preston's sneer turned into an ugly smile at the surprise Jackson wasn't able to hide. "Oh yes. I know all about the doings in Denver. Had quite a chat with the Pinkerton fellow when he came snooping around with a picture of Claire and her sister. How do you think he knew where to find her?"

Fire roiled in Jackson's gut. The little snitch. He clenched his fist but forced himself to remain calm. Losing his cool wouldn't help Claire.

Instead, he let out a long, slow breath and narrowed his eyes. "Two can play your game, Preston. It's not like you don't have secrets of your own. You gossip about Claire, and I'll have a talk with Jane. I'm sure she'll be very interested to hear where you spent your nights this week. I can't imagine news like that would go over well with your pregnant wife."

Preston lunged at him, but Jackson was ready. Propelling forward, he caught him mid-punch. Using his momentum, he threw Preston back into his seat and held him there with an arm to his throat.

"One week, Preston, then I go to Baldwin. Believe me, it'll go much better for you if you're the one to tell him first."

He held his arm to Preston's throat a split second more, then released him. Straightening, he made his way up the aisle toward the next railcar without a backward glance.

He couldn't get home soon enough.

CHAPTER 35

Darkness. Soul-numbing darkness. Every morning when she opened her eyes, except for that split second before awareness set in, before she remembered, before reality returned, Claire woke to the darkness that was her life now.

She was living her nightmare, only backwards. Before, the nightmare would come at night. Now her only reprieve was when she slept. Jonas was back. There was no waking up from that fact.

To be fair, living with Jonas now wasn't anything like it had been before. Miles was right. Jonas had changed. Irrevocably. But that didn't change the facts. She was trapped in a marriage she thought she'd escaped two years before. If it weren't for Sadie and Ella, she'd pull the covers over her head and never get out of bed again. Instead, she did what she'd done the past twenty-three days, twelve hours and seventeen minutes. She pushed herself out of bed to face another day.

Mechanically, she washed her face, combed and pinned up her hair, and pulled on a skirt and shirtwaist. Then she went downstairs to the kitchen, where Sadie was already starting a fire in the kitchen stove.

"Is Jonas awake?"

"I haven't heard him."

They would. Her husband might not have the mental capacity he once had, but he hadn't lost any of his demanding nature. As soon as he woke in the morning, he'd call out her name, over and over, and wouldn't stop until she answered his call. He wasn't as crippled as she had thought that first day. He could walk in a slow, lurching shuffle. He'd plant his left foot, then drag the right one forward. But he couldn't get in and out of bed on his own and couldn't dress or bathe himself. Luckily, she'd been trained to provide for the needs of patients far bigger than he. From a nursing perspective, she had the situation well in hand.

If she considered his condition merely from a medical standpoint, she would have to say he'd improved since he arrived at the cabin. His speech, though garbled, was mostly intelligible if you knew how to listen. He had little to no strength in the right side of his body, but he could feed himself slowly with his left hand. He spent most days in the rocker by the woodstove. Ella considered him her own personal playmate and was forever bringing him her dolls or Mr. Cuddles to hold on his lap while she played on the floor beside him.

One day Claire had found the two of them engaged in a rather one-sided tea party. Ella had the teacups and teapot spread on a footstool beside his chair. She would pretend to fill a cup with tea and hand it to him. He, in turn, would lift the cup to his lips. Whether his actions were automatic or on purpose, she could not ascertain. Whatever the case, the two seemed content, so she hadn't intervened.

She had no idea what he remembered from before the accident. He knew their names, but if he remembered anything about his previous life, he gave no indication of it. For the most part, he focused on the present, letting them know if he was hungry or if he needed to visit the chamber pot. But there were times she would catch him watching her with a look of clarity in his eyes that scared her. As if he knew what had put him in this condition and was only biding his time before he got his revenge. Then, his eyes would glaze over, and his head would loll to the side, leaving her wondering if she had imagined the whole thing.

"I've made up a basket with a jar of my chicken noodle soup and pan of biscuits to send to Granny." Sadie placed a tea towel over her basket and looked over at Claire. "Why don't you take it to her this visit? Make sure she's doing better."

Petie had stopped by the day before to tell them Granny was feeling poorly. Sadie had immediately gotten busy in the kitchen.

"I thought you planned to go."

Sadie still tried to visit Granny at least once a week.

"I did, but I got to thinking if she's really not well, you'd be able to help her more than I would."

"I can't leave you and Ella with . . ." Claire nodded toward the bedroom door.

"Why not? I can care for him as well as you. You can get him up and ready and settled in his chair, then there's not much for me to do other than feed him. You know I can handle that."

"You know I don't like leaving you all alone with him."

"You did it before."

Yes, and regretted it. After that debacle in Lander and the gossip it caused, she hadn't ventured away from the cabin again.

"You need to leave the ranch from time to time." Sadie wasn't one to give up easily. "You haven't gone anywhere for at least three weeks. It's not healthy. You move around here like one of Ella's wind-up toys—just going through the motions. I can't remember the last time I saw you smile."

Claire shrugged. "What do I have to smile about?"

"Precisely why you should get away. Get your mind off things. Even if it's only for the day. You know Granny will be delighted to see you, and I'd feel a lot better knowing she's had a nurse look in on her."

A bellow from the bedroom alerted them that Jonas was awake.

Claire sighed. "Let me get Jonas situated. If it looks like he's going to have a good day, I'll think about it. No promises, though."

"All right. I'll quit pestering you if you at least think about it. Now go before he wakes up the whole county."

THREE HOURS LATER, CLAIRE TOOLED THEIR BUGGY UP THE RED canyon road, Sadie's basket for Granny on the seat beside her. Jackson had brought Malachi and the buggy over from his Pa's before heading to Omaha market.

"You'll need a horse to get around," he'd said. "I'll be taking Boaz with me to Casper, and I don't trust Duchess or Calliope enough for either Sadie or you to ride. Malachi's easy to handle. You can use him as long as you need."

She remembered the gentle gelding from her early days at Granny's when she rode him back and forth to nurse Jackson and Louis. An eternity ago, it seemed. He'd been easy to hitch to the buggy, and she found herself enjoying the drive. Sadie was right. She needed this.

She drew in a deep breath of the crisp, fall air. They'd had an early snow a week ago, but the weather had warmed again since then. Not a cloud marred the deep blue of the sky. With just a nip of cool in the air, Claire reveled in the warm sun on her skin. Yellow and gold still clung to the trees along the creeks and gullies. The Winds to the west, white-topped now from the recent snow, reminded her of Jackson and the wild horses. Petie had told them yesterday that he, Jackson, and Louis would head out soon to bring home more of Hippolyta's band. How she wished she could go with them.

The dark heaviness returned. She couldn't escape it. Even away from the cabin, away from Jonas, the reality of her circumstances weighed her down.

Before long, she turned into the lane toward Granny's cabin. The orchards on both sides of the narrow lane were heavy with apples. Petie had also mentioned their small community was gathering this weekend to help with the harvest. Apparently, Granny's apple harvest had become a tradition for the neighbors ever since Granny's husband passed away. Once picked, the apples would be sent to Lander, Riverton, and Shoshone to be sold.

As the cabin came into view, she spotted Granny on the porch, peeling apples. Baskets, pails, and buckets of apples littered the porch beside her. She waved and stood as Claire pulled Malachi to a stop.

"You must not be feeling too poorly if you're sitting out here." Claire climbed down from the wagon and pulled the tiny woman into a hug.

"Oh, child, it's so good to see you." Granny's voice was hoarse, but her movements were still spry. She placed her hands on both sides of Claire's face and smiled.

The minute she did, Claire burst into tears. That simple touch, the love in Granny's eyes, somehow breached the dam of her dark emotions, and sobs burst forth in torrents. She couldn't control them. Part of her was mortified, but the other part sank into the Granny's tight embrace, hearing the familiar comfort of "There, there, child. There, there."

After an eternity, but what was probably only a few minutes, the tears subsided, and she pulled away.

"I'm so sorry. I didn't mean . . . I hadn't planned . . ."

Granny took hold of her hand and patted it. "Now, now. Don't say you're sorry. I've always said a good bout of crying can do the body good." She took a handkerchief from her pocket and handed it to Claire. "Come. Sit down. We can talk while we work."

"What are you working on?"

"I'm peeling some apples for a batch of pies I'm making for this weekend's harvest party."

"See? I told Sadie she should come instead of me. She'd have been able to help with the pies much better than I can."

"Nonsense. Anyone can peel an apple. There's another paring knife over by that bucket of apples if you'd like to help."

Claire found the knife and sat on the stoop beside Granny. She'd peeled apples before, but never with Granny's expertise. She watched in awe as Granny's knife and fingers flew around the apple. Within seconds, all that was left of the peel was a curled ribbon of red that fell at Granny's feet in one long strand.

Claire picked up an apple and tried to emulate Granny's motions with very little luck. She finally settled for peeling the apple as she always did. Slow and steady, but it did the trick.

"Petie told us you'd been feeling under the weather."

"Just a bit of a head cold. Nothing to be concerned about."

"You do sound a bit congested. I brought along some ginger and honey for tea,which will help with that. Sadie sent some of her chicken noodle soup."

"Bless you, child. You girls take such good care of me."

"Sadie said to be sure to tell you she misses you."

"And I miss her. Nothing makes an old lady feel young more than having a young 'un around to keep her company."

"Once things settle in a bit, maybe she can come stay with you again."

"Now, don't be thinking I was hinting around about that. A girl should be with her family, and I'm pretty sure you need her a lot more than I do."

"She *is* a big help."

"Will you be coming to the apple harvest on Saturday?"

"I plan to send Sadie and Ella, but I'll need to stay home with Jonas."

"You could bring him too. The neighbors would like to meet him."

"Maybe at some point. He's still too fragile right now." Other than Jackson, Petie, and the Skivingtons, no one had met Jonas yet. She didn't know how much they really knew of Jonas's injuries. Some days he could be so difficult, fighting against everything she needed him to do. The thought of bringing him to a community event at this stage was more than she wanted to contemplate, both from the work it would involve and the gossip it would generate. It was so much easier just to stay home.

"You can't hide in that cabin forever, dearie. Have you thought of what your future might hold?"

No, because her future held nothing but vast darkness. Tears threatened again, but she blinked them back. It was hard to think about tomorrow when it was all she could do to get through today. Jackson's cabin had become both a refuge and a prison, but she knew deep down they'd eventually have to leave. She couldn't take advantage of Jackson's generosity forever.

"It's all so heavy and dark right now. I'm having trouble imagining a future."

Granny reached over and patted her hand. "I know, dearie. I remember feeling that way when Hiram died."

"My husband didn't die." If only he had. Was it terrible of her to admit that?

"No. But your dream of a marriage with Jackson did. Sadie told me what your first marriage was like before your husband's accident, and I can understand the pain you're feeling right now. It all seems so unfair, especially after you thought you'd escaped all that and moved on to something so much better."

Except she never really had. She'd never truly believed herself married to Jackson. Sadie might have told Granny part of their story, but she obviously hadn't told her their part in Jonas's "accident." No one knew about that other than Jackson.

Granny looked off into the distance, her fingers resting on the apple in her hand. "Sometimes I think it's those fledgling dreams, the ones that haven't even had a chance to fly, that die the hardest."

"What do you mean?"

Granny gestured toward her apple groves. "On the east side of our orchard is a family graveyard. Hiram is buried there, but it also has three other graves. Small ones. The graves of our babies. Not one of them lived to see its first birthday. The girls, Hattie and Etta, came far too early and died before they were born. Finally, I delivered a healthy baby boy. Little Johnny was a beautiful child. Hiram and I doted on his every move. But one morning, when he was just eight months old, I bent to pick him up from his cradle and realized he was gone. Just gone. No reason. He hadn't been sick. He just left us while he was sleeping."

Claire brushed back tears. Why? Why, Lord, couldn't Granny have kept just one? She would have made a wonderful mother.

"How did you cope?" Claire forced the words past the tightness in her throat.

"Not well, at first. Like you, I couldn't even imagine a future without my babies. After Johnny died, I was in a very dark place. I was so angry with God. I didn't eat. I couldn't sleep. I remember thinking I didn't want to live if I couldn't have Johnny."

Claire gave Granny a sidelong glance. Had the woman read her thoughts? "How did you get past it?"

"Hiram. I'd snapped at him one day for something. Something little, I'm sure. Seems like all I ever said to anyone after Johnny died was something sharp and angry. Well, he sat me down, took hold of my hands, and said to me, 'I can't do this anymore, Lettie. I can't. I've lost Johnny. Please, don't make me lose you too.' And then he cried. Cried! My Hiram never cried. It about broke me.

"You see, I'd let bitterness and anger take over my life. God can't use a life like that. A life like that ain't no use to nobody. See all these apples?" She gestured to the buckets surrounding them. "They're my windfalls. I went out and picked them up off the ground after that big wind we had a couple of nights ago. All of them are bruised and battered in some way because of their fall. I won't be able to sell them at market, but that doesn't mean they are useless. Not yet. But I'm guessing if you went back and looked under those same trees today, you'd find some apples I missed that are rotten clear through. They've sat in their bruises too long, letting the sickness spread through the whole apple until they aren't of any use anymore."

She held up the apple in her hand. "But see this one? It has a bruise here." She pointed at a dark spot with her knife. "And here. And a wormhole here, but when I cut them out, the apple is perfectly good and will make part of a wonderful pie for everyone to enjoy. I could have stayed in my bitterness and lived a useless life, but instead, I let the Good Lord cut out the bad parts. Hiram and I never had children of our own, but I did have four little neighbor boys that desperately needed my mothering." She looked over at Claire and smiled. "And a couple of lost girls and a child who needed a home, even if it was only for a brief time. Child, don't let bitterness keep you from the joy of living a useful life for the Lord. He's given you a wonderful gift. The gift of healing. Use it. Find joy in it, even if it means using it to help the one who hurt you the most."

"You don't understand. What Jonas did . . ." Claire swallowed hard, not wanting to even look at Granny. "Some of the things Jonas did . . . they're . . . they're unforgivable."

"I'm not asking you to condone his actions. I'm asking you to give up the bitterness. Let go of the right to be his judge and jury and give it over to God. Remember, by God's holy standards, none of us deserves forgiveness, yet it's freely given. Your unwillingness to forgive does nothing to change the past, but it does keep you from fully understanding God's grace for you. Trust me, if you hold onto it, it will rot you to the core. Don't let the horrible things Jonas did destroy your life. If you do, then evil wins."

Evil. Wins.

She didn't want that, but forgive Jonas? She didn't have it in her. "I can't. Even when I try to forgive him, the old feelings just keep coming back."

"Ah. You're thinking forgiveness is a one-time thing. It's not. It's a decision you'll have to make over and over. And, you're right. In our own strength, it's impossible. With God's help, though? Anything is possible." Granny reached over and patted Claire on the leg. "Now, enough of this heavy talk. Let's take these apples inside and make some pies. I've found that rolling pie dough is another helpful way to let out anger and bitterness. Shall we give it a try?"

Claire laughed and pushed to her feet. "You'd better have a whole lot of dough then because I'm going to need it."

SHE THOUGHT ABOUT GRANNY'S ADVICE ALL THE WAY HOME AND for the better part of the next two days. Eventually, she prayed about it. At first, the prayers were more of a tirade against God and how unfair life was, but in the end, she surrendered. Granny was right. Her bitterness hurt no one more than herself. If she allowed it to control her, evil won. Jonas won.

The next day when Ella and Sadie were down at the barn feeding the chickens and playing with the cat, she sat down beside her husband.

"I don't know if you can understand what I'm saying, but

I'm going to say it anyway. You hurt me. Deeply. Without provocation or right. And for the longest time, I was glad Sadie hurt you. I was glad when I thought she had killed you. I wanted you dead. I don't excuse what you did to me, but I need to tell you I choose to forgive you because that's what God chose to do for me. I forgive you, Jonas. Can you understand that?"

He tilted his head to one side, working his mouth and lips to force out some words. "Huurt, Ah-na. Huurt, Ah-na." He began giggling and rocking back and forth. "Huurt, Ah-na."

Was he confessing that he hurt her or wishing he could hurt her again? Had he even understood anything she'd said? The gleam in his eye reminded her of the look he'd get right before he hit her. The giggling sounded almost maniacal.

Dear God. Help me. Help me. This forgiveness business was proving even harder than she'd anticipated.

"Mama." Ella bounded into the cabin and skidded to a halt beside Claire's chair. "Jackson's here. Can I go see him? Pwease, Mama? Pwease?"

Claire's heart skittered a beat. *Why now, Lord? Do I have to do all the hard things at once?*

Sadie followed Ella in the door. "He's down by the trees again. Ella spotted him from the barn. One of us probably needs to go tell him we're all doing fine. I'll be glad to take Ella to see him if you'd like, but we both know the only one he really wants to see is you."

Claire pushed to her feet, smoothing the wrinkles from her skirt. "No. I'll go. I need to talk to him. I need to tell him to stop dropping by. It's probably better if that comes from me."

Ever since he'd returned from Omaha, Jackson stopped in every two to three days to check on them. Because of the neighborhood gossip, he'd been careful not to visit the house or the barn. Instead, he'd stand just inside the strand of trees down by the stream until one of them came out to talk. Lately, she'd been sending Sadie and Ella. Talking to him was just too painful, too much of a reminder of what she couldn't have.

She knew he was merely keeping his promise to be there for her, but it was time to bring even this small involvement to a halt. Jackson wasn't part of their world anymore, and he never could be. The sooner she made the break, the better.

But the minute she caught sight of him leaning against one of the willows, arms crossed across his broad chest, hat low over his eyes, she was torn. Part of her wanted to run straight into his arms. At the same time, she was tempted to drag her feet in order to prolong their time together as long as possible. She forced herself to walk at a normal pace.

As she drew near, he straightened but said nothing, his midnight blue gaze seeming to devour her. Or maybe it just felt that way because she couldn't stop looking at him.

"I'm glad you dropped by today. I've needed to talk to you," she said.

Worry settled on his face. "Fitzgerald?"

"No. Jonas has been fine. Not much change, though he has been able to walk a little further each day. Exercising his leg muscles seems to help."

"You think that's wise? Wouldn't it be safer to keep him immobile?"

She shook her head. "He hasn't shown himself to be a threat in any way. I couldn't knowingly keep from doing what I know will help his wellbeing simply to make myself feel safe."

"No. The healer must heal." His voice was tender. Too tender.

"Jonas isn't what I wanted to talk about. Jackson, you don't need to keep checking up on us. We'll be fine. I appreciate that you are worried, but don't be. We're doing fine." She pulled her shawl tight against her body and hugged it close. The north wind was brisker today than she'd anticipated. It whipped her skirts against her legs and clawed at her hair.

"I don't mind." He gave a lopsided grin. "It's not like I'm not in the neighborhood."

"I know. But it's better for you . . . for me . . ." She choked on the words. She looked off toward the Winds in the distance, gathering her composure. "We . . . *I* can't go on like this . . . holding onto something that will never be. It's not fair to either of us." She drew in a deep breath. "I've decided to move back to Denver as soon as Jonas is a little stronger, maybe as soon as next month."

"No. Claire. You don't have to leave." His voice sounded clogged, tight. "I told you, you can stay in my cabin as long as you need. I'm fine using Skivington's old cabin. And I'll stay away if that's what you want. But, please, Claire. Don't go."

She forced herself to look at him. His eyes pleaded with hers, dark and hurt. She clenched her fists into her shawl to keep herself from reaching out to him.

"It's no use, Jackson. I have no future here. The sooner you and I accept that, the better."

He shook his head, the muscles in his throat and jaw working as he spoke through clenched teeth. "I don't think that's possible."

She swiped away a tear. How she hated hurting him. "I'm sorry. I never meant to hurt you. You're a good man, and I—" She cut herself off. She'd almost said she loved him. How stupid could she be? Of course, she didn't love him. He wasn't hers to love. "I pray you'll find a wife someday, someone who will be so lucky to share her life with you. But that's not me. It can't be me."

"You're the only wife I want." His words came out low and tender. "I love you, and that's not going to change. Even if you move away."

Tears ran freely down her face now, and she didn't bother to wipe them away. "It has to change, Jackson. Don't you see? We have no choice." She reached out and placed a hand on his arm, ever so briefly. "Goodbye, Jackson."

She forced herself to turn and walk away. No looking back. If she looked back, she knew she would run to him, hold on, and never let go. She could feel his eyes on her as she left and knew that she was hurting him. She hated herself for it.

God, I know you tell us you are a good God, but nothing about this feels good. Nothing.

Why bring her here at all? Why allow a good man like Jackson to fall in love with her if it wasn't meant to be? None of this made sense and her puny morsel of faith didn't come anywhere near to handling it.

Dear God, help me. Help us all.

CHAPTER 36

This was the last place he wanted to be today. Apple harvest at Granny's was always more of a party than a workday, and the last thing Jackson wanted right now was a party. But he and his brothers had been helping Granny harvest her apples for as long as he could remember. Even a broken heart was not going to excuse him from today's festivities. Thankfully, no one ever expected him to be the life of the party. Louis and Gabe were the social ones in the family. Out of the corner of his eye, he saw them up by the food table talking to a couple of the Bunce girls.

Turning his back to the crowd, he hefted a ladder from the pile and headed toward the farthest part of the orchard.

She was leaving him. No. She'd already left. He'd just been too dumb to notice. Just because a girl kissed you, even if the kiss rocked you to your core and left you reeling, didn't mean she was yours. Even if she cried in your arms and clung to you for comfort and protection, didn't mean you were the one meant to give it to her. Especially when she was married to someone else. Only a fool would try to hang on to a married woman.

Obviously, he was a fool.

In his head, he knew Claire did the right thing by walking away from him last night. In his heart, he felt like that ten-year-old boy who cried and pleaded with his Ma not to leave him and then watched her climb into that carriage and drive away without a backward glance. The circumstances were different, but the result was the same. He'd given his whole heart only to have it rejected, left behind like a worthless piece of rubbish. Pa had the right of it, after all. Women only brought pain.

"I should knock you right off that ladder."

He glanced down to see Preston's angry red face glaring up at him.

"What's stuck in your craw this time, Preston?"

"As if you don't know. I held my part of the bargain, Garrity. I expected you to do the same. Yet my wife won't even talk to me right now because she said someone told her I'd been visiting the brothels when we were in South Omaha."

"Wasn't me."

He'd given Preston a full week and a half before stopping by to see Baldwin.

"Yes. He came to me and told me about the cut he's been taking," Baldwin had said when he asked him if he'd talked to his son-in-law. "Clears up those questions we had with the books, at any rate, but my hands are tied. Had it been anyone else, I'd have fired him quicker than you could hog-tie a steer, but he's my son-in-law. You can't fire family. But don't worry. He won't be handling any business transactions unless I'm in the same room. Lesson learned there. And I do appreciate whatever it is you said to make him come clean."

Jackson felt sorry for his old boss. It couldn't be easy having a lying sneak for a son-in-law.

"Of course, it was you." Preston wasn't backing down. "Who else would it be?"

Jackson shrugged and continued to pull apples from the tree and add them to his basket. "I wasn't the only person on that trip. Half the ranchers in the county were at market the same time we were. Besides, I haven't even seen Jane since you two moved into Lander last June."

"We've been back on the ranch for more than a month."

He shrugged. "And I've been working at my own ranch since before that. I'm not the person who ratted you out, Preston. Seems to me, you'd make better use of your time trying to make things right with your wife than looking for a scapegoat."

"You sanctimonious prick," Preston grabbed hold of the ladder. "I ought to knock you off this thing. See how high and mighty you'd feel then."

"I'd like to see you try."

Preston shoved the ladder, tipping the basket of apples and knocking Jackson off balance. Apples flew in all directions as he jumped free of the ladder, landing awkwardly on his bad leg. Great. The last thing he needed was to injure it again. Before he could fully regain his footing, Preston launched at him, fists flying.

"Hey." Jackson caught Preston's right arm and held it. A second punch glanced off his shoulder. Wrenching his arm free, Preston jabbed an elbow into Jackson's jaw.

Pain radiated across his face and down his neck. That did it. He sent a fist into Preston's gut, followed immediately by an uppercut to the face that sent Preston backward. Jackson had been itching to hit something for hours. The impact of his hand against flesh felt good. Too good.

Before he could let loose another blow, someone grabbed him by both arms and pulled him backward.

"That's enough of that," Louis growled in his ear. "You know Granny's rules. No fighting on harvest day." A rule that came about solely because, as kids, he and his brothers would inevitably end up in some sort of wrestling match before the day was over.

Jackson shook himself out of Louis's hold. "Fine. Just keep him off me. What are you doing out here anyway? Shouldn't you be tending to a tree of your own?" Preferably on the other side of the orchard where all the other pickers were.

"Granny put Gabe and me in charge of the wagon. We came to get your apples."

Gabe stood off to the side, holding Preston back. The wagon with the empty barrels was parked just behind him. Jackson hadn't even heard them drive up.

"Might be a minute." He righted the ladder, then bent to pick up the spilled apples.

"Let me go." Preston struggled to free himself from Gabe's grip.

"You done fighting?" Gabe asked.

"I'm not stupid enough to fight three Garrity brothers at once."

"I'm surprised you'd even take on one," Louis said.

"Yeah, well. He had it coming." Preston's boots stopped just shy of Jackson's basket. Jackson kept on working, not bothering to look up. "This isn't over, Garrity," he said. "You'll see. You're going to be sorry you ever decided to pick on me."

Jackson didn't respond. He just kept picking up apples and putting them in his basket. Thirty seconds later, the boots turned and walked away.

Louis blew out a low whistle and squatted down beside him. "What did you do to get him so riled?"

Jackson shrugged. "Trust me. With that one, it doesn't take much." He took his refilled basket to the wagon and poured it into one of the barrels. "Come back in about ten minutes, and I'll have another basket for you. And while you're at it, keep Preston on the other side of the orchard. I'm not in the mood to be friendly today."

"That's a mighty fine band of horses you got there."

Pa and Jackson leaned on the top rail of Pa's corral, looking over the fifteen horses Jackson, Louis, and Gabe had rounded up on their last horse-hunting trip into the mountains. Once tamed and trained, this herd would go a long way toward building Jackson's stock for his ranch. He also hoped to sell a few at market this winter. The money would help toward settling his debt to Rob.

"Thanks for letting me corral them here until I can get pens built for them at my place."

Pa snorted. "Your place or Skivington's?"

He hadn't decided yet. Building at Rob's place didn't make a whole lot of sense because he didn't plan to stay there permanently, but building on his own ranch would be difficult as long as Claire was still living there.

"You need to get that woman off your property," Pa growled.

"First off, she's not 'that woman.' She's Claire, and she's allowed to live in my cabin as long as she needs it. She used to be my wife."

"She never was your wife. She was just using you to hide out until she thought it was safe to move on. She never had feelings for you."

"That's not true. She thought Fitzgerald was dead. She wanted to make our marriage work as much as I did."

"You sure about that? Last time I talked to her, after that Pinkerton fellow came sniffing around, she sounded like a woman ready to run. Face it. She played you just like your mother played me. Women bring nothing but trouble, son. I thought I'd taught you that. Could have saved yourself a boat-load of heartache if you'd listened."

Jackson clenched his fists around the rough bark of the corral's top pole. Pa wasn't saying anything he hadn't told himself a thousand times these past few days, so why did it rub him so raw?

"Are you telling me that nothing about your life with Ma was good?" That couldn't be true. They had four boys together. That had to be worth something.

"Once your Ma left, my eyes were opened. Everything about our life together had been a lie. So no, nothing about that life was good. I was a fool to think it was, but I'm not a fool now. You shouldn't be either. Tell that woman to move on and get your ranch back. Quit moping around like a lovesick puppy. I raised you stronger than that."

Jackson bit back the words he wanted to say. "I told you. *Claire* can have the cabin as long as she needs it," he said instead, through clenched teeth.

"Bah. You're more of a fool than I thought. Well, don't come crying to me when the lease to Skivington's cabin runs out and you have nowhere to go." Pa spun on his heel and took off toward the barn.

Jackson watched him go, then lifted the latch on the corral gate and walked in. He'd heard Pa's rants before. Why should his words bother him so much today? Maybe because he *had* been a fool to give his heart to Claire, and he knew it. The truth hurts sometimes. But dwelling on that wouldn't get these horses tamed.

An hour later, Pa's words still ran on repeat in his head, and the filly he'd chosen to work with showed little sign of responding to his instruction. What was wrong with him today? He'd never had a horse take longer than thirty minutes to respond to him. If he'd been the type to use a whip to correct, he'd have used it on this one by now. Instead, he cracked it into the dirt and turned away in disgust. He needed to get his head straight, or he'd never get these horses ready for market.

"Maybe you should take a break." Sikes stood outside the round pen watching him.

"How long have you been here?"

"Long enough to know you're not yourself. Might be best to leave it for today and try again tomorrow."

Sikes was right. No use wasting time on a lost cause. Jackson opened the gate that led to the main corral and let the filly escape back to the rest of the herd. Rolling up his rope, he walked out of the pen to where Sikes was waiting.

"Want to talk about it?"

Jackson sighed and shook his head. "It's just Pa." How many times had Sikes asked him that question over the years, and how many times had he responded exactly the same way? Some things never changed.

"Do you think Pa will ever get over what Ma did to him? How long should it take a man to get over a woman, anyway?"

Sikes cocked an eyebrow. "Maybe you should tell me?"

"Me? I'm the last person you should ask."

"Seems to me the problem isn't so much getting over the heartache; it's how you allow yourself to respond to it. If you're not careful, son, you might find yourself just as angry as he is."

Jackson huffed. "No danger of that."

"No? Then tell me why I found you attacking that horse taming session like a bear with a thorn in his paw. While we're on the subject, why'd you decide to brawl with Preston at the apple harvest? Oh, and did you know? Each of your brothers told me, individually, that going on the horse roundup with you was like taking a trip with your Pa. None of those things sound like a man who's not angry."

Wait. His brothers thought he was like Pa? Okay, so maybe he had been a little irritable on that trip, but it had been a bad week. A guy was allowed to have bad days. It wasn't like he would be this way the rest of his life.

"Anger can become a lifelong habit if you're not careful." Sikes always had an uncanny ability to read his mind. "Look. I'm not saying you haven't been dealt a rough hand lately. I'm just asking you to consider how you want to respond to it. Remember how you and your brothers used to love to listen to stories about David in the Bible?"

Jackson nodded. What kid didn't like stories about a boy who could take on a bear, a lion, and a giant and win?

"I've been reading in First Samuel recently. Remember the story where David and his men go off to war and come back three days later to find their homes burned to the ground? Their families, their livestock, everything was taken. All they had, gone in three days' time. David's men were so angry in their grief that they wanted to stone him. Then right there in the middle of the story is this phrase: 'but David encouraged himself in the Lord his God.' It kinda jumped out at me. Everyone around him was angry and grieving. He was grieving too, but he chose not to be angry. Seems to me that's the choice we all have to make when life brings tragedy. You either allow your grief to turn you bitter, or you turn to God for your strength."

Huh. He hadn't come here today expecting a sermon, but Sikes was good at that. Made him feel about twelve years old again, having been caught stealing gingerbread from the kitchen or smoking a cigar with Louis behind the barn. Sikes had a Bible story for every situation. The problem was, he was right. Jackson hadn't had much to say to God since Claire walked away. Nothing good, anyway. He may have done some complaining about the way He worked things out, but he certainly hadn't turned to Him for encouragement.

Was he really in danger of becoming like Pa? Dear God, he hoped not. But every time he pictured Claire turning and walking away from him, the hurt was almost more than he could bear. For the first time ever, he could imagine how his Pa felt. How he'd become the way he was. But Claire wasn't Ma. Not really. She hadn't wanted to walk away. He had to believe that. She'd chosen to stay with Jonas because she was a woman of principle. Her convictions and her strength of character were part of what he loved about her. He could trust her to do the right thing. He just wished the right thing wasn't so wrong for him.

CHAPTER 37

"Ten more gone this morning," Gabe said.

"Ten?" That made almost thirty sheep dead in three days. At this rate, he wouldn't have a herd left come spring. "Any luck finding a cause?"

"Yep. Found this down in a ditch by the spring." He held up a wilted plant.

"Dogbane? Where'd you find that? I know for a fact there wasn't any there last week. How could any have sprouted up so fast?"

"It wasn't growing there. It was spread there. Like someone picked a bushel of it and spread it around, knowing the sheep would be grazing in that area."

"You think someone did this on purpose?"

"I don't think. I know. Something like that doesn't happen on its own. Just like the gate at Pa's didn't *happen* to get left open."

Louis had ridden over the day before with news that the wild horses they'd gathered had escaped. Someone had opened the gate on the corral or left the latch loose, and they were all gone by morning. Yesterday, he'd considered it an unlucky accident. Now, he wasn't so sure.

The horses weren't irreplaceable. They'd rounded them up once. They could do it again. Maybe. It would mean another three-day trip into the mountains and hoping the band hadn't moved on to some other spot. Dead sheep were another matter. Thirty gone already, and no telling how many more had eaten the weed before Gabe spotted it.

"Did you move the sheep?"

"Yep. And raked the dogbane into a pile and burned it. I searched the new area and didn't see any other patches, but that doesn't mean whoever dropped the first batch won't try again. I've got George riding lookout with the dogs right now, but we might want to set up a night watch. I doubt whoever is doing this will make a move in broad daylight."

"It's almost like that business with the cattle ranchers two years ago, but I thought that died with Jake and his gang. Have you heard of any other trouble among the other herders? "

"I dunno. This seems more personal than that. Seems more like someone out to harass you. Preston was spitting mad at you the other day. Do you think he could be behind all this?"

"Preston? He wouldn't know dogbane from milkweed or any other plant for that matter. Besides, I can't imagine him sneaking within a hundred yards of the sheep without the dogs putting up a fuss."

"Well, someone's responsible. Better be on your guard for a while until we know who it is."

Yes. Someone. But who?

Hopefully, they weren't in for another battle between the sheep ranchers and the cattle ranchers. He didn't have the energy for that right now. He just wanted to be left alone to raise his sheep and horses. Was that too much to ask?

After his talk with Sikes, he'd read back over that story of David's fight with the Amalekites. Sikes was right. David had turned to God for his strength and encouragement at a point when he thought everything was lost. In the end, David had recovered it all—wives, children, livestock, everything. Jackson didn't expect to recover his wife and child, and the thirty sheep were already dead. For now, he'd be happy not to lose anything more, but with the news of the horses yesterday and the sheep today, he was beginning to feel a lot more like Job than David.

Still, he'd hashed it out with God last night. Hard as things were, he was determined to trust God no matter the circumstances. Today, he needed to get these corrals built so once he and Louis could round up another bunch of wild horses, he'd have somewhere to put them. Somewhere close where he could keep an eye on them.

"A night watch is probably a good idea. In the meantime, are you still willing to help me with those posts? I'd like to get them in the ground before the weather turns cold."

"You thinking we're gonna have a storm?"

"The way my leg's been aching, I'm sure of it. This leg's better at predicting a weather change than Scott and his fancy weather station in Lander any day."

"You're sounding like an old man, Jack. What's next. Rhumatiz?"

"Just wait. You'll break a bone someday, and then you'll know."

The afternoon was half spent when a voice calling his name drew his attention to the southwest. Claire. Running. Hair flying. Dress hitched high. Something was wrong. He ran to meet her, catching her as she threw herself into his arms. Tears streamed down her cheeks.

"What's happened? Why aren't you on Malachi?"

"He's gone. And we can't find Ella. Or Jonas. Oh, Jackson, I think he's taken my baby." Sobs wracked her body.

He held her tight, her words striking dread to his very bones. Hadn't he been afraid of this ever since the man returned?

"How long have they been gone?"

She pulled back, swiping her eyes with the backs of her

hands. "That's just it. I don't know. Sadie and I were doing laundry out in the wash house. Ella was in the cabin with Jonas. She's stayed with him before. She likes to play with her dolls while he sits in his rocker. She calls him her JoJo and makes him take tea with her and her dolls. They've always been just fine. But when we came back in the cabin for lunch, they were gone. We searched all over the cabin and the outbuildings and couldn't find them anywhere. And then we realized Malachi was gone too. He's taken her, Jackson. I know he has. And I can't even go after him. I don't know which way they went. I don't have a horse. You have to help me."

"Of course, we'll help." He glanced at Gabe.

"I'll head up the canyon road toward Dallas. I'll let the neighbors know as I go by. If they headed that way, we'll find them," Gabe said.

"I'll saddle Duchess and Boaz, and we'll look around the cabin area for signs. Chances are, we'll be able to track which way they headed from there. Don't worry. We'll find them. I can't imagine Jonas getting too far, given his condition."

"But what if he's stronger than he's led us to believe? What if he's been faking all this time? I should never have trusted him. Never."

He took her flailing hands and held them in his. "He couldn't have faked all of it. No one is that good. We'll find them. I promise. Come. You can saddle Boaz while I work on Duchess."

Minutes later, the three of them were galloping up the canyon road. At the lane leading from the road to Claire's, he and Gabe spent a few minutes checking for hoof prints in the soft, red dirt, but the road was well enough traveled. It was hard to tell if the prints they saw belonged to a single horse or several.

"Better just head toward Dallas," he said to Gabe. "Someone's sure to have seen them if they took the road. Meanwhile, Claire and I will head toward the foothills and check with all the sheep camps along the way."

Gabe nodded and cantered off.

"Let's find Sadie. Maybe they showed up while you were gone."

But Sadie met them at the porch, her face falling when she saw they were alone. "No sign of them?"

Claire shook her head.

"I searched down by the creek and went through the barn again. She's not in the loft or any of the stalls, but I did find something odd. Look at this, Jackson. You can see Jonas's tracks in the dirt here. See here's his left boot print, then here's where he dragged his right leg. But I don't see Ella's anywhere."

"Maybe he was carrying her," Claire said.

"How? His right arm is useless, and he holds his cane with his left hand. Look. He was using it. See? You can see where it left divots in the dirt just to the side of his boot print. But here's where it gets strange. You can see Malachi's prints coming out of the barn and heading around the side of the corral, then they disappear into the grass, but look here."

Jackson bent down to see what Sadie was pointing to. A small shoe print, the size of a child's marked the dirt just at the edge of the grass. Following it backward, he found another, partially covered by Malachi's hoof print.

"Ella's footprints were here before Malachi came this way."

"She could have been leading him."

"But her prints don't come from the direction of the barn," Sadie said. "If you look, you'll see one here . . . and here. But none over here on the path from the barn."

"Tough to know if those prints are fresh, though," Jackson squatted down and examined the dirt. "It's been so dry this week, they could be prints she left a day or even a week ago. She could still have been with Jonas on Malachi today."

"Yes. But I found more prints down by the creek."

Sadie led them down to the creek bed where two distinct boot prints marked the soft mud at the creek's edge.

"They could be my prints. From when I was here before." He didn't really want to bring up that memory of the day Claire told him goodbye, but he also wanted them to consider all angles before jumping to conclusions.

Sadie shook her head. "Too small. Your boots are larger by at least two inches."

He put his foot alongside one of the prints and realized she was right. The girl had a sharp eye.

"And there, on the other side of the creek, it looks like more than one horse rode up the bank."

He hopped to the other side of the shallow creek and studied the hoof prints. Definitely two separate horses, and some of the prints fell almost on top of each other as if the horses followed each other rather than walking side by side. Claire squatted beside him, her hand on his shoulder. Was it wrong to be glad to have her so close again, even in these circumstances?

"You think Jonas had help?"

"Sorta looks that way, but it doesn't make much sense. Has he ever been outside the cabin alone? Could he have communicated with anyone else?"

Claire and Sadie looked at each other and shook their heads.

"I can't imagine how," Sadie said.

"Well, speculating the hows and whys won't help us find Ella, but at least we have a clue as to which direction to take."

He looked off toward the northwest where gray clouds were building. The wind had picked up in the last half hour, bringing with it a distinct bite. They'd need to hurry if they were to find Ella before the storm hit.

"Let's ride up to the ridge there." He pointed to the west. "The ground's pretty high there. Should allow us to see a long way in either direction. Also, there are several sheep camps to the north of here. We can visit them and see if they saw anyone pass by. Gabe's covering the other direction. He said he'd pass the word on to all the ranches between here and Dallas, so we'll have eyes on the lookout to the northeast in case they doubled back that direction.

"Sadie, you stay here at the cabin. If anyone finds them while we're gone, shoot that rifle in the air like I taught you, and we'll head back. Otherwise, we'll check back in a couple of hours."

He and Claire mounted up and splashed across the creek.

"Dear Lord," he prayed under his breath. "Keep her safe."

CHAPTER 38

Daylight waned, and a sleety rain bit against Claire's cheeks as she and Jackson splashed back across the creek toward the cabin, nothing to show for their hours of searching but heavy hearts. They'd visited sheep camp after sheep camp and scoured the countryside for miles to no avail. Claire's soul was as numb as her toes inside her boots. The only thing keeping her going was the hope that the others had had more success, and Ella was waiting for her at the cabin.

Please, God, not my baby. Please, God, please. Those words had been her constant prayer the entire afternoon. Light and people spilled from the cabin as they approached. By the looks of it, every woman in the neighborhood waited on the porch or inside the open door for them to return. One glance at Sadie's white, pinched face told her all she needed to know.

No Ella.

She slid from the saddle and into Mrs. Baldwin's warm, comforting arms, no longer able to hold back her sobs. How could she have been such a fool as to trust Jonas again? She'd massaged and exercised his weakened arm and leg. She'd fed and bathed him. She'd knelt by his chair and offered forgiveness. All the while, he'd been plotting this. Whatever *this* was. She still couldn't fathom how he'd mustered the strength to take their daughter and completely disappear.

The sound of hoofbeats broke past her sobs. She lifted her head, hoping, praying. Quickly, she scanned the group riding into the yard. Gabe, Louis, Mr. Garrity, Sikes.

No Ella.

"Anything?" Jackson asked as the men pulled their horses to a halt.

"Not between here and Dallas. They didn't make today's stage for sure. I alerted the ticket agent, and he passed the word down the line. If Fitzgerald tries to take her out of the area by stage, they'll stop him and send word right away."

Within minutes, other groups of men rode in. Tavis, George Skivington, Petie, Daniel Cullen, and several of Baldwin's ranch hands. They'd scoured the county to the south and west with no success. It was as if Jonas and Ella had vanished into thin air. The sleet had turned to snow, and a light layer of white snow blanketed the ground. She wouldn't allow herself to think of Ella out in this all night. They had to find her.

As Mr. Baldwin and Preston cantered down the road and up the lane to the cabin, leading Malachi but neither one carrying Ella, the last of Claire's hope died. She sank onto the porch and buried her head in her hands.

"Preston has something he needs to tell you."

The harsh tone in Mr. Baldwin's voice made Claire look up, her stomach plummeting. No. Please, God. No.

"What. Have. You. Done." Jackson forced his words through a clenched jaw as he walked slowly toward Preston.

Preston, who had just climbed down from his horse, stepped back, arms raised in surrender. "Nothing. I mean, I didn't *mean* for anything to happen. I just wanted to scare you a bit. Make you worry for a few hours. I meant to bring her back. I swear."

Jackson grabbed Preston by the collar and shook him.

"Where is she? By God, if you've hurt her in any way, I'll–" He let the words trail off. "Tell me where she is."

"I don't know. She's not where I left her."

"What do you mean, she's not where you left her? Why in hades would you leave her? By God, man. She's only three years old. How could you leave her by herself?"

"Because of him . . . her husband." His gaze caught Claire's, and he quickly looked away. "He kept following us, so I hid her. Told her to stay put for a minute while I tried to lead him away. Then, when I doubled back to get her, she was gone. I looked all over, but he had disappeared. *She* had disappeared. All I found was his horse."

Jackson tightened his grip on Preston's collar. "Where." He shot the word like a bullet.

"Hall's Gulch."

"The canyon? Are you out of your mind?"

Claire could tell by the pallor on Jackson's face that Hall's Gulch must be a terrible place. *Please, God. No. Keep her safe. Keep her safe.*

"This isn't over, Preston. Not by a long shot, but I don't have time to deal with you now." Jackson shoved Preston into Baldwin's arms and spun toward his brothers. "Gabe, Louis, we'll need lanterns and dogs. George, go get Rosie. Tavis, can I borrow Laddie? Hurry, now. I'd like to be out of here within thirty minutes."

Mr. Garrity stepped forward. "Hold on, now, son. You're not thinking of going into that canyon in the dark. There's no way you'll find anyone tonight. You're likely to get someone killed if you try."

"You're right." Jackson's jaw clenched, and his throat worked as he forced out the words. "Louie, Gabe, you come at first light. I'll go alone and take the dogs."

"It's suicide, boy."

"Maybe, but my dau—, *Ella's* out there. I'll be danged if I sit on my heels all night while that baby is alone in the cold."

Claire pushed to her feet. "Wait. I'm coming."

Jackson swung around, looking as if he'd forgotten she existed. "No."

"Either you take me with you, or I'll follow. Either way, I'm coming."

"Claire. You have no idea what we're up against. Brown's canyon has dropoffs as deep as one hundred feet. A river runs through it. It's dark. It's snowing. You're not coming."

"Watch me."

She walked into the cabin to change into her split skirt, thick wool jacket, and leather gloves. Throwing a hooded cloak over it all, she grabbed a blanket and headed back outside. She was already seated on Boaz when Jackson came out of the barn carrying two lanterns and wearing his long, leather duster.

Before he could say anything, she said, "She's *my* daughter, and I'll be danged if I sit on my heels all night while she's out there alone."

His jaw tightened, then relaxed. "Fine."

He swung up onto Duchess and led the way down the lane.

An hour later, they reached the mouth of Brown's canyon after stopping to collect Rosie and Laddie from their respective sheep camps.

"These two can find a sheep buried in a snowbank. They'll be able to find Ella," Jackson had said.

Claire prayed it was so. *Please, God. Please, God.* Those two words had been constantly repeating in her head since they left the cabin. They were all she could manage. Surely God understood the words she couldn't say . . . couldn't even think right now.

Please, God. Please.

They followed a dry creek bed into a narrow valley. Steep, rock walls rose hundreds of feet above them to the north.

"Hall's Gulch," Jackson said. "This is where Preston said he left her. Might be best to tether the horses and take the rest of this on foot."

He dismounted and called to the dogs. Squatting, he held Ella's wool coat under their noses. Poor baby. All she had on right now was a light jacket. Hopefully, she still had her jacket. But in this cold, it would offer little protection.

Please, God. Protect.

Jackson gave the dogs a signal with his hand. "Find the sheep," he said.

Rosie and Laddie took off up the canyon, noses to the ground. Within minutes, she heard them barking furiously up ahead.

"Do you think . . . ?"

But Jackson had already taken off. "Watch your step." He called back to her.

Large boulders lay scattered across the path, some hidden already by the snow and darkness. Claire wanted to run toward the barking dogs but knew she would do Jackson and Ella no good should she twist an ankle. She forced herself to slow down, picking her way by the faint light of her lantern.

When she caught up with Jackson, he was kneeling in front of a small crevice in the rock face about two feet wide. Wide enough for a small child but not an adult. He shined his light into the dark hole, then pulled back, shaking his head.

"This might be the spot Preston left her when he brought her here, but she's not there now. The dogs must still be able to pick up her scent. That's good, though. I was hoping we didn't lose it with the snow."

He backed out of the crevice and stood up. One of the dogs, the little black and white one, bounded back into the opening and came out with something in her mouth.

"Whatcha got there, Rosie? Drop it." He held out his hand, and Rosie let go of her prize. He looked at it, then held it out to Claire. "Ella's?"

"Her shoe!" Claire snatched it from his hand and held it to her heart. She'd been here, but where could she be now? Poor baby, walking this rocky path with only one shoe. Surely, she hadn't gone far.

Please, God.

"Let the dogs smell it again," Jackson said.

She bent over to hold it under both dogs' noses.

"Find the sheep." Jackson sent them off again with a series of whistles. They bounded off into the shadows, where the canyon narrowed up ahead.

Jackson offered her his arm. "Keep your eyes on the path and step carefully. The dogs will let us know if they find something up ahead."

They walked for what felt like hours, but Claire knew it could only be fifteen or twenty minutes. The path was treacherous in the dark, in some places almost completely blocked by huge boulders they had to climb over or squeeze around. How could a partially crippled man and a tiny girl have navigated this on their own? Maybe they'd missed them somehow. Maybe they'd gone the other way and were lost on the vast prairie in the cold and dark. Maybe they rode right past them on the way here and didn't see them. Claire wanted to curl into a ball and sob out all her fears. Instead, she clung to Jackson's hand and put one foot in front of the other.

Please, God. Please, God. Please, God.

Finally, she heard the faint sound of barking in the distance. "Did you hear that?"

Jackson nodded. He set down his lantern and took both of her hands in his. "Do you trust me?" He asked.

Of course, she trusted him. Wait. No.

"I'm coming with you, Jackson."

"Claire, listen to me. I know what's up ahead. The path gets very narrow and even more treacherous than it's been so far. I could go much faster if I went alone. I promise. If I find her, I will send a signal right away. But if . . . *when* I find them, they're going to need shelter and warmth as soon as possible." He pointed his lantern toward the face of the rock to their north. "See right there? There's a shallow cave there in the rock." He dug in his pocket and set something in her hand. Her fingers closed around it. Flint and steel. "You stay here. Build a fire. Set up a shelter. I'll go see what the dogs have found and bring her back to you in a jiffy."

She knew what he wasn't saying. He was afraid for her to see what might lie ahead on that trail. There was no guarantee Ella wasn't hurt. She might even be . . . No. She wouldn't allow herself to think it. *Please, Lord. Please.*

"I don't need to be protected, Jackson. I can handle whatever we find." The words sounded brave, but she didn't think either she or Jackson believed them.

"I know you're strong. You're the strongest person I know. I'm just asking you to stay here and prepare a shelter and let me bring your daughter to you."

The dog's barking intensified. They were wasting precious minutes.

"Fine. Go. I'll get a fire started."

Jackson reached out and pulled her into a quick, tight hug, then set off down the path. He was right. Even with his slight limp, he could navigate the trail much quicker without her. She would let him do his job. She would do hers. Holding the lantern close to the ground, she looked for tinder and kindling. She wouldn't allow herself to dwell on anything else.

Please, God.

JACKSON TOOK OFF AT A SLOW JOG OVER A RELATIVELY CLEAR patch in the canyon. What he hadn't told Claire . . . couldn't tell Claire . . . was the dread he'd been feeling the farther they'd pushed into the canyon. Unlike Claire, he knew the dangers that lay ahead. He'd searched this canyon before. Not in the dark. Not for a child. But many a lost sheep had wandered this path. Many had not survived because up ahead, probably about as far ahead as where the dogs waited, barking, was a sharp dropoff at least twenty feet high. Anyone not familiar with the path, anyone traveling it in the dark, could easily not see it and fall. *Oh God, please. Let Ella be safe.*

He didn't know if he could ever forgive Preston if she wasn't all right. He didn't know if he could forgive himself. Because as much as Preston was culpable for what happened to Ella, Jackson knew he was equally to blame. He shouldn't have pushed the man the way he did, exposing his weaknesses and humiliating him, not once, but twice, in front of his wife and family. He couldn't help thinking that if he hadn't thrown Preston in the horse trough, hadn't thrown those punches at the apple harvest, Ella would be safely tucked in bed at home right now.

Preston was right. He had been a sanctimonious prick. He'd been so mired in his own pain and self-pity that he'd forgotten God's call to love *all* his neighbors. He knew God forgave him, but if something were to happen to Ella, he didn't know if he could forgive himself.

He dodged around a boulder and skidded to a halt. Rosie stood on the path in front of him, barking down into the darkness. Laddie's bark echoed up from down below. The dropoff. He knew Jonas and Ella were down there as surely as he knew his own name. This was the scene he was trying to spare Claire from seeing, yet now he was here, he wasn't sure he had it in him to see what lay below. *God, give me strength.*

Taking a deep breath, he walked over to where Rosie stood and peered down. Nothing but darkness. Seeing he had joined her, Rosie headed to where the rocks on the left side of the path made it possible to climb down. Hugging the rock face, Jackson started down after her. His boots slipped once on loose rock, but he caught himself and managed to pick his way to the bottom. Once there, he could see a dark mound on the ground over where Laddie was standing. Too large to be Ella. Jonas?

The man lay in a tuck position. A thin layer of snow covered his garments, so he must have been lying there for some time. Jackson squatted and placed his fingers on his throat. The skin under his collar was warm, pulse weak. He was alive.

Jackson blew out a breath and looked around. Where was Ella? He'd thought for sure the two would be together.

"Ella?" He called. "Ella?" He started to stand when a rustling sound drew his attention back to Jonas. The front of Jonas's coat gaped open, and a small head peaked out.

"Jackson! You founded me."

"Ella, baby. Are you hurt?"

She shook her head and wriggled herself out of Jonas's embrace, launching herself at Jackson. "I was cold. Jojo keeps me warm."

Jackson folded Ella into his arms and held her close. "You're squeezing me, Jackson."

"Sorry. I'm just so glad to see you. Your mama and I have been looking for you all day."

"Jojo came to take me home, but we got lost." She looked back at the man on the ground. "We falled, and JoJo held me close and made me fall on top of him. Is he hurt, Jackson? He won't get up."

"Yes, baby. I think he's hurt pretty bad. We need to try to help him." But how to do that tonight and who to help first was the question. "Hold on, sweetheart. You better cover your ears. I need to fire off my gun to let the others know you've been found."

He walked a few feet away and fired a shot into the air aiming to the southwest, away from Jonas and Ella. He waited ten seconds and fired another. One shot, she's found. Second shot, send help. The sound echoed off the canyon walls. Claire, for sure, would have heard it. Hopefully, she'd stay by the fire as he told her. They'd left Gabe and Louis at Pa's about a mile away with instructions to listen for a shot. Time would tell if it worked. He'd have to leave Jonas here until he could come back with help.

He knelt down beside the man. "I'm taking Ella to safety. I'll be back to get you. I promise."

He pulled off his duster and tucked it around the man, then told the dogs to lay down beside him. Their body heat should keep him warm until he got back.

He started to rise when he heard Jonas speak. Bending closer, he caught the words, slurred and low.

"Save . . . El-la."

He placed a gentle hand on the man's shoulder. "I will, Jonas. Thank you for helping her today."

Rising, he lifted Ella into his arms. "Shall we go see your mama?"

"Yes, Jackson. 'Cuz I'm cold."

"We've got a warm coat, a blanket, and a fire for you just up the path, but I'm going to need you to help me get you up these rocks. Do you think you can climb where I show you?"

"Yep. Let's go see Mama."

A GUNSHOT. CLAIRE SAT UP STRAIGHT. AFTER SOME TRIAL AND error, she'd managed to get a fire going on the outer edge of the cave. Already the rock inside the small alcove was heating up nicely. Building a fire had helped occupy her mind. Kept her from wondering every minute when Jackson would get back.

But that gunshot could only mean one thing. He found her. One shot meant she was found. That's what he had told Sadie earlier today. Another shot rang out.

Wait. Two shots? Why two? When they'd dropped his brothers off at their father's ranch, she remembered them discussing the signals, but her mind had been on Ella. On her two-word prayer. On getting to the canyon and beginning their search. What did two shots mean?

Maybe it hadn't been a signal. Maybe Jackson was in trouble. Maybe there was someone else down the trail with a gun. Pulling on her cloak and grabbing her lantern, Claire stepped around the fire and took off in the direction Jackson headed when he left. She needed to get to him. What if he was hurt and trying to get her attention?

The trail wasn't as rough as she expected. In fact, this area was one of the smoothest sections they'd passed so far. So why hadn't Jackson let her come with him? Did he sense trouble ahead?

Claire skirted a boulder and then skidded to a halt. A light flickered around the bend in the path up ahead. Jackson? No. He was tall, but not that tall. And then it hit her. It *was* Jackson with Ella on his shoulders.

"Ella!" She took off running, heedless of the rocks. "Ella. Oh, Ella, baby."

"Mama." That sweet little voice was the most beautiful thing she'd ever heard.

As she got closer, Jackson swung Ella off his shoulders and let her run to meet her. She caught her in her arms and held on tight. Oh, her little body felt so good. Was it only a few minutes ago that she wondered if she'd ever hold her again?

Ella pulled back and placed her chubby hands on both sides of Claire's face. "Mama, why you cwying? You sad?"

"No, baby. I'm happy. So happy. I've been very worried about you."

Ella puckered her lips and nodded. "The bad man who wasn't Jackson took me. He said he was going to take me to Jackson, but he didn't. Then Jojo came, and it was all right. But we got lost. And Jojo and me falled." Her eyes clouded with tears. "Will Jojo be all right, Mommy? Jackson left him sleeping."

She glanced over at Jackson, taking in his serious face.

"Is he . . . ?"

"No, but he's hurt pretty bad. We'll need help getting him out. Hopefully, Louis and Gabe heard my signal and will be here soon."

Oh, right. Now she remembered. Two shots, send help.

"Did you get that fire started? Ella and I could use a warm up."

She noticed he was no longer wearing his duster. And poor Ella in her light coat, and . . . she checked Ella's feet. No shoes. On either foot.

"Yes. Let's get you both warmed up."

Within minutes, they had Ella back at the cave wrapped in both her wool coat and the blanket. Claire held her in her arms. *Thank you, Lord.* Maybe that should become her sole prayer from now on. Because right now, in this minute, she had all she needed.

She glanced over at the man beside her. So strong. So solid. Their eyes made contact. The look in his dark eyes caressed.

And so not her husband anymore. She glanced away. Okay. Maybe she didn't have all she wanted, but she did have all she *needed.* She had her baby girl. That was enough. It had to be enough.

Jackson shifted and checked the time on his pocket watch. "I think I'll give Louis and Gabe about fifteen more minutes. If we don't hear them by then, I'm taking you and Ella to Granny's. I don't want to wait here too long on the chance they didn't hear the gunshots."

But ten minutes later, they heard hollering up the trail.

"Over here," Jackson shouted back.

Soon, Louis, Gabe, Petie, and George Skivington came into

view. They whooped and cheered when they saw Ella in her arms.

"You found her," Gabe said.

"She's not hurt?" Louis asked.

"No, but Jonas is. I'm going to need all of your help getting him out of here. He fell off the drop up ahead."

Louis let out a low whistle. "And he survived? Did Ella fall too?"

"From what I can make out, he must have held her in a way that broke her fall. She doesn't have a scratch on her. Did you happen to bring anything we could use for a stretcher?"

Gabe nodded. "Back at the wagon. Shouldn't take too long to rig something up."

"Good. I'll walk back with you. Petie, you should come too. I want you to take Claire and Ella to Granny's. The rest of us should be able to handle Jonas."

Forty minutes later, Ella sat in her chair at Granny's, happily munching on a slice of gingerbread, a little dirty, a little sleepy, but not much worse for wear after her day of adventure. Claire, on the other hand, felt like she could fall into bed and not wake up for a week.

When she, Petie, and Ella had arrived at Granny's cabin, the tiny main room had been bursting at the seams with all the women from the neighborhood. Apparently, shortly after she and Jackson had left, the men had moved to the Garrity ranch and the women to Granny's to be closer to the canyon and any news. She and Ella had arrived to a cacophony of cheers and well wishes, but little by little, the women's husbands had arrived to take them home, and the overstuffed cabin now held just her, Ella, Granny, and Sadie.

"You'll stay the night, of course," Granny said.

They might have to. After dropping them off, Petie had headed out to find Doc. From what Jackson had told her, Jonas was in pretty bad shape. She might be needed to help nurse him tonight. She still couldn't imagine how he'd managed all those boulders and that slippery wet terrain on his and Ella's trek up the canyon. She'd started the afternoon sure he was a villain and ended tonight with the realization he was a hero. She was having trouble wrapping her mind around that one. Maybe when she saw him, she would get a better understanding of her jumbled feelings. For now, all she wanted to do was hold her daughter and sleep.

~

"HE WON'T LAST THE NIGHT."

Doc's words struggled to find purchase in her brain. Not last? He was . . . Jonas was . . . dying? She sank into the chair beside his bed, the same bed Jackson had laid in when she'd nursed him and Louis last spring.

She took hold of the hand of the man who had caused so much havoc in her life. So much pain.

Jonas. Her husband. Her worst nightmare.

Jonas. The man who had saved their child.

If he hadn't been with Ella today, her precious daughter might be the one on this bed tonight, dying. Or worse. Already dead. She swallowed against the pain of that thought.

She believed she had forgiven him, but earlier today, when she'd thought he'd taken her daughter . . . *their* daughter . . . she knew she never really had. Not the old Jonas, anyway. All the bitterness, all the hatred, all the anger had come roiling back. *Lord, how can I forgive?*

How could she not? He'd given her Ella . . . twice. He would always be a part of the daughter she loved.

The man he'd been before the accident was so totally removed from the man who lay on the bed in front of her. It was almost as if he was two different people. She could forgive this man . . . easily. She could not forgive the other.

Do I have to, Lord?

Yes.

I can't.

But I can. With me, all things are possible.

She took Jonas's hand in hers. Doc said he had broken multiple bones in his fall. Arm, hip, ribs. Had he been a healthy man, maybe they could have saved him. Pieced him back together somehow. But his earlier head injury, coupled with his lying for several hours in the cold and snow, had proved too much. His body was in shock. According to Doc, there was no bringing him back.

She stroked the skin on his hand, running her thumb back and forth, back and forth. Turning his head, he opened his eyes and looked at her. Despite his pain, his eyes were clear. Knowing.

"Ah-na." He forced her name out.

"Yes, Jonas."

"Save . . . El-la."

"She is safe, Jonas. You saved her. Thank you for that."

"For-give . . . me." His words pierced like a knife.

I can't.

I can. God's words resonated from within.

Then help me, Lord. She drew a deep breath. "God forgives you, Jonas, and . . . I forgive you." She felt the burden lifting even as she said the words. The bitterness. The hate. The need for him to pay for what he did. She didn't realize how much those feelings had been hurting her, dragging her down.

Her bitterness, anger, and need for Jonas to hurt like he had hurt her were also forgiven.

She was forgiven and forgiving, and in that forgiving, she had been set free.

CHAPTER 39

They buried Jonas Fitzgerald on the bluff east of the cabin. Jackson had earmarked that area as a family cemetery when he bought the land. Jonas was Ella's father, after all, and had proved himself worthy of that title in the way he died. If Ella and Claire stayed in Fremont County, they'd be able to visit the grave any time they wanted. Ella especially. A girl should know where her father was buried.

A cold wind whipped at Jackson's collar, putting his Stetson in danger of flying down the hill. He clamped it down with one hand. Claire stood across the grave from him, looking beautiful, even in all black. The wind tore at her pompadour, pulling out tendrils and slashing them across her face. Ella clung to her mother's leg, face buried in her skirts. Poor little tike. Jojo had become very special to her.

Their entire community had turned out to bury Jonas. All the neighbors who had showed up to search for Ella days before now stood in respect for the man who gave his all to save her. Few of them had ever met him when he was alive. They knew and loved Claire, Ella, and Sadie, and that was enough.

The preacher who had ridden down from Lander to perform

the service said his final words and stepped back, allowing Claire, Sadie, and Ella some final moments before Jackson and his brothers lowered the casket into the ground. Claire crouched down beside her daughter and whispered a few words in her ear. Ella nodded. Taking something from her pocket, she placed it on the casket. Jackson swallowed hard and glanced away when he realized she'd placed one of her toy teacups there.

The women gathered around, offering hugs and condolences and spiriting Claire and Ella down the hill toward the cabin for the funeral dinner. He, Gabe, and Louis got to work on filling the hole with dirt.

"So," Louis said. "You ask her to marry you yet?"

"Kind of bad form to ask a woman to marry you the day she buries her husband, don't you think?"

"Probably. Can't say it hasn't happened, though. I wouldn't wait on it too long. Once the single men around here find out there's a young, pretty widow in the area, they'll be lining up in droves. Especially when they hear she's got her own money. Who knows? I may even try my luck."

He knew Louis was just trying to get a rise out of him, so he didn't respond. The truth was, he hoped to talk to Claire today. They hadn't spent a lick of time together since they searched for Ella, and the last time he'd told her he loved her, Claire had been a married woman. If he told her again, would she still walk away?

The thought of putting himself out there again and possibly getting rejected made him want to go to his sheep camp and never come back. But Louis was right. If he didn't speak up soon, it might be too late. Last he knew, she was making plans to leave Fremont County. He hoped he could convince her to stay put for a while.

He didn't have a chance to talk to her alone until late that afternoon. His brothers and Pa were long gone, so he'd slipped out to the barn to check on Malachi's feed and see if he needed to restock the woodpile. He came around the barn to find her leaning against one of the poles at the corral, gazing out toward the Winds.

"Everything all right?"

She jumped. "Jackson. I didn't know you were still here."

"Just checking your wood supply."

Her smile warmed. "You take such good care of us, Jackson. I haven't even thanked you for all you did to help me find Ella. I know everyone said today that Jonas saved her, and in his way, he did, but you were the one who brought her home. Don't think I didn't notice. I should have thanked you sooner."

"I don't need to be thanked. Believe me, I needed to find her just as much as you did. You know that."

She nodded and looked away. "You won't have to put up with us taking over your cabin for too much longer. I promise. Give me a few more weeks to get things in order, and then we'll be out of your hair for good."

So that was that? Nothing had changed?

"I don't want the cabin back. Not without you in it." He forced himself to say the words, even if it gave her the chance to rip out his heart and stomp on it again. "Claire, I know our marriage was never a real one, but you have to know, I'd like it to be. I love you. I love Ella. Can't you ever see us together? Won't you at least give us a chance?"

Tears pooled in her eyes. She swiped at them and swallowed hard. "I can't, Jackson. Not yet. Maybe not ever. A part of me is still broken, and I don't know if it'll ever heal. I went from being Jonas's wife to being your wife, to being Jonas's wife again. I don't know what I want anymore. What I want . . . what I *need* . . . is to not be anyone's wife for a while. I need to find out who I am as just me."

"What if I'm willing to wait?"

Finally, she turned to look at him. "I can't promise anything."

He reached for her hands and clasped them in his, his

thumbs tracing small circles on her silky soft skin. "I'm not asking for promises. All I ask is that you don't leave. Not yet. I asked you this once. I'm asking again. Give it until spring. Give me a chance to court you." He saw the reluctance in her eyes. "Slowly. I won't rush you. I won't even come around for a whole month if you'd like, maybe two. But give me a chance. Give us a chance. Please?"

"I don't want to hurt you."

"If you leave without giving me a chance, you already will." He swallowed against the tightness in his throat. He needed to get this out. Tell her everything. "When Ma left, I swore I wouldn't let anyone tear my heart apart the way she did. I put up walls. Didn't let anyone get too close. But slowly and surely, you've broken through those walls. I'm willing to take the risk with you, Claire. You're worth the heartbreak. I promise."

She looked down at their clasped hands, then she looked up and nodded, a tentative smile on her lips. "All right. Six months."

"And I can court you during that time?"

She took a minute to respond. "If we take it slow, yes."

He leaned in until their noses were almost touching. "I'll hold you to that, Claire Monroe."

He wanted nothing more than to kiss her, taste those soft red lips once again and, this time, savor them, but he forced himself to pull back. He couldn't promise her slow and jump right in with a kiss. He dropped her hands, then with a tip of his hat, he turned and walked away.

SHE MISSED JACKSON. WHEN HE PROMISED TO COURT HER SLOWLY, to not even come around for a while, she hadn't realized it would be six weeks without seeing him at all. Thanksgiving had come and gone. The Winds were more white than purple as heavy snow blanketed their peaks. Here on the plains, the red cliffs of the canyon looked like Sadie's gingerbread, lightly dusted with powdered sugar. But as many times as she looked down the winding red road toward the Skivington cabin and the sheep camp that lay somewhere to the south of it, she hadn't caught one glimpse of Jackson riding Boaz up that road.

He hadn't gone completely silent. True to his word, he was courting her. Just not in person. He wrote several times a week. For a man of few spoken words, he was a master with pen and ink. With his letters, he took her with him as he and his brothers made another trip to the mountains to recapture their band of wild horses. With his words, he made her see that multi-colored band, Hippolyta in the lead, churning up wisps of white powder as they ran wild and free in their winter mountain valley. He wrote of the silver mare with the black mane and tail and the healthy young colt who tailed her, reminding her of that glorious day they'd delivered the foal together.

He told of his adventures at his sheep camp and made her laugh, describing the stupid things the sheep would do and the dogs' antics. He told her his plans for his ranch. Introduced her to each of the horses he was training—their personalities and quirks.

In addition to his letters, he left little gifts. How he managed to hide them without her seeing him was beyond her. He must have given Petie some of them to hide when he came to restock the woodpile and leave more grain for Malachi. Shortly after he returned from his trip to the mountains, Ella ran in from the barn carrying a carved horse painted silver with a black mane and tail. A small card tied to its neck read Moonshadow. She said she had found it in the empty stall beside Malachi. Another morning, Claire discovered *Treasure Island* on the shelf in the wash house. The note tucked inside read: *Looking forward to reading this one with you.* One day, she stepped out onto the porch and almost tripped over a basket of biscuits. The note inside said he would always think of her when he ate a biscuit.

She'd laughed. Trust Jackson to tease her about those burnt biscuits in his efforts to woo her.

Each gift reminded her of the life they'd had together before Jonas returned. Each letter painted a picture of the life she could have with him if she were to stay. What surprised her was how tempting the picture was and how easy it was to imagine herself living it. She hadn't thought, once freed, that she'd ever want to marry again. That conviction was slipping a little more each day.

"All that sighing and looking out the window won't do you a lick of good," Sadie said from the kitchen, where she was kneading a loaf of bread. "You've absolutely no chance of seeing him today unless you can miraculously see all the way to Omaha."

"See who?"

Her sister rolled her eyes.

But Sadie was right. Jackson wasn't even in Wyoming this week. He and Louis had taken five of their wild horses to market in South Omaha. Jackson had written in his last letter that he hoped to use some of the profits to buy a small band of rams. Late December was the time to breed sheep for spring lambing.

She turned back to the sock she was mending for Ella. She needed to get her mind off Jackson. If she truly was going to leave here in the spring, she needed to start making a plan. She'd been helping Doc out on some of his visits, keeping her nursing skills fresh. The ranching community provided no shortage of patients. Maybe Doc would write her a letter of recommendation that would help gain her work with another doctor in a small town somewhere. Maybe he would know of someone who needed help. It wouldn't hurt to ask, but she had to admit the prospect of starting over somewhere new didn't appeal the way it once had.

The beat of horse hooves and a shout brought her attention

back to the window. Her heart quickened, but the horse wasn't Boaz, and the man wasn't Jackson.

Baldwin's hired hand dismounted, and she met him at the door.

"What is it, Shorty? Is someone hurt?"

"No, ma'am. It's Miz Jane. Miz Baldwin says to come right away. Baby's a'comin.'"

Finally. Jane had been more than ready to have her baby when Claire last saw her over a week ago. "Let me get my bag and change into my riding skirt."

"Yes'm. I'll go saddle your horse for you."

"Did someone send for Doc Stevens?"

He nodded. "Preston rode off for him right away."

Good. At least if there were complications, she wouldn't be on her own.

As it turned out, the delivery was smooth and uncomplicated. Two hours later, when Preston and Doc Stevens finally made it to the ranch, Jane was already cuddling with her new baby boy. Doc looked baby and mother over and declared them in perfect condition.

"Another fine job, Claire," he said as he left the room. Not that she'd had much to do with this one. Jane had done all the work.

As Preston stepped up to the bed to meet his son, Claire slipped from the room.

She hadn't seen Jane's husband since the day he admitted he'd purposely lured Ella away in an effort to hurt Jackson. Seeing him today brought all the emotions of that day flooding back. Would it always be this hard to forgive? After Jonas, she thought she'd learned how not to let the bitterness foster. Seeing Preston now, she wasn't so sure.

As she walked into the ranch home's large, warm kitchen, Mrs. Baldwin bustled over with a cup of coffee. Claire gave the woman a side hug and accepted the drink with a smile.

"Congratulations, Grandma."

"Thank you. And thank you so much for your help. I must say, it's always a relief when a baby finally gets here, and the mama and baby come through healthy and well."

"Something tells me Jane will grant you many healthy grand-children over the years."

"You're probably right. She's a lot like me. For some of us, birthing babies just comes easier than for others. And a boy, no less. Joseph's going to be so pleased to finally have a little boy around the ranch. But come, sit a minute. You don't need to rush off right away, do you?"

No. And visiting with Mrs. Baldwin was always a treat. She set a plate of cookies on the table between them before taking a seat across from Claire.

"Now, tell me what you and Sadie have been up to lately. I'm sorry I haven't been over to see you since the funeral, but I didn't like to leave Jane alone in her condition, and Lord knows, she was in no state to travel herself. How is Ella? You have to know, we were sick, just sick, at Preston's part in all of that."

Claire nodded. They already made that clear the day of the funeral. They weren't to blame for the actions of their son-in-law, and she certainly never held it against them. Preston was the one she had a problem with.

"Ella's fine." Claire took a bite of cookie, savoring its sweet-ness. "She misses Jonas, though. Some days she'll come into the kitchen right after she wakes up and ask for Jojo. I have to remind her he's gone."

"Poor, dear, to grow up without a father. Though I daresay, if Jackson has any say in things, she won't be without one for long. How is the dear boy? We sure miss him around here. We haven't seen him since he stopped working with Preston last month."

Though she couldn't stop the heat in her cheeks, Claire did her best to ignore her friend's subtle probing, snagging instead on the bit of news she'd let slip. "Jackson's been working with Preston?"

"Didn't he tell you? Yes. It about bowled me over when he showed up the day after your husband's funeral to mend fences with Preston. I expected him to come in with fists flying after what he did to your little girl. Instead, he asked *Preston* for forgiveness. Said he'd let things escalate and hadn't been fair to Preston by not giving him the training he needed when Joseph gave Preston Jackson's old job. Said he planned to rectify that, and he did. He came over every day for at least two weeks and worked with Preston on the books and all the other things that go into managing this ranch. Preston has been like a new man."

Once again, Jackson surprised her. And taught her something about forgiveness.

She and Mrs. Baldwin chatted for another twenty minutes or so. Long enough for Claire to finish another cookie and catch up on the news in their little community. But with sunset arriving earlier and earlier these days, Claire reluctantly pushed to her feet.

"I'd better be getting back if I'm going to make it before dark. You enjoy your new grandson, now."

Mrs. Baldwin pulled her into another hug. "Oh, I will, dearie. And you come back to visit real soon. And bring Sadie and Ella with you. It won't be too long before the snow comes, and none of us will be wanting to get out in it to go visiting."

A few minutes later, Claire straightened from having adjusted the last buckle on her saddle to find Preston standing a few feet away, watching her.

"Congratulations on your new son." If Jackson could treat the man with undeserved kindness, she could too.

He nodded and took a step closer, his fingers worrying the brim of his hat that he held in his hands.

"I . . . uh . . . I . . . I wanted to talk to you a minute before you leave. I . . . what I did . . . taking Ella away that day the way I did.

I was wrong. Very wrong. I'm sorry. I never meant to hurt her . . . or you. But I did. And I'm sorry. I just wanted you to know that."

He spun on his heel and hurried toward the barn.

"Wait."

He stopped but didn't turn around.

"I forgive you, Preston."

Again, just saying the words was freeing. But she knew forgiveness would never be a one-time thing. She would have to choose, with God's help, to forgive her debtors over and over. Maybe with every prayer. Just as her Father had chosen to forgive her and continued to do so.

CHAPTER 40

Aweek later, Claire found another package tied to one of the poles on the round pen when she came out to do the morning chores. Jackson was back. She untied the leather pouch from the pole wanting to tear into it. Instead, she forced herself to put it in her pocket. She hurried through feeding the animals and gathering a couple of buckets of wood to replenish the wood box in the kitchen before racing toward the house.

Once back in the cabin, she ducked into her room and closed the door. She pulled off her gloves and blew on her fingers before fishing the packet out of her pocket. Feeling inside, she found a slip of folded paper and a small box. She opened the note and read: *I'll bring you real ones in the spring.*

Intrigued, she opened the box to find a dainty gold brooch nestled on a bed of cotton. Seed pearls and purple stones formed a bouquet of wildflowers. Claire smiled, remembering their picnic in the field of flowers last spring. Another memory. Another reason to stay. She ran her finger gently across the brooch. Jackson had held this not too long ago. How she wished he had stopped to see her.

"He's back?"

Claire jumped and turned toward where Sadie stood in the open door.

"Can't you knock?"

"I did. I guess you were too busy mooning over whatever is in that box to hear me." Sadie took the box out of her hand and looked inside. "Ohhh. Pretty. He must have bought this in Omaha. So, are you going to go see him?"

"What do you mean?"

"Well, he's obviously not coming here anytime soon. At least not openly. You should go see him. You know you want to."

"And say what?"

"That he's won. His courtship worked. You'll be his wife."

"I couldn't say that!"

"Why not? You moon around here all day long, no good to anyone, waiting for him to come to you. Who knows how much longer he's going to take? You may as well put him and you and all of us out of our misery and go see him. You don't honestly think it's going to take until spring for you to make your decision, do you?"

Sadie was right. Somewhere between the field of wildflowers and the wild horses, she'd fallen in love with Jackson, but it had taken until now for her to admit it to herself. She didn't want any other future but the one he'd been painting for her these last six weeks. She wanted baby lambs and wildflowers in the spring, adventures in the mountains hunting wild horses, nights beside the fireplace talking and reading books aloud. She wanted Jackson. Now that she knew, now she was certain, did it make any sense to wait?

"I don't know where he is."

Sadie pointed south. "I'm betting if you find his sheep camp, you'll find him. Go on. Grab your happiness. After all you went through with Jonas, you deserve it."

No. She didn't deserve anything, but she was grateful, oh, so grateful, God had blessed her with the gift of Jackson, in spite of herself.

"All right. I'll do it. I have no idea what I'll say once I get there, but I'll go. Wish me luck?"

Sadie squealed and turned toward Claire's wardrobe. "You don't need luck. Just a warmer coat. Let's get you bundled up."

"Oh, no. I'll need a lot more than a coat. I can't possibly go talk to him with my hair looking like this. Get your brush. We've got work to do."

An hour later, Claire turned Malachi south toward the sage-covered bluffs.

THE TROUBLE WITH WATCHING SHEEP WAS IT GAVE YOU TOO MUCH time to think. Jackson clasped his arms around his bent legs and stared off across the herd of grazing ewes. He and Louis had gotten back from Omaha last night. After tying Claire's gift to a pole on the round pen, he'd headed out here to spell George and Gabe, who'd been in charge of the sheep while he'd been gone. He'd sent them off to find pasture for the twenty rams he'd bought. In a couple of weeks, he'd turn them in with the ewes, but not yet. Not unless he wanted lambs dropping in the middle of winter.

His thoughts, as they always did, turned to Claire. She should have found the brooch by now. What was she thinking? Did his gifts bring her joy, or had she come to dread them? Was this courtship of his having any effect at all? He'd promised her slow, but he didn't think he could go much longer without seeing her. She'd written to him a couple of times, long, newsy chronicles about life at the cabin, the patients she'd tended, Ella's antics, but not one word about the gifts. Not one word about the feelings he'd expressed in his letters. Not one word about her own feelings. Nevertheless, he'd read those letters over and over until the pages had become threadbare along the folds.

But they weren't enough. He wanted to see her. Watch the expressions play across her face as they talked. Lose himself in the gray depths of her eyes. Hold those silky soft hands in his again. Or, as he did in his dreams each night, pull her into his arms and taste her soft lips.

He groaned and shook his head to clear it. He needed to get his mind off his wants. He needed, for the moment anyway, to stop thinking about Claire.

The good thing about watching sheep was it gave him plenty of time to work on other things. He would need it if he were to get Claire's Christmas gift finished in time. He planned to deliver that one in person, on Christmas Day, to kick off the next stage of the courtship if she was agreeable. One where he would see her at least once a week. Maybe more. But if she still wanted slow, he supposed he could limit it to twice a month. It wouldn't be easy, but he'd do whatever it took to win her heart.

Rummaging in one of the saddlebags he had slung on the ground beside him, he pulled out a small block of wood and a knife. He'd been working on a simple nativity for Claire and would need every one of the next two weeks to finish it. Luckily, he had no more trips planned. Just two full weeks of sitting and watching sheep. Should be plenty of time. He already had the small stable built and had carved a simplistic Joseph and Mary. Next, he planned to fashion a tiny manger and the Christ child. Today, though, he was going to work on a few sheep. Other than the holy family, he only planned to add a couple of animals to Claire's gift this year.

If she accepted his suit, he planned to add to the scene each year with some wise men, shepherds, maybe an angel or two, and all the animals Ella would ever want. For this year, a few sheep and a cow would do.

He whittled away at the wood until the image of an ewe

began to take shape. Nellie, his lead ewe who sat a few feet away, made a perfect model.

He worked for a couple of hours, doing his best to keep his mind anywhere but on Claire. The first wooden sheep completed, he got up to fix himself a small lunch in the sheep wagon. As he sat finishing his last cup of coffee before heading back outside, he gave in to the temptation he'd been battling all morning and pulled a small jeweler's box from the pocket of his duster. Opening it up, he gazed at the ring inside. He should never have bought it. Seventy-five dollars was a lot to pay for something he might never have a chance to give. Were other men more confident of their woman's answer when they got down on one knee to propose?

Other men probably waited until they were closer to the proposal before buying the ring, but he didn't plan to be back in a city again until May. If all went according to plan, he hoped to need the ring long before then.

Horses' hooves pounding outside the wagon had him sending the ring back into the depths of his pocket. The last thing he needed was Louis or Gabe getting wind of his foolishness. They'd never let him hear the end of it.

He opened the top half of the wagon's Dutch door and peered out, expecting to see one of his brothers riding up. What he saw instead made his heart stutter, then pound in pace with the horse's gallop.

Claire.

He was tempted to rub his eyes in case she was a mirage. Had he somehow fallen asleep at the table and was simply dreaming all of this? But no, as many times as he'd dreamed about Claire, he'd never had a dream this real.

He hopped out of the wagon and grabbed hold of Malachi's bridle as Claire pulled to a stop.

"What's wrong? Is it Ella?"

"Nothing's wrong. Ella is fine. But goodness, Jackson. I

almost didn't recognize you." She slid out of the saddle and stood in front of him, those beautiful, gray eyes of hers laughing up at him. "What have you done?"

She reached out and stroked his beard.

Oh.

He'd planned to shave before he saw her in a couple of weeks. He must look a sight. Mrs. Baldwin tended to liken him to a bear this time of year.

"I never shave much in the winter." His growl probably didn't alleviate his bear-like appearance, but he hadn't planned on company.

"I can see that. You'll give your father's beard a run for its money if you don't watch out."

Hardly, since Pa hadn't shaved since Ma left and only trimmed his beard once a year. But the Garrity men were blessed with full, heavy beards. He could understand her surprise.

"I'm guessing you didn't ride all the way out here to comment about my beard."

"No, but you can't expect me to simply ignore it either."

"Why *are* you here?"

Sobering, she looked away. "I . . ."

"I'm sorry. That sounded rude. I didn't mean to be. It's good to see you." He wanted to pull her into his arms and hold her close. He fisted his hands at his sides instead. "*Very* good. I've missed you."

A smile lit her features. "That's why I'm here, Jackson. I wanted . . . I *needed* to see you. I've missed you too."

She'd missed *him*? Those words were ones he'd been longing to hear. Maybe he *was* dreaming.

"And I wanted to thank you for this." She gestured to the collar of her coat, where he saw she had pinned the brooch.

"You like it then?"

"I love it. Jackson, I've loved all your gifts. And they've made me realize something. I don't want you to court me any longer."

His heart plummeted. "What? Why not?"

"Because I don't need a courtship. Not anymore. What I need is to be married to you again." His shock must have registered on his face because she held up a hand. "Let me explain. When you left me all those gifts, you reminded me of all the special times we've had together and gave me a taste of all we could have in the future. I realized my marriage to you was more like a real marriage than anything I ever had with Jonas. I believed, after Jonas, that I never wanted to be married again. That life on my own would be much better than any marriage could ever be. You've shown me I was wrong. I want what we had before, Jackson. I want that type of marriage . . . only with more, of course." Her face turned a delicious shade of pink.

He closed the distance between them, pulling her into his arms. "More? Like this more?" He lowered his mouth to hers, barely touching at first, planning to take the kiss slow, but his control slipped the minute their lips connected. He sank into her, his mouth devouring hers. She moaned and entwined her arms around his neck, digging her fingers into his hair and pulling herself closer.

After several minutes, maybe longer, but not nearly long enough, he pulled back. "When?" he said.

"What?" He loved that she looked as dazed as he felt.

"When will you marry me?"

She reached up and stroked his mustache. "As soon as you shave off your beard."

"Tonight then?"

She laughed. "Better make it tomorrow at least. We need to give the preacher time to make it out from Lander. And let the neighbors know. How about Friday at the very latest?"

"Done." He reached into his pocket and pulled out the jeweler's box. "Let's make this official then." Dropping to one knee, he opened the box and held it out to her. "Claire Monroe Fitzgerald—"

"Montgomery."

"What?"

"Not Monroe. Montgomery."

All right. He'd sort that new information out later. "Claire *Montgomery* Fitzgerald–" He stopped, eyebrow raised until she nodded for him to proceed. "Would you do me the honor of becoming my wife, just like before, only with . . . more?"

She laughed. "Yes. I do. I will." She helped him to his feet. "I can't believe you already had the ring."

He took it from the box and placed it on her finger.

"Oh, Jackson. It's beautiful."

"You're beautiful," he said as he pulled her in for another kiss. "And just so you know, I'm really, really looking forward to the more."

ACKNOWLEDGMENTS

As always, the production of a book does not take place in a vacuum. My thanks go out to all the following:

To my husband, Kurt, for putting up with all the times I'm off living in my imaginary worlds.

To my editor, Kristin Avila, you continually make my stories stronger.

To my sister, Marjorie, your awesome copy-editing skills make my stories shine.

To Evelyn LaBelle at Carpe Librum Book Design, thanks again for the beautiful cover design.

To my MBT Huddle group—Pattie, Linda, Dalyn, Mary, and Geri—your daily prayers and encouragement are priceless.

To the Scribe Tribe—Dalyn, Elizabeth, Kim, Jennifer, and Sara–thanks for all your gentle input and support for this writing journey we're on.

To my family and friends who encourage and cheer me along, I value each and every one of you.

To my readers, thank you for taking the time to read my stories. I am honored.

ABOUT THE AUTHOR

A south-Texas transplant to the good life of Nebraska, Kathy Geary Anderson has a passion for story and all things historical. Over the years, she has been an English teacher, a newsletter and ad writer, and a stay-at-home mom. When she's not reading or writing novels, she can be found cheering (far too loudly) for her favorite football team, traveling the country with her husband, or spending time with her adult children. For more information on upcoming releases, visit www.kathygearyander son.com.

More by Kathy Geary Anderson
Wind River Chronicles, Books 1 & 2

At the turn of the 20th century, New York socialite Jenny Westraven is in trouble . . . again. This last escapade has her guardians washing their hands of her and sending her to live with her brother in Wyoming. Lawyer, Lester "Ben" Bennett, has been getting Jenny out of trouble since they were ten. When their paths meet up again in Wyoming, Ben must decide whether to risk his heart to rescue her once again or cut his losses and let her go.

The year 1900 promises to be a good one for newlyweds, Rob and Maddie Skivington, until a doctor's diagnosis turns their comfortable world upside down. When Rob's doctor suggests a change in environment and climate, they sell their jewelry business and head to Wyoming in a desperate quest for health. But soon, despair, loneliness, and tragedy strike. The couple must turn to God to help them weather those onslaughts or risk being torn apart.

Made in the USA
Coppell, TX
17 February 2023